WITHIN THE CIRCLE

ALSO AVAILABLE BY ARNE DAHL

The Intercrime Mysteries

Europa Blues

To the Top of the Mountain

Bad Blood

Misterioso

The Detective Sam Berger Mysteries

You Are Next

Hunted

Watching You

WITHIN THE CIRCLE

A NOVEL

Arne Dahl

CROOKED LANE

NEW YORK

This is a work of fiction. All of the names, characters, organizations, places and events portrayed in this novel are either products of the author's imagination or are used fictitiously. Any resemblance to real or actual events, locales, or persons, living or dead, is entirely coincidental.

Published by agreement with Salomonsson Agency

Published in the United States by Crooked Lane Books, an imprint of The Quick Brown Fox & Company LLC.

Crooked Lane Books and its logo are trademarks of The Quick Brown Fox & Company LLC.

Library of Congress Catalog-in-Publication data available upon request.

ISBN (hardcover): 979-8-89242-070-9
ISBN (ebook): 979-8-89242-071-6

Translation by Agnes Broomé

Cover design by Nebojsa Zoric

Printed in the United States.

www.crookedlanebooks.com

Crooked Lane Books
34 West 27th St., 10th Floor
New York, NY 10001

First Edition: February 2025

10 9 8 7 6 5 4 3 2 1

To Ioanna

Prologue

1

That has to be a bloody woman up there, he thinks, and accelerates, passing the nearest EV, shooting the slowpoke driving it a dirty look. He chooses to save the finger for later.

You have to pick your battles.

Division Head Alf Stiernström woke up on the wrong side of the bed this spring morning. Granted, it's been a long time since he woke up on any other side. And of course the first email he read on his phone—head burrowed deep into his pillow and eyes full of sand—was from his lawyer, an inveterate morning person.

These early mornings are what he hates most about the position he has strived for his entire life and finally reached. But there's no escaping the fact that he, a top manager for one of Scandinavia's leading companies, must embrace early mornings. In fact, managers need to go even further: early mornings need to be seen as a sign of having the upper hand, as though they've already taken a solid lead by the time the competition wakes up. It's about beating the enemy to the battlefield, as legendary strategist Sun Tzu once said.

Stiernström had tried to embrace that management philosophy while he read the email from his lawyer, but when he realized his ex-wife-to-be was demanding even more money, the philosophy instantly evaporated. He'd made concession after concession, but nothing was ever enough. The bitch wouldn't be happy until she'd taken every penny he'd ever made.

Feminism has gone too bloody far.

Now, on the motorway outside Uppsala, Alf Stiernström sees one EV preparing to overtake another in the distance. He opens the throttle, sending diesel fumes swirling out across the billowing rapeseed fields, and sets his sights on the tree hugger. He notes smugly how hesitant the hippie in the passing lane becomes when he finds himself staring at the elegant, fast-approaching grille of Stiernström's BMW in his rearview mirror. The artificially accelerating EV gadget shudders, unable to sustain any power. Stiernström sees the no-doubt-overpaid, immigrant IT nerd cut in front of the slower driver in the inside lane with terror in his eyes.

When Stiernström overtakes the so-called car, he's a fraction too slow getting his middle finger up. He's already passed the driver, who'll barely be able to see it, but he flips him off anyway.

He has picked his battle.

Just as Stiernström reaches peak acceleration, he notices the BMW handling oddly.

* * *

The binoculars find the cars just as the overtaking happens. They watch from an elevated angle. Watch as the car in the outside lane loses control almost immediately after passing the EVs, watch it veer the wrong way when it reaches the bend in the road, watch it catch fire before it has even started to pull back into the inside lane, watch it careen into the bright-yellow rapeseed field instead, ploughing through it in a ball of flame.

They watch a raised middle finger burning like a torch behind the windscreen. Then, the binoculars are lowered, and the remote control.

The universe hears a deep exhalation. It has begun.

2

It's a beautiful spring day in a typical Swedish forest. Tentative rays of pale light trickle down between tall trees. The small pond is like a dark mirror, as though it's hiding the deepest of secrets. The air is humming, chirping, purring, suffused with all kinds of odors, smells, scents. A swell of melancholia ripples through the forest as it comes back to life after a long winter.

As if it knows it's doomed.

On one side of the large pond, the trees open into a clearing. Another side is bordered by dense thicket. There's unnatural movement in the thicket, but even once it becomes clear a human is crouched next to the shrubbery, the contrast with the surrounding nature is still not particularly stark. Not only because the man's clothing is khaki but also because he simply looks as though he belongs. This is his world.

He finishes shearing gray handfuls of hair from his scalp, rinses his freshly shaven face with water from a wooden bucket, stands up, and slips his large hunting knife into the waistband of his trousers. He appears to be in his fifties, sinewy, flinty faced, and weatherworn, and when he turns his face toward the pale blue sky and sniffs the air, it's clear his precision- trained olfactory sense picks up everything it needs to.

He's grateful it's not another bear, but rather two or more deer that have moved within range of the trap. Thankfully, he has already removed the explosives.

Because he's leaving this place too. He has made a life-altering decision. He has followed the path of his conviction as far as it would take him, and it's time.

It has begun.

He feels it's important to remember his name now. Living in nature, he didn't have one. There are no names in nature, only scent trails, distinctive calls, changes in behavior. But it's time for him to reclaim his name, and everyone will know it.

He raises his binoculars and peers down at the water. Nothing there. When he moves toward the pond, its surface like tar, he has a name again.

Lukas Frisell.

He remembers it.

With the name comes civilization, a history, a life that should have turned out differently. He takes down the empty trap at the water's edge, detaching it from the trees, doing his best to brush the traces of explosives from their trunks before letting the trap drop into a burlap sack. Then he gazes out across the black water.

He has to return to the ruins of destruction.

Which he left once, intending to never see again.

Lukas Frisell slings the burlap sack over his shoulder and takes in the world he has been allowed to be part of for so long. Nature let him in, made him a participant.

His gratitude will always be without end.

He starts walking, to stave off the melancholy. He's only partially successful. The time has come to revisit the ruins, to take the next inevitable step in life.

Nature keeps him company as he walks, as if to say goodbye. As if to make sure he knows what he's doing. He feels overwhelmed by the richness of the planet, and for a moment it seems as though nature is trying to stop him, trying to keep him from taking the drastic step he feels forced to take.

Lukas Frisell has never been alone here. Through all the long years with no human contact, he never once felt lonely in earnest.

It takes experienced forest eyes to recognize the vague outline next to the hill before him as anything other than constantly shifting nature. But it's something else. Where the hill turns into a ravine, the foliage has taken on a faintly unnatural shape. That's where he's going.

To his house.

As he slides down the slope, another knife's edge of melancholy slices through his leathery skin. His dwelling, his refuge. The center of his life for so many years. Until he finally came to the only viable conclusion after witnessing the increasingly visible devastation of his surroundings.

He passes through his large garden. Vegetables, herbs—everything is sprouting, straining toward the sun once more. But this year, he'll leave the harvesting to the animals.

He has almost reached his heavily camouflaged dwelling when instinct strikes.

Something's different. He grabs the heavy hunting knife hanging from his belt. And then he sees it. There's a fresh carving in one of the doorposts.

A circle inside another circle.

Once more, he turns his bright blue eyes to the sky and inhales. The only unfamiliar smell is so fleeting he can't be sure it was really there. It may have been the smell of horse chestnut, but there are no chestnut trees nearby.

A gust of wind sweeps through Lukas Frisell's part of the forest; fresh shavings from his doorpost whirl on the ground.

3

Autumn 2008

In the dimly lit interview room, two people are seated on the same side of the interview table. The chair across from them is empty. And there's no one in the observation room behind the one-way mirror on the wall.

Eva Nyman is a detective inspector at the National Criminal Investigation Department and her boss's right hand. She slowly smooths her unusually elegant designer clothes, and when she meets the gaze of her aforementioned boss, she can tell he's trying hard to contain his impatience.

Patience has never been Chief Inspector Lukas Frisell's forte. "Any word from Peter?" he asks.

Eva Nyman shakes her head, her thick brown hair billowing when she adds a shrug. "He said he was chasing down a lead. That he'd check in."

Frisell lets out a derisive snort, then nods, swipes at his wispy medium-blond hair, and taps his pen against the table. It's the same case as always. Everything in the autumn of 2008 revolves around the kidnapping of Liselott Lindman, a photograph of whom was sent to the press a week ago, tied up on a dirt floor next to a copy of that day's paper. She was visibly emaciated and clearly no more than semiconscious at that point. The perpetrator had celebrated the one-month anniversary of her kidnapping by sending a fresh photograph of his victim to the media.

The worst part is that they know who the kidnapper is. They're all but certain the man who pulled off the spectacular abduction a month ago, in public and broad daylight, is Liselott's ex-husband Dick. It's just that they don't know where he is.

A person who in all likeliness does know is Dick's best friend Robban Svärd, who was recently arrested for tax crimes in the Maldives. But he's late. This is their second day interviewing him, and he's annoyingly late.

"We'll get him today," Lukas Frisell says, and stops tapping his pen, moving on to turning his wedding ring round and round his finger instead. Eva

Nyman watches his fidgeting, aware of everything contained in it, then counters by putting her new phone down on the table in front of her.

It doesn't look like any other phone in the year 2008. It's an iPhone, only just launched on the Swedish market.

Frisell glances at it, pulls a face, sticks his hands in under the table, and instead fixates on the carving in the wood next to the smartphone. He interprets the four crudely carved letters as F-R-E-E. Free. Perhaps an aspiration carved by a prisoner who was still clinging to hope, although he'd be damned if he knew how someone managed to get a sharp enough implement into the interview room.

Maybe that's the freedom it refers to. Then, he says: "This new technology is going to have us all brainwashed."

"It's the future," Nyman replies, "whether we like it or not."

Neither one of them really wants to argue about this. They just want to get the interview started and use anything they can drag out of Robban Svärd to find Liselott Lindman. But for now, they have only each other.

"You know how all this started," Frisell continues.

Eva Nyman nods. With Facebook, yes, she knows. Liselott had been in the protected persons program. Then, someone posted a picture of a neighborhood party on a new social media platform called Facebook. Liselott was visible in the background. Two days later, she was taken from the street outside her new, top-secret home.

Eva Nyman is glad there's no discussion this time. Lately, they've been ending up in that particular dead end far too often. The way she sees it, at the end of the day, Frisell is her boss—simple as that. His word goes. But not everyone shares that sentiment. Peter, for instance, most definitely does not.

"So, he's chasing down a lead?" Frisell says, reading her mind the way he tends to a bit too often for comfort. "Peter, he was going to be in touch?"

Nyman shrugs. She knows there's more coming.

"We can't outsource our police work to untested and integrity-violating technologies. Besides, triangulation is a bloody unsafe method that promises to turn our mobile phones into unreliable informants. We forget the tried and tested investigative methods, in the same way we're pulling away from nature. We're moving through the ruins of destruction, straying further and further from our origin. Securing crime scenes, conducting interviews, that's what solves a case, not computers and . . . those things . . ." Frisell points contemptuously at Nyman's brand-new iPhone.

"Just wait until those things reach their full potential," he adds, falling silent when he hears the familiar sound of footsteps in the hallway outside the small interview room.

The tension rises markedly. Two guards escort Robban Svärd into the room. A sarcastic smile is once again curling the left corner of his mouth. His lawyer enters behind him. Svärd throws himself onto a chair.

Just then, a clear but discordant alarm sounds. A few moments of confusion follow. Lukas Frisell is struck by the fact that he's never heard an iPhone ring before. More to the point, however, is that the thing should obviously be turned off in here.

Eva Nyman answers the device.

"Eva. Bloody hell, Peter, you can't call me . . . What? Okay, hold on."

Frisell has already sprung into action. He physically shoves the guards, the suspect, and his lawyer out the door and slams it shut. Nyman has managed to turn the iPhone to "Speaker," and she puts it back down on the table as Peter's voice rings out in the room. It sounds different from usual, and the information it relays is cryptic.

"Start over from the beginning," Frisell cuts in sharply.

They can clearly hear Peter composing himself, taking a few deep breaths. "The triangulation finally turned up something," he says.

Frisell turns to Nyman, frowning. She just shakes her head. Sure, she suspected Peter and his team may have been secretly running a triangulation search behind Frisell's back, but she didn't know it for a fact.

Peter continues: "It led us to an address outside Järna. A house in the middle of nowhere. We went in. There was no one there—at least no one with a mobile phone. But there was a basement. When we got down there, we noticed it had a dirt floor."

An unarticulated sound escapes Lukas Frisell. He already knows what's coming. In her heart of hearts, Eva Nyman probably does too.

"She's so small," Peter says quietly. "Like a baby bird. A tied-up baby bird."

For a long moment, there's only silence. Dead silence. Both in the interview room at the Police HQ in Stockholm and in the basement outside Järna.

Then Peter resumes in a steadier, slightly angrier voice: "She's still warm, Frisell. If we'd just started the triangulation sooner—"

Nyman lunges for the phone and ends the call.

But it's too late. Frisell heard it too.

"If we'd just started the triangulation sooner, Liselott Lindman would still be alive."

His voice is a whisper. He stares at the carved word in front of him.

Free.

Nyman gently walks over, tries to put her arm around him. As he calmly pushes her arm away, her phone dings. A photo is briefly visible before Nyman manages to get it off the screen.

The late Liselott Lindman really does look like a baby bird. With his eyes closed, Lukas Frisell whispers: "I don't think I should be here."

I

The First Hunt

4

Every time he turns down Dalagatan from Odengatan, he looks up at Astrid Lindgren's windows. The fact that this is where she penned her classic children's books lends the entire area a creative aura. These days, Jesper Sahlgren would go so far as to say that on occasion, his own desk, with its view of Vasaparken, feels like the creative heart of the neighborhood. This is one of those occasions. The company's spring campaign is already making waves in the world of Swedish advertising.

That campaign is what prompted Jesper Sahlgren to get up uncharacteristically early this Sunday morning in May, leaving his family still sound asleep in their house in Täby as he hopped into his Tesla and drove into a Stockholm that even now, at 6:23, feels completely deserted. On the other hand, that gives him a chance to park on the left side of the street, against traffic. With his iPad Pro in hand, he heads through the front door, climbs a couple flights of stairs, and strides up to the sturdy metal door on which trendily square letters spell out "Flat Broke Ltd" and underneath, in smaller script: "Not necessarily the PR company for you." He remembers when he pitched that slogan to the board. He remembers the moment their skeptical faces lit up with understanding.

Sahlgren punches in the code, stares into the retinal scanner, and hopes the text he received the night before is reliable, that indeed the company's assistant, whatever her name is, really did come in to work on a Saturday from Vallentuna or Märsta or wherever it is she lives, to accept delivery of the print proofs.

When the security door finally swings open, he can't resist the temptation anymore. As he moves through the familiar office—which he still remembers missing terribly during the pandemic—he pulls up on his iPad the series of ingenious photographs showing the leaders of every conservative party standing next to petrol pumps.

He can't wait to see the campaign in hard copy.

Without so much as a glance in their direction, he passes window after window overlooking Vasaparken. Save for a small movement, possibly a shadow, next to one of the trees nearest the street, the world still seems uninhabited.

Jesper Sahlgren reaches his desk. His sigh of relief echoes through the office when he spots the cylindrical parcel sitting on it. The assistant came through indeed.

He allows himself to savor the moment ever so briefly. His eyes fall on his heavy wristwatch. It tells him it's now 6:28.

He was on a wait list for over a year to get the genuine Omega Speedmaster Moonwatch Titanium, possibly the world's most shatterproof watch. It's the titanium version of the watch Neil Armstrong wore around his wrist when he stepped down onto the lunar surface.

A small step for mankind, but a big step for humanity, Jesper Sahlgren thinks as he starts unwrapping the cylindrical parcel.

* * *

When the binoculars catch the movements in the window, the shadow retreats behind the tree. Taking cover.

The binoculars are lowered.

The universe hears a deep exhalation followed by a deep, hollow bang, then the distorted sound of broken glass shatters the desolate morning. Something flies astronaut-like through the air, landing with a thud on Vasaparken's lawn.

In Vasaparken's lawn.

When the shadow silently slips away from the tree, the thing in the grass is an utterly shapeless, smoking, deformed hunk of charred flesh.

The only human thing about it is a wristwatch that stubbornly keeps ticking. It's now 6:29.

Scattered around the roots of the tree are a number of fresh wood shavings.

5

On her way to the stack of today's post, Chief Inspector Eva Nyman happens to glance over at the Gustavian mirror that constitutes the apex of her attempts to zhuzh up her dull-as-dishwater office. But the glance turns into a lingering look.

Eva Nyman's not the type to tell people much about herself. Her reticence had become firmly cemented fifteen years earlier, when the shit hit the fan. She knows she's something of an enigma to most of her subordinates; they're likely not even sure which side of fifty she's on. Consequently, she hasn't addressed the reason her hair is suddenly turning gray, even with her only real friend.

But she knows why. Their bond wasn't meant to be broken. It went against the universe's intentions. They weren't supposed to go their separate ways. Nature itself is protesting.

She knows all of that. And yet she pauses in front of the mirror. Has exactly half of her hair really turned gray now?

She traces the lines that make her features unnecessarily grim until she reaches the hair at her temples. She pulls it back a little, tilting her head this way and that for a better look.

And there it is, gray and brown by turns, in patches.

She chuckles and continues toward her antique desk. When she reaches it, she straightens her classically cut, color-coordinated outfit; takes a seat; puts on her reading glasses; and heaves a sigh before pulling the pile of letters closer. *How is it that there are always so many? Aren't we living in a digital age?*

Partway through the pile, she comes across a letter that seems to confirm her thinking.

When she sees the old-fashioned, typewritten enveloped addressed to Chief Inspector Eva Nyman, NOD, Police HQ, Stockholm, she says aloud, "Like a greeting from a bygone era."

She opens the envelope with her letter opener and pulls out a wild-looking, typed letter. Her brow furrows as she skims the text.

The Police Authority receives far too many letters from swivel-eyed cranks.

Apparently, email just doesn't scratch the same itch. It probably has something to do with the crafting, the physical nature of it.

A handful of phrases stand out: "It's time to let holy wrath wash over the defiled land where people once dwelt." "The mildest of the blasts has already scattered the man of steel across a sea of yellow." "The guilty must be held to account, on the other side of the ruins of destruction." Surprisingly well written—but that's not enough to prevent the letter from slowly sliding into the bin.

Eva Nyman has more important things to do.

Except, to be completely honest, she doesn't. She and her team are currently "between cases." Granted, there are still some loose ends to tie up, but it won't be long before what few investigators she has left are reassigned to investigations in other corners of—or even outside—the National Operations Department, more commonly known as NOD.

This Tuesday continues to be dominated by what happened on the Sunday preceding it. The explosion, the charred man whose remains were blown into Vasaparken. Eva Nyman has seen the pictures. The case belongs to the Stockholm Police. Big, enviable. National news that has even generated some international interest.

Why would anyone bother to blow up the offices of a PR company? And in the early hours of a Sunday?

She shakes her head and continues to scan the list of crimes committed over the past month. Something's gnawing at her. She has no idea what it is, just a feeling that she's overlooked an item of importance.

Then, she comes across an internal update. Granted, it's over twenty-four hours old, but the reclassification of the case in question is notable. What had been presumed to be a matter of a leaking fuel tank had now, after closer examination by the National Forensic Center, been confirmed as a bombing.

Eva Nyman almost keeps swiping. But then she stops. There's one detail. A field of rapeseed. Of yellow.

That rings some kind of vague bell.

She sits there for a minute. A field of rapeseed. A sea of yellow. Man of steel.

Who was the victim? A division manager at steel manufacturer SSAB, who was racing down the motorway from Uppsala when he exploded and careened into a field of rapeseed where his car was devoured by the flames.

So? Recent crimes are often fodder for the frustrated fantasies of dyed-in-the-wool cranks. Why would it be significant?

Eva Nyman sits for a while longer.

Then she reluctantly bends down and pulls out her bin. Her fingerprints are already all over both the letter and the envelope, but she still exercises extreme caution when she picks them up and places them on the desk.

The typewritten text has an intense, dense, cramped look, running all the way to the edges of the sheet of A4, the short message repeating over and over, completely filling one side of the sheet. The back is blank. The text reads:

> *Beware, you present-day descendants of homo sapiens. It's time to let holy wrath wash over the defiled land where humans once dwelt. Soon, the light of the sun will no longer reach the soulless ones through the ruins of destruction. It has begun. The clock no longer ticks by its own volition; it has to be wound with violence. Eliminating impediments is necessary to ensure our survival. The mildest of the blasts has already scattered the man of steel across a sea of yellow. As I write, the baldfaced liar is plummeting into his green grave in the park. And before long, the hall of hell will be filled with dread. This is only the beginning. The fight-back is only in its infancy, the guilty must be held to account on the other side of the ruins of destruction. Beware, you present-day descendants of homo sapiens.*

Chief Inspector Eva Nyman pushes her reading glasses up into her graying hair and just sits there, staring at the letter in front of her.

It's more well written than she remembered from her quick skim, a kind of ominous and apocalyptic twist on the generic climate rant. These are the end of days, the clock can no longer run on its own, impediments have to be eliminated. But surely what follows after that are cryptic descriptions of two recent attacks? The thing that scattered the "man of steel" across the field of rapeseed was a bomb. And it was another bomb that sent the "baldfaced liar"—the ad man—into his green grave in Vasaparken. And then there's the "hall of hell."

That one hasn't happened yet.

But there's another time marker that interests her even more. "As I write this."

Eva Nyman pushes the letter aside to focus on the envelope. She studies the stamped barcode on it and then picks up her phone.

She dials. While she waits for someone at Postnord to answer, she ponders two things.

The first is: Why the hell is this letter addressed directly to her? How can this be personal?

The second is one of the phrases, and somehow, the two things are connected.

"*The ruins of destruction.*"

6

The head of NOD, the National Operations Department, is sitting in his not particularly grand office. Now he looks up from the letter, his face grim. The sheet of paper is sealed inside an evidence bag, which he waves around and says, "This is a bunch of nonsense."

Sitting across the desk from him, Chief Inspector Eva Nyman is surreptitiously trying to pry her reading glasses out of her hair. She answers with a question: "Have the two explosions been linked before?"

The head of NOD frowns, shaking his head slowly.

"No," he admits finally. "But any lunatic can find a way to connect two crimes that have both featured in the media. Especially if at least one of them is spectacular."

Nyman is forced to stop messing with her hair. "The barcode," she says, doing her best to keep the fact that her glasses are now dangling from her hair from becoming too conspicuous.

The head of NOD stares at her. She points and says, "The other bag, Peter."

He picks up the other evidence bag and peers at the envelope through the plastic. "There's a barcode on it," Nyman says. "The modern version of a postmark. Today's Tuesday. That machine-stamped code on the envelope says the letter was posted on Friday."

The head of NOD nods and grunts. "And the ad man in Vasaparken wasn't blown up until Sunday morning."

They exchange a long look, a look filled with mutual respect and mutual skepticism.

Eventually, Eva Nyman says, "The author of the letter not only claims responsibility for two lethal bombings—one of which had not yet taken place—he also indicates there will be another attack, on some 'hall of hell,' which will be 'filled with dread.'"

The head of NOD shakes his head. "I'm still not sold."

"SSAB, a big steel manufacturer, could count as Sweden's worst climate offender, depending on your criteria, and PR firm Flat Broke Ltd has just put the finishing touches to an ad campaign for the oil industry, with pictures of various party leaders grinning next to petrol pumps. Worst-case scenario, the author of the letter could be some off-grid critic of modern civilization like the Unabomber in the US. Or even an extremist climate activist group."

She's not going to beg. She'll argue until she's blue in the face. But she will not beg. Not with Peter. Anything short of begging.

He frowns, tapping his pen.

"What I want to know is why the letter is so unambiguously addressed to you, Eva. Is there a personal connection?"

Eva Nyman has been waiting for that question. She wants to kick it down the road, wants to make sure she's secured the case first. But how is she supposed to answer without lying? Without making a statement that may very well come back to bite her.

"I'm trying," she says, "but I really can't put my finger on it."

The head of NOD nods, grimaces, then clears his expression.

"There's not enough here to justify taking these cases away from the local jurisdictions," he says. "As things stand, I'm not prepared to say they're linked."

Eva Nyman has a deluge of arguments ready. But she bites her tongue. Her boss looks as though he might not be done talking.

"But," he continues, "it may be worthwhile to follow up the terrorist angle more narrowly."

Nyman doesn't move, doesn't breathe.

After a long pause, the head of NOD continues: "Your team's been idle for a while, and people are about to be reassigned. You'll have to gather them back so you can follow the activist lead. This means you'll also be given an official name, which will be relayed to you after this morning's management meeting. But not a word about terrorism or activism in public. We can't allow ourselves to even hint at the possibility of some kind of climate terrorism unless it's been one hundred percent proven. Are we clear?"

Nyman nods. The head of NOD fixes her intently. He holds her nut-brown gaze for a good long while before he continues.

"But I'm not so sure you're up to leading a team right now, Eva. Given everything that's happened."

Nyman closes her eyes as an unexpectedly powerful surge of joy ripples through her, then replies as firmly as she is able: "I'm absolutely certain I am."

When she opens her eyes, the head of NOD still hasn't taken his eyes off her. It's as though he's searching for the truth somewhere deep inside her. In the end, he nods curtly. "Good," he says. "Then your team will cover that angle, Eva. But discreetly. Try not to interfere with the main investigations."

Nyman tries to keep her face stern. She stands up as steadily as she can manage. As she turns to leave, the head of NOD stops her, saying, "But I think you're going to have to do something about those glasses."

She clears her throat to conceal a chuckle and pauses in the doorway. A phrase poised at the tip of her tongue.

The ruins of destruction.

But she manages to bite it back. She'd be a fool to shoot herself in the foot now. She's just going to have to find a way to solve it.

Behind closed doors, she thinks, as she closes one behind her.

7

Chief Inspector Eva Nyman is perched on the desk at the front of the auditorium that for reasons unclear has become known as the Waiting Hall. She's waiting for her team, small as it may be. At present, it has zero members.

Logically speaking, the room likely got its name from the fact that it's a hall where people wait. For colleagues, sure, but also for retirement perhaps, or death—or a stalled career.

But linguistically, it's also possible that it's the hall itself that waits. The waiting hall. The hall that despite its severely neglected state has been forced to wait for an eternity.

In the middle of Eva Nyman's spiritual musings, Annika Stolt—who is invariably and in all contexts simply called Ankan—enters, looking around in surprise. She's not exactly known for being the first to arrive anywhere. On the other hand, Nyman thinks the powerful blonde, who looks as though she was born to wear a police uniform, seems to have recovered surprisingly well from last year's life-altering shock. She doesn't know exactly what has changed, but in the past few weeks, there's definitely a glow about Ankan.

Glow? Nyman thinks, smiling at herself. Maybe she has a new glow too, because when Shabir Sarwani steps into the hall, his eyes linger longer than usual on his boss. On the other hand, maybe it's just that the group's ever-observant, perpetual-motion man is noting that something's amiss with Eva Nyman's hair. Specifically, with the area just above the fringe, where she was eventually forced to cut her reading glasses free.

Then Anton Lindberg joins the group, bringing with him the dark storm cloud that's almost always accompanying him these days. The burly family man sits down and, force of habit, attempts to tame his long, unruly, light-brown hair.

While Eva Nyman waits for the last member of the team, her thoughts once again circle back to the phrase "ruins of destruction." Surely it must be a coincidence. Surely it's as far from tangible proof as a person can get. Surely she's running the risk of developing an obsession here. Surely there's also a risk her fixation could jeopardize the main investigations.

When a muscular woman with a shaved head and slightly baggy clothes finally steps into the Waiting Hall, Nyman still hasn't decided how to proceed.

Sonja Ryd gives her a curt nod before taking a seat between Ankan and Sarwani. Thankfully, she looks to be in decent shape, Nyman muses, once again marveling at Ryd's unique dichotomy between fiendishly disciplined exercise and . . . well, the bad habit. And at how Ryd has managed to move beyond her past, working their worst imaginable sex crime investigations.

Eva Nyman wants to size up her team's reaction, to gauge exactly how excited they are to hear the news.

"It's been a while since we've gathered here," she begins, sliding down from the desk and moving in behind it. "Last time we were here, we were working a real case, as a team.

We're close to doing that again now—a proper, high-profile case that will reverberate through the media for a long time to come."

All eyes are on her. No fidgeting; intent focus. Ears pricked. Anticipation. Good. "We're close to working a case?" Sonja Ryd asks after a pause.

"We're looking into a possible connection between two cases, which may soon become three," Nyman says, just as she prepared. "And if there is a third, the three will become one."

"Sounds like an awkwardly constructed riddle," Ryd comments.

Eva Nyman contextualizes: "We may have an active serial bomber on our hands in Stockholm right now, possibly even a terrorist group, motivated by climate change."

"So, we're talking Vasaparken?" Anton Lindberg asks. "Aren't the Stockholm Police dealing with that?"

"They're running the investigation," Nyman replies. "But the terrorist angle belongs to us. And we're going to keep things on the down low. We're going to investigate whether there's a link between Vasaparken and a much less public case that was dismissed as a traffic accident until recently." Nyman lays out the pertinent facts. "A week before a bomb sent thirty-seven-year-old Jesper Sahlgren flying through a window on Dalagatan, a BMW exploded on the motorway outside Uppsala, with sixty-year-old Alf Stiernström, a division manager at steel manufacturer SSAB, inside." She pauses, looking at each of them. "We're also going to assess whether there's any substance to the threat of a third attack . . . And we've been given an official name."

"A name?" Ankan exclaims.

She nods. "From now on, we're Nova."

"What the fuck?" Anton Lindberg blurts out. "What kind of a sick joke is that? Our bloody IT support's called Nova."

"I know," Nyman says. "We have the honor of sharing our name with the internal reporting system. But the important thing is that we've been recognized as an official working group. That makes it harder to fire us."

"Wow, Nova," Sarwani says incredulously. Then follows a long silence in the Waiting Hall.

"You said 'motivated by climate change,'" Sonja Ryd finally says, breaking the quiet. "So, we've had some kind of manifesto?"

Nyman studies her. And in that moment she realizes Ryd is what she needs. Ryd at her best.

Not that she knows how to make that happen.

"I'm not sure *manifesto*'s the right word," Nyman says, turning on the laptop on the desk in front of her. The letter projects onto the wall behind her. She reads aloud:

> *Beware, you present-day descendants of homo sapiens. It's time to let holy wrath wash over the defiled land where humans once dwelt. Soon, the light of the sun will no longer reach the soulless ones through the ruins of destruction. It has begun. The clock no longer ticks by its own volition; it has to be wound with violence. Eliminating impediments is necessary to ensure our survival. The mildest of the blasts has already scattered the superman across a sea of yellow. As I write, the baldfaced liar is plummeting into his green grave in the park. And before long, the hall of hell will be filled with dread. This is only the beginning. The fightback is only in its infancy, the guilty must be held to account, on the other side of the ruins of destruction. Beware, you present-day descendants of homo sapiens.*

When Eva Nyman trails off, another dense silence settles over the Waiting Hall. No one seems to know where to begin.

Eventually, Nyman kickstarts the discussion herself: "The letter was sent to me personally, here at NOD."

"Do you have any idea why?" Shabir Sarwani asks.

"Not really, no. So, what are your immediate thoughts about the letter?"

"Literary," Sonja Ryd replies. "A reasonably educated person."

"Big vocabulary but completely off their rocker," Anton Lindgren puts in.

"Feels like genuine conviction," Ankan surmises.

"The two victims could be viewed as climate offenders," Sarwani says. "Maybe this is some kind of Unabomber? Twisted idealism?"

"Unless it's just a garden-variety lunatic," Lindberg counters.

"Good," Eva Nyman says, nodding. "It's good you're pumped. The core question is, of course: How did the bombs get into Alf Stiernström's car and Jesper Sahlgren's office? If we find out how, we find out who."

"But surely our top priority has to be finding the 'hall of hell?'" Ryd points to the text behind Nyman and continues: "'And before long the hall of hell will be filled with dread.' 'Before long' indicates—if this is to be believed—that we don't have much time. I mean, a week between the first two, right? Maybe even less this time?"

"Bloody riddles," Lindberg bellows. "What the fuck is a hall of hell? Is it this? Is the Waiting Hall the hall of hell?"

After a short collective chuckle, Sarwani asks, "Is it even possible to prevent something so vaguely worded?"

"We'll do our best," Eva Nyman replies. "But we're going to start by getting as full an overview as possible of the entire situation. We're going to start by talking to the active investigators and crime scene technicians. That's the best way to bring us up to speed with any potential terrorists. So, starting today, Nova's going to work until we drop, and assignments are as follows: Anton will take the BMW and the scattered man of steel. Ankan's on Vasaparken and the barbecued ad man. Shabir will look into the vaguely worded 'hall of hell.'"

As Shabir Sarwani raps his knuckles on the table, Eva Nyman makes her decision: "Sonja, in my office."

8

Having made it to Eva Nyman's office, Sonja Ryd immediately walks over to the sofa by the window and throws herself down on it, leaning back and looking around.

"You really do have an eye for decor."

Nyman laughs and takes a seat in the armchair across from her.

"I suppose you could call it a challenge," she says, gesturing toward the beige seventies wallpaper.

Their eyes meet. The unlikely friends have sat exactly like this ever since Nyman was promoted. A private sphere of mutual trust and confidence between the well-dressed chief inspector and the baggy detective inspector. A sphere in which nothing has to be held back, where the hierarchies are suspended. Nyman is around fifty, Ryd several years younger, but that difference, too, is temporarily erased in here. For once, Eva Nyman's not an enigma. Not even to herself.

"Did you just want to check up on me, or am I really slated for a secret mission?" Sonja Ryd asks, vigorously rubbing the stubble on her head.

"The two aren't mutually exclusive," Nyman replies. "Though 'secret' is overstating it. At most it's unofficial. But you know I do have to check up on you too. How the hell do you stay so fit?"

Sonja Ryd's eyes turn grave.

"One addiction is much the same as another," she says. "When I feel the urge at the end of the day, I have to work out. Otherwise, I drink. Now tell me what's so hush-hush."

"Just at the end of the day, though, right?"

"As far as exercising goes, the mornings might actually be more acute. What with all the anxiety having accumulated overnight. But you know it doesn't affect my work."

Nyman's face betrays her, prompting Ryd to lean forward and say, "You've made significantly more serious professional missteps than I have, Eva."

Nyman's grimace deepens. Then she says, "'The ruins of destruction.'"

Ryd nods. Nyman notes her acuity.

"Two occurrences," Ryd says. "The only repetition in the entire letter."

"I figured you might catch that. It's a very distinctive phrase. And you have a very distinctive way of looking at things, Sonja. Have I ever told you about my first year as a detective?"

"Not nearly enough."

"I had a boss who taught me pretty much everything I know. He's still the best detective I've ever worked with. He really loathed technology. He saw the risks of it far earlier than most of us. But he took it too far. He refused to use triangulation to find a kidnap victim. It led to her death. A fairly gruesome death, at that. And the perpetrator's still on the loose."

"Oh, so we're talking about Liselott Lindman?" Sonja Ryd says, sounding surprised. "That's a classic case. I had no idea you worked on that."

"The top brass put a lid on it. The team was scattered to the winds."

"And your boss?"

"He quit."

"So, what does he have to do with this?"

Nyman keeps her eyes on Sonja's.

"He was a nature lover and a climate activist. And his favorite phrase was 'the ruins of destruction'. It was his nickname for our rotten modern times."

"Bloody hell," Ryd exclaims.

"Obviously, two instances of 'the ruins of destruction' isn't enough to justify a separate investigation. But I've never heard anyone else use that phrase. More generally, the language in that letter, it's his. Plus, he's the type."

"Then I really need to know everything you remember about him. But first things first: Why would he send his manifesto, or whatever we want to call it, to you of all people? Were you that close?"

"I was his right hand."

"And you did what men's right hands usually do? Come on, Eva. Did you shag him?"

Nyman clears her throat and, instead of answering, launches into a lengthy biographical statement. "He was married and a dedicated detective who grew up under difficult circumstances and was close to becoming a career criminal before his love of nature saved him. That and a stubborn police officer who met him at a juvenile detention facility. The cop badgered him onto the straight and narrow. He attended some kind of agricultural university at first—I don't remember which one—but then he dropped out to join the academy. He contacted his old police friend, who pulled some strings to get him into the academy, where the cop became his mentor."

"Sounds as though there are two people I need to talk to . . . But what happened to him after the kidnapping debacle? Where is he now?"

“I honestly don’t know. We drifted apart. He went back to the agricultural university. Then I heard he’d become a prepper or something like that. I googled him, but there’s no trace of him online. He’s not registered as deceased.”

“A prepper? Seriously? Like a survivalist? Living in the woods with no electricity or running water? Practicing self-sufficiency? Hostile to all forms of civilization?”

“That part’s a rumor at best. See what you can dig up. Start with the two people you correctly identified: Frisell’s old mentor, Edward Rasmusson, a now-retired detective whose recruiting efforts at juvenile detention facilities are legendary, and his ex-wife, Nina Strömblad. Keep a low profile.”

“With the others as well? With the . . . Nova Group?” Nyman makes a face. It’s hesitation masked as a grimace.

“For now,” Nyman says. “If this turns out to be a dead end, we’ll just drop it.”

There’s a pause. Sonja Ryd contemplates the small but classically decorated office. “I’m going to find your old boss,” Ryd says at length, “if only to find out what the two of you were to each other. Why did he send this to you personally, Eva? There’s no way around that question.”

Eva Nyman blinks slowly, her brow creased. Then she says, “I think Lukas Frisell is trying to bait me.”

9

Shabir Sarwani arrived as an unaccompanied minor during one of the Afghan refugee waves and was subsequently shuttled between deeply inappropriate foster homes. The conclusion he drew was that he needed to become Swedish as quickly as possible.

He'd be lying if he claimed that his self-assigned mission hadn't run into its fair share of hurdles, but by the time he was accepted to the basic training program at Umeå University's Police Education Unit, he had top marks in every subject. According to the independent assessments of several police historians, that had never happened in Sweden before.

When Sarwani had celebrated his thirtieth birthday a few weeks earlier, however, it was without a single Swede present. He has secretly made it his mission to coax at-risk youth back from the brink, using their own language to talk them around just as they're about to slide into the criminal networks of their segregated neighborhoods. After all, it was in one such neighborhood that he himself had finally ended up with a functional family, where he'd had the opportunity to attend a good school and fill his free time with constructive activities. Granted, times had changed since then, but his conviction that segregated suburbs were perfectly able to produce productive members of society remained unshaken.

And it was with those young people that he celebrated his birthday.

Clearly, that's not what Sarwani should be thinking about, sitting all alone in what is now Nova's office. But keeping your eye on the prize isn't easy when everyone else is off on real assignments in the field. What he should be thinking about is the "hall of hell."

The one that will be filled with dread before long. A proper shit assignment. But potentially an important shit assignment.

If this even was a real case . . .

He starts over from the beginning. What characterizes hell and what constitutes a hall? Hell is hot, a place where evil people are punished, but what is a hall? A large, open venue? A concert hall, a town hall, a dance hall, a dining hall, a waiting hall that will be filled with dread and thereby turned into a hall of hell?

Sarwani's mind turns idly to Stockholm's grandest halls. He thinks about City Hall, he thinks about Grand Hôtel, he thinks about the Palace of the Hereditary Prince; he even thinks about the Royal Palace, floating off into Swedish opulence and luxury, before reining his thoughts back in.

Is that really what the letter said? Is that the chronology? First feast hall, then hell hall? Doesn't it actually sound more as though the place were a hall of hell from the start? Which will then be filled with dread?

So, a hot hall. A hot, open . . . industrial facility, maybe? The opposite of the opulence of the feast hall.

What could it be? A steelworks? The first victim, Alf Stiernström, had been a bigwig at steel giant SSAB. Picturing a blast furnace full of rivers of molten steel as a hall of hell is easy enough.

Except the ad man was more into petroleum.

Sarwani takes a mental step back. If the letter and all three attacks—two executed, one forthcoming—really are linked, which is to say if they really are the work of a single perpetrator, who is he? A first sketch at a profile.

The climate rage seems genuine, and possibly complex—perhaps the attacks are intended to throw a spotlight on different types of environmental crimes. So far, the perpetrator has pointed fingers at the steel and oil industries. What else is there? Another climate offender with a connection to a hot hall?

That rings a tiny bell inside Shabir Sarwani. The internet. The internet, which already consumes twenty percent of the world's electricity. Sweden's electricity crisis. The cloud. The digital giants: Facebook, Google, Amazon, Microsoft, which all operate massive, energy- guzzling server halls in Sweden. The romantic-sounding cloud doesn't exist, in reality it's a bunch of hot, loud, energy-wasting "halls of hell," disproportionately found in the little country in the far north that is so flattered by the giant companies' interest that it grants them enormous financial incentives, even though relatively few jobs are created.

If his Google search is to be believed, there are at least ten major server halls in the country, from Luleå in the north to Staffanstorp in the south. Facebook has invested in the north; Microsoft, all over the map; Amazon, around Stockholm; and Google, in Dalarna. And the domestic IT firms have their own server halls as well, but that makes the number unmanageable.

The internet has very few pictures from inside the biggest halls, and Sarwani suspects the kind of strict secrecy that has more to do with the United States than with Sweden. He calls Eva Nyman and is given—in addition to a small helping of well-deserved praise—the news that she will ask for an emergency meeting with the head of NOD. Hopefully, they'll be able to come up with a strategy to quickly and discreetly warn the digital giants.

Shabir Sarwani makes a list of as many halls of hell as he can find, and then he suddenly sees them through the eyes of a climate terrorist: hot, noisy, enormous facilities housing what will, in the end, be what breaks our civilization.

He feels increasingly certain one of the halls on his list will be filled with dread before long.

10

A few too many of Anton Lindberg's colleagues were injured in the Easter Riot for him to just be able to drop it and move on. His soul is stuck there. It's a trauma he can't get past, the storm cloud that has become his constant companion.

The Easter Riot took place in April 2022. Sweden was busy with Russia's grotesque attack on Ukraine and its own potential need to join NATO. Of course a right-wing extremist and provocateur had had to celebrate Easter by popping up in segregated suburbs to burn the Quran. His provocation had been unbelievably successful. Violent factions among the protesters went on the offensive—except not against the provocateur, but against the Swedish police.

Very few of the attackers were injured. But at least three hundred police officers were.

Anton Lindberg wasn't one of them. But he'd been there. He'd been on the ground in Rinkeby on April 15th. He'd figured his burly, imposing physique would have been deterrent enough, but instead he'd witnessed several colleagues get hit in the head with cobblestones.

He'd seen the bottomless hatred in the attackers' eyes. The top brass had been weak—but he still supports the decision not to open fire on the protesters. He only wishes there had been an alternative to passively taking rocks to the head.

Having followed his train of thought thus far, he reaches the exit near Uppsala, where a police car is waiting. His uniformed colleague has a relatively fresh scar on his face. Why does he want to ask if it's from a rock? What's he trying to confirm?

He stops himself. Instead, he pats down his uncooperative light-brown hair and follows his colleague's pointing hand out across the bright yellow field of rapeseed.

"The diesel car flew straight into the biodiesel," his colleague quips before retracting his hand and stroking his scar.

"Biodiesel?" Lindberg asks. "And it's blooming early too."

He can tell his colleague's local despite the immediate vicinity of two larger cities. They have a dialect out here in rural Uppland.

"Rapeseed methyl ester," the man clarifies in that distinctive accent.

Only then does Anton Lindberg notice what his colleague's hand had been pointing to before he pulled it back. The rapeseed hasn't had time to fully cover the charred path that cuts through the yellow. It leads to the remnants of a large fire.

"What are you telling me?" Lindberg asks.

The uniformed officer suddenly seems wary. In a far more reserved tone, he replies, "All I'm saying is that this would be the perfect place to make a point. The rapeseed's blooming unusually early this year. And unless I've been misinformed about why we have to keep NOD up to date about our case, that point has something to do with the climate."

"And why would this be the perfect place for it?"

"Rapeseed methyl ester, RME, could become the biodiesel that replaces fossil diesel—or at least a useful additive to it—and it was a fuel-guzzling BMW that went up in flames in the field. That's all I'm saying."

"And why did it take you so long to figure out it wasn't an accident?"

"All the signs pointed to it," his colleague replies with a vague gesture.

"Let me guess," Lindberg says. "BMW, witness statements about speeds approaching one hundred and thirty miles an hour, a wildly accelerating division manager of upper middle age?"

"Plus, the finger," his scarred colleague adds, and starts walking toward his car.

"The finger?"

"Talk to the technicians, they'll tell you all about it."

* * *

Driving back to Stockholm, Anton Lindberg circles again to the question of what being a police officer really means. True, he's very close to changing his opinion on whether an officer in danger should be allowed to use lethal force. But he was, after all, raised in the democratic and humanitarian tradition. He's a police officer who didn't become a police officer to kill people, but to make the world a teeny, tiny bit better. To set things right. That was Sweden before the Easter Riots.

Now, with the older of his two daughters about to start middle school, fear has sunk its claws into Lindberg in earnest. He can't allow his children to ever become victims to the dangers he knows too well. He won't.

At the same time, he knows he has several highly skilled colleagues of foreign extraction at his disposal, including Shabir Sarwani, though Sarwani's actually unusually annoying.

Lindberg has seen plenty of people live productive, normal lives in the segregated suburbs. And yet, he still wakes up at night sometimes with horrible images in his head of a daughter who is no longer only verbally called a whore, but also attacked. Physically attacked. He knows what he's *supposed* to do in that situation. But if such a thing happened, it would already be too late. The only thing left in him would be vengeance.

Prevention is the word he's looking for: "pre-empt, forestall, thwart." It can never be allowed to happen.

But how do you stop this shit? he thinks as he turns into the National Forensic Center's campus in Solna. *Legalize drugs?*

He's shown inside the building to meet with the acting head forensic technician, after being told the regular head forensic technician is otherwise engaged. He finds the acting head forensic technician standing in front of a computer, inputting data. Just as she's about to speak, Anton Lindberg says, "I'm primarily interested in the finger."

She stares at him. But not as though she doesn't understand. It's just masked as incomprehension. Half decently masked.

"All we know is that's how he was found," she says at length.

"Would you mind expanding on that?" he says with a smile.

She seems to pick up on the fact that it isn't a smile to play around with.

"His middle finger was extended," she says reluctantly. "He was probably flipping off the driver he was overtaking."

"Do you know who that was?"

"Not yet. But the charred right hand is very clearly positioned to give a 'fuck you.' See for yourself."

"The perfect horror film scene," Lindberg says, studying the image on the screen. "Tell me something intelligent about the bomb."

The acting head forensic technician's jaw drops briefly. Then she tells him something intelligent about the bomb:

"A lot of things are pointing to it being remotely detonated. Effective main charge. We don't know exactly what it consisted of, but it seems to have been well balanced. The primary explosive may have been picric acid, and the secondary, potentially diazodinitrophenol, DDNP."

"So the primary explosive activates the secondary explosive?"

"It's very unstable, yes, and it detonates the more stable and powerful secondary explosive of the main charge."

"Homemade?"

She shrugs. "Most likely," she replies. "If so, there'll be fertilizer. You'll have a report in due course."

"But you're saying someone was standing within a certain range with a remote control and detonated the explosive?"

"We're not sure yet exactly how it happened. But conceivably, yes. They definitely make remote triggers with the requisite range."

Lindberg nods and suddenly spots the NFC's head forensic technician farther down the hallway. Wasn't he supposed to be too busy to talk? And behind him, a woman as robust as she is elegant, with her blonde hair in a bun and palpable pep in her step.

"Ankan!" Lindberg exclaims.

Ankan turns to him, makes a quick face, and then bounces on to keep up with the head technician.

Anton Lindberg feels slightly confused.

"A paradigm shift," the acting head forensic technician comments with a grin. Lindberg stares at her. She shrugs.

"Don't worry—it's happening everywhere. The women are taking over."

He chuckles and admits to himself that she's probably right. And that it's far from the worst alternative imaginable.

She gives him a faintly pitying look and offers a few words of consolation: "I'll email you all the documentation."

11

The head forensic technician leads Ankan into his office at the National Forensics Centre in Solna, invites her to sit down in a low swivel chair across from his desk, and turns his computer screen toward her without a word.

Over the past month, she's seen enough of human behavior to realize this is a power move. And enough to not give a shit.

Besides, she's already experienced the shock of her life. The image that covers the screen is a spring breeze in comparison.

It shows a badly burned corpse on a lawn.

"May I introduce Jesper Sahlgren," the technician says with a smile.

"Hi, Jesper," Ankan replies calmly before turning to the slightly more animated of her two interlocutors. "The cat seems to have got Jesper's tongue, so maybe you wouldn't mind filling me in on his story."

The technician clears his throat, sounding faintly disappointed, and says, "Our preliminary analysis shows that the primary explosive was picric acid; and the secondary, DDNP."

"Would you say the explosives used in Vasaparken are similar to the ones found in the BMW in the rapeseed field?"

"Well," the technician says slowly, "we're still far from being able to draw any firm conclusions."

"Do it anyway," Ankan tells him.

The technician grunts and says, "Reasonably similar, yes. On the other hand, it's a fairly typical setup for a homemade bomb. It's the kind of thing you can easily find on the internet."

"Same explosive power?"

"No, the one in Vasaparken was considerably more powerful than the one on the motorway. If we were willing to entertain vastly premature conclusions, we might say the bomber has achieved a more effective blend."

"He's improving?"

"I still wouldn't go so far as to—"

"And a different type of trigger?" Ankan breaks in.

"Two different functions, yes. Remote control on the motorway, mechanical switch at the PR company. Nothing out of the ordinary, really."

"Doesn't the victim look a bit too deformed?"

The technician seems to have recovered from his initial disappointment at Ankan's failure to be shocked and seems to be beginning to work up some professional enthusiasm.

"There were screws, nuts, and nails in the package. The coroner pulled one hundred and twelve foreign objects out of the body. Pretty similar to a classic suicide bomb, actually."

"The package, yes," Ankan says, so as not to add to his eagerness. "Did it come in the post?"

"According to our information, it was proofs from a print shop. Hard copies of ads that were going to be part of an ongoing campaign for the oil industry. But you'd have to get the details from the detectives handling the case."

"I intend to," Ankan says, rising from her chair and exiting into the hallway.

* * *

Driving away from the NFC, Ankan allows herself to marvel a little at her new attitude. At how quickly it changed. She tightens the bun holding her blonde, shoulder-length hair back and gives her reflection a quick glance in the rear-view mirror. She wouldn't have thought it possible six months ago. She'd been thirty-seven then, with a fifteen-year-old daughter, and had been dead. At least spiritually speaking.

Now, she's thirty-eight, her daughter's sixteen, and Ankan's alive. Spiritually as well as physically. And living life to the fullest.

She has no reason whatsoever to try to shake the nickname she's had since her academy days. Annika Stolt proudly embraces Ankan.

No one who hasn't experienced it could possibly imagine what it's like to be told a loved one has died. Completely out of the blue, with no warning. To be standing there with a whisk in your hand when the doorbell rings. Smiling, in the middle of making dinner. She vividly remembers the béchamel sauce dripping from the whisk, slowly, like in some kind of absurd slow motion. And that her daughter, Lina, had been in the kitchen and had heard it all.

Jörgen had been a construction engineer, and it was a work-related fatal injury: a block of concrete had fallen on him from a crane. There had been nothing left to bury.

As though it would have made any difference.

Ankan had been back at work just a couple of weeks later. Working was the one thing she still knew how to do. What she'd been clueless about was grieving. She's not sure she's any better at it now.

But all of a sudden, she does know how to move on.

After not letting herself live for over a year, she had quite a bit of life pent up inside her. And now, she has opened the floodgates.

Online dating. It was as easy as that.

Jörgen had been her only one. No one before him, no one during, no one after. Until now. It was like a revelation.

She turns down Dalagatan, peering up at the buildings until she spots the big black hole where a window had once been. The police cordon is gone, and the hole in the wall's hidden behind plastic sheeting; and yet small crowds seem to continually gather along the edge of Vasaparken. There's no denying it's a spectacular sight.

She spots the two men she's there to see, parks halfway up the pavement, climbs out, and shakes their extended hands.

"Detective Inspector Stolt," the older of the two says with a nod, then points from the hole in the wall to a black spot on the lawn, adding: "Quite a trajectory."

"Is it true Jesper Sahlgren opened a package?"

The younger of the two Stockholm detectives has caught her eye. He has black hair and uncommonly sharp dark brown eyes. She doesn't quite want to look away.

"He was expecting a delivery on Friday afternoon," he answers in a deep baritone, "but the package wasn't sent until Saturday evening, by courier. The firm's junior assistant, Frida Söder, came in from Rimbo to accept delivery, and says she spent several hours waiting for it to arrive. When it finally did, she texted Sahlgren, who was eager enough to drive in early on Sunday morning."

"Around six, yes, and probably dead sober." Ankan nods. "I assume you've talked to both Frida Söder and the courier service?"

"We'll send you copies of the case file," the older man mutters. "Since NOD's apparently going to insist on meddling."

"And?" she says, turning to the younger detective. Who is not wearing a wedding ring.

He replies, "Söder comes across as very trustworthy. The messenger—a Dedik Jaya, Indonesian citizen—on the other hand, has proven impossible to get hold of. He did one last Saturday shift before going off on holiday. But there's nothing suspicious in his past. The only thing worth noting is that his delivery van was parked somewhat carelessly in the DHL car park in Västberga and that he left the keys in the glove box. But those kinds of things happen when drivers are in a hurry."

"But surely someone has to know where he is . . . I'm sorry—what's your name?" "Detective Sargeant Rahim Adbulhamid. His friends tell us northern Norway; Dedik Jaya dreamed of seeing fjords. We've contacted the Norwegian police, but things are still unclear."

"All right, Rahim," Ankan says. "And what do you think?"

The young detective looks slightly taken aback, as though it has never occurred to him that someone might be interested in his opinion.

"The print shop, which is in Jordbro, was under pressure," Rahim Abdulhamid replies after a brief pause. "Jesper Sahlgren was hounding them. They were working overtime on Saturday to finish up. When the proofs were ready to go that afternoon, the person in charge contacted their usual courier service and, as requested, informed Jesper Sahlgren, who in turn contacted Frida Söder."

"And you've sat Frida Söder down with a forensic artist to create a composite sketch of the messenger who delivered the package to Flat Broke Ltd? And then you compared that sketch with a picture of the messenger, Dedik Jaya, who picked up the package from the print shop in Jordbro? And of course you also verified the time it took from when the package left the print shop to when the courier delivered it to the PR company?"

When Rahim Abdulhamid fails to reply with anything but a sheepish look, Ankan makes a snap decision. No online dating tonight.

"All right," she says. "I assume the two of you have put your numbers in this folder so we can reach you at any time?"

It's been approved. Sanctioned. In fact, it was her daughter, Lina, who eventually shook some life back into her mother, who was spending yet another evening staring into the wall, by saying, "I miss him too, but you can't go on like this, Mum." It was like something out of a feel-good film.

The two Stockholm detectives nod reluctantly and walk off. Ankan manages to catch Rahim Abdulhamid's eyes. He stops. She tries to gauge his dark brown gaze, not completely sure he's caught her drift. But maybe clarifying would insult his intelligence? She does it anyway, by making a phone with her right hand and raising it to her ear.

He smiles, nods briefly.

Also smiling, Ankan watches their car accelerate off toward Kungsholmen. Then she takes a short walk around the neighborhood, in expanding concentric circles centered on the burned spot on the lawn.

For once, she feels pleasantly undisturbed. She's looking up at the building across the street, when she reaches a tree set back slightly from Dalagatan.

Something has been carved into the bark. Just below eye level.

This is Vasaparken, Odenplan, Central Stockholm, a part of the world where there are people moving about at all times. What she's looking at could have been carved there at any time.

But Ankan's a detective, a proper detective. And her gut tells her it might be a clue.

She pulls out her phone and snaps a picture of the carving in the bark.

It's two circles.

One inside the other.

12

Sonja Ryd has taken a seat in a living room that smells like widower. It's not an unpleasant smell, but it still strikes her as strange that the homes of all well-preserved widowers smell the same. The home of a widow, on the other hand, has a completely different smell.

The spring sun is streaming in through unwashed windows, illuminating the old man as he carries in coffee cups and a coffeepot, creamer, sugar bowl, and a plate of biscuits. Even though both the service and his movements belong to a bygone era, the shadow he casts seems to belong to a much younger man, his younger self.

Ryd runs a hand over the stubble on her head and smiles at Edward Rasmusson as he sits down on his shadow.

He'd been the chief superintendent of the City Police District when the big police reform struck in 2015 and had seized the opportunity to retire. That's as far as they'd made it in their conversation when he'd shuffled out to the kitchen to make coffee.

"And I've never regretted it," he continues now, as though twenty minutes hadn't passed since he last spoke.

"The reform didn't turn out to be everything people had hoped," Ryd admits.

"More than anything, I was sick of being an administrator."

They sip their coffee. Ryd finds herself dunking.

Rasmusson says, "Lukas Frisell was one of the most promising detectives I've ever met. He was from the right place. He could see through the criminals."

"I'm told you saved him from a life of crime."

The scrawny man looks almost birdlike when he smiles mildly, shrugging his shoulders.

"He saved himself. But it's true my position at the time allowed me freedoms that would be unthinkable nowadays. A police officer, visiting juvenile detention facilities, talking to at-risk young people. Lukas was sixteen and most definitely at risk. It was the early eighties, and he'd grown up rurally, close to nature up north. Alcoholism killed his father, and his mother took her son and relocated to Vällingby. Culture clash, failure to fit in—all that stuff. I especially remember this one conversation I had with him; suddenly, I saw a light in his eyes. It was about nature."

"Nature? His interest in nature?"

"Yes, and I told him there were ways, so long as he made sure he didn't get a criminal record. It took a long time to get him to open up. I suggested the Norrland Rangers; they're as close to nature as you can get within the military. But first he had to finish upper secondary school. He was accepted into a two-year program, some kind of chemical technology thing. I think his time as a ranger actually did reconnect him with nature. Afterward, he applied to the Swedish University of Agricultural Sciences, SUAS, to study agronomy."

"Agronomy? To become a farmer?"

"Well," Rasmussen replies with a smile, "sort of a farmer, sure. He learned to work the soil. But then something made him want to change careers. He called me up, asking how he could join the police."

"And you got him in?"

"That's overstating it. At most, I made him realize how valuable his experience would be to the Police Authority."

"So, if we could just pause here, Frisell possesses the following qualities and skills: practical closeness to nature, criminal experience, chemical technological know-how, ranger training, agronomical knowledge. Even before joining the police, he matched our profile pretty well."

Rasmusson heaves a deep sigh and reluctantly adds, "And that's not taking into account the hostility toward technology he would later develop."

"The hostility that cost Liselott Lindman her life in 2008?"

"We'll never know. But it destroyed Lukas. He left the police and plunged into a personal crisis. Then, he found some meaning in the climate crisis. He was one of the first to sound the alarm about us destroying our own planet. He made his way back to nature, to SUAS, and studied all kinds of things there and became an instructor."

"An instructor at the Swedish University of Agricultural Sciences?"

"Yes, he wanted an offline existence. I continued to keep an eye on him from afar."

"Even after he became a hermit prepper in the woods?"

"Well, no, that was impossible, of course," Rasmusson says with another smile. "But . . . hold on . . ."

Rasmusson gets up. It's as though he and his shadow have traded places. He nimbly disappears through a different door. Ryd can hear him rummaging around on the other side of it.

She thinks. Wonders what it is that feels so off. Isn't it almost as though the old chief superintendent is holding back? Or is it a generational thing? Facts before feelings?

When Rasmusson returns, his shadow is still in charge. He sits down heavily, pulls a newspaper clipping out of a plastic folder, and reads:

> *We know it's time. There are vast cities on our planet into which the sunlight can't reach. The time for sitting back is over. Each one of us has to act. The people responsible must be made to answer for their crimes if we are to survive. The guilty must be held to account.*

Ryd finds herself blinking more times than she'd intended. The cadence is unquestionably familiar. Slightly more direct, true, but surely the spirit of the letter is the same. Even some of the words.

"A short letter to the editor from 2013," Rasmusson says, adjusting his reading glasses. "Greenpeace's membership publication. Lukas wrote quite a bit during his years at SUAS. Fairly irate stuff."

Ryd leans across the table, fixing on him intently.

"Do you recognize the phrase 'the ruins of destruction'?"

"No," Rasmusson replies, frowning. "But it certainly sounds like something he might write."

Ryd nods slowly, then says, "I still don't feel as though you know who Lukas Frisell is."

Rasmusson lets out a giggle; his shadow is pushed back into the sofa.

"When I was young, I always felt a bit odd," he says. "Far too late, I heard about neuropsychiatric disorders and realized how well I fit on what is nowadays called the autism spectrum. Imagine navigating a fairly complex professional life without ever having a clue. Would you forgive me, Sonja Ryd, if I were to ask you if you have a diagnosis?"

Ryd doesn't answer at first, just strokes the stubble on her head. "HSP," she says finally without breaking eye contact.

Rasmusson nods with a smile that might possibly be fatherly.

"You're a highly sensitive person," he confirms. "I have a granddaughter who also feels things very intensely. But I'm not like that. Lukas Frisell is as close to a son as I got in this life. And yet, I don't know him very well—you're right about that. I never fully learned about feelings and attachment. For that, you'll have to talk to his ex-wife, Nina."

"That's where I'm going," Ryd says, standing up.

Edward Rasmusson walks her to the door. They say goodbye, and there's a slightly awkward handshake. When Ryd is halfway down the garden path of the terraced house, Rasmusson says, "There's help to be had—you know that, right? Better help."

She nods with her back to him; hurries around the corner; reaches her car, which is parked next to a simple football pitch; squeezes into it. She fumbles for the half-full bottle of mineral water between the seats. What's left inside is pale yellow and flat.

The taste of lukewarm sauvignon blanc doesn't swirl around her mouth for long; she swallows a bit too quickly, a few too many times. Sonja Ryd stares at the bottle, wincing. It's almost empty. She walks a brisk lap around the football pitch—once, twice, three times—before returning to the car and pulling a small black object out of her pocket. She blows into it, hard. Watches the light flicker between red and green until the green diode emerges victorious.

Sonja Ryd cracks her neck. As she starts the engine, she hears a voice. The voice of a shadow.

"There's help to be had, you know that, right? Better help."

13

As usual, the majestic building is ridiculously hot. It's also almost deserted; it doesn't exactly take a lot of people to run the place. Even though it was originally pitched as a job creator.

Mehrdad Golbahar, data center manager at Amazon's server hall in Västerås, is halfway through his round, inspecting each individual server. The heat is bad enough, but for him, the noise has always been worse. He has tried all kinds of noise-canceling headphones, but so far to no avail. Besides, headphones make him even hotter.

These days, he makes do with standard ear protectors. He just has to save listening to music for his free time.

Unfortunately, the ear protectors aren't very good. Sound tends to leak in. Like now.

A text dings from the shipping department. A new package from HQ has been delivered to the usual collection point.

That collection point is not on the way to Golbahar's next checkpoint, but he could take a slightly roundabout route. He hopes that won't set off any alarms in Seattle, where all the real activity is happening, in a data center that monitors all other data centers. On the other hand, he has no real reason to go over there other than an urge to break with routine, stage a mini rebellion. And it's an unexpectedly strong urge.

Mehrdad Golbahar deviates from his route. He turns left instead of right between the large, rumbling servers. Then he winds his way toward the location where packages from HQ are usually dropped off. As a rule, it's upgraded memory cards, not exactly thrilling stuff.

As he turns the corner of the last of the narrow aisles and steps out into a wider corridor, he glances up at a high-tech CCTV camera, wondering if Seattle is watching him.

A few steps down the corridor, he reaches a table placed between a couple of dimly flashing server racks. On the table is a fairly sizable package.

From HQ.

Nothing life altering.

* * *

The CCTV camera shows a corner of a nondescript industrial building. Since there are no reference points, it's hard to gauge how large the building is. Everything is still.

Completely still.

The absence of sound makes the events that follow ghostly.

The corner of the industrial building is blown outward and sucked toward the ground. Everything is covered with swirling dust. Then, the swirling stops. It's as though the connection has been cut. There's nothing to be seen.

But eventually, the dust does settle.

It's looks like drone footage from Iraq. A very small person staggers out of the building and topples forward. Something rolls away from him or her.

It might be a head.

The laptop is shut, the video disappears.

The only sound is the deep breathing of the universe.

14

Sonja Ryd takes an instant liking to Lukas Frisell's ex-wife. Not least when she's led through the living room of the detached house in Nacka with the words "I'm particularly fond of the word *re-divorced*."

Upward of eighty percent of all patios in Sweden are intended to impress. The one Ryd lets herself be shown onto is definitely one of them. Two glasses of champagne are sparkling in the spring sun, as though they'd been placed there by a butler so discreet as to be invisible. Ryd slumps into something resembling a hammock as the image of her breathalyzer flickering between red and green flashes before her.

"So, you're re-divorced?" she asks, fixing her gaze on Nina Strömblad, who, with the grace of a lifelong ballerina, takes a seat on the other side of the table.

"That's correct," she replies, raising her glass.

Even though Nina Strömblad's main focus seems to be appearances, she strikes Ryd as highly intelligent. If nothing else, she has survived two divorces without falling apart.

"Here's to divorce," Strömblad says.

Ryd raises her glass, touching it to her lips but stopping at that. "So, shall we move on to Lukas Frisell?" she asks.

"Touched a nerve, did I?" Nina Strömblad says with a smile. "You're surrounded by a faint divorce aura. I thought that the moment I saw you. Tell me."

"Is that the key?" Ryd counters. "To get you to talk to me?"

"Sure, why not. The key, the password, the code—whatever. Quid pro quo, darling."

Sonja Ryd's first instinct is to lie. But instead, she says, "I cheated and he left me."

"And then you shaved off your hair?" Strömblad says, still smiling. "Because you felt like a tyskertøs? A traitor?"

Ryd is unable to suppress the compulsive gesture. She energetically rubs her stubble, saying, "I'm actually starting to like it. Is the door open now?"

"A crack," Nina Strömblad replies. "What do you want to know?"

"Where to find Lukas Frisell."

Strömblad leans back in her chair, nodding slowly, taking another sip of champagne. "I see," she says. "I assume you know he was a very good detective."

"That's what I'm trying to understand. We just need to talk to him."

"His favorite phrase was 'We just need to talk to him.' It made him laugh out loud. This will go easier if you're honest, Sonja."

Ryd studies her opponent. It's an entire marriage ago, but surely there are all kinds of feelings flailing about there still.

"It's about crimes committed in the name of the climate," she says.

"I see," Nina Strömblad says, changing before Sonja's eyes.

"What do you see?"

"Just that he became implacable about that particular subject. With everything else, the relentlessness was just for show."

"He became implacable when you discussed the climate?"

"But that was then," Strömblad adds quickly. "Not now."

"How do you know? What kind of contact do you have with him now?"

Strömblad slips back into her urbane, re-divorced persona, smiling wryly. "The spiritual kind, of course."

"I'd be grateful if you could refrain from wasting my time."

"No contact at all, my dear Sonja. He's kept his promise to never come back. Saying we were an odd couple would be an understatement."

"Opposites attract?"

"At first, always. In the long run, never."

"And the rift between you was about his passion for the climate?"

"I had no problem with the passion—passion is passion. It was his unhappiness that bothered me. He simply didn't like living in town. He wanted to buy a rural summer house, but to me all of Stockholm was a rural summer house. Why buy another, you know?"

"I suppose there's quite a bit of nature here," Ryd says, indicating the vast and obscenely tidy garden.

"Tamed nature," Strömblad says, smiling. "You really think Lukas would have liked this? The gardener tends to the bushes every two days."

"So not the old urban Nina Strömblad, then?"

"I was Nina Frisell back then. Nina Frisell, born Silfversparre, ballerina. Lukas could have taken half of everything in the divorce—I didn't know what a prenup was. But he didn't want anything. He even left some rubbish behind that I took with me and put in the attic. I will leave it to you, since you clearly have some experience with therapy, to psychoanalyze the reason why."

"There are still lingering feelings?"

"Lukas was a force of nature, authentic to the core. In the men I've met since, I've only found tamed nature. I think I looked for the opposite of him after he was gone, and old man Strömblad was a perfect fit. Not an authentic bone in his body. And this time it was my turn not to sign a prenup. Which is why I'm sitting here now with a gardener and a butler, enjoying my solitude amid the ruins of destruction."

"As Lukas liked to put it?" Strömblad studies Ryd.

"You 'just want to talk to him'?" she says after a long pause. "And yet you're familiar with one of his favorite phrases? Borrowed from a eulogy by Romantic poet Franzén, in which 'only the glory of memory still illuminates the ruins of destruction.' Which is to say the present."

Sonja Ryd is taking notes. She presses: "But you don't know where to find him? You're telling the truth?"

Nina Strömblad nods without any sign of being upset.

"It doesn't feel like it, but it was a very long time ago. We got divorced in the spring of 2009. Since then, we've had no communication whatsoever."

"What about friends? Contacts? Anyone we could talk to?"

"His old mentor, I suppose, Edward Something-son. Lukas wasn't very sociable. Parents dead, no siblings. There was someone called Rudolfsson, possibly Aron; they ran, like, marathons together. A couple of eccentrics he talked to in various contexts, Kalle Råman and Lelle Bergis. And that female detective. What was her name? Eva Nyström, maybe . . ."

"Eva Nyman?"

"Yes, I guess that was it," Strömblad replies, her voice suddenly sounding strange.

"And what was his relationship with this Nyman?" Sonja Ryd asks neutrally.

Nina Strömblad studies her with a curious, somehow probing smile. Then she says, "He called her his only female friend."

"And you never suspected there was more to it?"

"I had no reason to. Our mutual passion was the one thing that survived right until the end. He was fucking me when I flushed my wedding ring down the toilet."

Ryd manages to disguise her laugh as a cough. "Sounds like he didn't fully accept the divorce?"

"He did. The divorce was a failure to him, yes, but something inside him also longed for a proper . . . I don't know . . . bachelor period. He never really had one. I guess he needed it. Unlike me."

"You went for old man Strömblad instead?"

Nina Strömblad chuckles. "That was more of a financial decision."

"And there was never any talk about . . . children, with Lukas?"

Strömblad smiles inwardly, shaking her head. "Neither one of us actually wanted any, so no. For completely different reasons. Lukas refused to bring a child into the ruins of destruction. I was simply too egocentric. Or just not fit to be in a nuclear family. Much like yourself, I'd wager."

Sonja Ryd stares straight ahead for a moment. Then she says, "Would it be too much trouble to go up to the attic?"

It takes Strömblad several seconds to connect the dots. Then she smiles her slightly mischievous smile and stands up. Ryd follows her, knocking back the rest of her champagne on the way.

While Nina Strömblad is rummaging around the hot, dusty attic, Ryd receives a text. It reads simply: *Reconvene in Waiting Hall immediately. Hall of hell, Västerås. Check the news.*

Ryd leaves Nina Strömblad's house more abruptly than planned. As Sonja Ryd walks through the meticulously kept garden toward her car, she peers down into the cardboard box in her arms and that holds a bunch of rubbish from Lukas Frisell's past. She can make out a couple of limp notebooks, a tangle of cables with various plugs sticking out, a far too well-used hairbrush, and a wedding photo.

She pushes the box into the back seat and climbs in behind the wheel, holding the photograph. Before starting the engine, she spends a minute studying the picture.

Nina the ballerina is adorable in her bespoke wedding dress. Lukas with his wispy hair is sternly handsome in his police uniform. Ryd studies his bright blue eyes. Then she throws the photograph in the back and grabs her water bottle.

To her disappointment, it's almost empty.

15

Sonja Ryd is the last to arrive in the Waiting Hall. She's rewarded with a pointed look from Eva Nyman, who's standing behind the desk at the front of the room. Something's going on behind Nyman, projected on the wall, but it's vague, a peculiar, barely visible graininess.

But then things begin to emerge out of the diffuse haze. It's smoke, dust, and dirt settling. A toppled wall appears, a building partially demolished. And out of the ruins staggers a very small person. The person stumbles and topples forward. Something rolls away.

It might be a head.

A collective groan ripples through the Waiting Hall. At length, Chief Inspector Eva Nyman clears her throat. Amid the horror, she's allowing herself to look a little bit too smug.

"Three cases become one?" Sonja Ryd asks with a wry smile.

Nyman feels lightly irritated that her face is so transparent, but she nods slowly. "This is the exact moment that confirmed there's a violent climate terrorist on the loose in Sweden. Let's wait and see what happens now. This case just took on completely new dimensions."

She looks around the Waiting Hall. It's as though it's suddenly occurring to everyone what has just happened. The Nova Group has gone from peripheral to pivotal in one crazy bang.

Nyman continues: "So, this is an Amazon server hall in Västerås. It's almost like a war has begun. Anyway, the hall of hell has been filled with dread. Sarwani, Lindberg, and Ankan, get over there. Now."

* * *

Anton Lindberg does the driving. His burly body hunched over the wheel, driving fast, not hesitating to use the unmarked car's hidden blue lights, and the sirens too, on and off—anything to push through the rush-hour traffic.

"They should have let us use the helicopter," Shabir Sarwani mutters from the back seat. After all, Nova's in charge of the country's most high-profile investigation now."

Ankan's in the passenger seat, silent and torn. True, she's at the center of a case that's shaping up to be big, but she has also been looking forward to meeting up with young Rahim Abdulhamid tonight. Identifying differences, similarities, analyzing the overarching vibe. She met Jörgen at sixteen and never had a carefree period.

She's making up for that now.

She's still hopeful she might still be able to get away later tonight.

Lindberg's fully focused on driving. They roll into a congested Västerås. They can navigate by setting their course for the smoke signal, which, almost two hours after the explosion, is still wreathing its way into the sky.

What greets them is a battlefield. The uniformed officers guarding the police cordon are composed but pale in front of an enormous facility that looks like nothing so much as a prison. One of the corners has been blown out. That's where the loved ones have gathered, at a safe distance. Six, seven fire engines are busy putting out the fire, but the column of smoke stubbornly continues to rise. A number of crime scene technicians and plainclothes policemen are also active on the scene. Ankan thinks she recognizes a fit-looking bloke from Security Services, but it's a classically pudgy copper who comes sauntering over to greet them.

"So, NOD?" he asks without asking. "We've been waiting for you."

"Rush-hour traffic," Lindberg mutters during the introductions.

"What do you have so far?" Sarwani, asks, ever direct.

The pudgy copper introduces himself as lead investigator Nilsson and gestures toward the smoking data center.

"They're keeping their cards close to the vest—put it that way. The local head of operations is said to be on his way after a day of meeting in Randers, of all places. The only thing we've managed to pry out of them, other than the CCTV footage, is another video, this one from inside the building."

Nilsson pulls out an iPad, carelessly scraping it against the hood of their car as he opens a file. They crowd in around him.

The image quality is unexpectedly decent. A robust man in shorts and ear protectors shoots the camera a skeptical glance and then takes a few steps over to a table between rows of blinking servers. The man bends down and begins to open a large package sitting on the table. The last thing they see before darkness abruptly falls is the brief but clear cracking of the camera lens.

Nilsson rewinds the footage, slowly, slowly, until the man's fingers reach the package. Then he pauses it and starts zooming in on a spot on the left side of the image. Behind a row of servers, something that might be a small patch of skin becomes visible.

"That's an elbow," Nilsson clarifies.

They stare at the elbow sticking out from behind the server.

"The man opening the package is data center manager Mehrdad Golbahar. There's not much left of him. The man with the elbow was called Andreas Grahn. He's the person you saw staggering out of the destroyed building in the previous video."

"The one with the head . . . ?" Ankan asks tentatively.

"I'm afraid so," Nilsson nods. "But despite the extensive damage, Grahn and Golbahar appear to be the only fatalities."

"Injuries?" Anton Lindberg asks.

Nilsson shrugs and says, "Nothing serious. According to emergency services, five people with smoke inhalation were evacuated. To the best of our knowledge, there are no other victims inside."

"And what do we know about the package?" Shabir Sarwani asks.

"At 2.43 PM, the shipping department sent a text indicating that a package from HQ had been placed in the location where the technical staff always picked up deliveries from the United States."

"Have you tracked the package's journey across the Atlantic?"

"As a rule, these are top-secret deliveries that aren't handled by regular freight companies. They're flown by the in-house airline, Amazon Air. At this stage of the investigation, we've not been able to track the package's route online. But the plane did land here in Västerås."

"The bomb's unlikely to have come from the United States," Sarwani says. "Sometime between landing at Västerås Airport and being delivered to the data center, the contents were switched, just like in Vasaparken. That's what we need to focus on. The person who delivered the package has to be identified."

"I suppose he's on holiday in northern Norway too," mutters Ankan, who at this point is forced to accept that her date just got canceled.

Shabir Sarwani gazes out at the partially destroyed hall of hell. It was on his list. Were they not warned? Did they ignore the warning? Either way, what happened here is an escalation. This prick's growing big and powerful.

What's more, he's technically skilled, knowledgeable, smart. It's expected packages he's blowing up, not unexpected ones. Somehow, he knows the packages are en route before they arrive, nicks them, and swaps out the contents without anyone noticing.

Do they really not have a single suspect? Sarwani wonders. *No technically skilled climate activist in their database who might conceivably resort to violence? Is anyone even looking into that?*

What is Sonja Ryd doing, for example? They think no one notices, but the Nyman-Ryd duo is playing their own game, as usual. What are they up to?

Sarwani studies the enormous, partially destroyed building. He can smell smoke, sure—but isn't there also a faint whiff of cover-up in the air?

The only thing he knows for sure is that it won't be long before they have another letter.

16

Chief Inspector Eva Nyman tumbles into her office after a day of emergency meetings—but also of quiet praise. After all, NOD's top brass knows Eva Nyman was the person who put the investigation on the right track.

The whole day has been about Västerås. Not just in the conference rooms, but possibly even more so in the hallways between them. You can tell just by looking at the staff, officers as well as civilians, that something has happened in Sweden. That a series of terrorist attacks is about to escalate. That practically anything can happen.

In the conference rooms, the discussions have revolved around what happened with the warning Nyman and the NOD sent out just over two hours before the explosion. No answer has been forthcoming from Amazon; they've been unable to get in touch with anyone senior.

Eva Nyman slumps down behind her antique desk and hears herself sigh. Several different divisions within the NOD are working on the case now, but at least her own group, her Nova, is still one of them. So far, they've been instructed to keep investigating the terrorist angle, which affords them certain liberties. But that's not what she wants to think about right now.

What she wants to think about is policework, not politics. She thumps a stack of photos down on the desk. She likes real photographs, the kind you can hold in your hand, that have a smell. She slowly flips through them, astonished by the destruction in the server hall.

They should have listened. They should have taken Sarwani's warning seriously. They should have been more wary of deliveries.

Her mind wanders. The big multinationals are far larger than most nation-states. They are nation-states with their own laws, their own judiciary and police—nation-states that have never been touched by such things as democracy or codetermination. They're worlds unto themselves.

Eventually, Eva Nyman runs out of photographs and instead stares down at a different type of paper at the bottom of the pile. It must have been sitting on the desk already when she brought out the photographs.

And it looks the same as the last letter, with its typewritten address: *"Chief Inspector Eva Nyman, NOD, Police HQ, Stockholm."* She's been ordered to hand any further letters straight over to the NFC, but long before this one turned up, she'd decided she'd hold off on that.

She pulls on latex gloves, picks up her letter opener, and slices the envelope open.

Peering in, she can make out parts of the text, running all the way to the edges of the paper, an endless loop of typewritten words. She gingerly pulls the letter out of the envelope and reads:

> *Beware, you climate skeptics. Which is to say all of you, because in your heart of hearts, you have no desire to make even the smallest change to the way you live. Nothing. That's what climate skepticism is—not what you say, the claims you make. The reverberations from the hall of hell are echoing still. We must reject these lives of mass consumerism, and we must do it now. Soon, the wave that will wake you from your selfish stupor will wash over you. The wave is building. It will wash away parts of the dying city of bridges, and God's white dwelling will gaze down upon the ruins of destruction. What you have witnessed is only the beginning. And in that beginning, your woefully brief future will behold its reflection. Perhaps it will even catch a glimpse of its truest self before it ceases to exist. Beware, you climate skeptics.*

Eva Nyman stops reading the letter aloud but leaves it projected onto the wall of the Waiting Hall. After a brief pause, she continues: "Thank you all for working late tonight."

"Like we had a choice," Ankan grumbles.

Shabir Sarwani jumps in: "And by that she means anything else would be unthinkable. Västerås is on its own; all information is being relayed to us."

"Unthinkable indeed," Nyman agrees before changing tack. "The press has already given our guy the moniker the 'Terrorist Bomber,' whatever that's supposed to mean. So, what do you have to say about this letter?"

"'The wave is building,'" Anton Lindberg quotes.

"We noticed," Nyman replies. "Look deeper."

"The hall of hell gets a mention," Ankan says.

"That's old news too. Come on now."

Sitting apart from the others, in a darker corner, Sonja Ryd says, "I guess it's obvious the core message is that the larger wave 'will wash away parts of the dying city of bridges, and God's white dwelling will gaze down upon the ruins of destruction.'"

"Yes, but what does it mean?" Nyman asks.

"The city of bridges has to be Stockholm," Lindberg offers. "God's white dwelling should be a . . . church?"

"Certainly possible," Ryd agrees with a nod. "And if that's the case, the threat is not aimed at the church, which seems to be there to bear witness, but rather at something in the vicinity of a church in Stockholm, which is about to be blown up."

"A white church," Sarwani says, launching a quick google search on his phone. "There must be fifty white churches in this town," Ankan objects.

"Hundreds," Sarwani replies, still googling. "If you take all of Stockholm County, there are hundreds of white churches."

"The county extends far beyond the bridges, though," Ryd notes. "Limit your search to the inner city."

Sarwani activates an image search while Nyman wheels out an old-fashioned whiteboard filled with information. She attaches a copy of the new letter in a fourth column—to the right of the Motorway, Vasaparken, and Västerås—which she names "The White Church."

"There's a lot of information missing here," she says, pointing to the third column. "I expect all of you to—"

"Not just there," Sarwani cuts in without looking up from his phone.

"Oh?" Nyman says, trying to catch his eye, but to no avail; he's busy with Stockholm's many churches. Which doesn't prevent him from seemingly distractedly answering, "You're working on some kind of lead, right?"

Nyman makes no reply. She avoids Ryd's attempt at eye contact too. Only then does Sarwani look up.

"I'm right, aren't I? But what's with the secrecy?"

Everyone's undivided attention is on Nyman now. She lets the silence stretch out, frantically trying to think of a way out. Then she blinks and settles for a confession. "It's still very tentative. It's about my personal suspicion of a former colleague. There's no concrete evidence of any kind."

"Colleague?" Lindberg exclaims. "A police officer?"

"Former," Nyman clarifies. "Sonja can explain as soon as we're done discussing the letter."

"I'd say we're getting somewhere," Ryd curtly puts in.

Sarwani studies Nyman for a few more seconds. Then he says, "The result of my at-a-glance search is four."

"Four?"

"Only four of Stockholm's churches appear to be more or less white, as in 'God's white dwelling': Adolf Fredrik, Gustaf Vasa, Djurgårdskyrkan, possibly Matteus—it's hard to tell from these pictures. And then there are evangelical churches like Filadelfiakyrkan and Sankt Peters Kyrka. I don't know if we should count those."

"That's excellent news," Eva Nyman says with relief. "So, what do these divine dwellings gaze down upon? That will be your next task, to narrow down potential targets, and I don't care if it takes all night. Because we're talking central Stockholm now, my friends, and if this bomb is allowed to go off, the attention of the entire world will be on us. And with that, Sonja, why don't you introduce our so-called suspect."

Sonja Ryd's steps are very measured as she walks up to the front of the room. She moves over to the whiteboard; the magnet snaps as she puts up a photograph in an empty corner. The picture looks ancient, like something from the Second World War.

"This is the last known photograph of Lukas Frisell."

17

The weights move up and down at breakneck speed. From the sound, it's clear the black plates aren't meant to dance so recklessly along the cables. But Sonja Ryd's alone. The best thing about the gym located a hundred yards from her flat is that there's never anyone else there this early.

She works out furiously, keeping up the high pace throughout the entire session.

Today needs to be kick-started, because it got so late last night. And consequently, so unhealthy. It's possible she's punishing herself. She tries to pump both the hangover and the word *tyskertøs* out of her spine, fighting against the tension of the upper-back machine.

The last twenty reps completely wipe her out. She slumps over, panting, pain radiating through the muscles of her upper back. After a moment of stillness, she rubs the stubble on her head vigorously and pushes up onto her feet. As she staggers toward the changing rooms, a single image is seared into her mind. It feels ancient, like something from the Second World War.

That image is her sole focus now. Nothing else.

* * *

Even though it was past midnight when they left the station, everyone's back in by eight. How the altarpiece of their shrine, the large whiteboard, got to the office remains a mystery.

Eva Nyman moves between the desks. She can feel her team's energy. She knows that energy is what she needs to spend her day tending. Because there's no one better than this ragged crew. Than Nova. But she knows there are other larger, more powerful organizations that want to take the case away from them, not least the one that "prevents threats against Sweden's national security and the freedoms and liberties of its citizens." Even just within NOD, other divisions are eagerly positioning themselves to take over.

She quietly slips out of the room without anyone noticing.

Ankan tightens her blonde bun while continuing to communicate with Västerås. The crime scene investigation has, by means unknown, been fast-tracked; the evidence collection has already been completed; and the rebuilding of the server hall is in full swing.

Replacement parts were flown in overnight from Seattle. How much of the so-called cloud, which is to say regular people's files and documents, was annihilated remains unclear. Ankan has been trying to get hold of someone senior in the shipping department. So far, no luck. She turns her attention back to Derik Jaya, the DHL courier who is purportedly on holiday in northern Norway.

Anton Lindberg has been in touch with the NFC, the National Forensic Centre. Their preliminary analyses indicate that the explosives used in Västerås were similar to the ones used in the two previous blasts. His attempts to push the head forensic technician to say more than that fell flat. They'll get back to him when they know more.

Instead, Lindberg turns to Shabir Sarwani.

"You take the evangelical churches," Sarwani says. "Identify possible nearby targets."

He himself is doing the same for the four white churches that belong to the Swedish Church. He's decided to be thorough. What does each steeple "gaze down upon?" He draws circles based on the height of each tower.

If his hypothesis is correct, large parts of the city are under threat.

Even tiny Djurgårdskyrkan, a wooden church that looks more like someone's house, can, despite its complete lack of elevation, gaze down upon parts of the Gröna Lund, though arguably not so far as the Abba Museum or up to Skansen. Adolf Fredrik, for its part, "gazes down upon" the Social Democrats' party headquarters and a large publishing house on Sveavägen, as well as parts of pedestrianized Drottninggatan, including the exact spot where the truck used for the Islamist attack a few years earlier was stolen. Gustaf Vasa gazes down upon one of the city's transportation hubs, Odenplan Square, and parts of Vasaparken, an interesting but probably farfetched connection. Matteus, which is at least almost white—Sarwani stopped by on his way to work to make sure—"gazes down upon," among other things, Vanadisplan Square and the other entrance to Odenplan's metro and commuter train station.

Sarwani studies his map and the four circles on it, then watches Lindberg work on the two white evangelical churches.

Sonja Ryd is working the Frisell lead, asking herself if Frisell knows enough about homemade explosives to pull these things off. He made it halfway through the agronomy program and can probably be assumed to be familiar with fertilizer. He completed the chemical technology program in upper secondary. She needs to find out exactly what he did at Sweden's University of Agronomical Sciences after quitting the police. But first, Frisell's potential contacts, as identified by his ex-wife, Nina Strömblad. The supposed running buddy, Aron Rudolfsson; the "eccentrics," Kalle Råman and Lelle Bergis.

Rudolfsson was likely not a police officer, or Nina Strömblad would have said so. The only match Ryd has turned up is the CEO of a lighting company in Sorsele. She makes the call. A bad-tempered Aron Rudolfsson doesn't know anyone by the name Lukas Frisell. She moves on. There are a handful of Karl Råmans in the country, a couple in Stockholm. She dials both numbers, no answer. And Lelle Bergis is a silly name. Lelle is likely short for Lennart, but Bergis could be Berg, Bergström, Bergman, anything, really.

Instead, Sonja Ryd calls the Swedish University of Agricultural Sciences in Ultuna outside Uppsala. After being passed around for a while, she's told a close colleague of Frisell's from the year 2009 to 2014 still works there, a Leif Stierna. She calls, texts, and emails him, but hears nothing back. But she's told Leif Stierna is expected to be in his office later that day.

A phone rings discreetly somewhere in the office. Ankan answers, listening intently before shouting, "That was the technicians working on the Vasaparken blast. They've found unidentified DNA in what's left of the bomb."

"Fuck me," Anton Lindberg exclaims. "The prick cut himself while he was making it?"

"Do we still have Lukas Frisell's DNA in our elimination database?" Sonja Ryd asks. "Doubtful," Sarwani replies. "It's been too long since he was a copper."

Ryd stares straight ahead for a moment, it feels as though she should have reacted already. Then, she does. She dives in under her desk and rummages through the box of Frisell's belongings, the one Nina Strömblad kept in her attic.

When Ryd reemerges, she's holding a far too well-used hairbrush, studying it. After confirming that it contains hairs complete with follicles, she slips it into an evidence bag, hands it to Ankan, and says, "Time to give the technicians something real to do."

18

The main campus of the Swedish University of Agricultural Sciences in Ultuna, on the outskirts of Uppsala, is extensive. While parking her car, Sonja Ryd marvels at its size.

It's a sunny early-summer day. While walking through the pleasantly calm campus, it strikes her just how unnecessary all the stress and anxiety is. The things that have forced her into what might be an addiction are all illusions, possibly figments of her HSP, her "highly sensitive personality." Suddenly, she can see where Lukas Frisell is coming from. Imagine just leaving everything stress inducing behind. Sinking into nature. Returning to the origin.

Contributing only minimally to the end of the world.

Once she reaches the main office, she's given a small, nondigital map with directions to Leif Stierna's office.

He looks like a scholar. A generic scholar, from any subject or discipline. The same furrowed brow Ryd knows so well from back when she was on the verge of plunging headfirst into the chasms of the academic world herself. But she was heading in the direction of philosophy; Leif Stierna's an agronomist. And he has a goatee.

"We worked together on some things," Stierna says with a nod, swiping on his phone. "We were jointly in charge of several programs and courses. That being said, Frisell didn't mind teaching virtually anything you can think of, including things on the fringes of our discipline."

"Fringes?"

"SUAS runs courses in several other locations too: Umeå, Alnarp, Skinnskatteberg, and a few other places. At first, Lukas was happy to go there—the more remote locations were where they do forestry anyway, the things that ought to interest a prepper—but toward the end, he spent most of his time here in Ultuna."

"Would you say you and Lukas Frisell were friends?"

Stierna bobs his head slightly, his frown deepening. Then his face relaxes. "Yes, here it is," he says, holding the phone out to Ryd as he adds, "This picture must be ten years old now."

She takes the phone, recognizing a slightly more time-worn version of the man with the wispy hair from Nina Strömblad's wedding photo. Leif Stierna, on the other hand, looks exactly the same, and they have their arms around each other, beaming, surrounded by a group of about ten students.

Ryd nods and gives him the phone back.

"Is this in response to my question asking if you were friends?" Stierna flashes her a quick, mirthless smile.

"We went out together reasonably often, for dinner, a pint. We had a shared interest in nature and were both single."

"So why the scholarly frown?"

"Pardon?"

"You hesitated. Why the hesitation?"

"I suppose our personalities were rather different. He was driven by this intense zeal.

I'd already accepted the teacher role, dedicating most of my time, both then and now, to theoretical agronomy. In all honesty, I found him a bit frightening."

"Frightening how?"

"His overly intense zeal. His slightly volatile tendency to aggression. Always dead certain and ready to fight for his conviction."

"So what was Frisell's degree in? Agronomy?"

"I actually don't know. When he returned to SUAS after his time as a detective, he completed a bunch of courses very quickly and then began teaching agronomy, forestry, fossil-free farming, environmental science. He was popular, not least among the female students. His lectures on crisis preparedness, which presumably built in part on skills he'd picked up as a police officer, were extremely popular and even videotaped so they could be shown at other campuses where Frisell was active. I can't tell you if they ever were, though."

Ryd looks down at her phone, which is sitting out on the desk between her and Stierna. It's recording. Without it, she wouldn't have a chance of remembering everything. She's not a scholar anymore. And very far from a philosopher.

What's more, her handwriting's illegible.

"What did he tell you about his past as a detective?"

"Not much. It was as though he wanted to bury it. But it was certainly noticeable, at first by how frustrated he was about how his time there ended. He said the Police Authority had been turned into a digital and bureaucratic institution. But in time, he leaned into his calm academic existence in nature's bosom here at SUAS. You might say he shifted his zeal from the Police Authority to fighting climate change."

"And he did a lecture series on crisis preparedness? What is that?"

"How to survive large global crises. Like war, floods, earthquakes. If the internet and the electrical grids are knocked out. If we're forced to return to a Stone Age state."

"Did the preparedness lectures include elements of violence?"

Stierna shrugs. "I have to admit I never sat in on those lectures. It wasn't my cup of tea, I like structure, order, neatly ploughed fields. But sure, there were clear self-defense components in Lukas's syllabuses. He used his police background. Firearms were definitely discussed. But primarily hunting knives."

"Homemade explosives?"

"Not that I recall, but explosives could conceivably fall under the headings of both self-defense and hunting. I seem to remember him talking about hunting with simple explosives once."

Ryd's silent for a while, letting that information sink in. Then something buzzes inside her.

"The photograph you showed me," she says. "Where is it from?"

Leif Stierna eyes her, looking surprised. "I got it from a student. Via Facebook, I believe."

"Facebook, eh?" Ryd says. "Would you mind if we have a closer look at the account you got it from?"

With a measure of reluctance, Stierna opens his computer, without letting Ryd see the screen, and begins to scroll.

"Ten years ago," he says, shaking his head.

After a few silent minutes, he finally slows down and seems to find what he's looking for.

"Here," he says, pointing. "The picture was shared on a Facebook page called 'Fun with Farming.'"

"Cute," Ryd comments tartly. "Is the page still active?"

Stierna clicks around briefly, then replies, "Seems like it. But the last post is from 2015. It might have been a student, documenting his or her years at the university."

Sonja Ryd nods and goes beyond staring at her phone on the desk by also committing something to memory before changing the subject.

"Did Frisell live here?"

Stierna scratches his little goatee and replies, "He had a flat on campus, yes. In fact, it might have been a student flat. But he was also building some kind of dwelling somewhere in the woods."

"A dwelling? Do you know where?"

"I'm afraid not. We weren't that close. But . . ."

"Yes? But?"

"I'm remembering some kind of rumor. I think there was someone, some—I don't know, some prepper 'guru,' who led him down the survivalist path."

"So he did become a survivalist?"

"I really don't know. He just disappeared after . . . spring term 2014, I think. But there was a rumor."

"Apparently SUAS is positively swirling with rumors," Ryd says with a smile. "Did you ever meet this 'guru'?"

Stierna shakes his head. "No, never."

"Do you remember if the rumors gave him a name?"

Stierna seems to be reaching far back into the marshes of his memory. "I'm afraid I'm just terrible with names," he says.

"Take your time," Ryd tells him, fighting every instinct she has.

"Mark something," Stierna finally says.

"First name Mark? With a Swedish surname? Or a foreign one?"

"No, Mark as part of a surname. Like, Marklund, Lundmark."

"Markström, Stenmark, Markberg, Sundmark, Marklind, Bergmark, Lindmark . . . ?"

"I don't know . . ."

A miniscule mite of a thought takes off inside Ryd's head. It buzzes around, unable to find a place to land.

"Are you sure you can't remember, Leif?" she asks, playing for time. "Do you know if he was an old or new friend of his?"

"Old, I think. I believe he was mentioned early on in our acquaintance. But I don't recall the context."

Just then, the mite lands in the right nook of her brain. And as it does, it activates a word. The name *Bergis*.

Lelle Bergis.

"Could it have been Bergmark?" she asks. "Lennart Bergmark?"

19

Eva Nyman studies herself in the Gustavian mirror hanging next to her custom built-in bookshelf. What's lurking behind that furrowed face that always looks grimmer than she wishes it did? What's there under that thick mane of hair that can't decide whether it's brown or gray?

Is it a team leader who can handle a case that just keeps growing? How long will it be before the media dig up the dark parts of her history? Will she be able to stand strong in that storm?

And how certain is she about Lukas Frisell? Certain enough to waste her primary resource, Sonja Ryd, on a lead that's Eva Nyman's and no one else's? There won't be anyone else to blame if things go sideways.

She takes a deep breath, resisting the temptation to dial that number that she—contrary to its owner's express wishes—has memorized. She has to see this all the way through, all by herself, there's no other option.

Just as she's about to step back into the office, and her phone rings. It's Sonja Ryd's number.

* * *

Each of them enters the Waiting Hall with their mind elsewhere. Ankan is thinking about the two couriers who seem to have vanished without a trace, Dedik Jaya from Vasaparken and Wilhelm Bock from Västerås. Anton Lindberg is pondering matching explosives. Shabir Sarwani's preoccupied with the idea of an impending explosion in central Stockholm.

"I want a very quick update on the latest," Eva Nyman says from the desk at the front of the room. "Brief and to the point, please. Ankan?"

"I have two missing couriers," Ankan replies, opening her laptop. "Dedik Jaya, the courier who delivered the Vasaparken package, didn't go on holiday to norther Norway. And Amazon's in-house courier, Wilhelm Bock, who drove from the airport to the server hall, is also missing. In other words, both of them have disappeared. And the sketch artist has finished the composites. Can I put them up?"

Nyman nods, Ankan clicks. A reasonably realistic face appears on the wall next to Dedik Jaya's passport photo. It's immediately obvious they're not the same person. Even so, a sigh or two is heard in the Waiting Hall. The Nova Group has seen enough phantom images to realize the sketch is far too abstract to be used for facial recognition. Ankan moves on to the next drawing. This one elicits no sighing. Not because the second portrait is any more concrete than the first one, but because they look distinctly alike. And the composite definitely doesn't look anything like the passport photo next to it, which belongs to courier Wilhelm Bock.

"I hear you," Ankan says, even though no one has said a word. "No, none of the witnesses can remember any defining characteristics; in both cases, the man in question kept his face slightly averted. But it seems to have been the same man. In his thirties."

"Are we prepared to say he's an immigrant?" Lindberg asks.

"That would be jumping to conclusions," Nyman says, glancing at her watch. "What we can say is that he appears to possess some features commonly associated with people from the Middle East."

"And we have no idea who he is," Anka concludes. "I'll distribute these nationally, and we'll see if that turns up anything."

"Thank you," Nyman says with another glance at her watch. "Anton?"

"I'm afraid I don't have much," Lindberg replies. "The explosives used in Västerås appear to be consistent with the two previous blasts. I'm waiting for more detailed info from the NFC. But I've been working up a threat assessment of the areas around a couple of evangelical churches."

"Wonderful," Nyman sighs. "Shabir?"

"Yeah, so Anton's been identifying potential targets around a couple of white evangelical churches in inner-city Stockholm. I have a few more I could put up on the wall right now?"

Nyman presses her lips together but then nods.

"Here's the list," Sarwani says. "And given as how my previous list was spot on, I think this one's worth taking seriously."

Just as around twenty potential terrorist targets in Stockholm appear on the wall behind Nyman, a phone rings loudly. Nyman nods curtly and clicks her keyboard. Sarwani's list is replaced by a woman with wireless headphones and short brown stubble on her head, who seems to be calling from a library.

"Hello, everyone," Sonja Ryd says, and is met with no response whatsoever. "I'm at the Swedish University of Agricultural Sciences in Uppsala."

A palpable lack of interest quickly spreads through the Waiting Hall. Unbothered, Ryd continues. "I think I've managed to dig up the name of Lukas Frisell's survivalist mentor in the woods of Uppland. He seems to have worked on Frisell for a good long while before he managed to persuade him to leave civilization. His name is quite likely Lennart Bergmark."

The lack of interest is slowly fading.

"There are three Lennart Bergmarks of roughly the right age and proximity," Ryd goes on. "We need to talk to them. I believe the right one would know where Frisell can be found."

"Shouldn't Bergmark be a hermit in the woods himself, then?" Sarwani asks. "And consequently, as lacking in home address, identity as Frisell?"

"Are you suggesting there's no point trying?" Ryd asks, staring into the camera.

"No," Eva Nyman intercedes firmly. "If he was Frisell's mentor, he's likely older than him. That's your thinking too, right, Sonja? The person we're looking for is maybe ten years older than Frisell. Is a person still physically able to do the survivalist thing, living completely outside of the society, at the age of sixty-five? He may very well have moved closer to some form of civilization."

Up on the wall, Sonja Ryd nods and says, "Either way, all three Lennart Bergmarks live in rural locations. One is near Uppsala—I'll take that one. And then there's one south of Stockholm, outside Ösmo. And one near Åkers styckebruk."

"Do you have anything else on them?"

"These old geezers are not the type to flaunt their lives on Facebook," Ryd replies. "Here's what I've managed to dig up: Lennart Bergmark in Åkers styckebruk owns a very large piece of land that seems to be located on the outskirts of the village proper. The Lennart Bergmark in Ösmo lives in the middle of the woods and is a member of some kind of hunting team. I'd say he's our most likely candidate. The only info I can find on Lennart Bergmark in Vänge, outside Uppsala, is an address."

"All right, great," Nyman says. "Anton and Ankan, you take Åkers styckebruk. And Shabir and I will head out to Ösmo."

"Don't you have, like, a thousand meetings today?" Sarwani asks.

20

A bad feeling creeps up on Sonja Ryd before she even enters Vänge. When the village appears around a wooded bend in the road, it looks like a bourgeois idyll, hardly a place where a hardened old prepper like Lennart Bergmark would settle. She soon finds herself driving down winding back roads. Her GPS manages to guide her to the right address but has her approach the large building from the back. It may have been a manor house once—it has a derelict, slightly warped aura, as though she's stepped straight into a long-lost era.

Ryd parks her car and climbs out, pausing to see if her arrival has stirred up any evil spirits. But nothing moves; even the aspen leaves hang motionless. She starts up a short flight of stairs that leads to an old kitchen entrance, pausing again when she reaches the patio in front of the peeling back door. Then she makes a decision and pushes down the door handle as quietly as she is able.

The door swings open without a sound.

* * *

The piece of land outside Åkers styckebruk is enormous. Anton Lindberg and Ankan drive along the stone wall for several minutes before reaching a sturdy gate, which, to their surprise, is open. Farther up the road, they can see a red house. After passing through the gate and driving another fifty yards or so, a white-haired man in an undershirt suddenly appears on the patio. Over his shoulder, he's carrying something that looks like a rifle, and shoots them a brief glare before racing down the steps and disappearing around the corner.

"What the fuck," Lindberg roars, accelerating toward the house.

Ankan checks her gun and slides it back into its shoulder holster before throwing open her door and sprinting after the man.

"Lennart Bergmark!" she bellows. "Freeze!"

She's already gone by the time Lindberg stops the car, heaves himself out, and runs after her. He rounds the house and barges through a stand of trees before abruptly pulling up short.

At the bottom of a long slope, he sees what must be at least ten unpainted cabins. It looks like an unfinished ski resort. And there's no trace of the white-haired man or Ankan.

Anton Lindberg takes out his gun, heaves a deep sigh, breaks cover, and slips down the hill toward the cabins.

* * *

Eva Nyman and Shabir Sarwani are standing by a row of letterboxes outside Ösmo. One of them is labeled "Bergmark." From there, they're going straight out into the woods, according to their property search.

It's an effort for Nyman to keep up with Sarwani. Thankfully, he has to stop from time to time to check their course on his phone. It's supposed to be less than a mile, and at first there's decent reception.

They still haven't located Lennart Bergmark's cabin when the last bar disappears from Sarwani's phone.

"But from what I recall, it's straight ahead," Sarwani says. "No more than a few hundred yards."

"And what exactly counts as straight ahead out here?" Nyman whispers back, waving at the dense forest.

She should feel uncomfortable, so far from her natural habitat in the conference rooms of the police HQ, but the opposite is true. She feels exhilarated. She's doing real police work. She's out in the field. She's quite literally moving closer to the truth.

Then, without warning, she's pushed down so hard her knees buckle. She looks up at Sarwani as they lie prone behind a mossy boulder. He lets go of her shoulder and shushes her. She follows his finger diagonally skyward. Her head comes up a fraction too fast from behind the boulder; Sarwani's attempt to hold her back is too slow.

She catches a glimpse of a camera high up in a pine tree before a loud bang rings out. Even though it's deafening and continues to echo through the forest for a good long while, it's another sound that burrows all the way into Eva Nyman's core. It's low and dry, and when she throws herself back down behind the boulder, she can see the bullet hole and has to work hard to keep breathing.

It's in the tree trunk right behind them. A wisp of smoke is rising from it.

* * *

Sonja Ryd knows full well she's not allowed to enter this house without identifying herself. Even so, she slips in through the back door.

The pine floorboards inside the manor don't creak under her feet. She has stepped into a nondescript hallway with three doors and a staircase leading up to the first floor. She chooses the stairs. She still has no idea where she is. There are no people here, not a sound. And a smell she can't quite identify.

She reaches the first-floor landing. A long corridor extends in both directions. Still no people. But next to a closed door on her left is a numbered list. Each number is followed by a name. The list is printed on a terrible color printer; the logo at the top of it is oval, purple. There are words on it she can't make out.

But she can make out one of the names, after the number "8": Lennart Bergmark.

Ryd walks over to the nearest door, which is marked "14," and then continues down the hallway. On her right, it widens into a kind of bay window overlooking the front of the building. She walks up to it and looks out, noting a number of parked cars and a sign with a logo that's purple and oval. And on it are the words "Skogstjärnen Nursing Home."

She heaves a deep sigh and moves back into the corridor, passing door after door on her left: 12, 10, and 8. There's a rhomboid window in door number 8. She peers inside. Sees a silhouette against a large, unwashed window.

The silhouette of a person in a wheelchair.

* * *

As he races down the slope, Anton Lindberg expects to be shot. He expects it as he sprints toward the nearest cabin. Not even when he presses his back against the untreated wood of its back wall does he stop expecting it. But no shot rings out.

Assuming the quick count he did while barreling down the slope is accurate, there are three rows of cabins with a number of cabins in each. The likelihood of their fugitive hiding inside or between them is considerable. The likelihood that Ankan is in there somewhere as well is also significant. The risk of him and Ankan being shot is not negligible.

Lindberg glances left, down the path between the cabins. He sees nothing, hears nothing. He tiptoes over to the other side of the cabin, peers down the other path, catches a brief glimpse of movement a couple of cabins down, pulls back, conducts a quick analysis.

What did he see? Someone lunging across the path, from one cabin to the next? He strains his ears, hears a few muffled sounds, possibly a groan. He can't remain passive any longer.

He slips out onto the path between the cabins, gun raised, jaw clenched. It should have been behind the third house. He quickly rounds the first one—nothing there; hugs the wall of the second, picking up splinters; pauses behind the corner and peers around it. Nothing. Time for the third cabin. He moves silently, waiting behind the corner with his gun raised, the ice-cold barrel nearly touching his nose. He can smell sulfur and feel death licking his ear.

Then he hurls himself around the corner.

The white-haired man is biting the dust. His face is deep in the dirt, and next to his hand is a walking cane that could be mistaken for a rifle from afar. Ankan is straddling his back.

Anton Lindberg has never seen her look so imposing, a shield maiden with a radiant halo of blonde hair around her face. Never has the nickname Ankan felt more inadequate.

She slips her gun back into her shoulder holster and pulls the old man's head up by his white hair.

His face is smeared with dirt and grass, and the whites of his eyes are glowing with terror.

In a hoarse voice, Lennart Bergmark says, "I take it you're not from the planning commission?"

* * *

Shabir Sarwani doesn't hesitate before taking out the camera up in the pine tree. The shot echoes through the trees for a long time.

"We have to split up," he hisses. "Otherwise he can get behind us."

"How?" Eva Nyman asks in a voice that's not her own.

"I can see the cabin. Unless he has more cameras, he can't see us. The entrance seems to be on the other side of the house. There's more cover on the right—over there. You go that way. I'll go left. Be careful. Don't do anything rash."

Then Sarwani's gone. Nyman grimly watches him go.

She peeks up from behind the boulder. Yes, she can make out the cabin in the distance, and she has a vague idea of what Sarwani meant by "on the right." So she pushes herself into motion, controlled motion, scurrying from boulder to boulder. There's no sign of additional cameras, no sign of life at all. Slowly, she creeps closer. She has no idea where Sarwani is anymore. Shouldn't he have reached the house by now? She speeds up a little without doing anything rash. Sarwani's words echo in her mind, making her want to do something reckless. She feels more like a defiant teenager than his superior.

She's close now, level with the right side of the cabin. Sarwani should have covered the distance much faster than this. Where is he? Inside the cabin? Why is he not giving her any kind of signal? She moves in as close as she dares, stopping when she spots something that looks like a wooden shoebox, attached to a rack at waist height. Just then, she hears a shot ring out very nearby. The echo ripples through the vegetation.

* * *

It's shot to bits.

Sarwani studies the wreckage; maybe the shock hasn't reached him yet. Everything's completely twisted.

His Glock 45 is lying in pieces on the ground outside the cabin's only door. How precise a shot does a person have to be to shoot the gun out of his hand, and with a weapon as inaccurate as a shotgun? As far as he can judge, his hand's unharmed, despite the pain. He wraps his left hand around his right wrist, staring at the unkempt old man whose shotgun is now squarely aimed at his chest.

"You know I have one bullet left," Lennart Bergmark hisses, slowly backing away toward the nearby tree line.

Sarwani suspects that's a lie. It's a double-barreled shotgun, and two shots have been fired. But the man could have reloaded after the first one. Bergmark continues to back away, reaching for something at waist level he seems very eager to find.

He simultaneously opens his rifle and a wooden box behind him, fumbling about inside it. He stares at what he pulls out of it. It's not two cartridges.

It's two pinecones.

Then, Eva Nyman coldcocks him with her gun.

When Lennart Bergmark comes to, he's handcuffed and staring up at them wildly. In a hoarse voice, he says, "Bloody thieves. I've already called the police."

* * *

Sonja Ryd opens the door with the rhomboid window and enters. The silhouette in the wheelchair slowly turns toward her. He turns until he's no longer a silhouette. Sunlight illuminates his face. The smell she's been trying so hard to put her finger on is, quite simply, urine.

A large scar hollows out the man's left cheek beneath his gray eyes. In a hoarse voice, Lennart Bergmark says, "I assume you're here to talk about Lukas Frisell?"

21

Somehow, Sonja had managed to miss that the address belonged to a nursing home. Her googling had been inadequate.

But it's clear enough that Lennart Bergmark was once an imposing man. He's stooped now—shrunken, even. And yet, Sonja Ryd can see the other man inside him, the one who survived alone in the woods for years, without electricity and running water.

"Why would you assume I'm here to talk about Lukas Frisell?"

His steel-gray eyes don't leave hers for even a moment.

"He's the only person from my past the police could possibly be interested in," Bergmark replies in a low, hoarse voice.

Ryd doesn't have to ask how he knows she's a police officer. She shows him her ID as confirmation and simply notes that he has good instincts.

"Is Lukas Frisell such a hardened criminal, then?" she asks, pulling over a chair and taking a seat so close to Bergmark that the reek of him makes it hard to breathe.

"I know I stink," he mutters. "My insides were pretty badly mangled when I fell off a cliff on Fulu Mountain. It was six days before a hiker found me. You might say it was a bit of a challenge."

"Fulu Mountain?"

"Northern Dalarna. I had a dwelling there. But that was the end of that."

"Does Lukas Frisell have a dwelling—whatever that is—there too?"

Lennart Bergmark studies her intently.

"You probably wouldn't categorize it as a house or even a cabin, so I just call it dwelling. You'll have to imagine the rest. Assuming your imagination is as vivid as I suspect it is. And no, Lukas Frisell isn't such a hardened criminal. But I don't know a lot of people, and he's a deeply bitter, unyielding man with extensive survival skills and a past as both a Norrland Ranger and a copper. We both know he could become a very dangerous individual."

"Do you follow the news, Lennart?"

"Not if I can avoid it."

"You haven't heard about the so-called Terrorist Bomber?"

Bergmark makes no reply, just studies Ryd. She waits him out.

"No, I haven't," he replies. But he sounds defensive.

"Does Lukas Frisell have a dwelling in northern Dalarna too?"

The old man turns to gaze out at the nature outside the window and doesn't move again. Ryd has no intention of disturbing him this time either.

"The point," Bergmark says eventually, "is that he doesn't."

"The point?"

"I offered. It was a one-time event in my life."

"But . . . ?"

"I'd selected a spot about ten miles away. It wasn't like we would have been stopping by each other's places to borrow cups of sugar or anything. But when I finally persuaded him, he wanted something all his own."

"So he was hard to persuade, then?"

"Mentally, he was there from day one. The way we live is unsustainable; he was deeply aware of that. None of us can actively participate in the accelerating destruction of this planet. But even though he grew more and more disillusioned with his soul-deadening academic life, there were aspects of it he appreciated. He liked going out to dinner with his students, for instance, not least the female ones."

"And he eventually set himself up with something all his own?"

"It looked like shit. On the other hand, he was only just starting out. There were things not even he knew how to do. Build a house, for instance. Establish a dwelling, to use a term I'm sure you're familiar with."

"So, you know Frisell's dwelling looked like shit because you've been to it, Lennart?" "Call me Lelle," Bergmark says. "And yes."

"'Yes' as in 'Yes, I've been to it'?"

Lelle Bergis is about to reply, when he looks as though something has suddenly occurred to him. Previously invisible lines appear as a faint smile spreads across his sun-wrinkled face.

"I don't know," he says. "I think my memory's failing me."

"What do you mean?"

"How many people has the Terrorist Bomber killed?"

"At least four. Four innocent people, Lelle. And unless we stop him, it's going to be a lot more."

"And how many people have died just this year because of climate-related disasters?

How many will die over the next decade?"

"That has nothing to do with this."

"Maybe it does. Maybe drastic measures are needed to open the eyes of a lobotomized population. I'm increasingly feeling like I'm on Team Terrorist Bomber. I have absolutely no recollection of where Lukas's crappy dwelling is located. Mongolia, perhaps? Who knows?"

Sonja Ryd checks herself and meets the by now blazing steely-eyed gaze. She gauges it as best she can, and no, that's no extremist she's looking at. It's a man who once upon a time made a decision for himself. An extreme but not an extremist decision.

"The bombings are undermining their own purpose," she says. "The Terrorist Bomber's never going to turn the public's attention to anything but his own bestial attacks. The real extremists are the people who keep going, even though we all know where things are headed. This lets them get away with it, Lelle. This gives them carte blanche."

Lines have appeared on Bergmark's forehead. He stares down at the floor, shaking his head.

"I don't know," he says slowly.

Ryd forges on: "Lukas Frisell is giving the real perpetrators, the real climate offenders, a free pass. Come on, Lelle."

Bergmark takes a deep breath.

"You might be right, you know," he says.

"You know where Frisell's dwelling is, Lelle. Which forest he built it in." Lennart Bergmark looks up, his gray eyes clear.

"No," he says.

"No?" Ryd repeats with a deep sigh.

"No," Bergmark insists. "I don't know the name of the forest. But I could draw you a map."

22

Nyman and Sarwani are the first ones back in the office. Their Lennart Bergmark had in fact called the police, and there had been a minor debacle when the local uniforms arrived in the woods outside Ösmo. As compensation for NOD's unwarranted involvement, the constables were allowed to haul Bergmark off to the local detention facility—after all, he had opened fire on an officer and was a nice trophy.

Sarwani takes a seat at his desk. He's still waiting for the pain in his right wrist, but it doesn't seem to be setting in, so it's as though none of it really happened. Eva Nyman is sitting across from him—partly to wait for the rest of Nova, partly to stare at the computer. He shoots her a grateful look.

She swapped two cartridges for pinecones, and she knocked his assailant out cold. In a way, he's happy he's been underestimating his boss.

On Eva Nyman's computer screen is not only a long list of missed calls, urgent texts, pressing emails, and critical memos; there's also a picture of a page from a road atlas, with a rectangle drawn in ballpoint pen on the map. The road on the map narrows gradually from motorway to forest track, which then comes to an abrupt end in the middle of the woods. A footpath appears to lead from there to the rectangle.

That was where Lukas Frisell had, once upon a time, driven the "real" Lennart Bergmark. It was as far as the car would take them. They'd left it there and hiked the last couple of miles. To the rectangle containing the approximate location of Frisell's home.

Bergmark estimated it at about two or two and half miles.

Somewhere in there.

That's what she learns from Sonja Ryd's report. The way lies open to raiding Frisell's dwelling in the deepest, nameless forests of Uppland.

Except that they don't have a shred of concrete evidence against him. The whole thing rests on Eva Nyman's hunch. She can't escape the nagging suspicion that it's all in her mind, that it's based on events fifteen years in the past. Could it even be that her subconscious is trying to punish Lukas Frisell? For letting his obstinacy not only condemn Liselott Lindman to death but also split up the best team she'd ever worked with?

Until this one.

That thought pours oil on Eva Nyman's troubled inner waters. The fact that Nova was given a name so quickly is enough on its own to instill a measure of confidence.

At that point, Lindberg and Ankan walk in the door, both mildly out of breath.

"All the way to the police station, our Lennart Bergmark remained convinced we were from the planning commission," Ankan puffs.

"Well, he's sleeping it off in a cell now, Lindberg puts in. "He'd secretly built twelve cabins to rent out, completely without planning permission. And he was stoned out of his mind too. Just to make matters worse."

The two of them sit down in unison, open their laptops at the same time, and disappear into cyberspace together, and yet so alone. Nyman looks from the map to them and back to the map.

The hand-marked map of Lukas Frisell's forest.

Damn it. She can't decide. Should she risk it? Should she risk her entire future?

She can't reasonably sound the alarm about Lukas Frisell without concrete proof. So far, it's been fine—she's kept that part of the investigation internal. But a raid in the forests of Uppland would require more resources, possibly the National Task Force. It would certainly have to be cleared by higher-ups. And as far as the top brass goes, it's not just that her reputation's tarnished, she's also already neglecting her duties. More and more she feels like she's caught in a bear trap. She needs time to think; time she doesn't have.

And then, Sonja Ryd strides into the office, shooting her boss a sullen look. As soon as she'd emailed Nyman the map, she'd started for Frisell's forest and was halfway there when Nyman told her to turn around. They would have to decide on the raid soon, but nothing could happen right now. Driving back to Stockholm had felt like a waste of time.

And yet Ryd understands; she understands Nyman's caution, can sense how close Nova is to having the case taken away. She knows they have no evidence, that Nyman's past doesn't do Nova any favors.

Eva Nyman sees Sonja Ryd's sullen face relax, turn into a smile. Shabir Sarwani watches them, thinking he gets it. He'd like there to be a raid too; they could do it themselves, even knowing their target's an experienced survivalist. He glances over at Anton Lindberg, sees the same thought in him. It's still early—it's May—and the sun sets late. They could do it. Ankan, in turn, sees the looks the two of them are exchanging. She has already canceled all dates for the foreseeable future; right now, this is what she lives for. And they could nick Lukas Frisell today, before sunset.

A strange, unsettled mood reigns. As though everyone's waiting for some kind of high sign.

Ryd hasn't even sat down yet when a shrill ring tone no one seems to recognize at first slices through the office. Ankan belatedly throws herself at the jacket she's hung up and pulls out her phone. She answers. Then she's completely silent. The seconds crawl by.

Ankan's face is impassive. At length, she ends the call and turns to her colleagues. "That was the NFC," she says neutrally. "Calling about the results of the DNA analysis."

All eyes are on her. Her face remains expressionless. Then she bellows, "We have a match."

They're on their feet now, waiting for the rest. Which comes. "The DNA found inside the bomb in Vasaparken is the same as the DNA from the old hairbrush Lukas Frisell's ex-wife gave us."

"The bastard actually did it," Anton Lindberg exclaims.

The ruins of destruction, Eva Nyman thinks to herself, and says, "Let's go."

As she stands, she can feel herself slipping out of the bear trap, with her skin only lightly grazed.

23

By the time the dark van turns down an even narrower road for the fourth time, the word *road* has really become a misnomer. The narrowest line on Lelle Bergis's map might have been a road eight years ago. Since then, nature has firmly reclaimed it. Despite his impatience, Anton Lindberg manages to drive relatively carefully, mile after mile over roots and rocks. At this point, however, it's so bad the Nova Group has to stop every few hundred yards to assess whether it's even possible to keep going.

This time, though, something's different outside the van. Ankan has caught a glimpse of something a few hundred yards down the track, in the shadows under some dense foliage. They climb back in and drive over to it, across terrain that can no longer really be called traversable.

What they find under the tree is a car, a dirty black Volvo that at first glance appears to have become one with nature. A closer look, however, reveals that it's neither abandoned nor overgrown, just filthy. There are no registration plates on it, but a rectangle of dirt clearly shows it wasn't long since they were removed.

"Good old Lukas wants to be anonymous when he leaves the jungle," Lindberg says, running a finger across the paint.

"We don't know that it's his car," Eva Nyman says, looking down at her phone. "But this is where we start walking."

Sarwani is also studying the map on his screen. He's put in the rectangle Bergmark gave Ryd on a map and shared it with the others. They all have it on their phones.

"Just under two and half miles to go," he says. "Is everyone's GPS up and running? You can see the rectangle? The network providers claim the reception's decent out here, but you never know."

Leaving the van behind, they strike out into the wilderness, suitably equipped thanks to the unexpectedly well-stocked stores of the police HQ. It's not long before the forest feels virginal. And as though they're being swallowed up by it.

It turns out to be two and a half very long miles. The smells and sounds of the forest keep pushing in closer. Never have they seen so many shades of green. Birdsong fills the air in a forest that constitutes its own discrete universe. And the farther in they go, the more clearly it feels like Lukas Frisell's universe. Somehow, they can sense his presence. They can tell from looking at each other that they're like a single organism invading an already perfectly balanced system. They need to stick together to form their own system. Their own strength.

"Two and a half miles," Sarwani says eventually. "We're at 2.2 now. Close enough?"

"We don't know how precise Bergmark was," Lindberg says.

"He did live in the woods for years," Ryd says. "I could see it in his eyes; he knows what he's talking about."

"Then why the hell doesn't he know exactly where this place is?"

But Lindberg's protest is barely more than a grumble. A seemingly exhausted Eva Nyman gives Sarwani a nod of confirmation.

"I spent a lot of time in the woods back when I was trying to become Swedish," he says with a wry smile, taking off his backpack. He pulls out three rolls of ribbon, each a different color.

"Ariadne's thread," he continues. "Trail-marking ribbon. Biodegradable, might I add.

Three teams: blue for Eva and Anton, green for Sonja and Ankan, red for me. Sonja and Ankan will walk the length of the rectangle; Eva and Anton, the width; and I'll cut through it along the diagonal. You trace the outside edges while I zigzag my way in, then you do the same, but from your directions. We'll leave ribbons every fifty feet so we know who's been where. We can do two ribbons along the sides and three in each corner. That way, we should be able to home in on Frisell's dwelling fairly quickly."

"And we're going to proceed with extreme caution," Nyman urges while each team ties a triple ribbon around the trunk of the nearest tree—blue-green-red at the origin—then Sarwani bounds away along the diagonal of the rectangle, tearing off a second marking ribbon and securing it around a tree before disappearing into the dense forest.

Eva Nyman waits, watching as Ankan and Ryd head off into the trees too. Then she nods to the visibly impatient Anton Lindberg and thinks, *I'm not entirely sure what I've authorized here.*

Then she sets off too.

24

They manage to keep true along what Sarwani termed the rectangle's width. So far, the landscape seems completely untouched by human hand. It's really only at this point that Eva realizes just how fit Anton Lindberg really is. Or possibly how young he is. She has trouble keeping up with him in the difficult terrain. Thankfully, he has to stop every fifty feet to tie two blue marking ribbons around a tree.

She hears a strange bird call she recognizes. It's low and raspy. The shivers it sends down her spine have their roots deep in her past. Very deep. The sound is coming closer.

A rustling is growing louder as it approaches through the nearby treetops. A large black shadow sweeps out between Nyman and Lindberg. For a split second, it's as though she's staring at a still. A silhouette. A bird in jet-black profile, like in a poem.

A raven.

Then it's gone.

Lindberg turns around, unperturbed, and mouths, "Get a move on, Eva."

* * *

Sonja Ryd watches Ankan's shapely backside swaying ahead of her, and her thoughts momentarily stray. She's seen her colleague swiping on her dating app and knows what she's doing. Ankan has belatedly realized she's a catch. And it seems like she's milking it for what it's worth. Ryd compares it to her own life. It must be roughly the same amount of time, just over a year, but she hasn't been able to pick herself back up like Ankan has. And her ex isn't dead and buried, just betrayed. It takes her a few seconds to recall his name, Jonathan, and when she tries to summon his face, it comes to her as sinewy, flinty, and weatherworn, with wispy hair.

She needs a drink.

But it's too early to pull the thermos out of her backpack. The thermos she's filled with bag-in-box wine from her locker at the station.

For once, the dense foliage above their heads is opening up a little. When Sonja Ryd raises her eyes to the heavens, she realizes it's grown noticeably darker. She shudders.

Anything but rain. When she looks back down, she sees Ankan is walking backward, watching her.

"Are you sure you're not distracted, Sonja?" she asks in a whisper, with a look that's equal parts skeptical and warm.

"Don't worry about me," Ryd mutters, just as the first raindrop finds its way through the dense canopy.

* * *

Sarwani moves diagonally through the rectangle. He moves quickly and stealthily, but what started as more of a workout slowly becomes a matter of life and death as the forest deepens. Every time he stops to tie red ribbons around a tree, he feels as though he's being watched.

He looks around. The forest is thick around him, and he can't see very far. But the forest seems to see him, as though it were a single untamed organism.

Or maybe there are eyes out there of the human kind. Except with all the qualities of a wary animal.

For the first time in a long time, Shabir Sarwani feels desperately alone.

Pushing on, he pulls his gun out of his shoulder holster, peering this way and that. He's not sure he'll spot Frisell's dwelling, even if he walks right into it.

But at least he feels safer with the gun in his hand.

* * *

They've reached a clearing in the woods. Anton Lindberg consults his GPS and confirms that they've walked almost two miles, that it's getting to be time to make a ninety-degree turn, from width to length. While he tears off three ribbons of the same length from their blue roll, Eva Nyman catches up to him. She's breathing heavily.

"Time to turn inward," she pants.

Lindberg nods. She's beginning to bother him. Why doesn't she just stay in her office and shuffle papers like all other managers? Why does she have to be out here, holding him back?

"Looks like it's getting denser over there," she says.

"This is a fairly small clearing," he answers without answering.

They push on. The forest does grow denser again. Time seems to stretch out endlessly. Rain begins to trickle down through the foliage above their heads. Cold water that seeps into every nook and cranny. The air is cooling quickly. In one way, it's nice, in another, it's frightening. The world around them grows hazy with rain. Their visibility shrinks to less than ten feet.

Eva Nyman shudders. It feels like they're close. Close to something ominous. The silhouette of a bird flashes before her mind's eye.

Anton Lindberg sinks into a squat. This time, Nyman doesn't dawdle; she instantly squats down behind him, thinking she's learned from her mistakes. He raises his khaki binoculars, peering at a faint brightening further into the forest. Without a word, he then hands the binoculars to Nyman. She wipes the rain out of her eyes and from her forehead and sees another clearing, this one larger. She thinks she can make out a small pond through the cataract of precipitation. It's not on her map, but there's definitely water there, like a bubbling witches' brew in the deluge.

Anton Lindberg leans over.

"I sense signs of life down there," he whispers. "You stay here."

"Signs of life?" she hisses, but he's already gone.

She sinks down next to a boulder. This feels like a repeat of something she just did. That time, her life was suddenly in danger. With Sarwani and the wrong Lennart Bergmark in Ösmo Forest.

In the autumn of 2009, Lukas Frisell turns to her. His wispy medium blond hair frames a powerful face that has forgotten that it's well on its way to middle age. His head is very close to hers, she hopes this is when he's going to say something to change her future. Instead, he heaves a heavy sigh and seems to stiffen.

Eva Nyman studies her hands. The rain is making her palms bubble like two beds of lava. The jet-black outline of a bird appears between them, turning its eyes to stare into hers.

Suddenly, she can clearly see the raven that flew straight into her when she was ten years old and had dared to go into the woods around her grandpa's house for the first time.

Something snaps behind her.

* * *

Ryd and Ankan move quickly between the trees. When they turned from length to width, their scouting morphed into some kind of competition. Three green marking ribbons, and off they went. They both know they can't let their attention slip for even a moment, so they both pretend no starting gun's been fired. But it clearly has. That feeling of becoming more animal, of being skin to skin with nature, it's stronger than most things the newfangled logic of civilized humanity can achieve.

Ryd realizes she's competing against something almost superhuman. They've worked together for four years, since the group was formed, and only now does she realize that behind Ankan's self-effacing persona, there's something else entirely. In the past month, it's as though she's been emerging from her chrysalis. And yet, Sonja Ryd's the fitter of them. She's the one who's in the gym at five in the morning to drive the demons out of her body. Ankan works out too, but more traditionally. For Ryd, exercise is self-flagellation; for Ankan, it's elegance.

Maybe that makes a difference.

They push up the pace, and the looks they exchange are those of two animals, female against female, two narrow, tight fields of vision. Who will catch the perpetrator's scent first? There's prey to fell. A male with no genetic value.

They run like lunatics. Ankan and Sonja, Sonja and Ankan, forces that are no longer directed outward; now it's all about their internal struggle.

That's when a figure suddenly appears before them. That's when it looms over them.

They both stop dead. The solidarity of the competition ceases to exist. They have only themselves. And the creature.

Out of the corner of her eye, Sonja Ryd sees Ankan pull out her gun.

* * *

Shabir Sarwani keeps his center of gravity low as he moves. His gun is practically dragging across the soaked ground. This was how he used to move through the woods back when he always had to be the best, when he learned Swedish better than the Swedes. But he doubts he learned anything about the woods other than that he wants to get out of them as quickly as possible. That strange presence is making itself increasingly known.

That's what he's trying to outrun.

He doesn't feel like his focus is slipping, but his field of vision has changed, grown narrower, sharper, denser. Anything that's not a threat or prey is filtered out. He is one with nature.

The last remnants of civilization are the red marking ribbons he increasingly rarely ties around the trees.

The forest seems to be pressing in closer. It's as though he's in its maw, about to be devoured.

Civilization has ended—we just haven't noticed yet.

Suddenly, Sarwani catches a glimpse of something out of the corner of his eye, nothing more than a vague blur through the rain. And for a fraction of a second, his focus does slip after all. His foot gets stuck under a root. As he topples forward with a strange slowness, he hears a loud snap coming from his shins.

* * *

Anton Lindberg slowly creeps down to the small pond. He definitely saw something moving in the clearing by the water's edge. Now, he can see nothing, the rain feels both grayer and more impenetrable. He has his gun raised in a two-handed grip, ready to fire.

He can't tell where the pond begins. For a moment, it feels like he's walking on its surface.

And then, it's there: small, dark, with untold depths. What little he can make out of the surface looks like boiling tar.

Then he sees the movement again, the same shadow, darting by at the edge of his vision. He turns and comes incredibly close to firing his gun before managing at the last millisecond to stop the shot that would have given them all away.

There's nothing there. The shadow's gone.

But Lindberg spots something else. He sees markings on a tree that can't be anything but human-made. Next to the pond, something seems to have been stretched between two trunks—there are several scuff marks on the bark. Possibly a trap of some kind, recently removed. He runs a finger across a charred patch and smells some kind of explosive.

They're close now.

Lindberg turns around. The rain seems to have eased a little, and he can see the gun in front of him again. He climbs back up to the large boulder where he left Eva Nyman. He looks around, the words ready in his mouth.

But she's not there.

Heart rate rising, he searches the immediate area for a few minutes. There's no trace of the head of Nova. Eventually, there can be no doubt.

Eva Nyman's gone.

When Anton Lindberg raises his phone to his ear to contact the others, it's visibly shaking.

25

Eva Nyman has been reduced to just hearing. She doesn't even feel pain. And yet, she must have been unconscious for a good long while. Something should be hurting by now, no matter what substance was used to knock her out.

She came to abruptly, managed to suppress the panic by doing yoga breathing as she worked on lowering her blood pressure and assessing the basic facts of her situation.

The facts: She's sitting up, with her arms and legs tied to a chair that appears to be screwed to the floor. She can tell she's indoors; she's dry and relatively warm, and she can hear the rain beating against something that must be a roof, but not a tin roof, because then it would have been louder. The blindfold lets in as much light as the rag in her mouth lets out sound, which is to say none at all. She still has her hearing; in fact, she has become hearing.

And yet, she can't hear much. So maybe that suggests she isn't very much at all anymore, that she's ceasing to be.

She's sitting in the Terrorist Bomber's dwelling, and she can hear him, but faintly, as though through a closed door. He seems to be busy with something she hopes she'll never find out anything about. There's chopping and bubbling, and a liquid is poured. Now and then, there are shuffling footsteps.

Eva Nyman can't help but picture Lukas Frisell. How has he changed over the past fifteen years, of which he's spent maybe eight in the wilderness? Has he become a hermit, a wild animal, a lunatic, a sadist? No matter which, what's likely is that she's sitting in the home of a man who has killed at least four people and is threatening to kill far more. In the name of the climate.

His DNA was found inside the Vasaparken bomb. He's addressing his letters to an old colleague.

The letters are written in his words. Directly to her.

"The ruins of destruction."

It's him. It's Lukas Frisell. He abducted her from the woods. All she noticed was a twig snapping behind her, likely on purpose. Then, silence, darkness, emptiness.

And Anton Lindberg didn't notice. Frisell must have moved like a stalking predator through a forest he knows like the back of his hand. Of the five people bumbling about out there, he took the one he wanted. The one he wrote his letters to, the one he hoped would come after him, the one he has a past with.

Maybe this is all part of his plan.

Maybe it was Eva Nyman he was after all along. Maybe he's preparing to torture her.

There's a bang, muffled, probably still on the other side of a door. Then the aural landscape changes, opens up. Everything that was muffled becomes immediate, unfiltered. It's as though the damper's been taken off the trumpet, and the harsh notes are piercing her eardrums.

The steps are no longer shuffling; now they have authority, power. Eva Nyman stops breathing when she senses his presence.

There's a smell.

Warmth spreads along her right side. She identifies the smell as something kerosene-like. There must be a kerosene lamp on the table in front of her.

Then, as though by magic, anything akin to petroleum fumes fades away. Even after fifteen years, she knows his scent so well.

26

Ankan has the majestic stag's flank in her sights. Just then, her phone buzzes in her pocket, making her gun twitch. It's enough to give the stag time to whip around and disappear into the dripping foliage. Before she can get her phone out, Sonja Ryd says hoarsely behind her:

"Eva's missing."

* * *

Shabir Sarwani has just landed heavily on his knees in the moss when his phone buzzes in his back pocket. The snap that accompanied his fall was so loud he wonders when the real pain will hit. *How the fuck are the paramedics going to transport a man with a compound fracture out through this forest?*

But when the pain fails to materialize, he takes out his phone and turns to look. He sees the root he tripped over. That's what snapped, not his shin bones. With a sigh of relief that quickly evaporates, he reads: *Eva's missing. These are my coordinates. Meet up immediately.*

* * *

The rain has slowed to a drizzle now. Sarwani's the first person to reach Anton Lindberg, who is sitting on a boulder with his face in his hands, shaking his head.

"How could I be so fucking stupid?"

"Let's not even go there," Sarwani says with a hand on his shoulder. "We just have to get her back before nightfall."

Within minutes, Sonja Ryd and Ankan join them, both winded, as though they ran the whole way. Or raced?

Sarwani takes an iPad out of his backpack and pulls up a larger version of the map. He draws three approximate lines, one green, one blue, one red. The red one's diagonal and reaches almost from corner to corner. The green and the blue both bend at a ninety-degree angle. At the end of the blue one, Sarwani draws a small circle.

"That pond down there," he says, pointing toward the water, making a small X next to the circle. "And we're here. Do we have any way of assessing where Frisell might be?"

They lean in, heads touching, studying Sarwani's markings.

"The largest unexplored area is to the northeast," Ryd says, pointing.

"Does that make the northeast more likely?" Sarwani asks.

"If we assume he's a proper survivalist, he won't have electricity," Ankan puts in. "Which means no cameras. We can still catch him by surprise."

"That would make this even creepier." Lindberg sighs. "If that's the case, he found Eva without cameras."

Sarwani straightens up and throws out an interpretation: "The most likely scenario is still that he noticed us because we got too close. His dwelling's nearby. Let's spread out—but not so far that we can't see each other. We'll do this like a grid search, moving south until we reach the green ribbons. Then we'll turn back north, but a hundred yards or so farther east. That way, we can't miss him."

"A hundred feet apart, maybe?" Ankan suggests. Sarwani nods.

"There are four of us. Luckily, the rain has slowed, so we can walk slightly farther apart than before. I'll take the right flank, then Sonja, Ankan, and Anton on the far left. Ankan, Anton, and I will do the ribbons, Sonja's off the hook for that. None of us will take our eyes off the others. Sound okay?"

The others nod and spread out. While Ryd waits for the others to get into position, she takes a long swig from her thermos.

When they set off, she pulls out her gun, sensing the first hint of dusk spreading through the damp spring air.

27

The blindfold is being pulled away from Eva Nyman's eyes. Even though she knows roughly what to expect, she still has no idea. Not really. What kind of impressions will greet her?

How long will she live?

When the blindfold comes off, she's thrown back to the autumn of 2008. She's watching the back of a man's head. She wants him to turn around, wants the chiseled face beneath the wispy medium blond hair to move in close to hers, she wants him to say something that will change her future.

But now, the back of that head is gray. His hair seems to have been awkwardly sheared with a knife, leaving a jagged half inch. And he doesn't turn around. He's busy with something on his lap.

A silence the like of which Eva Nyman has never experienced spreads through what now comes into focus as her eyes adjust to the light.

It's a bare, primitive room with doors leading off in three directions. All forms of ornamentation are lacking. Even the boards the walls are made of seem to have been hewn by hand. There are no windows, and a single kerosene lamp illuminates the space; at the other end of the room, there's a fireplace with no fire. It, too, looks homemade.

The man who's sitting with his back to her stops what he's doing. Without turning his head, he slams a large hunting knife down on the table. While he turns around, he also tosses down the rag he's been polishing the knife with. There are red stains on it.

And so, Eva Nyman finds herself face to face with a weathered, haggard man in worn khaki clothing.

It's a strange experience. It's unquestionably Lukas Frisell, but it's as though he's spent years wandering through purgatory. The only thing that seems unchanged are his clear-blue eyes.

Maybe they're in purgatory right now. On their way up. Or down.

Their eyes meet for a good long while. There's something in his gaze she's never seen before, perhaps something only lonely years in the woods can give rise to. She's looking straight into a primeval era.

"What are you doing here, Eva Nyman?" he asks in a voice that must be at least one octave deeper than fifteen years ago.

How does one control one's voice in advance? she thinks and says, "I'm glad you remember me, Lukas."

He scrutinizes her. It really is the gaze of a predator.

"Though I suppose you should, considering the letters," she adds, scrutinizing him right back.

"Letters?" he rumbles.

She tries to read him. She can't. She adopts an official tone. "We just need to talk to you. You have to come with us—or stay on the run forever."

For the first time, he smiles. A wry, sardonic smile, true, but she still recognizes the contours of his old smile. It's so strange to witness the passage of time in a face. It's the only way a person can really see the fourth dimension.

"You just need to talk to me?" he repeats with a chuckle. Then he slowly strokes his clean-shaven chin and continues: "I suppose I committed a crime when I grabbed you, Eva. So what do I have to lose?"

"This is nothing compared to the bombings, Lukas. Four dead so far, maybe as many as six. There's physical evidence against you. There are letters written in your words addressed to me personally."

"My words?

"'The ruins of destruction.'"

He eyes her with the same wariness as before. Possible slightly more sharply. Then, with a sideways nod, he says, "The other four out there are younger than you. They're looking for their boss. Night's falling. And you've been kind enough to leave marking ribbons around the forest so I can find you more easily."

Eva Nyman winces involuntarily. Frisell continues: "A tight-knit little team, Eva—the way you liked it even back then. And if you learned anything from me, this is some kind of unsanctioned operation. Otherwise, I'd be hearing helicopters and seeing the National Task Force boys."

She feels the blindfold being pulled back over her eyes. The last thing she sees before the world is plunged back into darkness is Lukas Frisell picking up his hunting knife. For a split second, it's the shape of the jet-black outline of a bird.

"I'm sure they're proceeding in close formation by now," Lukas Frisell says, standing up.

28

Their formation is closer than planned. The rain has stopped falling, and yet the hundred-foot distance they agreed to has shrunk significantly. On the other hand, night is falling.

They turn around for the third time. From south to north. They've kept a high pace, but it's getting hard to make out details on the rocky, uneven, waterlogged ground. They're slowing down.

The smells of nature have grown stronger.

Sarwani and Lindberg are holding the flanks, Ryd and Ankan are scanning the area between them. They're slowly pulling closer and closer together like a shrinking fabric.

Sarwani still can't shake the feeling of being watched. It's as though the forest itself is following his every move. Ryd feels almost a bit exhilarated by the terror surging through her, as though she's earned it. Ankan can feel her battle lust growing, but she really doesn't want to be shot—that's been a fear of hers since the first day of her police training. Lindberg has turned this hunt into the one he really wants; for him, it's a war against the criminality that's undermining Sweden's future.

They look at each other as much as the forest. At what point do they have to knuckle down and contact their colleagues? A senior member of the Police Authority has been kidnapped. The fact that they haven't raised the alarm already could mean the end of all of their careers.

Which is nothing compared to what would happen if Eva Nyman were to die.

Sonja Ryd thinks back to the autumn of 2008, to kidnap victim Liselott Lindman, to the hell Lukas Frisell and Eva Nyman worked so hard to put an end to. She briefly shuts her eyes.

Eva might be her very best friend. What is she going through right at this moment? Is she even alive? Staying focused under these circumstances, attacking with everything she has, requires something the proximity of the others makes impossible. The thermos has to stay in her backpack.

Ankan's the one who tilts her head back to greet the first new raindrops. And she's also the one who spots it.

Who sees the streaks of even deeper black against the darkening sky, an inverted dark lightning bolt that's unquestionably rising from below.

They pause briefly, watching the phenomenon, all together. "That's smoke," Sarwani eventually whispers.

"And it's coming from somewhere nearby," Ankan whispers back.

They slowly move in that direction. Soon, they can smell the smoke too. Someone very nearby has lit a fire. Something's burning in the late May evening.

They push through the dense forest until they reach the bottom of a hill, where the trees thin out slightly. It looks like a mirage. Black smoke can't be puffing out of the hillside. And yet, it does.

Sarwani has their only set of night-vision binoculars. They're not professional grade, but he can see something. He whispers, "It's some kind of building, camouflaged by the slope. He's built his dwelling into a man-made hill. I can see a door. Does everyone have reception?"

They check their phones. Everyone nods.

"He's a bloody prepper," Sarwani continues. "I'd be surprised if there were just one entrance. Sonja, you're with me. Ankan and Anton, see the door?"

They follow his index finger, Lindberg spots what he's pointing to through his inferior binoculars. Likely a front door. He nods.

"Wait for my signal," Sarwani says.

Ryd follows him, Ankan and Linberg stay put. Waiting.

The trail of smoke has taken on the look of a bony finger emerging from the underworld. Sarwani and Ryd move around it in a semicircle.

Sarwani stops Ryd. Raises the night-vision binoculars. Inches forward, peering through the binoculars. She follows him, crouching low. She can see almost nothing.

Then he stops, abruptly. She can barely make out his pointing hand, but she can hear his excited whisper: "There's another door here."

Sarwani's face is illuminated by his phone screen. It looks very pale in the deepening dusk. There's no hint of a moon. After a moment, he hisses, "Anton and Ankan are going in."

Ryd only understands half of what Sarwani's saying. She's not present—not properly. She's in the grip of near-death panic as she follows him. But somehow, she's still ready, still able to convert her panic into determination. To find her way back to professionalism.

She's sweating in the chilly woods. Her gun's welded to her hand.

Very slowly, they set off in the direction of the hill, toward the smoke that's still just about discernible in the enveloping darkness.

And then, they reach a wall. Ryd reaches out to touch it. It feels like moss. But she can't see anything at all anymore.

Night has come.

Sarwani's face is lit up again. It's even paler now.

He nods to Ryd, reaching out toward the wall. She can't quite see it, but she can hear it, a faint click, like when a door handle is pushed down. If it is a door, it swings open without a sound.

A faint, faint light is flickering deep inside an interior that neither of them can make out yet. Ryd and Sarwani move silently down a kind of hallway.

Anything can happen.

Eventually, they reach a larger room. It's revealed as though a curtain is slowly parted.

The first thing Sonja Ryd sees is Eva Nyman.

Maybe it's because Sonja's subconscious has already decided Eva's dead, but sitting there, Chief Inspector Eva Nyman really does look dead. Her face is gleamingly white in the light of a kerosene lamp on the table in front of her.

Ryd quickly glances over at the second source of light in the room. It's a fireplace. She sees Lindberg and Ankan push into the room from the other end.

In the shadows next to the fireplace, a man in his fifties is sitting on a chair, his hands fully visible.

A woman's voice yells out something about a bomb.

II

The Interview

29

He traces the carving on the table with his index finger, letter by letter. The first one is *F*. The second is *R*. The third and fourth are *E*'s.

Free.

He is still smiling wanly when he once again raises his gaze to the large mirror on the wall. It's the first time in eight years he's seen his own smile.

It's enough to make him stop smiling.

* * *

Eva Nyman notes the smile. She's sitting behind the mirror, which from her side is a window, watching the smile wink out. Then she asks, possibly rhetorically, "Are we ready?"

Every member of the Nova Group is gathered in the small observation room behind the interview room. The computer that does the video recording has been activated. The clock above the one-way window says 3:42 AM.

The room is full of paper cups with brown stains. A lot of coffee has been drunk.

"That trap on the chair really did look like a bomb," Ankan says again, sheepishly, suddenly her old, self-effacing self.

"He'd probably retrieved it from the pond," Anton Lindberg offers. "There were trace explosives on both it and a tree. Some kind of homemade explosive trap stretched between a couple of trees.

"It's going to be a long night for the technicians," Nyman says with a nod. "They're keeping us in the loop, of course, and we'll have more weight behind our arguments tomorrow. But it's important to conduct an initial interview now. While everything's still fresh."

"Are you sure you're up to this?" Shabir Sarwani asks from behind the computer screen. "That prick drugged and kidnapped you just a few hours ago."

"I've been examined by a physician," Nyman replies curtly, standing up.

Sonja Ryd is standing by the door, holding a folder. Tapping it impatiently against her left hand.

"Yes, yes," Nyman mutters, picking up her own folder from the desk and pushing her way to the door Ryd is now holding open for her. Ryd follows her toward the weatherworn man with the knife-shorn, wiry gray hair. He sits motionless, staring down at the ancient interview table. The only thing that moves is his index finger.

Nyman and Ryd sit down. Frisell still hasn't looked up. Nyman opens her folder and announces sternly: "Lukas Frisell, you have been arrested on suspicion of several crimes. Do you understand what you are accused of?"

Only now does he look up. His eyes are clear blue and drill into Eva Nyman's. He shakes his head.

"As you know, you need to answer our questions aloud," Nyman continues. "And you have waived your right to counsel?"

Frisell turns his face to the ceiling and sniffs the air. "Smells like ethanol in here," he says.

Ryd and Nyman exchange a quick glance.

"Just answer the question," Nyman says in her frostiest tone.

"You've asked two questions," Frisell says without taking his eyes off the ceiling. His finger keeps moving across the tabletop, as though he were writing something.

"Then answer both, Lukas."

"I don't belong in a world where there are lawyers."

"Is that a 'Yes, I wave my right to counsel'?"

"Yes. And I more or less understand what I'm accused of. Though legally speaking, it was far too vaguely worded."

"Good, then we can move on. This is my colleague, Sonja Ryd."

Nyman turns to Ryd, who immediately grabs the bull by the horns. "Speaking of smell, you don't smell nearly as bad as I thought you would." Frisell turns to Ryd. Even though it's the first time, she doesn't flinch.

"What I mean by that is that you seem to have more creature comforts in your dwelling than most preppers. Do you have a hot shower hidden away somewhere? A sauna, maybe, or a spa section? An exclusive selection of eau de toilettes?"

"I don't know what a prepper is," Frisell replies.

"But you know where I'm going with this, don't you?"

Eva Nyman leans back, hoping it won't be too obvious through the one-way window. Despite the horrors of the evening, there's something gratifying about sitting between her old mentor and the person she has mentored in turn. It's like three generations. How do the old interrogation techniques stand up against the modern ones? Will Frisell be able to handle Ryd's sometimes unexpected changes of subject in the interview room? She and Ryd have never talked about it, but surely her approach must have something to do with her peculiar philosophical background.

"Going?" Frisell says, and Eva Nyman knows she's not the only one to notice the microscopic smile playing at the corner of his mouth.

"I think you're visualizing the big reveal right now." Ryd smiles back. "I think you're even imagining what it looked like when we discovered your secret. Not to mention what the technicians are going to turn up. But we'll get back to that. Do you prefer the term *survivalist*?"

Lukas Frisell stops tracing shapes with his finger and leans in across the table instead, saying, "All of this is terribly difficult for you to imagine, isn't it?"

"All of this?" Ryd says. "Your whole . . . plan?"

Frisell sneers faintly and leans back again.

Ryd continues: "Yes, I suppose I do have a hard time comprehending your plan, Lukas. Explain it to me. We're talking about murdering people at random and striking fear into a country for the purpose of opening the eyes of the general public?"

"Is that what I'm accused of?"

Ryd and Nyman study him closely. Does he remember enough of human interaction to fake surprise?

"You know we can't reveal any pivotal details," Nyman replies, her manner more tentative. "But if it's about murder and terrorism, you should have informed me of that, shouldn't you?" She directs this to Ryd.

It feels like 2008 again. Before the disaster. Frisell's hair is medium blond and wispy. The weight of his authority is pushing Eva Nyman down under the surface.

But no weight is pushing Sonja Ryd down.

"Since this relates to several unspecified violent crimes, the head of the investigation, Prosecutor Sten Robert-Olsson, has decided to keep the potential charges as broad as possible for now—nothing unusual about that," Ryd says. "Back to the smell."

Frisell studies Ryd. Then he tilts his head back to sniff the air again. But he says nothing.

"Why don't you stink?" Ryd asks.

Frisell snorts derisively. Then he says, his fingers drawing air quotes, "Any 'survivalist' could tell you hygiene is a top priority."

"So you do secretly have running water?"

"Of course not. I have a pond less than a mile away."

"Ah," Ryd says. "Where the trap was?"

"I bathe every day. Wash my clothes every third. If I have to, I cut a hole in the ice." "Do you have soap, shampoo, detergent?"

"There are better methods."

"And you clearly took the trap down recently. It looked intact."

"And not at all like a bomb," Frisell replies with a wry smile.

"Why did you take the trap down, Lukas?"

"It no longer fit in with my plans."

"So your plans changed recently? After eight years in the woods?"

Frisell ignores the questions, just angles his face up toward the ceiling again.

"You know what we found, don't you?" Ryd continues calmly. "It rather changes the premise of this conversation."

"I think I'm done talking," Frisell mutters.

Nyman and Ryd exchange a look that contains many things.

"How did your plans change, Lukas?" Ryd asks.

"No comment."

Ryd stares at Frisell. What she sees is absolute determination. What she'd really like to know is why it wasn't there from the start.

Frisell is playing some kind of game.

Ryd nods briefly to Nyman, who lets out a deep sigh, closes her folder, and says, "It's been a long day. This interview is concluded at 4:06 AM, to be resumed tomorrow morning at 8:00 AM."

30

There's only room for one chair in the small observation room behind the one-way mirror. But no one wants to sit down anyway. They're all lined up, staring at a seated Lukas Frisell. It's like a film still.

Eventually, Sonja Ryd moves toward the door, but this time, Eva Nyman stays put.

Instead, Sonja Ryd holds the door for Shabir Sarwani. When the clock strikes eight, they walk side by side toward the motionless figure at the interview table. Collectively, they open their folders.

"The interview is resumed," Ryd says neutrally. "This is my colleague, Shabir Sarwani."

Sarwani points to the wall across from the mirror. There's a screen there. It flickers to life, showing an image that after a moment turns into video. Before long, the main room in Frisell's dwelling, where Eva Nyman was held captive, comes into focus. The video, devoid of both people and sound, moves toward one of the homemade doors. It swings open, revealing a storage space. A handful of shelves that hold all kinds of jumbled junk, a number of rags dangling above the rough wooden floor. A hand reaches into the frame, pushing the rags aside. Exposing—an electrical outlet.

"This is what we found yesterday," Sarwani says. "This is a video recorded by the technicians, I'm sure there will be more coming over the course of the day, revealing what you've been using that electricity for. We were quickly able to establish that there's no official account associated with your dwelling, but now we know where the electricity's coming from, which is to say a clever hookup to the nearest farm, just over six miles away. You're racking up quite a few crimes here, Lukas."

Frisell fixes his interlocutor as though he were prey; Sarwani shudders with déjà vu from last night's deep forest, which seemed to be watching him. He tries to ignore it, pushing on: "We'll obviously come back to your possible possession of a computer, the internet, a mobile phone, but in a way, it's what doesn't run on electricity that interests us, which is to say a typewriter."

"Do you own a typewriter, Lukas?" Sonja Ryd asks.

"Wouldn't your technicians have found it if I did?"

"You seem to have secret hidey holes in all kinds of places around your home," Ryd replies. "The technicians are slowly discovering them, one after another. And as I am sure you're aware, all typewriters have their own unique fingerprints."

"So you're saying I wrote letters on a typewriter?" Frisell asks.

Ryd studies him for so long that Sarwani starts flipping through his papers, pulling a couple out and taking over. "You wrote quite a lot of letters to the editor during your final years at the Swedish University of Agricultural Sciences, didn't you?" he asks, handing Frisell the papers. They're copies of journal articles. "Can you read the highlighted passages aloud for us?"

Frisell's eyes are squarely on Sarwani. He doesn't make the slightest move to look at the articles. Sarwani continues: "My favorite has to be 'We know it's time. There are vast cities on our planet into which the sunlight can't reach. The time for sitting back is over. Each one of us has to act. The people responsible must be made to answer for their crimes if we are to survive. The guilty must be held to account.' What does 'held to account' mean in this case, Lukas?"

Ryd watches Sarwani. *Don't make Frisell clam up,* she thinks. *Pique his interest, don't make him clam up. Open the door for more.*

"You were an academic with a genuine interest in nature and the climate," Sarwani says. "Why didn't you write proper articles instead? Why letters to the editor, like some garden-variety tinfoil hat wearer?"

Silence settles heavily over the interview table. Sarwani continues: "Fine, I'll tell you. Because you sounded like someone who'd be wearing a tinfoil hat. The tone of these letters is that of a swivel-eyed crank. No editor worth their salt would publish your submissions in any other section than Letters to the Editor. You became a survivalist in a state of overwhelming rage. The guilty had to be made to answer and held to account. Why would that rage have subsided during your time as a hermit in the woods? It's not as if the climate's doing any better today than eight years ago. Your rage must have been growing day by day. Until it finally exploded."

The sharp eyes Frisell has kept fixed on Sarwani throughout the entire interview are suddenly averted. He shakes his head and says, "Nothing soothes anger like nature."

Sarwani opens his mouth but feels someone pinching his thigh and checks himself.

From Ryd's hand on his leg, he turns his eyes up toward her mild smile.

After a short pause, Frisell continues: "You experienced it yourselves out there. The primal power of the hunt. The sharp threat of nature. The closeness to the origin. You especially, Shabir Sarwani, came very close to nature."

Once again, Sarwani's overcome with the intense feeling that the forest was watching him, that it kept pushing in closer. The strong feeling of being watched.

"The red ribbons were yours." Frisell flashes him a brief smile. Sarwani closes his eyes.

It had not been his imagination. Frisell continues: "Yes, I'm furious that we're letting our planet die. Year by year, month by month, I've witnessed the devastation. It's visible to the naked eye now—that's how far it's gone. But nature is also peace. Threats and dangers, yes, death and destruction, yes, but above all a powerful serenity. Which allows you to handle the dangers. You become nature."

Ryd and Sarwani exchange a look. Ryd nods.

"You let us catch you," Sarwani says. "You lit the fire in your house so we'd see the smoke. You were in charge the whole time. You could have taken us all down. Why didn't you?"

Frisell turns to the mirror, smiles fleetingly, and says, "Then I would have had to be on the run forever."

"So part of your stolen electricity is used to power CCTV cameras?"

"Can't your technicians tell you that?"

They have, Ryd thinks to herself. They found nothing of the sort. The outlet in the storage room was the only connection.

"Cameras can run on batteries too," Sarwani says.

"So you've found screens for video surveillance?" They haven't. Yet. Frisell sighs and says, "I had to find out why you were out there in my forest. I could tell straight away you were cops. And then I recognized Eva. I had to try to figure out what you wanted. It didn't look particularly official."

"What type of explosives do you use?" Ryd asks abruptly.

Frisell stares at her, momentarily knocked off balance. Before he can answer, she takes things in a different direction: "Why are there no registration plates on your car?"

The fact that he quickly recovers does nothing to erase the split second of bewilderment. The animals of his world are probably more predictable than Sonja Ryd.

"My car?"

"The black Volvo with the scrubbed chassis number."

"I don't own a car," Frisell replies.

"Hmm," Ryd mutters, pointing up at the screen on the wall.

It appears to be the same camera, now moving through the forest. A path has been cleared to a previously inaccessible area. Two large boulders stand on either side of what appears to be a camouflaged section of wood. A hand reaches for the wood, which turns out to be a hatch, lifting it. The hand brushes away the debris underneath the hatch, revealing six flat metal rectangles. Once removed from the hideaway and turned right side up, it's clear they're registration plates for a vehicle.

"Oh dear," Sonja Ryd says. "Caught in an irrefutable lie. Your dwelling's like an advent calendar, a gift that keeps on giving, door after door opening. Lie after lie laid bare."

Frisell actually looks shaken. But he says nothing.

"If we ignore the fact that you've just added yet another crime to the list, Lukas, I have to ask: Why do you need to be someone else when you leave the woods?"

Frisell shakes his head, answering slowly. "I take my anonymity very seriously. I live off the grid. I'm not part of society."

"'The grid' actually refers to the electricity grid, though, doesn't it, so that's not an entirely true statement, is it?"

"I don't want to be registered in any kind of database. So I use the plates of several different demolished cars when I'm forced to acquire provisions."

"And here I thought you were a proper prepper. So it's not that you've been disguising yourself when you've headed out to execute your bombings?"

"The information I've been given about these so called 'bombings' is still far too vague."

"Or when you met up with your accomplices?"

"Do I look like a man who has accomplices?"

"You look like a man who belongs to a terrorist cell, yes. A man who was already radicalized and who has been further radicalized by his life outside society. You look like the Terrorist Bomber, Lukas. Who is this?"

Ryd slams a document down in front of Frisell. It's an amalgam of the two police sketches of the courier who delivered bombs to Vasaparken and Västerås, the thirty-something man with "some features commonly associated with a person from the Middle East".

"That's one weak police sketch," Frisell mutters.

"Who is he?" Ryd demands.

"I genuinely have no idea."

"Maybe you drove him in your car with the false plates? To make sure he took proper care with the volatile explosives and didn't blow himself up?"

Frisell watches her in silence. She forges on: "We're obviously going to do a search on these plates. And then we'll know all about your movements during this wave of terrorist attacks."

She takes a deep breath.

"You've been experimenting with various explosives for a long time. You used them for your damn animal trap, where you blew up your beloved moose. Then it was time. Time for you to leave your dwelling in the woods and head into town to execute the Terrorist Bomber's epoch-defining attacks. I think we caught you just as you were about to vanish into the ether. Because you clearly have a place somewhere in town."

It's Sonja Ryd's turn to fix her fierce eyes on the man on the other side of the interview table sternly.

"You're guilty as sin, Lukas Frisell."

31

In the cramped room behind the mirror, Ryd and Sarwani share a kebab. Nyman's sitting by the computer with a salad. Ankan and Lindberg have, understandably, made themselves scarce. It must be at least thirty degrees in the room. On the other side of the glass, Frisell has just been led back into the interview room after enjoying lunch in his cell.

"I wonder what he ate out in the woods," Ryd says.

"I wonder if we really want to know," Sarwani replies.

"It's the same table," Nyman says.

Ryd and Sarwani stare at her.

"The way he moves his index finger across the tabletop," Nyman continues. "It intrigued me. So, I went in and had a look while he was away for lunch. There's a carving in the table. His finger's tracing it. He wants to be free. Four letters. *F-R-E-E.* I remember them already being there in 2008."

"Maybe he wanted to be free back then too," Sarwani mutters. Nyman chuckles and changes the subject:

"No computer found, no mobile phone. But why would he have tapped that farm's electricity if not to keep an eye on the outside world? A search is being conducted; apparently finding out if someone in that location ever connected to a 3G network is a bit of a challenge, but that's the only type of network that sometimes works out there. And there doesn't seem to have been a land line."

"So you're saying the prick really did lay over six miles of cable through the woods?" Sarwani exclaims. "By himself?"

"And buried it fairly deep," Nyman says, nodding, her eyes on the screen. "It obviously required a heavy-gauge cable, which he spliced professionally three times per mile. Apparently, the kind of cable he used is typically purchased on spools that hold three-tenths of a mile each, which he likely pushed through the terrain like some kind of Sisyphus."

"And no hits on the registration plates," Sarwani says. "Does this guy even have a weakness? We keep coming up with theories in there, but we can't seem to nail him."

"I'll nail him," Ryd says.

Both Nyman and Sarwani turn to her. Something about her tone jars.

"I'll nail him" is all she offers by way of clarification.

She stands up and opens the door for Sarwani. Before they've even sat down across from Frisell, Ryd says, "I recently spent several hours with a former ballerina whose name was once Nina Frisell."

While slowly taking her seat, she watches Frisell with almost over-the-top interest. "She told me a lot of interesting things," she continues after a long pause. "Might you, for instance, remember an incident with a wedding ring?"

Frisell heaves a deep sigh, shaking his head. "What could that possibly have to do with my supposed terrorism?"

"Just answer the question."

"I remember it, sure. It was a difficult separation. A lot of feelings spilling over every which way."

"Who asked for the divorce?"

"You spent several hours with her and didn't find that out?"

"No, I know," Ryd says with a crooked smile. "But I'd like to hear your version."

"Like so many women, Nina was unable to look beyond her most immediate context."

"To the climate issue, you mean?"

"To the universe! Bloody hell. To have the capacity to feel awe, some basic damn reverence at the mystery of existence."

"I assume you realize how misogynist you sound?"

"So you're a member of the thought police, are you? The morality police?"

Ryd sees the opening; for the first time, she has a glimpse of Lukas Frisell's so-called passion. She wants to see more of it. Of the force of nature Nina Strömblad talked about. If it's really there, he hides it very well.

"I've heard you described as the opposite of reverential. As implacable and unhappy in Nina's company. What could be more of a turnoff than that?"

Frisell shrugs.

"That's when we parted ways, that's correct." He slips out of her net. She needs to tighten it.

"Since then, she has only encountered tamed nature."

Frisell sits there in silence for a while, unreadable. And yet, Ryd can sense that her words have struck a nerve, that she has scored a hit. He closes his eyes.

"You know what we've opened the door to now, don't you, Lukas?" She can tell that he does know. She can see it despite his granite face.

"You got divorced in the spring of 2009," Ryd continues. "In the autumn of 2008, something else happened, didn't it? Something as spectacular as now, when, after eight years in the woods, you took down your old trap as a symbol of the fact that an era was over. The explosives in your trap are being analyzed as we speak, by the way. We'll know if they match the bombs soon enough. So, what happened in the autumn of 2008?"

"Something called an iPhone appeared."

Ryd sees Frisell's little smile. His walls are back up. But there's scaffolding now; They'll be easier to tear down.

"And there was someone called Liselott Lindman too, right?"

"You already know about that—you all know about it," Frisell says, waving toward the mirror.

A minor outburst, at least. But "passion"?

"Professional misconduct that serious is unusual," Ryd says, fanning the flames.

He's stone-faced again. Eyes gazing far beyond the interview room.

"You were fired, weren't you, Lukas? You didn't go willingly?"

Silence.

"But this time, it was your choice, Lukas. You left the woods willingly. The woods you've loved for so many years. You'd had enough. You know how right you are. Now the world has to be convinced. No matter the cost. Species are going extinct out there, in nature. You've watched it up close, season by season. The insects are disappearing, the trees are dying. Society's decision-making processes are toothless. Extreme measures are needed to rouse the public. And you've only just begun. The guilty must be held to account."

Ryd pauses. Shoots Sarwani a quick glance. He nods. Frisell is silent and closed off. She pushes on. "We've seen your stubbornness, Lukas, your determination. You built your dwelling almost entirely from what nature has to offer. You cultivated an amazing garden outside, with root vegetables, cabbage, lettuce, potatoes, herbs—the technicians have made a list of everything you're growing. And you laid mile upon mile of cable so you could steal electricity. Then, you used that same determination to plan a series of bombings in and around Stockholm. You quickly realized you couldn't do it on your own. Do you have just one accomplice? This particular one is likely a murderer, since both couriers are missing. Do you do any of the dirty work yourself, or are you just the brains of the operation?"

Still no response from Frisell.

"You're a practical man. Of course you do most of the dirty work yourself. You drive around with stolen registration plates for some reason—and in a proper petrol guzzler of a car too. How do you justify that kind of environmental transgression?"

"I need to get around," Frisell replies suddenly.

Ryd is briefly taken aback, her rhythm disrupted. Maybe that was his intention. "The heat is on, Lukas. The traffic police are busy going through their digital archives. Soon we'll know everything about your movements and your internet activities in the woods. Technology has come a long way since you were fired. There's a kind of irony in the fact that, in the end, it will be digital technology that takes you down."

"The technology that has brainwashed us all. The technology that devours all our electricity and sends our carbon dioxide emissions through the roof," Frisell retorts.

"Much like your old Volvo, Lukas. Don't play innocent. Even if you were to die, your corpse would still have a sizeable bloody climate footprint. It's not as though we get to choose whether to be born into these 'ruins of destruction.'"

She studies the statue in front of her. Somehow, it's clear he can hear her, possibly even that he understands. The way he's studying her has changed.

Sonja Ryd stands up, planting her hands on the interview table as she leans across it and says: "'*God's white dwelling will gaze down upon the ruins of destruction.*' We need to talk about that, Lukas."

32

She'd had him. Sonja Ryd is standing at the back of the small observation room, rubbing the stubble on her head, thinking, *I had him.* But then what happened? Where did it go wrong? At what point did Lukas Frisell manage to squeeze the open cut shut and suture the edges?

It had been a few more hours of talking in circles after that. She'd been treading water, getting nowhere. Sarwani had taken over. He hadn't gotten one step further; if anything, it had been the opposite. Reluctantly, she's forced to admit that what's happening now may be the right strategy. Eva Nyman knows her inside and out, can read her like an open book.

Or is it Lukas Frisell Eva's reading?

The relationship between Frisell and Nyman is still impressively unclear.

Ryd peeks out of her corner. There are six of them in a room intended for two. And one of them is elderly, though a shadow from a long-gone era seems to be holding him up.

Is this man Eva Nyman's secret weapon?

Nyman nods to him, opens the door, and follows him into the interview room, shutting the door behind them.

Ryd watches from the other side of the glass. She watches Lukas Frisell look up and sees his mask slip. Only for a split second, but that's enough to let her know it's possible. It's possible to pry Lukas Frisell open.

The past suddenly suffuses the interview room.

"Edward," Frisell says, not just standing up. He rounds the table too, managing to get in a hug before Edward Rasmusson sits down. The door opens, and Lindberg and Ankan barge in, but Frisell has already returned to his chair.

"You're going to sit down," Ankan bellows.

"Looks that way," Frisell mutters.

"No more light touch," Lindberg says, handcuffing Frisell to a couple of sturdy metal hoops under the table.

The pair of them quickly withdraw again, closing the door. In the calm after the storm, Edward Rasmusson's voice emerges: "I'm sorry, Lukas.

These weren't exactly the circumstances under which I'd hoped to see you again."

"Me neither," Frisell replies. "But you look good, Edward."

The old man smiles wryly. "I suppose 'good' is a relative term," he says.

From the small observation room, Sonja Ryd peers into the space between the two men. Trying to catch what's going on there.

"You have to tell me what you've done, Lukas," Rasmusson continues after a pause. "Remember that day at Tysslinge? When you finally opened up to me and told me what you like?"

"You know I remember."

"You were this crackling firework display of frustration, but after several attempts you managed to get out what you liked, what you'd like to do instead of being locked up in a detention facility, wasting your life on violence and crap. You wanted to get closer to nature."

"Your visits were—"

"I'm not here for validation, Lukas," Rasmusson interrupts. "I'm completely impervious to sentimentality. But I can see that you're the same person you were then, that it's impossible to squeeze the truth out of you. But you have to tell us now, Lukas, you really do."

"You think I . . . ?"

"I have no idea what to think, Lukas. What I see is that sixteen-year-old at Tysslinge, the one who was so sure the world was against him, who was extremely hard to get through to. But you wanted someone to get through, Lukas. Do you still? Or can no one reach you anymore? What happened to you out there in the woods?"

"I've come far closer to myself."

"And yet, you were on the verge of breaking camp when we got there," Eva Nyman says.

Ryd can see what she's doing. She sees the timelines bending in Frisell's head, she can sense Nyman probing for openings, using Rasmusson's pinpricks into his childhood.

But Ryd misses the tempo, the quick twists and turns. Maybe she's being unfair.

Maybe even jealous.

"So you keep telling me," Frisell replies. "But all I did was take down a trap that no longer fit in with my plans, that's all."

Your plans, Ryd thinks to herself, and feels her nose touch the glass.

"You have to talk to me, Lukas," Rasmusson says, taking over again. "Where were you going? What made you suddenly decide to leave after eight years in the woods?"

"Blue, green, and red marking ribbon suddenly appeared on the trees. My forest was poisoned."

"They're biodegradable," Eva Nyman counters calmly.

We have your fucking DNA, Ryd thinks far less calmly, rubbing her nose against the one-way window. Then she pulls back, thinking, *You promised me, Eva. You promised you'd let me drop the DNA bomb. When it's time. When it won't drive him into total silence.*

Eva Nyman clenches her jaw. Watches Frisell. Looks over at the mirror. Shoots Rasmusson an encouraging glance.

"Remember the first time we met, Lukas?" Rasmusson asks. "Remember how you were feeling? Remember the situation?"

Frisell stares up at the ceiling. If Nyman's goal is to sow chaos in his brain, she seems to be succeeding. Ryd's starting point is that Frisell is utterly untrained socially but is animalistically sharp. She's not sure what this is doing to his brain.

Frisell says nothing. But he also won't meet Rasmusson's eyes. The old man continues: "I've never seen anything so broken, Lukas. My first thought was about your father, a minor criminal and alcoholic living in the woods of Hälsingland. I obviously didn't know him, but I always read up on the young people I was scheduled to meet."

At that, Frisell turns to his old mentor, who continues. "Your father's death was an opportunity to break free. Instead, you became your father. I woke you up, Lukas, when you were lost and on your way to an early grave."

"The Norrland Rangers, yes," Frisell says, and there's actually a hint of wistfulness in his voice.

"But first you went back to school," Nyman says. "The applied chemistry program. Was that where you learned how to make explosives?"

Frisell just shakes his head curtly. Nyman continues. "Your neighbors at the farm didn't know someone had been stealing electricity from them. But twice in the past five years, they've reported fertilizer stolen. With that fertilizer, a person with your chemical knowhow could make diazodinitrophenol, DDNP. Is that the type of explosive you've been using for your trap in the woods?"

Frisell remains silent. Alarmingly silent, Ryd muses on the other side of the one-way mirror.

They can't have him clam up now.

"The farm has a big yellow rapeseed field too," Nyman adds. "Drew some inspiration from that, did you?"

Edward Rasmusson leans forward and says, "You also told me you learned quite a lot about booby traps when you were in the Norrland Rangers. And guerilla warfare, covert strikes, kidnapping. You really have to tell us what this is all about, Lukas. What was the straw that broke the camel's back?"

Frisell still doesn't speak, but the handcuffs rattle faintly. He's not fully the stone-faced man from the wilderness anymore.

Nyman explicates: "Abducting a police officer in the woods. You pulled that off expertly, Lukas—there's no denying that. You grabbed me without anyone noticing, knocked me out, dragged me back to your lair, tied me up, subjected me to a campaign of terror. And now you're claiming you're innocent."

Their eyes lock. Eva Nyman reads a word inside him that never makes it to his mouth.

She's pretty sure that word is *sorry*.

"You do realize, don't you, Lukas, that we wouldn't have come for you if we didn't have solid evidence?"

Then she turns to the mirror and nods briefly.

Sonja Ryd sees the nod from the other side. And understands. The table has been set for her.

33

This time, Sonja Ryd's the only cop in the interview room. Sonja Ryd and Lukas Frisell. Sitting across from each other at the interview table. Nothing moves. Not until Frisell slowly turns his face to the ceiling.

"Smells like ethanol in here again," he says, sniffing. Ryd pretends to be too focused to listen.

"Shall we return to the incident with the wedding ring, Lukas?"

Frisell shifts in his seat as though mildly unsettled.

"I'm trying to picture the scene," Ryd continues. "I assume we're talking about a distressing row. Nina probably runs up to the toilet to flush down her wedding ring. You catch up to her, but you don't stop her. What is it you do instead? Rip her clothes off?"

"Who says we were wearing clothes?"

Ryd can feel herself blink but doesn't let that stop her.

"Nina says the passion the two of you shared was a stronger force than your separation. Though I'm not so sure that was really what—"

"You weren't there. No matter how interested you sound."

"There's something kind of rapey about the whole situation. Is punishment fucking something you're into, Lukas?"

"You'll never make me believe Nina would have told you that's what happened."

"It's nice to see you have at least some human emotions, Lukas. It's going to help you to come off as at least minimally sympathetic in court. Happily, there's an alternative scenario."

Is there hatred there now? Frustration? Disappointment?

"Shagging Nina over the toilet might not have been about her at all. It might have had more to do with your impending bachelorhood. You never did get to sow your wild oats, did you? You and Nina met young, and you were already looking forward to that new phase of your life. Let's have a closer look at your background."

Frisell observes her as one does a snake.

"Things started out poorly in the forests of Hälsingland. And moving to the big city didn't improve matters. At least in Hälsingland, you were able to escape into nature whenever your dad, the alcoholic, beat you black and blue. In Vällingby, you were sucked into petty criminality instead. And you weren't much of a chick magnet either. The upper secondary you eventually attended was a technical college—back then, there wouldn't have been many girls there. And none at all in the Norrland Rangers. So you never had a chance to indulge the bachelor in you."

"And what could this possibly have to do with me being a 'terrorist'?"

"I'll try to explain," Ryd says with a small smile. "The Terrorist Bomber's driven by sexual frustration. He might be telling himself he has a noble purpose, but in reality, he just wants to fuck. That urge never subsides, does it? Not even in older men."

"Out of the two of us, you seem to be the one who likes that word, Sonja Ryd."

"It wasn't just a yen for nature that made you go back to SUAS when you were fired from the police. It was the students too, not least the female ones, the ones whose hearts beat for nature and animals."

"I wasn't fired," Frisell mumbles.

"That's what you're focusing on? Isn't there some other part of that you should be objecting to?"

Frisell falls silent. A familiar threat is hanging over their conversation like a pall, the threat of *"No comment,"* the threat of *"I want a lawyer."* But it doesn't look like that's what his silence is about this time.

"Shouldn't you be objecting to my hypothesis that you became a teacher to get closer to the female students you so enjoyed taking out to dinner?"

Frisell just shakes his head. But it doesn't feel like he's done talking. She sets her jaw and forges on: "There are a lot of pictures of you on a Facebook page called 'Fun With Farming.' Did you know that?"

Both the silence and the headshaking continue.

But Sonja Ryd has staked her success on this card now. She has to keep going.

"The page belongs to a former student at SUAS who posted things between 2013 and 2015. You're featured in about a dozen pictures, some from nights out. You should remember her. Her name's Jonna Carlgren, and she attended the landscape architect program at SUAS. Women are the reason you made your way back to the university after your divorce, right?"

"Don't play even stupider than you actually are," Frisell snaps. "I studied agronomy, forestry, fossil-free farming, environmental science. That was the draw. Solid, practical knowledge. Knowledge that later helped me survive in and love nature in its rawest, purest form."

Ryd's pleased. She's pleased there's still communication, after all.

"But above all, it's all about Liselott Lindman, of course," she says quietly. Frisell stares into the outskirts of the universe.

"2008," Ryd continues. "Such an unbelievable debacle. Was it the very first time you were trusted with such a high-profile investigation, Lukas?"

Pause. Silence.

"Either way, you put all your eggs in one basket. You were going to save Liselott without relying on any new-fangled technology. She was a protected person, but a picture on Facebook had revealed where she was. You led the investigation. You were high and mighty and bet the house on 'natural' police methods being enough.

At that moment, in the autumn of 2008, you were the alpha male, Lukas. You had Eva Nyman by your side, a young, female sidekick always ready to validate you. But disaster struck. Liselott Lindman died, you were both blamed and fired, Nina left you. The alpha male crashed. And the person who witnessed your castration from the front row was Eva Nyman."

Frisell sits motionless, listening. His face is stony again, but now there are thin, fragile cracks streaking the granite.

"That's why you send her letters, isn't it?" The silence is solid now. Ryd continues, "But there was a way to regain your virility, Lukas. You remembered the girls at the university and decided to resume your interrupted studies. You rebranded yourself, and finally, you were ready. You were an instructor. An admired, well-preserved ex–police officer who, even though he constantly toyed with the idea of exiting society, never actually took the decisive step. You were torn between the female students and real life in the woods. It was against your libido Lelle Bergis had to fight."

"I suspected Lelle was the one who told you where to find me."

"Just like you, he's a shadow of his former self. It was a few years before you were done with the ladies at SUAS, it was hard to turn your back on that constant supply. But in the end, you were ready. You managed to transform your sexual urges into lust for the ultimate MILF, Mother Earth."

"You'll never understand what that closeness is like."

"That's probably true. But it's over now, I take it? Why? Had you had enough of fucking beavers?"

The noise is unexpected. It sounds like a jet engine but lasts only seconds. Then Lukas Frisell is done laughing. "There are no beavers out there," he mutters. "Of any kind."

"But you'd had enough of celibacy, right?"

"Why do you people always have to turn big questions into trivial ones?"

"Us people?"

Frisell demonstratively stops talking. Sonja Ryd exhales, shakes her head, gestures resignedly at the mirror, and continues. "If I didn't know you, Lukas, I'd say your years in the woods have turned you into both a nutcase and a misogynist. But the more I get to know you, the clearer it's becoming that you were always those things."

"The earth is dying out there and you're bickering about trifles."

"By all means, keep proving me right. The misogyny is unmistakable, but maybe nutcase isn't the right word, after all. More like fixated. Maybe obsessed. An obsession that grew as the celibacy became more difficult to bear and as nature continued to show you her unhealable wounds. Taken together, a perfect hotbed for radicalization. What finally flipped the switch?"

"What switch?"

"The one that made you decide to put all your disparate skills, frustrations, and convictions together and start attacking society?"

"That's not what I decided to do."

"Then what did you decide to do?"

Frisell makes no reply. Ryd tries to catch his eye. To no avail.

"Do you recognize these three points in time?" she asks, passing him a note from her folder.

Frisell looks at the piece of paper but says nothing, face impassive.

"Those are the dates and times when three times lethal bombs were detonated. I want to know if you have an alibi for any or all of them."

Frisell sighs and says, "I've lived alone for eight years. You know full well I never have an alibi."

"And yet we know you have accomplices."

Frisell shakes his head, his face despondent.

"Soon enough, we'll know when you began stealing electricity from the farm," Ryd says. "That will give us an approximate start date for your planning process. You realized you needed access to the internet to execute your plan. To select symbolically important victims and, not least, to start putting the bombs together. Somewhere in the forests of Uppland, you have a laboratory, Lukas, and it's only a matter of time before we find it. That lab is where you messed up."

Frisell looks up, curiosity in his clear blue eyes.

"Did something out of the ordinary happen when you were working on the second bomb?" Ryd continues. "It was rather unique, wasn't it, oblong, with a mechanical detonator."

Nothing but attentive silence from Frisell.

"It was quite powerful, Lukas, you can take my word for it. You should have seen what Jesper Sahlgren looked like, lying there, burning away the grass in Vasaparken. But the explosive force wasn't enough to blow up your DNA. It's still there, in what's left of the bomb. What happened? Did you cut yourself building the bomb?"

Ryd doesn't expect eye contact, but when she turns to him, his gaze meets hers. She can't say what she sees in it. A new kind of seriousness?

"I didn't build any bombs," he says.

"Except we know you did. You built an explosive trap that you subsequently disassembled when it was time to leave the forest, to reunite with your accomplices and start your terror campaign in earnest. This was just a prelude, wasn't it, Lukas?"

"That's not why I took the trap down. That's not what I decided to do."

"Then what did you decide to do, Lukas?"

"I wasn't fired."

"And?"

"I don't think I should say anything else now."

34

The glasses Anton Lindberg is carefully carrying toward the far corner of the pub create a resonate melody as they slide around the tray. When, against all odds, he manages to set the tray down safely on the table, he notes smugly that it's bone-dry.

Which is more than can be said about the people sitting around it. This is not their first round.

"I don't understand who this guy is," Shabir Sarwani says, picking up his beer. I see him, I hear him, I talk to him, but I have no fucking idea who Lukas Frisell is."

"Guilty," Sonja Ryd announces from the deepest sofa. "That's what he is. Guilty. I've never been surer about anything."

"What do you base that on, though?" Ankan asks, grabbing her tankard like some Munich beer wench. "He mostly seems surprised at finding himself there."

"But like a surprised animal," Sarwani says, taking a swig. "Constantly on the alert. As though he's studying an unexpected but potentially traversable bit of terrain. As though he's gathering information."

Eva Nyman sips her Singapore sling and says, "He has changed a lot."

"Alright, so what do you think?" Lindberg says, grabbing the last pint. "You knew him really well. Is he our Terrorist Bomber? How good of a liar is he?"

Nyman sighs, shrugging. "I honestly don't know. Everything points to him."

"Including hard evidence," Ryd adds, raising her glass of red wine.

"That too," Nyman admits. "But I just don't know. Could someone be trying to frame him?"

"You know as well as I do how unlikely that is," Sarwani says.

"What's abundantly clear, amid all this chaos," Ryd declares, "is that once upon a time, he was a bloody good detective."

"And probably a proper babe magnet," Ankan adds.

There's tentative laughter around the table. Ryd watches Nyman.

"You would know," Lindberg says, patting Ankan on the arm. "But after eight years in the woods, he looks like one of those walking trees in *The Lord of the Rings*. What is it you women are drawn to?"

"Danger," Sarwani hisses.

"Aren't you always bragging about how you've never had a girlfriend?" Ankan retorts. "No, it's not danger, it's how a man . . . carries himself . . ."

"It's not Shabir's fault he's gay," Lindberg shouts, raising his tankard to his lips before pausing and turning to Ankan. "How he carries himself? Seriously?"

"Even you have to admit it, Sonja," Ankan says, turning to Ryd, who takes a big swig of her wine.

"I don't have room in my life for that shit," Ryd says. "But maybe Eva can tell us what Frisell was like fifteen years ago, as a detective and as a man."

"And I'm not gay, by the way," Sarwani puts in. "I'm just not into commitment."

"I think I'd like to change tack, actually," Eva Nyman says calmly. "Here we are, in a bar, it's late, the whole team came out, even after a monstrously long workday. Surely what we should be doing is taking a moment to celebrate a little. So far, we've done really well, no matter how this ends. And tomorrow, we'll have more videos to show him."

"I just need him to take the bait with this white church thing," Ryd mumbles.

"Eva's right," Lindberg bellows. "Nova's the new fucking vanguard of NOD. Who would have dared to guess that a couple of weeks ago?"

"Vanguard?" Sarwani exclaims. "We're nothing short of NOD's core team."

"The core team." Nyman giggles. "That's us, that's Nova. The stars of NOD."

They chuckle at that for a minute. Then Nyman knocks back the rest of her cocktail and adds, "Besides, I could personally use a victory. More than a few members of the top brass would like to see me gone."

Silence follows. Her subordinates exchange looks. In the end, Ankan's the one who speaks.

"We've all heard rumors. But we're not sure exactly what they're about."

"I know," Anton Lindberg blurts out. "And you know I support you, Eva."

"Well, I don't support me," Nyman replies quietly. "I made a mistake. And followed it up with even more."

"Every crime these days is linked to criminal gangs, every last copper knows it. Sometimes one snaps—that's perfectly understandable," says Anton Lindberg.

"That's actually not at all true," Ryd mutters from her sofa.

"But you did snap, Eva?" Sarwani asks.

"It was about a year ago," Nyman replies. "This guy was mocking me in the interview room. For hours on end."

"Anyone would have ended up hitting that prick," Lindberg says.

"Sure, but maybe not with a statute book," Nyman mumbles, shaking her head.

"A statute book?" Ankan repeats.

"For some reason I can't remember now, his lawyer had placed one on the interview table. That gang leader was sitting there, spewing all kinds of sexual innuendo while his lawyer went to the bathroom. I struck him on the side of the head with the book."

"Wow," Ankan says. "And then there were more mistakes?"

"I tried to cover it up. Some of the members of my team, which was subsequently dissolved, helped me. We managed to keep it from going public. But the top brass obviously found out. There was political concern, put it that way. There still is."

"But you're still here, Eva," Anton Lindberg says, slamming his phone down on the table. Lit up on the screen are the police sketches of the two couriers who delivered the bombs to Vasaparken and Västerås.

"I would bet anything they're the same person and that he's Frisell's hired gun," Lindberg continues. "I would also bet anything he's linked to the escalating gang criminality in this country. And that he's an Arab."

The first thing Anton Lindberg sees is that Ankan knocks back what's left of her beer and stands. The second is a pair of dark brown eyes watching him.

"I didn't realize you were out with your friends," the dark-haired man says to Ankan, his eyes still on Lindberg.

"We're done for tonight, Rahim," Ankan replies, turning the large man's face to hers, kissing him on the mouth before nodding to her colleagues. Then she links arms with him and starts walking toward the exit. He only glances back over his shoulder once, at Lindberg, who has stood up and is watching them go, looking as though he wants to say something but has forgotten every word in the Swedish language.

From the depths of the sofa comes Sonja Ryd's slightly sleepy voice: "I would bet anything that bloke's a copper."

"You know him?" Sarwani says, putting down his half-empty tankard and standing.

"I know the type," Ryd replies.

Eva Nyman gets up too, with a sigh. Sarwani puts his arm around the rigid Lindberg and turns to Ryd.

"We'll get him tomorrow," he says, giving her a thumbs-up.

Ryd nods and to her surprise feels her own thumb extending toward the ceiling.

Nyman pats Lindberg on the shoulder as he's led away by Sarwani. She herself stays put for a moment, studying Ryd.

"I wonder how deep the racism really runs in the police," she mutters, but then she shakes off her dark musings and asks with a gesture toward the exit: "Coming, Sonja?"

"I just have to make a call," Ryd says, holding up her phone.

Nyman studies her for a while longer. Then she breaks into a big smile, shakes her head, and leaning forward to ruffle Sonja Ryd's stubble to the extent that's possible, follows Lindberg and Sarwani.

Once they're gone, Sonja Ryd slips her phone back into her pocket, takes a deep breath, walks over to the bar, readies her vocal chords, and says, "A half bottle of red, please."

On her way back to the sofa, she says under her breath, "Nova's a shitty fucking name."

35

On this May morning, the sun rises at 4:20 AM in Stockholm. The members of the Nova Group don't wake up quite that early, but eventually the sunlight reaches each of them, one after the other.

Shabir Sarwani opens the blinds in his Solberga flat and is almost knocked over by the light as he slinks out onto the balcony, coffee in hand. In his terraced house in Huvudsta, Anton Lindberg is hit by the rays just as children's feet hit him in the solar plexus, and he hears the shared, not entirely friendly laughter of his two daughters. On Frejgatan, Eva Nyman feels the light trigger a headache as she fumbles for her phone under her pillow and then, for some reason she can't fathom, looks down at the number she absolutely mustn't call. In Stureby, Ankan watches Rahim Abdulhamid's olive skin reflect the early morning rays and realizes she's not going to be getting up just yet. Finally, when the light reaches Sonja Ryd, it finds her doing her best to parry her nausea in the rowing machine at the twenty-four-hour gym on Hornsgatan, driving the toxins out of her body one pull at a time so she won't smell of ethanol.

* * *

An hour or so later, Sonja is reading aloud: "'We must reject these lives of mass consumerism, and we must do it now. Soon, the wave that will wake you from your selfish stupor will wash over you. The wave is building. It will wash away parts of the dying city of bridges, and god's white dwelling will gaze down upon the ruins of destruction. What you have witnessed is only the beginning.'"

When she's done, Shabir Sarwani takes over, pointing and saying, "If we could turn our attention to the screen on the wall."

Ryd sees Frisell obey, and a black-and-white map of Stockholm slowly emerges from the whiteness. The last thing to appear are six circles dotting the city.

"This is what one can gaze down upon," Sarwani says. "From the white steeples, that is. From 'god's white dwelling'. Could I have some assistance, please?"

The door to the interview room opens. Lindberg and Ankan enter. They take off Frisell's handcuffs; remove his shirt, not entirely gently; and attach wires from a device to his arms and chest. Then they leave almost as quickly as they came.

Sarwani continues, "We're going to have a look at each of these six circles and gauge your reaction, Lukas. Are you ready?"

They begin before Frisell has a chance to answer. It's only after zooming in that the name of each church becomes legible. First on the list is Matteus, followed by Filadelfiakyrkan, Adolf Fredrik, Sankt Peter, Gustaf Vasa, and Djurgårdskyrkan.

"Thank you," Sarwani says, and as if on cue, Ankan and Lindberg reappear to remove the measuring equipment from Frisell's body. They pull his shirt back over his scarred torso, cuff him to the table again, and leave. Sarwani says, "Okay, your reactions to the six potential crime scenes have been recorded. It won't be long before they've been analyzed by experts in the field."

"Your heart is likely to have sped up at the sight of one of these points," Ryd explains, with a mirthless smile. "Whether or not you choose to speak. Because we have to move beyond what you're willing to say, Lukas. No one believes you anymore. You've burned your bridges."

Frisell shakes his unevenly shorn head but remains silent.

"Let's turn back to the screen," Ryd says.

A video starts. It shows the forest. It appears to be dusk as the camera rounds a slope and reaches the base of a ten-foot moss-covered precipice. A latex-gloved hand reaches into the frame as the camera moves to ground level. A patch of moss has been scraped away, revealing another almost invisible wooden hatch leading into the hill. The hand scrapes away even more moss, then grabs the bottom edge of the hatch and heaves it up. A torch slices through the twilight, then the perspective dips toward the ground. The hand reaches into the opening, and the camera's operator seems to wiggle into a space that, from the outside, looks like a dark cavernous hole. As the torchlight grows stronger, it illuminates a space that contains not only a chair and a simple desk with candle stubs on it, but also, sitting on the desk, a laptop with a USB modem, which is to say an internet dongle inserted into the USB port. Then the camera zooms in on a stack of printer paper on a shelf, but there's no printer to be seen, and no typewriter. What the camera does capture is a significant amount of tiny paper chads on the dirt floor.

"You must have felt really sure no mushroom pickers would ever stray into your part of the forest," Sonja Ryd comments.

Frisell stares at the now paused video. Not least at the chads on the floor.

"I'm assuming you charged your laptop before you took it to this study, which has no electricity. But I haven't been able to find any chargeable printers," Ryd says. "Which begs the question of what the stack of printer paper is doing there and, more importantly, makes me think maybe those little flakes of paper didn't come from a printer at all, but were, rather, punched out by an old-fashioned typewriter. Correct me if I'm wrong."

Frisell just shakes his head.

"I'm sure you've realized by now that we're going to find everything?" Ryd asks without asking. "We're going to find the typewriter too. We're going to prove it was used to write the letters. And very soon, we're going to get into your computer and have a look at your entire search history. It would be very cooperative of you to give us the password right now. Save us the work."

Frisell looks up at Ryd and says, "That's my writing den."

"Your writing den?" Ryd exclaims. "And what were you writing? Other than the threatening letters addressed to the police and your one-time partner?"

"I write about living skin to skin with nature. And I do it on that computer, not a typewriter."

"What's it like, then? Explain it to a dyed-in-the-wool urbanite."

Frisell chuckles briefly. "This is all really hard for you to imagine, isn't it?"

"So, help me."

"You must get to know every inch of your surroundings, the way you know close friends. You have to learn how each part is doing, ups and downs, what mood they're in. Nature has to let you in—you can't force it. You have to get to know every tree, every stone, every moss, every plant, not to mention the animals. Being truly close to them, looking a stag in the eye and knowing it as it knows you."

"And yet, you didn't mind blowing them up in your trap."

"Only when I had no choice, when I was starving. I considered making food runs with the car a failure, I only left to buy food a handful of times. A couple of the winters were really tough."

"So you're saying you kept the car for other purposes?"

Frisell makes no reply. Ryd is hopeful. Don't clam up. You're talking. Keep talking. "You were right before," Frisell says at length.

"Before?"

"About the celibacy. I was prepared for everything else. Not that." Ryd nods. She knows all about celibacy. Tyskertøs.

"So, how did you deal with it?"

"It's the only thing you're going to find on that computer, aside from 'my book,' if I can call it that: online conversations with women."

"With whom you met up? Prostitutes?"

"Of course not. Regular women on dating sites."

"And where did you meet up with them?"

"If they wanted to go to a bar, it had to be one that takes cash. Usually Flustret in Uppsala. Sometimes I went to their houses."

"Did this happen often?"

"Not often enough," Lukas Frisell replies with a smile. "And in a way, it's still somehow a fundamental part of nature, wouldn't you say, Sonja Ryd?"

She's just about to put on her sternest face and push on with her questions, when Frisell continues: "You know nothing about what humanity is on the brink of destroying until you've lain in the moss, gazing up as the stars begin to emerge against a darkening sky while the first snowflakes of winter drift down to settle on your face. You know nothing until you've seen half a dozen red squirrel kits race down a bare pine trunk to explore the world under the gentle supervision of their mother. You know nothing about . . ."

It takes Sonja Ryd a couple of seconds to realize what's going on. Frisell's nature vignettes paint such vivid pictures, it's only when Sarwani tugs on her arm that she notices the wildly waving Ankan in the door to the room behind the mirror. The last thing she sees are the guards dragging Lukas Frisell out of the room, back to his cell.

"Major incident," Ankan shouts as she ushers Ryd into the small observation room.

36

The inner room is crowded. Eva Nyman's standing on tiptoe, phone to her ear. She's trying to reach the head of NOD but keeps being passed off to civilian staff. Since she never curses, she doesn't curse, but she's treating her phone fairly roughly. Everyone's calling their own contacts to have the major incident confirmed. In the end, it's Anton Lindberg who bellows, "I have confirmation from colleagues on the scene. There's an abandoned backpack on the commuter train platform at Odenplan, right now, in the morning rush hour."

"Odenplan," Shabir Sarwani says. "That's one of the places where God's white dwelling can gaze down upon the destruction."

"Except it's underground," Sonja Ryd says, frowning. "Out of sight."

"I have a live feed here from an officer on the scene," Lindberg shouts, holding his phone up.

They crowd in so close they're like one giant creature. A shaky video feed on the screen shows people pouring out of the underground entrances as emergency vehicles begin to arrive.

"You three, get over there right now," Nyman says, pointing. "Sonja and I will stay here and consolidate. We'll be right behind you."

Sarwani, Lindberg, and Ankan rush out of the room, heading for a car. Odenplan's not far; they arrive in minutes. By then, the entrances to the commuter trains and metro have been cordoned off, the station fully evacuated.

Lindberg squeezes the car through the roadblocks on Odengatan. They stop partway up Odenplan Square, jump out, and approach the inner cordon on foot. Uniformed officers guard the entrances; the bomb squad have arrived and are already setting up their equipment outside the main one. Sarwani, Lindberg, and Ankan greet them curtly and are led over to a screen that has just been set up inside the police tape.

The uniforms out on Odenplan are doing their best to keep people back, and tape has been set up while they wait for crush barriers to be delivered, and yet there's chaos out there. Curious onlookers are pushing forward like the audience at a rock concert. A billowing semicircle with as many phones as people is forming in the shadow of Gustaf Vasa's white bulk.

Sarwani shouts in vain to the insufficient number of uniformed officers: "Make these people disperse."

The screen next to Sarwani, Lindberg, and Ankan suddenly lights up, and an image emerges from the nothingness. It's the commuter train platform, completely deserted. A bomb disposal robot, operated by a man with a joystick standing next to Sarwani, is slowly approaching a bench on which sits an abandoned army-green backpack.

Sarwani hears a voice inside. It belongs to Sonja Ryd. It says, "Except it's underground. Out of sight."

Out of sight of God's white dwelling.

But it can't be out of sight, because "God's white dwelling will gaze down upon the ruins of destruction."

Sarwani peers over at the crowd pushing against the police cordon. He ignores the screen and the robot inching across the platform. Instead, his peripheral vision briefly catches something indistinct among the curious, phone-wielding onlookers, and then it's gone again, a patch of army green that has already slipped out of his field of vision.

His eyes rove frantically across the curved line of people, searching their faces, seeing acquaintances where there are only strangers. Then there it is again, flickering at the edge of his vision. He hears raised voices from the sea of people. In one spot, people are parting, like the Red Sea before Moses.

Sarwani is already on his way. Toward that point.

Sitting on the asphalt is an army-green backpack, identical to the one on the platform.

Shabir Sarwani shouts wordlessly at the top of his lungs as he sprints toward the backpack sitting there in the middle of Odenplan, waving his hands wildly, trying to make people scatter.

He's still running toward the backpack when it explodes. And God's white dwelling gazes down upon the destruction.

37

Klara Sjö is sparkling in the morning sun, promising the city's residents a beautiful Stockholm day. The patrol car, on the other hand, hurls harsh blue light across the southern end of Barnhusbron Bridge before turning on sirens that join a growing chorus of others as it turns down Dalagatan.

Sonja Ryd and Eva Nyman are in the back seat. Ryd's trying and failing to reach Sarwani, Lindberg, Ankan; no one's answering. Nyman has two screens with different newsfeeds open, both relaying chaos, blood, destruction, but no context.

The patrol car passes Vasaparken and is let through the now expanded police cordon around Odenplan. Several ambulances have already arrived, their paramedics engaged in something akin to combat medicine.

The car stops. Ryd puts a hand on her forehead as her own ridiculously racing pulse thumps through her. She and Nyman both take a deep breath, exchange a look of what might be called mutual understanding, and throw themselves out of the vehicle.

All in unison.

They wrestle their way through the chaos on Odenplan. People bending over other people. Screams and noises only half recognizable as human. Bodies twisting in panicked contortions, held still, pushed down. A strangely large part of their field of vision is red. Blood, guts—everything's red.

Nyman realizes they need to focus on finding the other members of the Nova group. Otherwise, they'll lose their minds. Ryd stops, and looks up the white facade, the black dome, finally reaching the copper-green lantern tower. It really is as though the church is haughtily gazing down upon the destruction.

Nyman pulls her along. Soon, they're in the trenches of the First World War. It's a time warp. The only thing missing are sturdy amputation saws.

There's no shortage of morphine, though.

Finally, Sonja Ryd spots Anton Lindberg. He's putting bandages on an injured person lying on the ground; it looks dire, blood's pumping out of a partially ripped-off arm. Lindberg sees them but keeps working.

Closer to the church, Eva Nyman spots a familiar blonde mane. It's Ankan, kneeling next to an ambulance stretcher. They run over. Paramedics are moving around the stretcher with impressive speed. There's someone on it. An ashen Ankan is clutching a bloody hand, staring vacantly straight ahead.

At first, Nyman thinks what she's looking at is a severed hand. A blown-off hand. But then she notices that it's coming out from under the light-orange hospital blanket covering the stretcher.

That's when Nyman realizes the person on the stretcher is Shabir Sarwani.

His eyes are closed, his face perforated by small wounds, like from a spray of shot from a shotgun. At least twenty little extra mouths, all leaking, rivulets of red streaming down his pallid face.

Eva Nyman squats down next to the catatonic Ankan. Then a scraping sound behind her makes her turn around.

She sees Sonja Ryd tripping over a person stretched out on the ground, her head hitting the asphalt with a thud.

38

No daylight ever reaches these corridors. A very different eternity is stretching out before Lukas Frisell than the one he was confronted with in the forest. This is an eternity of tedium. He could never have imagined how miserable he'd be in the corridors of the Kronoberg Detention Facility. And yet that's nothing compared to how he feels in his cell.

His cell is hell. The small window in it seems to have been installed mostly as some kind of cruel joke.

He's walking between two sturdy guards. Their steps echo cinematically between the walls. Eventually, they stop. The younger of the guards unlocks a door, pushes Frisell into his cell, and removes his handcuffs. Frisell walks toward the window, toward the dissonant howl of sirens. He can't make out any of what's going on. All he can see is an infinitely dull rooftop.

He can see tedium itself.

The older guard lingers in the doorway while the younger steps back out into the corridor. The one who stays is around the same age as Frisell; neither one of them has commented on the fact that they knew each other once upon a time. Not friends exactly, but their paths crossed often.

How far they've since diverged.

The guard fixes Lukas intently, and for a long moment, neither of them moves or speaks. Then the guard braces himself and says, "Tell me you didn't bloody do this, Lukas."

Frisell heaves a deep sigh and gestures toward the window. "I don't even know what this is."

The guard still doesn't leave, just shifts impatiently from one foot to the other.

Apparently unsatisfied with his answer, he continues: "Seriously, you have to promise me, Lukas. The whole world's turning rotten, and I don't know what I'm supposed to do if someone like you turns rotten too."

Frisell turns away from the window. He looks the guard straight in the eye and says,

"I was just on my way back."

"Back?"

Frisell looks at him, unable to hold back a short, bitter laugh. "Back to this fucking place."

He pauses briefly before he continues: "To policing."

39

They're no longer in the trenches of the First World War. They're back in Medieval times. The screams and howls ripping through the large hall—which is normally a combined reception area and waiting room—could just as easily have emanated from a plague house in fourteenth-century Florence.

Sabbatsberg Hospital, located just a few hundred yards from Odenplan, was built in the 1870s, electrified in 1884, and chosen as the home of Stockholm's first X-ray department in the year 1900, but the screams are timeless. Chaotic scenes like these have dogged humanity since the dawn of the species. They are its history.

Sonja Ryd is sitting in a corner of the large room. She's not convinced the woman treating her for the severe scrape on her forehead is really a health-care worker. It feels more like she might have snuck in from the street. Her lab coat doesn't fit her right; she probably just grabbed one at random from a hook in some hallway.

On the other hand, Sonja Ryd admittedly can't see very well. And the world's spinning too.

"Any dizziness?" the nurse asks. "Impaired vision?"

"No," Ryd replies, struggling to focus and stand up. "No dizziness," she continues, "no impaired vision."

Eva Nyman leans past Ryd and asks, "Can we see him now?"

The nurse studies her archly before replying, "You may have noticed that you're not the only people here."

"But we're the ones in charge of the investigation into all of this," Nyman insists, holding out her police ID again.

The nurse shakes her head contemptuously before turning and walking off. They follow her into a six-bed room. While they wait for a makeshift curtain to be pulled back, Eva Nyman says, "By the way, the backpack on the platform was filled with two very environmentally unsound pink balloons and a note that simply read: 'Booom, motherfucker.' With three *o*'s."

"Smart," Ryd says, fighting the dizziness that seems to want to swallow her whole. "While our attention was on the platform, the bomb was planted in the crowd."

Just then, the nurse is given the go-ahead and opens the large curtain a crack. They've reached Tuscany now, as the plague came sailing in with the rats via Genoa, from the far shores of the Black Sea. Moans from bygone centuries seep through the thick, putrid air.

At the far end of the room, they see a figure with closed eyes and bandages wrapped all around its head, like a white parcel on its shoulders. Splotches of red have bubbled up through the bandages.

Ankan is sitting next to the bed. Some color has returned to her face. She says hoarsely, "The doctor claims he's okay, that he's going to wake up any minute. But I'm not so sure I believe him."

Eva Nyman gives her a hug and nods with relief. "And you're okay, Ankan?"

Ankan holds up her bloody forearms.

"I don't know if I'll ever be okay again. This blood can't be washed away." She points to the unconscious Shabir and continues: "But you're going to read your fill about this guy over the next few days. God knows how many lives he saved out there. He warned the onlookers with no thought to his own safety."

Ryd can feel the room spinning. She can't seem to focus on Ankan. Maybe she shouldn't have lied about how she's feeling. But seeing Sarwani wrapped in those mummy bandages does something to her. More than anything, she feels genuinely happy he's alive.

Ankan grabs Nyman's arm and stares deep into her eyes, their faces inches apart. "We have to find this bastard," she says. "Lukas Frisell was behind fucking bars when this shit went down."

40

For once, Sonja Ryd's alone in the small room behind the mirror. Not by choice. She sees the door in the far wall open as two guards escort Lukas Frisell into the interview room.

She hadn't just wanted to be in the interview room; she'd been needed. Urgently needed. There's an uncontrolled, angry ticking behind the compress covering her forehead. But the world's no longer spinning. It still was during her confrontation with Eva Nyman in her classically clean-cut office. Ryd had refused to accept Nyman's suggestion—which was only masquerading as a suggestion. What's more, she'd missed parts of the unmistakable order because the dizziness had finally claimed her.

But a couple of hours has gone by since then. Some kind of normalcy has settled in.

Statistics have replaced chaos. Five people died at Odenplan, and fourteen were injured, three critically.

It was a terrorist attack to equal the 2017 Stockholm truck attack.

And Eva Nyman was passing the buck when it came to Ryd's current station. The decision had been made by the higher-ups. This was Nova's only chance to cling onto some small part of this case. Besides, it was an opportunity to utilize Lukas Frisell's unique expertise and insights. So. Much. Crap.

Now, Nyman's in the interview room. Ryd's boss, her friend. Frisell's there. He actually looks eager. But they're not alone. There's also a stern-looking middle-aged man in a suit. He slowly opens his briefcase. Frisell takes a seat and says calmly, "I'm sensing I should be preparing to be released."

Nyman gestures toward the well-dressed man. "This is Prosecutor Sten Robert-Olsson. We want to make a proposal." She pronounces *Robert* in flawless French.

Frisell clearly has something he wants to say. He manages to bite it back. Instead, Nyman says, "You were in this interview room when the bomb went off on Odenplan, that much we know. But we also know your DNA was found inside one of the bombs and that you could have any number of accomplices out there. The fact that the bomb exploded while you were under arrest far from proves your innocence."

"Do I look like a man with accomplices?" Frisell says again.

Ignoring him, Prosecutor Robert-Olsson says, "In other words, you're still a suspect, and in theory the DNA evidence is enough to keep you detained indefinitely—which is what's going to happen."

The pause is so obviously for effect that even Frisell, after eight years in the wilderness, seems to recognize it as such. All the things he might want to howl out like a wild animal are firmly pushed back down.

They always are, Sonja Ryd thinks.

"What we're proposing is a modified version of detention," Robert-Olsson continues, "as part of the ongoing investigative work. Continued detention, yes, but with an ankle bracelet rather than in this facility."

"Doesn't that require a home?" Frisell asks darkly.

Prosecutor Robert-Olsson studies him with his unreadable fish eyes and replies, "What you probably don't know is that electronic tagging has come a long way. The application of detention by means of ankle bracelet ought therefore to keep pace with said technological advancements. The version whose effectiveness has been established involves an ankle bracelet with limited freedom of movement within clearly defined parts of Stockholm."

Robert-Olsson continues: "With a GPS-equipped ankle bracelet, you can, in other words, move freely within most of the inner city. But there's a condition: you will put yourself at the service of the Nova Group."

"What the fuck is the Nova Group?" Frisell retorts.

Sten Robert-Olsson ignores him the way only a lawyer can and continues, unperturbed. "In addition to the standard intensive surveillance by the relevant authorities, all members of Nova will be able to track your position on their mobile phones and tablets. An alert will immediately sound if you overstep your predefined boundaries by so much as a foot—or enter any prohibited areas, such as internet cafés, electronic shops, and so forth. You will be provided with a list of prohibited areas. You are not allowed to use the internet or computers, and you may not go near any mobile phone other than the one provided to you by the authorities, a basic phone whose outgoing and incoming calls will be logged and can be monitored in real time by Nova."

Eva Nyman leans across the interview table and says, "Too many things still point to you for it to be coincidence. If you're not guilty, Lukas, someone must be trying to frame you."

Frisell leans back in his chair, staring up at the ceiling. He slowly shakes his head and says, "The thought has occurred to me."

"And do you have any inkling who that might be?"

He continues to shake his head, saying at length, "I can't think of anyone. I have no contact with people."

"Do you accept these conditions, Lukas Frisell?" Sten Robert-Olsson asks formally. "Do you agree to make yourself available to the lead investigative team, to Nova, at any time of the night or day?"

"Nova," Frisell says.

Prosecutor Robert-Olsson waits silently for another long moment. Then he continues sternly: "As this agreement is affirmed, you, Lukas Frisell, are provided with an old, basic, pay-as-you-go phone, a Nokia 3310, which you must keep with you at all times and which is the only one you're allowed to utilize, as well as new clothes, toiletries, towels, and the key to one of the Police Authority's flats close to this station. The Nova Group may call you in for a meeting at any time, and you may never arrive late without calling to provide a valid reason for the delay. I repeat and stress that you may under no circumstances acquire or borrow an alternative mobile phone or computer or any other equipment by which you can communicate without the knowledge of the authorities. Do you accept these conditions?"

Frisell very deliberately turns his face to the large mirror in the interview room. Then he slowly begins to nod. "I accept," he says with a wry smile, and is given a set of keys, a bundle of clothes wrapped in paper, and an old maroon Nokia phone.

Nyman clears her throat and announces, "Your liaison will be Detective Inspector Sonja Ryd. Together, you will sit down and scour your past for possible suspects."

Lukas Frisell nods to the mirror and says mockingly, "Sonja Ryd . . ."

Ryd slams her hand against the one-way glass. Everyone in the interview room turns to stare.

III

The Second Hunt

41

The office looks different. Ankan pauses in the doorway. Of Nova's five members, only four are present, but to compensate, the group has been augmented overnight by almost twenty investigators, both police and civilian. More desks and computers have been brought in. The space gives a very different impression.

"Bloody hell, Nova's hit the big time," she exclaims, setting her course for a table Eva Nyman's sharing with three newcomers. Ankan has seen them around, but she doesn't know their names.

Nyman stands up and comes to meet her, pulling her aside to ask, "How is Shabir?"

"He's awake. His body's taken a beating, but behind the bandages, he's definitely the same old Shabir Sarwani. We're going to have a tough time keeping him away."

"That's good to hear," Nyman says. "Well, as you can see, things have changed quite a bit. We're still here, and Nova's leading the expanded group investigating the terrorist and activist aspects of this case."

"What other aspects are there?" Ankan asks.

"I'd say the rest can be characterized as, quite simply, a power struggle. Someone in the top brass has staked their reputation on this not being terrorism."

Ankan nods so violently her blonde bun comes undone. While she pins it back up, she asks, "And who are the people sitting with you, Eva?"

"Coordinators," Nyman replies with a smile. "It's the price we pay. But they can come in handy, keeping a bird's-eye view of things."

"So, like, your secretaries?"

"More like stand-ins," she says with a shrug. Since I'm barely ever here. "It's nonstop emergency meetings and press conferences for me."

Then she walks over to the whiteboard. It, too, has been expanded in every dimension. Across the top, the header simply reads "Nova."

"More clearly defined sections," Nyan says, pointing. "Four columns: Uppsala, Vasaparken, Västerås, and now Odenplan. The latter's being filled in at a rapid clip right now. But that doesn't mean we stop investigating the previous bombings. Until Shabir returns, we have four groups. Odenplan is led by Anton; the Frisell angle, by Sonja; and the three previous attacks, by you, Ankan. And the team of coordinators is headed up by me. You're listed as team leaders here."

"Shouldn't that involve a promotion?" Ankan asks, studying her name on the whiteboard.

"If we bring this case home, I reckon that's a realistic expectation. Now, come along."

Nyman leads Ankan over to a corner where the sturdy Anton Lindberg is sitting with six other people. He looks up, asks about Sarwani's condition, and then says, "Pictures, videos, and witness testimonies from both the platform and Odenplan itself are pouring in. I need quite a few bodies. The moment we spot something that might be worthwhile, I'll send one of my slaves to the whiteboard. We agreed to call you guys my slaves, right?"

Anton Lindberg's entourage grumbles briefly. Nyman leaves, dragging Ankan with her to four people sitting at a table in the middle of the office.

"This is your team, Ankan," Nyman announces. "Your task is to keep the three previous attacks up to date. I'm going to leave you here, so you can introduce yourselves and discuss assignments."

Ankan shoots Nyman a slightly surprised look as she walks away, but then makes herself comfortable in her new environment.

Nyman moves on to Sonja Ryd, who is seated between two detective constables, typing on a computer with her phone wedged between her cheek and her shoulder. Nyman taps her on the other shoulder.

"Are we keeping an eye on Frisell?"

Without pausing her phone conversation, Ryd pushes over the open iPad sitting next to her computer: a red line is winding its way across a map of inner-city Stockholm. In one location, there's a flashing dot, by Hornstull. When Nyman makes a small gesture of bewilderment, Ryd gives up on her phone call, saying into her mobile, "I'll call you back in a couple of minutes, Nina." Then she turns to her new coworkers and asks, "How would you people like a five-minute coffee break?"

The constables are used to following orders, and quickly get up and leave. Ryd turns to Nyman and points to the iPad.

"The flashing red dot is Frisell's current location, and the line shows his movements. In other words, he's remaining within the authorized zone, but as you can see from the line, he has approached the station a couple of times already. He'll be here before long. Me notwithstanding."

"It's important that you understand that this technology is one hundred percent reliable, Sonja."

"No such thing," Ryd mutters, shaking her head. "You know how I feel about this idea, Eva. That prick's guilty. This is just good old Swedish naivety."

Eva Nyman glances around and leans closer to Ryd. She whispers, "I'm having him tailed."

Sonja Ryd can feel how incredulous the look she shoots her boss is.

"I know," Nyman nods. "I have, extremely unofficially, managed to appropriate a surveillance team that will be following him around the clock. Like us, they're able to monitor the position of the ankle bracelet in real time. They won't lose him."

Against her will, Ryd feels slightly impressed by Nyman. Securing a surveillance team without the higher-ups knowing about it is a challenge, to say the least.

Nyman changes the subject. "When is Frisell supposed to be here?"

"We just said before the end of the day, to give him a few hours to get acclimated. It's four o'clock now. The longer he stays away the happier I am. Bloody hell, Eva, making me his babysitter . . ."

"You know that's not what this is about. I watched you interact with him."

Ryd frowns briefly, shaking her head. "The important thing is that we're still on this case," she says through gritted teeth. "But what we're doing in this part of the room is collecting evidence against Frisell. For example, I'm currently in the middle of a conversation with Nina Strömblad, who definitely has more to say. And I don't know about interaction."

Nyman briefly looks flustered but quickly composes herself. "Oh yes," she says. "Interaction. Whether you like it or not."

"My feeling was more that he was interviewing me," Sonja Ryd says.

42

Lukas Frisell discovers them the moment he steps out of the borrowed police flat on Agnegatan, a stone's throw from police HQ. By the time he reaches Flemingatan, he realizes he's never going to be able to drop the note into the letterbox without being seen.

They move the way surveillance officers usually move. Just to make sure, he takes a roundabout route, to map how the officers take over from each other when there might be a blind spot.

He estimates that it might be possible if he cuts through the Sankt Erik neighborhood and takes the winding backstreets to Inedalsgatan. Along the way, he sits down on a park bench and adds a few notes to the slip of paper.

It works. He manages to create a thirty-second window before Officer 1 appears out of a shrubbery and a winded Officer 2 catches up out on Flemingatan. That's enough to race down the short flight of stairs on Inedalsgatan and quickly slip the note into the slot in the door. Now he'll have to wait for an answer at the old drop-off point on the other side of town.

He gets there just over thirty minutes later—that should be enough—and repeats the blind-spot maneuver. Briefly out of sight, he reaches in under the bronze sculpture Kjolen in Fredhäll Park, pulls out a piece of paper, and waits for an opportune moment to read it.

Then, he goes to an electronics shop by Fridhemsplan Square that's on his list of prohibited areas. After a few failed attempts, he manages to talk a young girl into going in for him. He gives her a hundred-kronor note for her troubles.

While Frisell waits outside the shop, he furtively studies the two surveillance officers, whose attempts to stay inconspicuous make them appear as though they have ants in their pants. After a while, the girls returns with a small bag she hands him. And thus, he has spent a considerable part of his remaining cash to purchase something as outdated as a Dictaphone. He uses another shop window as a rearview mirror to make sure Officer 2 slips into the electronics shop while Officer 1 keeps an eye on him from the corner of the street.

Then, he takes a stroll through Rålambshov Park and across Västerbron Bridge, taking in Stockholm's most beautiful view, watching a figure in a gray hoodie moving about a small park at the southern bridgehead. He quickly strides past, not stopping until he reaches Hornstull.

It's the first time in a long time that Lukas Frisell is not on the move. He puts his foot up on a wooden tree seat and waits for the surveillance officers who are pretending to be strolling down from Västerbron. He adjusts his ankle bracelet, which has already given him eczema. Apparently, he's now allergic to plastic. A very of-the-times ailment.

Then, he pulls his khaki trouser leg back down over his old hiking boot, takes his foot off the bench, and gazes up at Hornhuset, whose steplike angles lead up to an enormous sunlit mural.

This is definitely not what Hornstull looked like when he left the city. And sure, there had been mobile phones back then too—after all, he'd been there for the introduction of the first generations of smartphones—but these days, no one ever looks up from them. During his long walk, he's even occasionally experimented with sitting down next to people tapping away on their phones; he's listened to people loudly discussing intimacies in public. And he understands these modern times even less now than fifteen years ago.

Social media seem to have taken over people's lives. Just like he'd feared back then. He turns and walks back up Långholmsgatan. There's a kind of panic in the air, which his sensitive olfactory organs registers. He can tell this is a city that has once again been the victim of a terrorist attack.

At the southern end of Västerbron, he returns to the small park by Pålsundsbacken.

It's empty now, the man with the gray hoodie is gone. Frisell finds the blind spot in his surveillance and quickly leans into it, dashing up to a sculpture in the middle of the park. The motif is exactly what the name suggests: cockfight. The two metal cocks fighting each other with everything they have.

From the base of the sculpture, he snatches up a small earbud, popping it into his ear before Officer 1 turns the corner.

"That sculpture could have been us twenty years ago, amigo," a hoarse man's voice says in his right ear.

Frisell catches himself smiling. Once again in motion, he says aloud, "Alonzo."

"Lukas," the voice replies,. "I don't think you should be talking too much right now. The important thing is that you listen. Besides, the microphone in that tiny earbud sucks. You look like hell, amigo."

Frisell chuckles but says nothing.

"Go to our old hangout," the voice says.

Frisell leaves the park, turning down the stairs and catching a glimpse of the man in the gray hoodie down on Pålsundsbron Bridge. Having crossed over to Långholmen, Frisell turns up the hill, passing between rows of little red wooden houses. Almost all the spring leaves have unfurled by now. This is as much nature as you can expect in inner-city Stockholm.

"The device is ready to go," Alonzo says in his ear. "Years of fine-tuning. Has already been tested in two neighboring countries."

Frisell nods slowly, as though to himself.

He reaches the Långholmen amphitheater, wooden benches with a seating capacity of three thousand, forming a large semicircle, an optimistic 1940s version of an ancient Greek theater. Five or six people are scattered on the benches, hunched over their phones. Among the trees in the nearby woods, he spots the man in the gray hoodie, who is by all appearances on the phone. The man briefly meets his eyes. Only now does he properly recognize Alonzo.

"Take out the Dictaphone," Alonzo says in his ear. "I can see them now. They didn't bring parabolic microphones. They can't hear you. I'll go around and come up the other side in a bit."

"They'll think I'm talking into the Dictaphone. Smart."

"I had to think on my feet, amigo. I wasn't exactly expecting to hear from you. You'll have to remember to record some nonsense later, just in case someone thinks to check at any point. Damn, I almost feel sentimental seeing you sitting there again."

"You were always my best informant, Alonzo."

"At the moment, it's best if we keep the device in the workshop," Alonzo says. "I need twenty-four hours. And you'll have to go over there. You obviously haven't forgotten where it is."

Out of the corner of his eye, Frisell can see Officer 1 over by the street he climbed himself, while Officer 2 seems absorbed in an animated phone call as he strolls across the amphitheater's stage. Frisell continues to speak into the Dictaphone: "I remember. And the phone issue is . . . ?"

"I'll leave a burner in drop-off location two," Alonzo says. "Remember where that was?

"Old Town, yes. I'll be spending about an hour at the station first . . ."

"I'll make the drop around half after five. It'll be safe there. As far as the other phone issue is concerned, we're going to have to get creative. What you want is for me to check a phone you've been given by the coppers and then give it back to you?"

"If I'm right, I can't leave here without it. Like I said in my note, it's a Nokia 3310."

"I have an idea of how to do it," Alonzo says in his ear. "I'm coming back around now. When I tell you, you record some stray thoughts on your Dictaphone, like a conclusion or whatever. Then you pretend to put it back in your pocket, but what you'll actually do is slip it down onto the ground, and then you put the Nokia next to it. Don't let them see. Then follow my route up into the woods. Once the two clowns are on your tail, keep going for three minutes, then do some acting when you realize you must have dropped your Dictaphone. "That gives me six minutes to check the phone, give or take."

"Thanks, Alonzo," Frisell says. "I wish we had more time."

"There'll be plenty once you're free of all this, amigo. Then you'll have to tell me all about what it's been like out there in the woods. For real."

"It's been . . . magical. But to everything, there is a season."

"Start talking into the Dictaphone now."

Frisell starts up the Dictaphone and says some bland words about returning to civilization. Nothing he says could ever come even close to the truth anyway.

Peeking over at the surveillance officers, he manages to place both the Dictaphone and the Nokia on the ground by his feet. Then he sets off at a decent pace, up toward the small stand of trees where Alonzo disappeared. The officers follow him without bothering to check the bench he sat on.

He amuses himself by heading straight up to the highest point on Långholmen, the lookout spot diagonally above Västerbron, a nightmare location for any surveillance officer. Before he can even start acting out his little scene about discovering he's missing the Dictaphone, he hears Alonzo's voice in his ear:

"There's a tracker on the Nokia, yep, and turning the phone off is not enough. But it can be fixed. I'll get you instructions. Now go pick up your stuff before someone nicks it."

"Thank you," Frisell says.

"You know which one of us owes an endless debt of gratitude, amigo. We'll talk soon, for real. And throw that fucking earbud into the sea."

Then he can clearly hear that Alonzo's gone.

Frisell acts out his little scene, a restrained version of a person discovering something missing and suddenly being in a hurry. Just patting his jacket briefly and expressing dismay is sufficient.

The officers follow him back to the amphitheater, like stalkers following an actor. The Dictaphone and the Nokia are both still there. He picks them up and then turns right back the way he came, just to make life difficult for the surveillance officers. But as the true professionals they are, they quickly come up with strategies that allow him to pass them by, through the stand of trees and on toward the stairs up to Västerbron, which takes him across the water to Kungsholmen.

To the police station.

He wanders up to the highest point on the bridge and pauses there for a while. The world of humans has become even more of a theater than he remembered.

He discreetly pulls the small earbud out and sends it plunging almost a hundred feet into the waves below.

What's down there is real water, at least.

43

Sonja Ryd's not neglecting her other duties, of course, but at the same time, she can't help checking her iPad from time to time. She avoids the news—she already knows panic is spreading through Stockholm. What she's making sure to keep half an eye on are the movements of Frisell, a man trying to reclaim a forgotten city. To her surprise, tracking the flashing red dot across the map has been therapeutic, at least until very recently. Until he left Fridhemsplan, cutting through Kronoberg Park on his way to the station.

That instantly undid any therapeutic effect.

Sonja Ryd walks over to the whiteboard, removes some of the information on it, and snaps a picture with her tablet. Then she puts everything back and heads down to meet him. On her way, she informs Eva Nyman. Via text.

Their relationship is ever so slightly strained right now.

She's standing just inside the entrance on Polhemsgatan when he steps through the door in his worn but odorless khaki outfit. He spots her through the bulletproof glass and points to her. She nods graciously to the guard at reception. But instead of letting Frisell in, the guard makes a sign as if to say, *"Hold on."* She waits, meeting Frisell's eyes, shrugging.

A few minutes later, another guard emerges from the depths of the building. The difference is that this one's heavily armed.

"Bodyguard," he says tersely. "As ordered."

Ryd stares at him while Frisell is let in. His eyes linger on the guard too. "Times change," he comments.

"Follow me" is all Ryd says.

They walk toward a nondescript conference room in an unassuming part of the building. The guard nods to Frisell in a way that can only be interpreted one way. Frisell spreads his arms and legs wide. The guard pats him down, relatively roughly, and hands the result of his efforts over to Sonja Ryd.

Ryd returns the Nokia to Frisell but studies the Dictaphone inquiringly.

"Random impressions," Frisell says, shrugging. "I try to catch them in flight. But I'm sure that's already been reported to you?"

While Ryd gives the Dictaphone back, keeping her face as expressionless as possible, the guard hands her a panic button and takes up position outside the door. Ryd and Frisell enter and sit down on either side of a table on which a coffee urn and dry cinnamon buns are waiting for them.

"What happened to your face?" Frisell asks, pointing.

"Have some coffee and a bun," Ryd mutters, successfully keeping her hand from going to the bandage after she puts her iPad and the panic button down on the table.

"Thank you. The armed guard and the panic button are quite something."

"We don't know what you're capable of."

Frisell nods without touching the coffee or the buns.

"So, how is this supposed to work?" he asks, spreading his hands.

"We've been ordered to put our heads together until you can dredge up someone from your past who combines climate extremism with a desire to see you behind bars. So, cue the free associations."

"I'm sure you know as well as I do that I need more to go on."

"Assuming that I accept your premise, sure."

"My premise?"

"That you're innocent."

Frisell falls silent and leans back. He looks into Ryd's eyes and she looks back.

"So, back to my original question." He exhales at length. "How is this supposed to work?"

It's Ryd's turn to shake her head.

"We'll have to act as though I do believe you."

"Except that means I need more to go on." They're at an impasse. Stuck.

"You really should just tell me everything," Frisell continues. Ryd sits motionless, arms crossed. Time passes.

Then, she makes her decision. She doesn't know if it's a good one. But if, against all sense and reason, Lukas Frisell is innocent, he might be able to help them, so she has to let him in. Just not into any high-risk areas.

She reaches for a remote sitting among the cinnamon buns, and a rectangle of light from a projector suddenly lights up the wall. Ryd quickly connects her iPad to the projector via Bluetooth, and a picture appears. She walks over to it, holding the tablet. Leaving the panic button on the table.

"The whiteboard containing our investigation," she says, pointing. Frisell shoots her a surprised look and straightens up in his chair.

"It's not everything and it never will be everything," she stresses. "I'll give you the info you'd have anyway if you were the perpetrator. Put differently, you won't know everything we know."

"Smart," Frisell says with a nod.

She contemplates him. He's different now. Could it be called relaxed? Or more like smug? Without making a final determination, she zooms in on the first column on her iPad. With a slight lag, the project does the same.

"Outside Uppsala," she says. "A remotely detonated bomb causes a heavy diesel BMW with an SSAB division chief behind the wheel to veer off the E4 motorway and plow straight into a rapeseed field. At first, this is believed to be a traffic accident.

"Vasaparken," she continues, zooming in on the next column. "The ad man behind a campaign for the oil industry goes into the office early one Sunday morning to check some recently delivered print proofs. The bomb goes off when he opens the package, and the ad man crashes, medium rare, into a lawn off Dalagatan.

"Västerås," she goes on, zooming out and back in again quickly. "A considerable chunk of an Amazon server hall is blown up when the data center manager opens a package that should have come directly from their HQ in Seattle. This is an escalation, both materially and in terms of the body count. This time there were two dead and five injured.

"And finally, Odenplan this morning." Ryd zooms in again. "A leap in the trajectory—random victims for the first time. Pulling the old switcheroo with double backpacks, of which the one on the commuter train platform simply moved people out into the open, where the real bomb could be planted in the crowd. This means at least two perpetrators are involved. Six people have now died in the Odenplan attack, and sixteen are injured, a couple critically."

Frisell studies the whiteboard as Ryd zooms out again. He shakes his head. "Ten dead in all," he says slowly.

"And all the evidence points to you, Lukas Frisell."

"I'm sure not even you believe that, Sonja Ryd."

"Then how the fuck did your DNA end up inside the Vasaparken bomb?"

"I genuinely have no idea. But I've never been near any bomb."

"Except you have, Lukas. We know you have. You stole fertilizer from the farm you got your electricity from for years, didn't you?"

"Not enough for them to ever notice. Only to make explosives for my trap. A shaped charge that kills the animal instantly as it passes. And I only used it when I was starving."

"And are there still explosives stashed away in some hidey-hole out there? Are our technicians going to be blown up?"

"Not anymore, no. But Sonja Ryd, you're still just interrogating me. Nothing has changed since the interview room. Surely that's not how you're supposed to move this investigation forward?"

Ryd pauses, touching the bandage on her forehead. This is the first time during their conversation she's felt the ticking pain. Ticking to the beat of her fury.

"Then let's try again," she says through gritted teeth. "I'd be grateful for some help now, Lukas Frisell."

"First thing's first: I need to read those letters," Frisell says.

44

It's a dream, but it's vivid. It's almost like a circle dance, a movement among people standing in a semicircle. What's moving is vague, evasive, army green, and it moves quickly, erratically, like a glint of reflected light. An army-green glint of reflected light.

Some kind of collision occurs, a face is revealed.

Shabir Sarwani wakes up abruptly in his hospital bed. He doesn't know where he is, but he remembers the face. The way it turned toward the glint of army green.

Why did it turn toward the glint of army green? The collision? Did they run into each other?

It's the man's face he not only remembers but also recognizes. The rest is blurry. But surely that face twitched, as though struck. While it turned toward the glint of army green being placed on the ground, the running Sarwani saw the face and captured it, storing it away somewhere in the depths of his subconscious.

There was a fraction of a second before the crowd parted and the army-green backpack exploded, ripping limbs off human bodies.

Sarwani tumbles out of bed, sees his reflection in a mirror above a washbasin, sees the bandage with the red blotches above the hospital gown, and freezes. How did he become this broken creature?

But he has something important stored inside him. While he searches what is quite likely a hospital room, he makes sure to sear the images deeper into his mind. Burning the man's face into his brain.

Only at this point do sounds find their way into his brain. He hears moaning, sees people writhing in the other beds. He finds some clothes thrown carelessly over a chair next to his bed. Even while pulling them on, he's unsure if they're his. He doesn't recognize them at all.

But Shabir Sarwani remembers one thing. He remembers the face from his dream, remembers the collision in the crowd. He will never forget.

Hopeful, he pulls the zipper in his trousers the right way before slipping out.

45

She has to shake this feeling, the feeling that Frisell's interviewing her, rather than the other way around. Although she hates it, she has to meet him halfway so the conversation can be constructive.

Even though she's convinced she's sitting face-to-face with a mass murderer.

Setting that to one side, she forces herself to change her point of view. Who could possibly know so much about him, have access to his DNA, and also hate him so much they want to put the blame on him and ruin his life?

"Come on, Lukas. You must at least have an inkling."

"It doesn't necessarily have to be someone from my past."

"I just read you the letters. You heard the tone. There's an unhinged kind of passion in them that hints at something extremely personal."

"I honestly don't think so. Maybe they just came across my story and felt I'd make a good scapegoat. They're clearly research criminals. They plan things out before they act."

"But that doesn't mean . . ."

"Try as I may, I can't think of anyone from my past who could possibly feel that kind of animosity toward me. I just can't. I don't think it's about that. I think these people have simply read up on me somehow and think framing a former police officer is a delightfully ironic twist. They've googled my letters to the editor and are trying to mimic my tone. My tone back then, the one Eva Nyman would recognize. They've come across a few phrases like 'the ruins of destruction' and made a big deal of them."

"Franzén, right?"

Frisell pauses, blinking several times.

"You're the research type too, Sonja Ryd. Yes, Frans Michael Franzén, a Romantically inclined Finnish-Swedish poet and priest. I came across the phrase when I was young and just beginning to feel revulsion at our modern consumerist society. 'The ruins of destruction' are our vain, despoiled times."

"Are you seriously suggesting the letters are emotionally neutral? If we accept that this is a group of some kind, would they really have ruthlessly exploited an unknown individual like yourself? To what end?"

"To the same end as any other terrorist: to sow chaos, fear, insecurity. To send the police charging off into investigative dead ends, sniffing their own arses. While the terrorist group carries on undisturbed. They're not in this to murder 'guilty' people—it just started out that way, to shape public opinion—but after the steel manufacturer, the oil ad man, and the server hall, they've set their sights on the public. Because we're all guilty."

Ryd finds herself reluctantly finishing Frisell's train of thought. But before she can speak, he continues. "They found my DNA somewhere—just like you presumably did—and planted it inside one of the bombs. My only purpose is to muddy the waters, I have no actual significance, I'm just misdirection. And all this talking isn't doing anything for us either. Put me to work instead."

"Work?"

Ryd studies him, asking herself how badly his years in the wilderness have really broken Lukas Frisell. She feels likes she's getting mixed signals about that. She clears her throat and says, "I'll talk to Nyman. But you, Lukas Frisell, are most definitely not an officer of the law anymore."

"Is that really a job a person can quit?" Frisell asks, looking her straight in the eye.

She catches herself smiling. Is this another attempt at misdirection? Or does he honestly believe he can rejoin the police? At his age?

She attempts to read his gaze. He doesn't look away.

It actually seems as though the lunatic believes he can become a detective again. "And I wouldn't half mind if you got rid of those useless surveillance officers that are following me everywhere I go," Frisell adds.

46

Eva Nyman notes that the whiteboard is drowning in pictures. She feels the selection from Odenplan that Anton Lindberg's "slaves" have put up could be culled considerably. Only critically important pictures belong on the board.

Since normal office hours are now over, her meeting schedule is clearing up. She hasn't even tried to keep count of how many emergency meetings she has sat through today. She's also not counting on making it home tonight. She has no urgent need for anything in her two-bed on Frejgatan anyway.

What she needs can't be found there.

She looks down at her buzzing phone, musing that the technicians are unlikely to see their homes tonight too. The words on her screen laconically inform her it's the NFC calling. The moment she picks up, a weary man's voice says on an inhale, "We might have something."

"From the woods or Odenplan?" Nyman asks.

"Neither. We've been forced to all but abandon the woods. We don't have enough staff to handle that in parallel with a national trauma."

"From where, then?"

"If I'm reading my screen right, the something's actually over at yours."

"Okay," Nyman says, moving out of the way in the slightly frantic office.

Back up. I don't understand."

There's a loud and uncalled-for sigh on the other end. When the man's voice returns, it sounds as though he's speaking to a small child. "The Terrorist Bomber has been using a primary explosive consisting mainly of picric acid and a secondary explosive reminiscent of the one used by mass murderer Breivik in Norway, diazodinitrophenol, often called DDNP."

Nyman adopts one of her wintriest tones. "This has been known for a while, yes."

"What hasn't been widely known is that the NFC put out an alert about both substances, in case they turn up anywhere in the country."

“And someone’s tripped the alarm?” Nyman asks.

“It would seem the Järva Police recently seized a shipment of good old-fashioned guns smuggled in from the Balkans—but they also found traces of picric acid in the van, which would have to be considered unusual cargo for that kind of smuggler.”

“Hmm. Does ‘seized’ mean there are suspects?”

“At least one,” the technician replies. “The driver. A man with links to a criminal network in Hjulsta is in custody. Over at yours, at Kronoberg. Järva’s own facility is apparently overcrowded.”

Eva Nyman thanks him and ends the call. While shuffling slowly toward the center of the room, she calls the station’s detention facility. Before she reaches Anton Lindberg, she’s done talking. She pulls him aside and opens a familiar police sketch on her phone. Lindberg stares down at it. Nyman says, “According to the guards over in detention, a man who could match this sketch is sitting in a cell in this very building. He was driving a van full of smuggled weapons through the Hjulsta Industrial Park when our local colleagues nicked him. They found traces of picric acid in the van.”

“I’m going over there right now,” Lindberg says with a shudder of anticipation. Nyman stops him, shaking her head.

“He’s demanded a well-known gang lawyer who isn’t available tonight. We’ll have to wait to talk to him until tomorrow morning, so make sure you study up. But Anton, you have to keep calm, I’m giving you this with a lot of trepidation. Don’t. Get. Worked. Up.”

Lindberg reluctantly stops, looking into her eyes. Then he nods and returns to his “slaves.”

As Nyman starts back toward her seat, she’s interrupted by some kind of commotion outside the half-open swing doors to the hallway. One of the doors is being held open, and through the crack she can see a heavily bandaged figure. There’s a brief exchange, then the mummy enters the office.

The door remains open a crack. The person holding it is Sonja Ryd. She turns to Lukas Frisell and half whispers, “You wanted to see the office. Now you have. I’m not letting you in there.”

“But you don’t mind your seriously injured colleague hobbling in?”

“He’s not a suspect. Besides, stopping him didn’t seem like a viable option.”

Eva Nyman goes to meet the bandaged Sarwani. It’s clear he can’t move unhindered.

His clothes are all askew too.

Ankan and Anton Lindberg join them. “Shabir, you shouldn’t be . . .”

“I have a witness,” Shabir cuts in, his voice surprisingly steady.

“Can you drive him back to the hospital?” Nyman asks Ankan. Ankan nods, grabbing Sarwani’s arm.

"I saw a man who saw the bomber," Sarwani continues, ignoring Ankan's hand. I've seen him before, either in real life or in a picture. That man knows who planted the bomb on Odenplan. They ran into each other."

Nyman gives Ankan a signal and she lets go of Sarwani's arm, saying, "Witness statements are pouring in from Odenplan. Anton and his group are going through them."

"There's a lot of material," Lindberg confirms. "I'm sure your witness is in there, Shabir."

To their surprise, Sarwani shakes his head.

"I've seen him before. I don't remember who he is, but he's definitely not the kind of person who talks to the police, who gives a statement. No, I need as much video as you can get me. People from Odenplan—police videos, TikTok, other social media, phone clips, news reports. Anything that shows people."

"I'll make sure my 'slaves' give you everything they have," Lindberg says. "But seriously, how are you feeling?"

"I'm fine," Sarwani says, pulling a little bit too hard on his facial bandages. "I need to look through mugshots of known offenders. We're talking Mediterranean. Or possibly from the Balkans."

"I'll email you the relevant ones from the database," Nyman says, rushing to her desk. From over by the swing doors, Sonja Ryd watches Ankan and Lindberg as they lead Sarwani over to a free chair. The silence that had descended on the office is gradually replaced by a soft din that soon returns to normal levels.

Ryd turns to Frisell. It's obvious the chaos of the office has found its way into the mind of the socially untrained survivalist, so differently calibrated. When he grabs Sonja Ryd's arm, he's pale in a way that can't be faked.

"This is too much for me. I need to be alone."

Sonja Ryd nods and watches him stagger toward the exit. At least he's going in the right direction.

Just as she pushes the swing door open and heads into the office, she sees Shabir Sarwani topple headlong from his chair.

47

Lukas Frisell ends the call on his new pay-as-you-go phone, the so-called burner, and goes back to the bathroom. He spots a vent cover in the washbasin ceiling and steps up onto the edge of the bath to remove it. Then he inserts the phone deep into the duct above the bath, securing it well out of sight before clicking the cover back in place over the vent opening.

Since he's under surveillance, he can't be sure they won't search the flat.

He looks out at the paved courtyard and feels claustrophobia creeping up on him. The small police flat on Agnegatan feels almost worse than his cell at Kronoberg. It has the trappings of freedom but feels infinitely cramped. The walls keep closing in on him. He needs to head out into the city. Even though he doesn't exactly like the city. And even though the surveillance officers will undoubtedly still be there. Except maybe they've been relieved by a new duo.

He's been given new clothes, toiletries, towels. At first, he barely remembered how to turn on a shower, but now he's nice and clean, and he looks longingly at the pile of his dirty forest clothes. When he trots down the stairs, the fresh-from-the-factory clothes cling to his fresh-out-of-the-shower body like a shroud.

He really needs to get out.

As soon as he steps out onto the short dead-end street, he's immediately cognizant, despite the reek and noise, of what kind of evening it is. The second half of May, a wonderful time of year in the forest. The changing colors have stabilized, the hatchlings have grown, that sharp edge in the animals' eyes is less desperate, and all kinds of edible plants are sprouting—ground elder, orpine, garlic mustard, shepherd's purse. Bees and other insects are pollinating the forest, and the olfactory landscape has moved away from decomposition and are sharing generously of themselves. This was the time of year Lukas Frisell began sleeping outdoors in earnest.

Sleeping outdoors is always best.

He steps out onto Fleminggatan. The traffic is roaring, even though it's already past eight. In the distance, he sees the sky widening between the buildings, so he sets off in that direction. Fleeing toward the celestial opening. That's one good thing about Stockholm. The water, the bridges. That there's always a certain amount of space just around the corner.

He lingers on Barnhusbron for a while. Shoots the bridgehead he just left a disinterested glance. There are a couple of potential surveillance officers there, but he doesn't care. This evening walk has no immediate purpose. It's movement from, not movement to.

He gazes out across Klara Sjö, toward City Hall. The sun's not intending to set for over an hour yet. It's a crystal-clear evening. The city seems a little bit more plainly visible than usual.

He turns up Dalagatan, passing the Adolf Fredrik School of Music, Sabbatsberg Hospital, and the blown-up PR firm Flat Broke Ltd across from Vasaparken before reaching the police cordon that still surrounds Odenplan. A handful of news teams are still hovering by the barriers. A large white tent complements the white dwelling of God that is Gustaf Vasa, as do the white-clad crime scene technicians moving in and out of it. Frisell briefly wonders if any of them have just come back from rooting through his forest, his life.

The police presence is, on the whole, considerable. He feels the ankle bracelet chafing against his leg and his stomach screaming with hunger. In the woods, he would have pulled out a piece of smoked meat by now, fried it up with some mushrooms from his autumn stores, boiled some pond water for his coffee. And if the sun was shining like this, he might even have dug a can of beer out of the secret stash they don't seem to have found yet.

He remembers a pub near Odenplan he used to like for some reason, but he doesn't remember the address. He navigates by instinct, meandering down back streets, constantly overtaken by young men on bicycles and mopeds, with large, colorful boxes in the back.

Eventually, he finds it.

It's definitely the same one. And yet, it's not. His old, humble pub has undergone a complete transformation. It feels like a student union. After being scolded by a nineteen-year- old for trying to order food at the bar, he manages to find a free table in a back corner of the pub that's almost as dark as back in his day. He successfully orders a pint, and the only thing he recognizes on the menu, a stringy pulled pork.

It's some kind of industrial pork that for inexplicable reasons has been shredded along the muscle fibers. But even though it makes him yearn for real meat from the forest, a pleasant feeling soon settles in, as though traces of the past have managed to cling to the fibers of the pub, after all. Even though they've been shredded.

By the time he's ready to pay, he's feeling pretty good. Then, the change happens in two distinct steps. When he's handed the bill, he can feel himself go pale. And when he manages to recover and pulls out his old roll of banknotes, the waiter barely hides his impatience as he says. “This is a cash-free bar.”

* * *

Sonja Ryd has recently made the switch to boxed wine in her small flat on Hornsgatan. In addition to being cheaper, it also conceals exactly how much she’s drinking.

She’s in the middle of topping off her cup when her phone rings. She jumps, spattering the white Ikea tabletop. Her phone shouldn’t be ringing. Eva Nyman has given her the night off on the condition that she drive Sarwani back to the hospital.

* * *

Despite the waiter’s suspicion, Frisell manages to order another pint while he waits. Strangely, it tastes even better than the first. He sinks a bit deeper into his chair and watches the pub transform around him. He allows the friendly atmosphere of the old days to envelop him and remembers why he was drawn here—this was the favorite pub of his wife, Nina. She drank in a way a ballerina probably shouldn’t. She’s there now, on the chair next to his. She’s wrapping her arm around him, moving her face in close to his. Her lips part slowly, and he hears a completely different woman’s voice say, “Smells like ethanol in here.”

* * *

Sonja Ryd has taken a seat on the chair next to his, and now she watches her wineglass being filled before raising it to toast his tankard. There’s an atonal clink when they knock together. As though they belong to different worlds.

“So, you don’t know what a cash-free bar is?” she asks, wiping some red wine from the corner of her mouth.

“I do now,” Frisell mutters. “Thanks for coming over.”

“Well, I am your babysitter,” she says, smiling grimly.

“Just don’t tell me you can pay with the damn phone now too?”

For the first time, they share a chuckle. Briefly. Then they sit in silence for a while.

“Did you get rid of the surveillance?” Frisell asks.

“You didn’t see them on the way over?”

“I didn’t bother to look.”

“I’m sure you can see why I can’t answer your question,” Ryd says. “But I do have a question that doesn’t belong down at the station, and even less in an interview room.”

“But fits right in at a pub?”

“I actually think it’s called a bar nowadays.” Frisell smiles. Ryd smiles too.

"Go on," he says.

Ryd clears her throat, frowns, and takes a sip of her wine. "What was the nature of your relationship with Eva Nyman?" Frisell pulls back slightly, nods, disappears into himself.

"I think . . ." he says, staring up at the wall.

Ryd has to forcefully remind herself they're not in the interview room anymore. She takes another sip. Practices restraint.

"I think," Frisell continues, "she had a bit of a crush on me."

"Crush? On you?"

"Sounds incredible, right? With that haircut?" Ryd tries not to laugh.

"Why don't you just shave that whole mess off?"

Frisell studies her with amusement and continues. "I believe Eva Nyman was a romantic, Sonja. I believe she still is."

"But what exactly was your relationship?"

"Nothing ever happened, honestly. I was in love with Nina. But we were drifting apart. Maybe Eva could see that. Maybe she was hoping something might happen. But I don't know."

"Would you call it a tense professional relationship?"

"I wouldn't, actually. Things were always easy between us. Eva Nyman was remarkably . . . loyal."

"Until disaster struck?"

"Yes. That made everything collapse like a house of cards."

"Were you fired, Lukas?"

He shakes his head slowly.

"No, I quit. Before it got to that. Nina had just left me. I figured I might as well start over fresh."

"So you'd have a chance to come back one day? Seriously?"

"If that was something I was considering, it was entirely subconscious. But the idea grew inside me out in the forest. That bridge actually wasn't burned. And I was never happier than when I was a police officer. After all. Those were the best years of my life. I have at least a good decade left to give. I can live close to nature and commute into town—it's doable. The best of both worlds."

"The job has changed beyond recognition since your day," Ryd says, flagging down the waiter.

"I'm a quick study," Frisell says as the young man reluctantly approaches.

"Want another?" Ryd asks, turning to the waiter and pointing to her own glass. Frisell stares at her.

Then he says, "Just one."

48

It's a lovely morning. Lukas Frisell lets his gaze glide out across the enormous, neatly kept garden. It's as though he's looking at himself.

Tamed nature.

The door to the house opens, and all color drains from Nina Strömblad's face. Her eyes dart wildly this way and that before she manages to focus on Frisell. Her frosty smile thaws slightly.

"You have to do something about your hair," she says.

"I just wanted to talk to you," Frisell says.

That turns her smile wry. "You 'just want to talk to me'? You're not serious?"

Only then does she notice the two uniformed officers behind Frisell. Grim-faced and armed, they nod to her.

"I've been given special permission to visit you," he says. "But I'm not allowed to come too close."

"Closer than six feet and we pull the plug," puts in one of the officers, a muscular man with a wide ginger moustache.

"Kind of like in an American prison film," Frisell adds with a smile.

With six electrically charged feet between them, she leads him through the house, out onto the patio. They sit down in the same chairs she and Sonja Ryd were seated in not that many days earlier. The officers position themselves strategically, ready to intervene.

"So, you're . . . what, Lukas? Under suspicion, arrested, detained?"

"All of the above, I think," Frisell replies, pulling up his trouser leg. Nina stares at the black ankle bracelet.

"But what did you do?"

"Nothing."

She turns pale again. Remembering her phone call with Sonja Ryd. Why hadn't Ryd said anything about him being arrested?

"Odenplan?" she says. "The terrorist attack. Oh my God, Lukas. Did you become dangerous out in the woods? Should I be afraid of you?"

"I'm just here to apologize. That's all."

"What for? For blowing up a bunch of people?"

Frisell pauses. Looks at her. Can't quite find the words. "For everything," he says.

Nina shakes her head. "No, Lukas. You're not going to get me to believe you've come here to do some kind of penance. You haven't changed that much. Was there something specific you wanted? Do I have something you want?"

Lukas blinks heavily a few times.

"You were always better at reading me than anyone else, Nina," he says.

"So, what is it I have that you want, Lukas?"

"I thought I just wanted to make sure you were doing okay. Now, I sense there's something else. But I have no idea what it is."

"Maybe we can find out," Nina says, smiling. "Anyway, I'm doing fine, as you can see. No man, if that's what you're wondering. Which is not to say I'm celibate. But that phase of my life is over. The strictly heterosexual phase."

Lukas gazes out at the gigantic lawn. The shadow of a miniscule cloud slowly glides across the garden.

"I went to your favorite pub yesterday," he says.

"The one near Odenplan?" Nina exclaims. "Returning to the scene of the crime?"

"Hardly. I was just curious."

"I haven't been to that pub in twenty years. Is it still there?"

"Fifteen," Lukas corrects her. "It's a bar nowadays."

"Please don't tell me you've grown ornery in your old age, Lukas."

He chuckles softly. So does she. The six feet between them feel like a mile.

"You seriously lived in the woods?" Nina asks at length.

"I tried to," Lukas says, nodding.

"You're going to have to explain that," she says, and Lukas lets out a snort.

"For eight years, I got closer and closer to nature. I learned to live in harmony with it. Tried to minimize my climate footprint."

"And then they came out there and nicked you in the middle of the woods?"

"And you know how, don't you, Nina?"

Her expression changes. A wariness creeps into it. Her quick glance over at the police officers says it all, makes them sit up and pay attention.

"I told them about your friends from our time together," she says slightly primly. "Edward Rasmusson, Aron Rudolfsson, Kalle Råman, Lelle Bergis. Your male friends, whom you never let me meet."

Frisell makes an apologetic gesture.

"I'm sorry," he says. "I didn't mean to sound accusatory. I'm just trying to get a complete picture."

"Why do you need a complete picture? It's not like you're a detective." He smiles, a brief flash of light in a now troubled face.

"Maybe that's what I want from you, come to think of it. As complete a picture as possible. Do you remember me ever telling you about anyone who hated me? Or maybe you caught wind of something somewhere? Someone who might have wanted to harm me?"

"You're not a detective, Lukas."

"But they let me wear the bracelet if I help them. If I don't, they'll put me back in a cell."

Nina leans back.

"If any of the criminals you put away ever threatened you, it wasn't something you shared with me."

"I wasn't thinking about work. Something else."

"You're grasping at straws, Lukas. We might as well admit we weren't close enough for me to have a clue."

It's as though all strength drains from Frisell. They just sit there for a moment. The divorced couple.

Then there's a flash of something in Nina's eyes. "Although there was one thing," she says. "But it was a while ago. I was in the middle of divorcing old man Strömblad. A woman called, looking for you. She gave me vague stalker vibes."

"Hmm. What did she want?"

"To get a hold of you. She said you were dating, but it didn't sound right."

"Do you know who it was?"

"I don't remember her name. But shouldn't you know, Lukas? Have you been with that many women since we were together?"

Frisell winces. Nina studies him and then keeps pushing. "You must have gone at it pretty hard up in Uppsala, Lukas."

An image of Sonja Ryd in the interview room flashes before him, making it difficult to focus. But then Nina Strömblad says, "Actually, I do remember her name. It was unusual." "Yes?"

"Rosetta."

Frisell takes a deep breath and nods. "Rosetta, yes, I remember her. She ended up killing herself. She had a lot of challenges in life."

Nina studies him intently. Then she says, "I hope you're more considerate these days, Lukas."

And at no point is the distance between them less than six feet.

49

They meet up in a cleaning closet just outside NOD's part of the building. Without a word, the powerfully built man with the wide ginger moustache and denim jacket hands her a USB flash drive. Sonja Ryd takes it, nods, and says, "Thanks, Olle. What's with the civvies?"

"Identity parade," the man replies with a grimace, checking his watch. "I'm playing the part of dodgy drug dealer. That's the kind of thing I can do, Sonja, but can't do this, it's just not me."

Ryd nods again.

"This was the last time," she says. "Did it go okay?"

"You tell me. The entire conversation is on there." He points to the USB drive.

"I have to go," he says, pushing past her.

Ryd gives it a minute before she, too, exits the cleaning closet and enters NOD's not inconsequential corner of the building, resisting the temptation to open the swing doors to the office, walking past them down the hallway instead, to the Waiting Hall.

The original Nova Group has gathered inside, the newcomers firmly confined to the office. Even Sarwani is present, sans bandages but with a number of smaller plasters on his face. She takes a seat next to him, and they exchange a brief smile. She can feel the flash drive burning in her pocket.

She can't wait to listen to the contents. On the other hand, the text from Eva Nyman has her equally curious. She barely managed to squeeze in her meeting with Olle, an old mate from the Academy, in the cleaning closet.

Then Eva Nyman steps resolutely into the Waiting Hall. The eyes of every member of the Nova Group follow her as she walks up to her desk, connects her laptop, and fires up the projector.

A densely typewritten sheet of paper is projected onto the wall:

Because the sun will not be extinguished. It will expand, swell into a red giant that devours Mercury, Venus, Mars, that devours the Earth. But when that happens, the Earth will be a desolate place anyway. And it will be your fault. You are the ones who can change our fate. Your guilt will be forever inscribed into the universe, and advanced lifeforms will remember you billions of years from now as a cautionary tale. After what God's white dwelling witnessed, the time has come to open the castle gate and spray the apathetic with pink microplastics. The greatest of all betrayals will be remembered when the red giant contracts into a white dwarf with space enough for all of us, all our faithless deeds, all of history as we know it, compressed into a minimum. Because the sun will not be extinguished.

Eva Nyman continues: "It's clear even to the naked eye that it's written on the same typewriter as the previous two. Have a look at the letters *p* and *b*. And the letter was addressed directly to me in the same primitive manner as before. Any immediate observations?"

"There's a riddle in there," Ankan says. "And I guess it's explicitly pointed to by our old favorite, 'God's white dwelling.'"

"The time has come to 'open the castle gate and spray the apathetic with pink microplastics,'" Anton Lindberg says, pointing up at the wall. "Which is utter nonsense."

"Before we start in on the riddle, is there anything to say about the rest?" Nyman asks. "The perspective's cosmic," Sarwani says. "It's all red giants and white dwarves and advanced lifeforms horrified by our remains billions of years from now."

"And how does that help us here and now?"

"Only in that it tells us the Terrorist Bomber's activities are ever expanding like the universe itself," Sarwani replies. "He's never going to stop."

"On to the riddle, then. In what kind of castle is a gate being opened, and what pink microplastics are going to be sprayed over which apathetic people?"

The silence that follows in the Waiting Hall has the density of a white dwarf. "Come on," Nyman coaxes. "Give me your wildest theories."

"It's obviously not a real castle," Ryd says. "But it probably is real microplastics, one of the great environmental scourges of our time. A growing percentage of our bodies consists of plastic. Which I guess you could say is noticeable."

"Plastic manufacturers?" Nyman suggests. "But are microplastics manufactured? Aren't they the result of regular plastic slowly disintegrating in nature?"

"Or blowing up?" Ankan suggests. "Plastic being blown up? What big plastic things are there that could be blown up?"

"Don't they make all kinds of new building materials out of plastic now?" Lindberg asks. "And plexiglass, I guess. Like at a hockey rink."

"There are manufactured microplastics," Sarwani says without looking up from his phone. "They're used in scrubbing materials and as an additive in cosmetics. And in AstroTurf, too, apparently—don't ask me how."

"So, both football and ice hockey," Ryd mutters. "Our Terrorist Bomber is getting folksier."

Sarwani reads on: "'Most of the microplastics in the world still come from plastic and rubber objects that have been broken down into smaller particles. Big contributors are roads, car tires, and synthetic textiles, such as nylon shirts, acrylic cardigans, fleece jackets.'"

"But when was this letter sent?" Ryd asks. "Was Frisell in detention?" Nyman flips through her papers.

"The barcode on the envelope shows the date and the letter's destination. In this case, the letter was stamped the day before Lukas Frisell was arrested in the forests of Uppland. In other words, it does not exonerate him. It also reveals which of the country's nine post terminals processed the letter: Rosersberg, just like the previous ones. Where the stamps were purchased is, on the other hand, impossible to ascertain."

"Uppland," Ryd notes.

"Unfortunately, that's all we have," Nyman says. "The letters may sound fanatic and appear deranged—but they've been written and sent in a way that means they can't be traced or identified. No fingerprints, no DNA, of course, but also no specific sender's location. And nothing at all regarding the paper or envelope. So, the microplastics are all we have to work with. But why pink?"

"Are there Swedish companies that manufacture pink plastic?" Ankan asks.

"We'll have to start there," Eva Nyman says. "And no matter how ridiculous this letter may seem, we have to keep two things in mind: First, the Terrorist Bomber's activities are escalating. Second, I get the feeling the next Big Bang is imminent."

50

Almost all interview rooms are occupied. Anton Lindberg has to make do with the smallest kind, a cramped cupboard barely big enough for the three people likely to be present.

That's okay. He doesn't intend to be long.

He pauses outside, rehearsing briefly. On the other side of the door are representatives of two of the categories of human being he has the least time for: a member of a criminal gang and a gang lawyer. What he has to do at all costs is to remain calm. He breathes slowly through his nose for a full minute.

Then he enters. Sitting on the other side of the table are a well-dressed lawyer and a thirty-five-year-old with black hair, olive skin, and baggy prison clothes, who seems more tense than arrogant. Lindberg gives them a brief nod, sits down, goes through the routine interview preparations, then presents the situation. "You, Elias Shariq, were caught red-handed driving a cache of smuggled firearms and ammunition from the Balkans in an area under active police surveillance outside Hjulsta.

"What's unusual about this situation isn't the weapons—they're pretty workaday—but rather that picric acid was also found in the van. Only trace amounts, as though you'd already unloaded the rest of the picric acid on your way to Hjulsta. And that particular substance has been used in no less than four bombs that over the course of the past few weeks have been used in terrorist attacks in and around Stockholm. Resulting in at least ten fatalities."

"My client doesn't understand what that has to do with him," the gang lawyer says laconically.

"It's very simple. You, Elias Shariq, were the person who drove the van into the depot in Hjulsta. It was likely brought up through Europe, you rendezvoused with it somewhere outside of town and travelled on to an unknown location to unload the picric acid before you took the rest of the arsenal to your gang's storage facility. Where did you unload the acid?"

Anton Lindberg doesn't even hear the lawyer's generic objections as Elias Shariq attempts to stare him down. He stares back. Calmly, verging on mildly, he continues: "Just before I came in here, I checked the arrest log. And wouldn't you know, there's a man who's being held down the hall right now who might be able to help us. His name's Hassan, and he's one of the members of a group that calls itself the Hjulsta Gang. Unless I'm reading this wrong, he's actually the leader of the Hjulsta Gang."

Lindberg stays focused. He notes the shifts in the seemingly deaf and dumb Shariq's facial expression. To his surprise, the lawyer says nothing. Lindberg continues: "It's a funny coincidence that you, Elias, have links to the Hjulsta Gang too. But you seem a bit old and experienced to be one of the group's foot soldiers. You have a long criminal record, suggesting you helped build the local narcotics organization: violent crime, drug offenses, blackmail, money laundering."

"He has served his time for those things," the lawyer says. "Everyone has a right to second chance after they—"

"Briefly put," Lindberg says without sparing the lawyer so much as a glance, "you, Elias, shouldn't have been driving that van."

The look they exchange is both forceful and probing. Elias Shariq seems to be searching for something in Anton Lindberg's eyes.

"You volunteered to drive because the picric acid wasn't on its way to the Hjulsta Gang at all, was it, Elias? It was unloaded somewhere else along the way. Are you running a side hustle? Maybe you've been using the Hjulsta Gang for your own ends, or even cheating them?"

Lindberg stands up demonstratively, closing his folder.

"Here's what I'm going to do," he says. "Hassan's tied up in some kind of drug trial today, but this afternoon I'll check with him about this whole van business."

He walks toward the door. Then he turns around with an angelic smile and asks, "Sound good, Elias?"

51

Sonja Ryd finally gets a chance to plug the flash drive into her laptop. She has fifteen minutes before she's due to meet Frisell in the conference room, surrounded by an armed security guard, cinnamon buns, and a panic button. She has taken a seat by herself in a corner of the office and put her earbuds in. Nina Strömblad's voice streams into her ears:

"Oh my God, Lukas. Did you become dangerous out in the woods? Should I be afraid of you?" And "You're not going to get me to believe you've come here to do some kind of penance."

Then she hears: "And then they came out there and nicked you in the middle of the woods?" Frisell: "And you know how, don't you, Nina?"

And she hears: "You must have gone at it pretty hard up in Uppsala, Lukas."

While she listens to the rest of the conversation, a memory slowly surfaces in her mind. Uppsala. Ultuna. SUAS.

Frisell's voice again: "Rosetta, yes, I vaguely remember her. She ended up killing herself. She had a lot of challenges in life."

Before the recording ends, Ryd hears: "I hope you're more considerate these days, Lukas."

Maybe there's more to his time at SUAS than Ryd had thought. And now, the memory is clear. That Facebook page where the picture of Frisell was posted, what was it called again? Something jokey? Right, "Fun With Farming."

She opens the page. She looked through it before, but only quickly. Frisell's in a handful of pictures, one of which was taken in a relatively sizeable lecture hall. Which prompts her to make a mental note to contact SUAS again regarding Lukas Frisell's public lectures on survival and crises preparedness, the ones Leif Stierna told her about. Having had no reply to her first email, she now fires off a brief but vaguely threatening reminder. That usually does the trick.

Other than that, "Fun With Farming" is a kind of student diary from three years in the middle of the 2010s. It seems to have been run by a single student. Ryd frantically searches for and eventually finds a name. The page belonged to a female student called Jonna Carlgren. Ryd has just managed to establish that

Carlgren's currently a city planner in Södertälje when she notices Sarwani waving at her from another desk, as discreetly as he's able. She goes over to him.

"Check this out," Sarwani says, angling his screen toward her.

Ryd leans in closer, watching a video that starts up immediately. The perspective's from behind the onlookers at Odenplan. Amateurishly and shakily filmed, it shows a semicircle of people held back by blue-and-white police tape. Officers can be glimpsed on the side of the crowd, one of them being Sarwani himself, but above all she can see something else. A collision between an unseen person and a highly visible one who lets out a silent roar.

Sarwani pauses the playback and proceeds more slowly until an angry man's face becomes visible. All the stereotypically male features are there: sharp cheekbones, hard eyes, disproportionate rage, violent tendencies, pure, unadulterated attitude. Ryd leans in even closer, so close her cheek touches Sarwani's.

"Am I supposed to recognize him?" she asks.

"If anyone in here does, it would be you," Sarwani says. "He's a criminal. I've seen him before."

"But you can't remember where?"

"No, I can't put my finger on it."

"Hold on a minute," Ryd says. "Back up. So, this is the man you saw in the crowd at Odenplan? The one who saw the guy planting the backpack with the bomb?"

"Yes," Sarwani confirms impatiently. "I've seen him before, maybe even talked to him, but God knows where. I'll have to run a facial recognition search on our entire database. And you know how well that usually works out."

He runs the clip again, in slow motion.

His and Ryd's heads touch again. Other than the brief collision, they don't see much of interest, though at one point there's a glimpse of the army-green backpack—but not the face of the person wearing it.

"Fuck," Ryd exclaims. "So close."

Sarwani starts comparing the video to other recordings. There's only one that shows the crowd scattering in a panic, giving them a brief glimpse of the green backpack. But there's no sign of the perpetrator in that one either.

Sarwani goes back to the first video, focuses in on the powerful face, activates the facial recognition software, and leans back with his hands behind his neck.

"This is going to take a while," he says, stretching.

Just then, Sonja Ryd's phone rings. It's the guard down at reception.

"I have a Lukas Frisell waiting. He was supposed to meet you here fifteen minutes ago."

52

Despite the early hour, most of the expanded Nova Group are already at their desks in the office. Everyone's hard at work, and no one reacts when a mobile dings, not even when two more go off in quick succession, but as more and more join in, there's soon a cacophony of noise.

It's push notifications from more and less serious media outlets. Ankan stares down at her phone and then shouts, "Some kind of explosion in Köldfors, Hälsingland, around ten dead. Is there really a town called Köldfors?"

"I have Källfors in Medelpad," Shabir Sarwani offers.

At that point, Eva Nyman bursts through the swing doors and calls for silence.

"Yes, there has been an explosion that may match our letter. Compared to Odenplan, it's small and peripheral, so our hypothesis about an escalation may have to be revised. Either way, it's a company that manufactures different types of plastic, Merplast Ltd, located in a small town by the name of Kallfors in Gästrikland—let's get our geography straight. Local police are on the scene, no fatalities have been reported, and no explanation for the explosion given."

Ankan exclaims, "They went from threat to action bloody quickly this time. We didn't even get a chance to solve the riddle."

"I don't think we were meant to solve the riddle," Ryd says. "At the end of the day, there is no riddle. They're not playing a game with the police, even though the letters are addressed to Eva. That's not what they're doing."

"I wouldn't mind heading up there," Sarwani says, ripping a plaster from his face. Nyman studies him for a moment. Then she says, "I'm going, and I'll take Anton with me. The helicopter's leaving in ten minutes."

"Hang on, I have my interview with Elias Shariq," Lindberg objects. "Take someone else."

"Shariq isn't going anywhere," Nyman counters. "We may have to stay overnight, so head downstairs and pick up a change of clothes."

"It would be better if you took someone who really wants to go," Sarwani insists. Nyman studies him again.

"You passed out in here not that long ago, Shabir. You should be on medical leave.

Besides, you don't exactly look very presentable."

"So an immigrant officer with superficial work-related injuries isn't presentable?" Eva Nyman lets out a sigh.

"Fine, Shabir, go with Anton."

Sarwani dashes toward the doors, followed by a slowly shuffling Lindberg. Nyman gives Sonja Ryd a long look, then says, "Ankan's in charge while I'm gone."

Ankan brightens visibly, then catches herself and nods sternly. Eva Nyman nods back and leaves the office to do some real police work.

53

She's sitting on a commuter train in the morning rush hour, working. Some quick calculations back at police HQ led her to conclude it was her most efficient travel option in the middle of the new bomb stress. Driving to Södertälje would take at least thirty minutes. Getting forty-five minutes of work done on the train was a far better choice. Although, what kind of work was it really, systematically going through an old Facebook page?

The Facebook page "Fun With Farming" is a grownup's attempt to be childish. It doesn't quite pull it off because the collegiate tone grates against a palpable need for order and control. Jonna Carlgren seems to have created the page mostly to exert control over her surroundings, which is to say her fellow students at SUAS.

Altogether, it's just over a hundred pictures.

Sonja Ryd had expected a tedious journey, but instead, she finds herself fascinated by the characters that flash by, without any context, without any real narrative, the students no less than the teachers.

Given the number of pictures, Lukas Frisell features in relatively few, which at least in part must be because he doesn't seem to have shared Jonna Carlgren's interest in landscape architecture. Nevertheless, several of the photos, not only the ones of Frisell, catch her attention. They all seem to somehow capture the mood at SUAS during Frisell's last year there, before he moved out into the wood. The closer to the end, the more exciting.

* * *

"The *mood*?" Södertälje's prim city planner repeats, as though she finds the word puzzling.

Sonja Ryd leans in over the desk, studying the young woman, whose hair is pulled back into a bun so tight it looks as though someone's standing behind her, tugging.

"The years you were active on the page 'Fun With Farming,'" Ryd says. "Wouldn't you say the mood was fairly . . . frivolous?"

"I studied hard, but I still took the time to run the page."

"But it looks like you partied quite a bit?"

"We were students. A lot of people partied. I took pictures. Though I didn't take all of them. Other people sent me their photos too."

"Did you have a lot of dealings with an instructor by the name of Lukas Frisell?"

"Not really," Jonna Carlgren replies without hesitation. "As I recall, he was primarily an agronomist. But he had this interesting lecture series about survival. I think there are a few pictures on the page."

"From a lecture hall, yes. But he also appears in several party pictures. Did he like to party?"

"That was the word around campus, but I didn't see much evidence of it."

"I've collected some of the party pictures," Ryd says, turning her laptop so Carlgren can see. "Would you mind identifying the students pictured together with Frisell?"

In the first picture, a red-faced Frisell has his arms around two young women.

"The one on the right," Jonna Carlgren says, pointing to a girl with a brown bob cut. "Her name's Josefin. I think she studied biology. And the on one the left might have been called Rosetta, Rosetta Ström."

Sonja Ryd marvels briefly at Carlgren's outstanding recall. Then she studies the short, black-haired woman staring intensely at Frisell. Other than that, the mood in the picture is excited—between the faintly illuminated silhouettes in the background, a hand is sticking out, forming a kind of gesture with its index and little finger raised like horns.

"Was there a lot of heavy metal at SUAS?" Ryd asks.

"If you're talking about Rosetta, I think she was an agronomy student . . ."

"I'm talking about the hard rock sign of the horns in the background, there. The fingers. The devil."

"I didn't take that picture, I'm afraid," Carlgren says. "But that's a corna symbol. An old Sicilian gesture to ward off Satan."

"What else do you know about Rosetta Ström?" Ryd asks.

"We took a few courses together. I heard she got really depressed later. But that's all I know."

Ryd checks to make sure her phone's still recording before moving on to a different picture.

Party pictures flash by, with and without Frisell in them. Ryd was right about Carlgren: she still knows her material like the back of her hand. While the names are recorded—Erika, Charlotte, Corinne, but also men like Anton, Albin, Urban—Ryd asks herself what the hell she's doing there. Another bomb has just gone off up in Gästrikland. Why is she sitting here? Does she even have time for this? If she's so convinced Frisell's guilty, why would someone from his past be interesting in the slightest? As an accomplice?

She can't put her finger on it. It has to do with the time when he finally decided to leave civilization . . . Something's not right about it.

A final party picture appears on the screen. Once again, Frisell's standing between two vivacious young women. The one on the left has a flaming red mane of hair while the one on the right has a brown buzzcut; a tangle of tattoos; and by all appearances, a split tongue. She's letting her tongue dance at the camera while the green eyes of the redhead seem to want to devour Frisell.

"Those are vet students," Jonna Carlgren says. "We went to the same university but didn't interact all that much."

"Like a separate part of SUAS, you mean? And you don't know their names?"

Carlgren shakes her head, beginning to signal that she has better things to do.

Ryd stares at the girl with the split tongue for a moment, trying to understand. Then she moves on to the next picture. What follows is a cavalcade of photographs from the hallways of SUAS. Carlgren continues to provide names and programs from the past.

She's impressive.

"That's vet students again, I think," she says, pointing to the current picture of six women around a café table.

At first, Ryd thinks she can make out the tattooed girl with the split tongue on the far left. But on closer inspection, the short hair isn't brown, it's ginger. It's not the same person. This is a seemingly sad young woman whom Ryd briefly thinks she recognizes. But then she moves on, finally reaching a picture of Lukas Frisell standing at the front of a classroom. He's pressing a marker to the whiteboard, drawing something Ryd recognizes. Two red vertical lines joined at the top by scrawled loops that are probably meant to represent foliage. On what must then be the tree trunk is a primitively rendered device.

"What's this?" she asks.

"One of Frisell's lectures on crisis preparedness," Carlgren replies, shrugging.

"Did you take this picture?"

"This particular one, yes. But I didn't go to all the lectures."

"Do you remember what he was drawing here?"

For the first time, Jonna Carlgren pauses, her eyes fixed on the screen. "I think it was about hunting . . ."

"Hunting?"

"Some kind of explosive device that was triggered when an animal walked by."

Sonja Ryd grows still. Something overlooked is stirring inside her.

"But you could just check the recordings," Carlgren says, standing up, as though to signal the audience is over.

54

As ordered, the helicopter circles the factory outside the small town of Kallfors in Gästrikland one more time. From above—as dark clouds gather—the building bears a remarkable resemblance to a medieval castle.

To make himself heard over the helicopter, Sarwani bellows a quote from memory: "'After what God's white dwelling witnessed, the time has come to open the castle gate and spray pink microplastics over the apathetic.'"

There's a seemingly newly poured concrete surface outside where the main blast damage occurred, likely some kind of loading area. A pink oval is still spreading across the concrete, lighter pink toward the edges.

"That's where the pink microplastics sprayed out of the castle," Anton Lindberg shouts. "But what the hell is that?"

Eva Nyman peers down mutely, shaking her head. Sarwani leans his forehead against the shaking helicopter window and yells, "Unfortunately, many things point to that pink oval being Merplast CEO Rikard Albrektsson."

Lindberg and Nyman turn to Sarwani, but before they can ask him to clarify, the helicopter shudders violently as it goes in for landing.

The trio run through the howling wind of the rotor blades to reach the assembled ambulances, fire engine, and police cars sifting blue light across the crime scene.

A large woman in uniform comes to meet them.

"Ulla Hultqvist," she says in a deep alto and is given their names equally tersely. "Anything new to report?" Eva Nyman asks.

"Let's start from the beginning," Hultqvist says, lifting a blue-and-white tape cordon. "Kallfors is a kind of upgraded industrial town, and Merplast is the factory that employs everyone around here. What was blown up is the storeroom where the company's PVC products, primarily pipes and related parts—are kept."

"Are they pink?" Sarwani asks.

"The pipes? No, I just saw a picture from inside the storeroom. The pipes were white for the most part. The pink stuff is . . ."

"Merplast CEO Rikard Albrektsson?"

The imposing Ulla Hultqvist eyes Sarwani with newfound interest.

"Nothing like that has been confirmed as of this moment. But we were just informed that the plastic debris from the blast is mixed with human tissue and that Albrektsson is the only person missing. And his office is adjacent to the PVC storeroom."

"No CCTV in the storeroom?"

Hultqvist shakes her head. "This has always been a safe place, virtually no crime. It wasn't considered necessary."

They pass the tightly cordoned-off loading area. The pink oval looks different from up close. It's not just plastic that's been blown up, but also, if you look really closely, a human being.

"A couple of crime scene technicians have already arrived from Gävle," Hultqvist says, pointing. I'm told the rest are on their way."

Two figures in white are on their knees next to the pink oval, scrutinizing it. Several uniformed officers are setting up a tent just outside the cordon. It's clear they're in a hurry; the dark clouds are continuing to build. Soon the first droplets of rain will be falling, contaminating the crime scene.

But before rain comes wind. A gust sweeps in from the distant forest, whirling through the factory area, picking up some of the pink microplastics and sending them flying, in over the nearby houses, scattering them over Kallfors.

"Over the apathetic," Sarwani says.

Ulla Hultqvist shoots him a skeptical look as she leads them on toward a small group of people at the heart of the factory grounds.

"I'll leave you to it," she says.

* * *

The first rain begins to fall while Anton is squatting next to a man wearing a yellow vest with the word "Doctor" across the back. He, in turn, is squatting next to a stretcher. The woman on the stretcher is visibly pale, and both her arms are wrapped in thick bandages. The doctor straightens up and nods to a man, who pushes the stretcher into a waiting ambulance and jumps in after it. It drives off before the back doors are fully closed.

"The least seriously injured," the doctor says with another nod, peeling off his latex gloves. "Which means she had to wait the longest."

"What's the injury count?" Lindberg asks, pulling out a classic police notepad.

"Five injured in the blast and one dead. The condition of two of the injured individuals is considered critical."

"Has anything stood out to you? Something all the injuries have in common, for instance?"

"Tri-Wing," the doctor replies.

"Pardon?"

"Sharp Tri-Wing screws in every wound. They have an unusual head with three wings that, as far as I know, are only used when you really don't want the screw to be unscrewed."

"And this type of screw was in the bomb?"

"All I know is they're rammed into the wounds. You'll have to talk to the technicians about potential bomb designs."

* * *

The technician exits the tent, walks about ten steps, then closes her umbrella and leads Sarwani in through the hole in the wall. Broken cement crumbles down on him.

The technician gestures toward the exploded storeroom, which contains what resembles nothing so much as an art installation of twisted and ripped-apart PVC pipes, then continues through a second hole in the back wall.

The destruction in the next room comes off as greater, not least because it was so clearly a nice room before the blast. A couple of newly arrived technicians are crawling around on the floor. The back wall of this room has been blown out too, revealing a chaotic and, in places, relatively bloody open-plan office.

"The injured were working in there," the technician says, pointing through the hole to the office area. "But the explosion itself took place in here, in the CEO's office. Both the back and the front walls were blown out. The bomb, if we assume that's what it was, must have been directed outward, and the remains of the main victim traveled through the storeroom, staining the pulverized PVC plastic, which then spread across the loading area outside."

"What do you mean by 'directed outward'?" Sarwani asks.

"The force of the explosion was greater in the direction of the PVC storeroom than the office. If the bomb had been aimed the other way, a lot more people would have died.

"But then there would have been no spray of pink microplastics?"

The technician studies him for a moment. Then she says, "I suppose you could put it that way."

* * *

Eva Nyman has just been handed a cup of coffee and is adjusting her umbrella. She has talked to and sent home the employees the local police had rounded up in the factory's courtyard. Not one of them had anything decisive to say; they'd all been in various stages of shock. She's jotting down a few concluding notes in her pad when she spots a woman in a secluded corner, sitting on the asphalt.

She walks over and squats down next to the woman, who's in her forties and dripping wet, her mascara running.

"Why are you sitting here?" Nyman asks, taking her hand.

"I'm sorry," the woman mumbles, letting herself be pulled to her feet.

Nyman takes off her jacket, holding the umbrella and her coffee in the same hand above the woman's head. Then she drapes the jacket around the woman's shoulders.

"And who are you?" she asks, giving the woman her coffee.

"Maria," the woman replies, her teeth chattering against the edge of the cup. "Rikard's secretary."

"And where were you when your boss was blown up?"

"I was running an errand on the factory floor."

"None of your coworkers know anything about a package being delivered to Rikard Albrektsson. Do you?"

"We have a freight desk. They would have been the ones to deliver it to Rikard if there was a package. But it was too early in the morning."

"And if I understand things correctly, you have to go through your office to get to Rikard's?"

Maria nods. She's sobbing but also drinking greedily from the coffee cup. Warmth seems to be returning to her body.

Nyman continues, "If something was delivered directly to Rikard, it must have arrived after you left your office, which is to say while you . . . Actually, what were you doing? What kind of errand was it?"

"I was talking to a friend down on the factory floor. A girlfriend. She's having marital problems."

"How long had you been away from your office?"

"Maybe twenty minutes, something like that."

"Could Rikard have taken out a package that was already in his office and opened it after you left?"

"Why would he have done that?"

"It almost seems as though he didn't want to be disturbed, doesn't it?"

55

The day passes strangely quickly up in Gästrikland. The NOD trio establish a temporary office in Merplast's cordoned-off manufacturing building and take on enough good old-fashioned policework to force them to spend the night. The no-frills, largely unstaffed hotel in Kallfors is closely associated with Merplast and normally houses out-of-town businessmen from the plastics industry. Now, instead—in three rooms—is more than half of Nova.

After a hearty dinner, Nyman, Lindberg, and Sarwani gather in Nyman's room, the biggest the hotel has to offer. They've managed to get a hold of a bottle of wine, which they intend to share. Lindberg and Sarwani have spread out on the sofa. Nyman has her own armchair. The silence has lasted so long, people less familiar with each other would have begun to feel a creeping awkwardness at this point.

"PVC is known as the most environmentally damaging plastic in the world," Sarwani says at length. "In terms of symbolism, Merplast Ltd is as straightforward as the previous crime scenes."

"Was Odenplan actually symbolic, though?" Lindberg asks. "Surely the victims there were the opposite of climate offenders. Weren't they mostly environmentally conscious commuters driven out of the underground and congregating on account of pure curiosity?"

"True," Sarwani says, nodding. "I suppose the message there was that we're all guilty. That's why I thought it was going to carry on like that, but instead, what we got was a return to the limited and overtly symbolic."

"Well, this symbolism is almost too on the nose, with microplastics slowly invading our corrupt human race, turning us all into plastic figurines," Nyman mutters.

"Except this particular invasion happened pretty fucking fast," Lindberg adds. "Besides, in this case, didn't the body invade the plastic?"

Nyman mutters, "Because the bomb was aimed that way."

"That's interesting, actually," Sarwani says. "The blast reached CEO Rikard Albrektsson first, and milliseconds later the PVC storeroom. If the Terrorist

Bomber had aimed the bomb differently, we would have had more victims behind the back wall, where the staff were—but we wouldn't have had any pink microplastics."

"And the message would have been off," Nyman. "And we would have considered our perpetrator unreliable."

"I suppose he took a chance," Lindberg says, shrugging. "People would have died either way, and that's the purpose, right? Seriously, I shouldn't be here. I should be leaning on Elias Shariq in the smallest interview room Kronoberg has to offer."

"Maybe there were instructions on the package," Sarwani suggests. "'Open here'? 'This side up'?"

"What kind of package was it?" Lindberg asks. "Where was it from?"

"We have a twenty-minute window from when Maria, the secretary, left her boss to when he exploded," Nyman replies. "During that time, he was unsupervised. Either the package arrived just then, delivered early in the morning and directly to him, bypassing the freight desk for whatever reason—or he waited to open the package until he was sure he was alone. Both options are interesting. If the latter's true, there was a secret or at least private package that had been delivered earlier. If the former, a courier timed their delivery to when Maria stepped away from her desk. And they did it unseen."

"And this time, the courier can't have been Elias Shariq," Sarwani says with a glance at Lindberg.

"But surely it's more likely that the CEO already had the package in his office," Nyman says. "Which one of you talked to the freight handler?"

Lindberg listlessly raises his hand.

"And did he or she say anything about a package of roughly the right size being delivered at some earlier point?" Nyman asks.

Lindberg shakes his head.

"Still, it's a company with a lot of deliveries going in and out. That its shocked staff would be unable to recall a specific package so shortly after the blast isn't really that surprising. But no one could remember a package even after they'd had some time to recover."

"Are we getting fixated on this whole package thing?" Sarwani asks pensively. "Just because it's always been packages before? Maybe it wasn't a package at all? Maybe it was a time bomb?" Maybe it was already in the room, already aimed just so?"

"Remotely triggered, then," Nyman nods. "Like the rapeseed field. Someone with binoculars who waited until Albrektsson moved into just the right position. That it coincided with the secretary's absence could just be happenstance. Albrektsson should have been visible through the windows and gates."

They pause briefly, thinking.

"That almost seems likelier," Linberg says after a while.

"But it requires local knowledge," Nyman counters.

"The apathetic," Sarwani says, jumping up.

Nyman and Lindberg stare at him. Sarwani sits back down on the sofa and continues. "We've forgotten about them. Why did the Terrorist Bomber write that the microplastics will be sprayed over the apathetic?"

"That gust of wind blew the plastic all over Kallfors," Nyman says. "Are the residents of Kallfors the apathetic?"

"Is it possible there was some kind of toxic emission from Merplast Ltd at some point?" Sarwani says slowly. "And that Kallfors, the town, which depends on Merplast for its survival, has remained apathetic vis-à-vis the company's environmental crimes?"

"If that's the case," Nyman says, "then maybe the Terrorist Bomber experienced that personally, because that environmental crime—if it happened—hardly made the national news. We would have heard about it."

"You're saying this is where it all began?" Lindberg asks.

"We're speculating wildly now," Nyman says, "but that would mean the Terrorist Bomber could have a local connection. That he's someone who was very upset by Merplast's environmental crimes and Kallfors's indifference."

"And who will therefore 'open the castle gate and spray pink microplastics over the apathetic,'" Sarwani quotes.

"If so, the man responsible, CEO Rikard Albrektsson, was deliberately targeted. But why now? Why start with four attacks in which innocent people were killed?"

"To hide the original crime in the middle of a series?" Sarwani suggests.

"Or to work himself up to the one that actually matters?" Lindberg says. "The one closest to his heart."

"The way I see it, there are two questions we need to tackle tomorrow morning," Eva Nyman says, reaching for the wine bottle. "Because now, we're done for the night."

Sarwani leans back and says, "I imagine the first question is, Was there active local opposition to Merplast Ltd? How do we find out?"

"If no one wants to talk, there must at least be some kind of local press," Lindberg says.

"But I don't know what the second question is," Sarwani says.

"How far is Kallfors from Lukas Frisell's dwelling?" Nyman asks, and finally uncorks the bottle.

56

The binoculars are raised behind the hill, peering at Merplast's blown-up castle through the factory gates. Then Sarwani lowers the binoculars and studies the map Lindberg's holding up.

"You're right, Anton," he says, nodding. It should have been possible to see Rikard Albrektsson moving about his office from this vantage point."

"The rain last night likely destroyed any tracks," Eva Nyman says, pointing down at the wet ground. "But I'm going to have to send our overworked technicians out here to see if they can find anything, all the same."

"I just know he was here yesterday morning," Lindberg says. "The Terrorist Bomber was crouched right here, detonator in hand, waiting until Albrektsson was in the exact right position to be turned into pink microplastic."

Nyman looks around at the morning mist billowing across the mud. "At this point, the technicians are about seventy-five percent certain we're dealing with a stationary bomb, not one that was delivered. And we know Lukas Frisell was in Stockholm during the relevant time period."

"We also know," Anton Lindberg counters," that if he is the perpetrator, he has at least one accomplice. Plus, it hasn't been established yet when the bomb was planted in the CEO's office. It could have been in there for weeks."

* * *

Soon after, they're in a rental car, driving south. Nyman says from the passenger seat, "If Anton's hypothesis proves correct, that the bomb was planted at Merplast some time ago, neither Lukas Frisell nor Elias Shariq has an alibi. But is that likely? Could a sizeable bomb really have been hidden in Albrektsson's room for days without him or his secretary noticing?"

"Well, it could have hidden inside a sofa or something like that," Lindberg suggests. "But the risk of it being discovered by a cleaner or accidentally going off would have been too great, don't you think?" Sarwani asks.

Nyman straightens up and says, "So, it follows that it should have been planted relatively recently by a third member of this group, one that not only has detailed local knowledge but also the ability to get into Merplast's offices, presumably at night; plant the bomb; take up position with binoculars and a functioning remote detonator; and then wait for exactly the right moment. That certainly wouldn't be an accomplice. If that person exists, he or she is a leader. And Lukas Frisell is their subordinate. How likely does that seem?"

"Not likely at all," Sarwani replies. "But Frisell could have come up with a detailed plan to make sure the others could carry on even if he was taken out. Frisell could have driven his old Volvo with its stolen plates to somewhere around the Rosersberg post terminal, posted the third letter, returned to his lair, and been nicked the next night."

"Safe in the knowledge that even if his killer-for-hire, Elias Shariq, was caught too, the plan would keep chugging along?" Lindberg asks.

"I highly doubt a man like Frisell would be unable to find a way around the prosecutor's internet ban," Sarwani says.

Nyman protests half-heartedly. "But we can see where Lukas Frisell has been at all times and for how long. I'm hoping to keep surveillance on him for another twenty-four hours at least, and entering any of the dwindling number of internet cafés in town, which have all been preprogrammed into his ankle bracelet, would immediately trip the alarm. The likeliness that he's in contact with any potential accomplices isn't nonexistent—I agree with you about that—but it has been minimized. That being said, I'm pretty sure we won't have surveillance for much longer . . ."

Sarwani's looking down at his phone. "Unless I'm miscalculating, it's about sixty miles from Kallfors to Frisell's home in the woods. Is that close enough for him to get worked up about Merplast's potential environmental crimes?"

"Doubtful," Nyman replies. "Nothing in his computer suggests he ever read the news. The search history of his ancient web browser consists exclusively of dating websites, going back years."

"So you think Merplast rules Frisell out?" Lindberg asks.

"It definitely doesn't rule him out," Nyman says. "But it has made him a less likely suspect. I think this attack points to someone local. Merplast's cynicism may have been the straw that broke the camel's back. Local apathy became emblematic of global apathy. A spark was lit. Inside someone who has yet to reveal themself."

Nodding thoughtfully, Sarwani adds, "And this local person or group has somehow selected Lukas Frisell as a suitable scapegoat and done extremely thorough research on him."

"Or knows him from somewhere," Nyman suggests.

"Well, we're here," Lindberg says, turning into a car park outside a low gray building from the seventies, located in something reminiscent of an industrial park. They enter, are given directions, make their way to a small office that houses the area's local paper, and are greeted by a woman who stands up from a cluttered desk.

"Yes, that's right," she says before another word has been exchanged. "I'm the entire staff, yes. Eva-Lotta Thelin. Welcome."

"Pleasure," Nyman says, launching into introductions. Once the formalities are done, Thelin says, "There have been two incidents at Merplast Ltd. I actually reported on both. The first was four winters ago. During the County Administrative Board's annual inspection, elevated emissions of polyvinyl chloride and phthalates were discovered."

"There's no way you remember that from four years ago," Lindberg exclaims. Eva-Lotta Thelin laughs reluctantly and confesses, "When you called, I hit the archive and dug up my old articles. The emission wasn't big enough to get traction in the Stockholm media, but it did stir up some local protests."

"In Kallfors?" Sarwani asks.

"I think most of the protests came from the surrounding countryside. But the second incident was bigger. It involved a significant leak of microplastics."

"Well, well, what do you know," Lindberg says. "Why haven't we heard about this?" Nyman asks.

"I actually tried to sell the national media on it, but it was February twenty-fourth, 2022."

"Ah," Sarwani says. "The war."

"It was the day Russia invaded Ukraine, yes. I couldn't even get through to the public broadcaster, TV or radio, and not the big papers either. The incident remained local news."

"But there were renewed protests?" Nyman asks.

"Yes," Thelin replies. "The same people. Beating their drum and inviting people to a protest in Kallfors. It was high time for Merplast's environmental crimes to resonate in the wider world. Do you know how many people came to the meeting?"

"Not a lot?" Lindberg hazards a guess.

"Zero," Thelin says. "Actually zero. They'd reserved the village hall in Kallfors and sat there, waiting. But no one came."

"The apathetic," Sarwani says emphatically.

"You have to have some sympathy for the locals. Their wagons are firmly hitched to Merplast."

"Do you have names, pictures?" Nyman asks.

Eva-Lotta Thelin walks back to her cluttered desk and turns the computer screen so they can see it.

"My articles," she says. "Only the second one had a picture to go with it. These days, we have to be reporter and photographer, so I took it myself."

She makes the photograph bigger. The Merplast courtyard is clearly recognizable behind a roaring man clutching a rolled-up banner in his deformed hand. Raised placards are visible behind him, but the focus is squarely on the man.

"Börje Sandblom," Thelin informs them. "Two or three people protested loudly—the most aggressive of them was definitely this Sandblom bloke. He was part of the first, smaller, protest too."

"And helped to organize the failed protest meeting, I assume?" Sarwani asks.

"That's correct, young man," Thelin says appreciatively. "I was going to write an article about it, but the powers that be made it clear it would be inappropriate, considering the outcome. I never did end up writing it, but I kept some photographs in the archive. I only have one picture from the protest out at Merplast's factory—the one I used in the article. But there was a serious confrontation between Börje Sandblom and Merplast's CEO, Rikard Albrektsson. Albrektsson was a CrossFit guy, and it almost came to blows."

"Where can we find this Börje Sandblom?" Nyman asks.

"I have no idea. I tried to find an address for him just over a year ago but came up empty. The only thing I had to go on was that he only has two fingers on his left hand. You can just about make that out in this picture."

"Would you mind emailing us the pictures from the meeting in Kallfors?"

"I already sent both of them, and the articles, to the address you gave me," Thelin says, looking as though she has more to say.

"Thank you," Nyman says. "And . . . ?"

"Well, look . . . I was the first journalist on the scene in Kallfors yesterday. Do you think the protests have something to do with the explosion?"

They've planned for this. As if on cue, both Sarwani and Lindberg pull back. Nyman moves closer to Thelin and half whispers, "We would be extremely grateful if you would refrain from writing about this right now. And in return, you may very well be given a scoop of the kind local newspapers in this country only dream of."

A few seconds of silence.

"All right," Thelin says. "I believe you."

"Good. And I would also be extremely grateful if your finely honed journalistic instincts could be put to work locating Börje Sandblom. And make sure you let me know directly if you do."

* * *

Anton Lindberg sets off toward Gävle. It's just over twelve miles away. Twenty minutes of undisturbed conversation.

"Why would it be so difficult to locate this Börje Sandblom?" Nyman asks.

"Could it possibly be because he's gone off-grid?" Sarwani asks.

"Like Lukas Frisell? Certainly possible."

"The severed fingers," Sarwani says, his eyes on his phone. "He really does only have two on his left hand. Check this out, for instance."

He holds the phone up to the front seats. It's a picture of a roughly forty-five-year-old Börje Sandblom in what must be the village hall in Kallfors. There are two other people in the photograph, a woman with short hair dressed in khaki clothes, who is half turned away, and a young man with freckles and a yellow baseball cap, who looks like he wants to take a bat to all of Kallfors. Together with the large man sitting in front of them, they are likely the entire Merplast protest, all gathered in one place.

The red-faced man in the front looks sullen, holding up his deformed hand like a heavy metal gesture.

"It looks like that hard-rock symbol," Sarwani says. Just the fore- and little fingers. The devil. What's it called again?"

"Corna," Anton Lindberg replies.

57

Ankan is reading Lukas Frisell's "book." Doing so in the office is a unique experience. She's a suburban girl, has always lived decently close to nature, is used to taking the dog for long walks surrounded by the smells of the forest. But what she meets in Frisell's text forces her much closer to all the things that grow, germinate, creep, live. A few minutes of reading is enough to transport her to a different world, here, inside our own. The world of origin. Face to face with biology. It feels as though she's just beneath the surface of the earth, burrowing through the soil.

She needs to take a break.

But the text doesn't contain what she's looking for. The only thing in it is a man who lets himself be swallowed up by nature while still surviving in it as a man and a human.

There's nothing else—even though she's cognizant of the fact that she hasn't yet managed to put any critical distance between herself and the material.

Something inside her admits that she would have loved to have met Lukas Frisell ten years ago.

* * *

After her visit to Södertälje to see the city planner the day before, Sonja Ryd had, with some effort, been able to get hold of an appropriate liaison at SUAS, a receptionist called Vanja Pärn, who had really retired but still came in to cover a shift from time to time. She had dug up the recordings of Lukas Frisell's lectures on crisis preparedness and survival from the mid-2010s, his last year at SUAS, and an ambitious IT technician at the university had then digitized them. Ryd's going through the videos when her phone rings.

It's Eva Nyman, calling from Kallfors to give her an update. After ending the call, Ryd just sits there, staring blankly into space.

What are they really dealing with here? How well-planned is this? Does this type of climate terrorism really exist? Well, why not? Isn't it actually more surprising that they haven't had to deal with it before now? That's probably down to the fact that climate activists are rarely physically aggressive, unlike fascists and Islamists, to take just two examples of male dominance movements.

Ryd snaps out of her philosophical reverie and pushes on with the recordings. She's only just started the lecture on "Health and Medicine in Isolation," watching a Lukas Frisell with wispy medium blond hair writing and drawing on a whiteboard, when she senses someone looking over her shoulder. She turns around, to be greeted by a familiar face.

"Found anything interesting?" Ankan asks.

"Not yet," Ryd replies, pulling her hands free out of her ear. "Frisell's considerably more loquacious in the lecture theater than in the interview room—that much is clear."

"He has a way with language. I'm reading his notes from the computer. He really did live close to nature, for real."

"And was passionate about it; that's also clear from watching these lectures. You'll have to guide me through his notes later."

"Did you see him this morning? The same armed guard?"

"Yeah, makes it kind of awkward. And we didn't get anywhere. It's as though he's wiped his memory. Sometimes it honestly feels like he might have gone a bit crazy out there in the woods."

"You still think he's guilty?" Ryd slowly shakes her head.

"I genuinely don't know. I *should* know. This is what I'm good at. Interviews, character analysis. I sit with him day after day, drilling down as far as I can, but I can't get a proper read on him. He's still hiding something. And it definitely has to do with his past."

"Well, he certainly looks . . . impressive," Ankan says, pointing to the screen where Frisell is continuing his lecture with obvious zeal.

Ryd realizes Ankan's not going to leave. She turns the volume up and lets her stay. The camera seems to be mounted up by the ceiling of the SUAS lecture theater.

Diagonally from above, they watch Frisell wandering around a desk. A section of the first few rows of seats in the auditorium are in the shot too, and they're packed. Just then, he's talking about sustaining an injury in the woods and how best to handle that. You have to make sure you have access to certain fundamental supplies: antibiotics, disinfectant, bandages, pain killers.

"But the forest also provides natural bandages and medications," he says, still circling the desk. "If you end up in a long-term survival situation, you will eventually be forced to phase out industrially manufactured products. Toward the end of this lecture, I will provide a list of herbs and mosses that not only staunch blood flow but also have various healing properties."

Ryd ignores his words. She watches him without listening. She sees his movements, the way he turns to the audience, at once extroverted and introverted. As though he wants to be seen and not seen, by turns. She can make out the backs of a couple of women in the front row, whom he seems to be using as a sounding board, whom he turns to and whose reactions he waits for. She doesn't immediately recognize either of them from "Fun With Farming."

The lecture keeps going. After a while, Frisell draws a diagram on the whiteboard.

First, he draws a circle. Then he draws a circle inside the first circle.

Ankan reacts immediately, wants to see it again, wants to turn the volume up. Ryd turns up the volume. Frisell is talking about "overlapping zones." "The world outside human society is so much bigger than the one inside it. The same is also true of the worlds outside and inside ourselves."

Ankan wants to pause the video to look at the symbol; Ryd manages to stop it at exactly the right moment. Ankan frantically swipes on her phone, eventually finding the right picture.

It feels like an eternity since she arrived on Dalagatan right next to Vasaparken and met Rahim Abdulhamid for the first time. After talking to him and his older colleague, she'd briefly walked around the park. Not far from the unpleasant scorch mark in the grass where Jesper Sahlgren had landed, she'd seen a symbol carved into the bark of a tree.

Two circles.

One inside the other.

Ankan holds her phone up to Ryd and explains.

"Well, fuck me," Ryd says.

"The bloody bomber was standing right there," Ankan says, "behind that tree on Dalagatan, carving this symbol into it while he waited for the explosion. A circle inside another circle."

"A symbol Lukas Frisell used in his public lecture series on crisis preparedness and survival in 2013 to represent things that are both inside and outside society: ourselves."

"Two possibilities," Ankan says. "Either Frisell is the Terrorist Bomber, or the bastard's somewhere in that auditorium."

"The beginning," Ryd says, rewinding.

The video starts over. They can hear people arriving, but only the ones who walk close by the empty desk at the front of the room can be made out, and even then, only from above and behind.

Then Frisell arrives, thumping his backpack down onto the desk. He pulls out a few books and fishes out a piece of paper that he hands to someone in the front row.

"Yes!" Ryd says, pausing the video. "An attendance list?"

"Looks that way. And if that's the case, SUAS might still have it. I'll give them a call." Ryd fast-forwards back to the moment when Frisell draws the circle inside the circle.

She lets the video run from there. He appears to have abandoned the stated theme of the lecture—"Health and Medicine in Isolation"—improvising his way into more abstract musings on general survivalist philosophy instead. Minutes later, he concludes his lecture with the words "See you next Friday, on the other side of the ruins of destruction."

58

The mood in the office changes when Nyman, Lindberg, and Sarwani enter. Eva Nyman walks straight up to the whiteboard, puts up a photograph, and writes in big letters: *Börje Sandblom*.

Without being expressly told to, the gathered detectives all move in closer. It's not long before they've formed a dense semicircle around the whiteboard.

"Börje Sandblom is as close as we currently get to a realistic suspect in the Kallfors bombing case. He's a large, bald man in his fifties, most easily identified by a maimed left hand. He's led two local protests against Merplast Ltd in the past few years, most recently in February of 2022. The company has on occasion handled toxins and microplastics negligently, and Sandblom and his group organized a protest meeting in Kallfors. No one came to it—which matches one of the phrases in the most recent letter, the one that talks about 'the apathetic' being sprayed with microplastics."

Eva Nyman pauses briefly, studying her team.

"The interesting thing is," she then says, "that Börje Sandblom doesn't exist. He's not registered anywhere in Sweden, but he also doesn't seem to have ever existed in the past. And yet, he's likely local, and we've put every officer in Gästrikland on searching for him locally.

What we need to do now is search for him nationally. You have this photo, and all other available pictures of him have just been sent to your inboxes. Start digging through every database you can think of. And it's not unlikely he's a prepper. The moment we have a lead, I'll be sending a couple of you back up to Gästrikland."

The informal meeting's over. Ryd walks up to Nyman and fills her in on their progress in terms of Frisell's notes and his drawing of a circle within a circle, a symbol that was also found in Vasaparken in conjunction with bombing number two.

"Very interesting," Nyman says. "But it could easily be coincidental; it's not exactly a unique symbol."

"I know," Ryd says. "Do you mind if I show Frisell the video? It might help him make the right connections."

Nyman ponders that for a minute, her eyes on Ryd. "Do it," she says at length, then rushes off to some neglected meeting with the top brass.

Ryd sits down at her desk and has a quick look at the latest news. Or, rather, the lack thereof. Frisell's heart-rate test yielded no results: none of the places that God's white dwelling gazed down on provoked a bigger reaction than any other. And the two registration plates that have so far been caught on a traffic camera seem to confirm his claims: twice outside a supermarket in Tierp, once in the car park of the bar Flustret in Uppsala.

She sighs and opens the pictures of Börje Sandblom. But her heart's not in it. The symbol with the circle within the circle has caught her attention. She needs to discuss it with Lukas Frisell. She takes out her iPad and opens the app that shows her the way his ankle bracelet has moved since she released him after their fairly useless morning meeting. He seems to be exploring the city.

At the moment, he's relatively nearby, but not in his flat on Agnegatan. He's standing still on nondescript Inedalsgatan, which leads down to Kungsholms Strand. He could be at the station in ten minutes.

She makes the call. He sounds surprisingly interested. That morning, a more accurate description would have been lethargic. Nothing new had come out of their meeting. The entire Frisell project seemed stuck in a rut.

She glances down at her tablet again. He's on his way. The flashing red dot is moving south on Inedalsgatan, making a beeline for the police station. She swipes right to a more or less identical map, page two of the app.

Two things distinguish page two from page one. First, the flashing dot lacks a line representing past movements. Second, the dot's green. This is the secret backup tracker in Frisell's Nokia 3310, the phone he always has to carry on his person if he doesn't want an alarm to go off.

There's nothing out of the ordinary there either.

She goes downstairs to wait for him. As if on cue, the armed guard appears. She nods to him, wondering if this is seriously his full-time job now. The Police Authority's allocation of resources is a thing of mystery.

Four minutes later, Ryd and Frisell are seated on either side of the same old conference table in the same old conference room, with the same old coffee thermos and possibly the same old cinnamon buns between them. Holding the panic button, Ryd asks herself if making coffee and buying baked goods might be part of the guard's job description. Or maybe just wiping the mold off the old ones.

Ryd walks around the table, opens her laptop in front of Frisell, and takes a seat on the chair next to his. The video starts a few minutes before the younger Frisell draws his double circle. She lets him get used to seeing his younger self first.

He actually looks touched, shaking his head.

"Right. Bloody hell," he says. "They recorded this."

"How do you feel watching it?"

"Strange. Like something from a different lifetime. Someone else's lifetime."

Ryd nods and points to the screen.

"You will soon abandon the stated theme of the lecture 'Health and Medicine in Isolation' and take off on what I would call a quasi-philosophical flight of fancy. Be ready."

He's ready. He watches himself draw the two concentric circles, hears a younger version of himself, in a more high-pitched voice, say, "In this context, we can talk about overlapping zones, which is to say that you exist both within and without. But the fundamental point is still that the world outside human society is so much bigger than the world inside it. The same can be said about life, and this thinking can be applied psychologically as well, inside and outside ourselves."

Sonja Ryd reaches out and mutes the video before returning to her side of the table. Frisell looks slightly nonplussed. He's staring blindly at the screen, colors flickering across his furrowed face as the video continues to play in front of him.

"That was some proper mumbo jumbo, don't you think?" she asks. "A philosophical analysis of that statement shows it's virtually devoid of meaning."

He shrugs.

"What did you mean by it?" she continues. "And was that circle within a circle a symbol you used a lot?"

"I think I was referring to something I'd discussed in a previous lecture," he replies hoarsely. "It's taken out of context here. Originally, that circle was a visual representation of escaping the narrow and stepping out into the grand. Into nature."

"So, you did use this symbol a lot?"

"A lot might be overstating it, but a few times, sure. I found it very useful."

"Then you should know that it has also appeared in conjunction with the Terrorist Bomber's activities."

She holds her phone out to him. It's Ankan's photograph from the tree in Vasaparken. A circle carved inside a larger circle.

"From attack number two," Ryd says. "Recognize it?"

Frisell takes the phone, putting it down on the table next to the laptop and staring at it as though entranced. His pale face is still illuminated by the constantly changing light from the computer screen.

"I obviously recognize it," he replies warily.

"It's Sunday morning," Ryd says. "Around twenty past six. The city's deserted. Behind a tree in Vasaparken, off Dalagatan, the Terrorist Bomber is waiting for his bomb to explode inside the offices of PR firm Flat Broke. While he waits, he carves this symbol into the tree. At 6:29 AM, the PR firm is blown up, the charred remains of a man are thrown out onto the lawn. And the Terrorist Bomber slips away unseen."

Frisell pushes the phone back toward her. He actually looks shaken. She takes the phone, discovers an unread email from Eva Nyman, and opens it. It's about new directives from the Head of NOD, and they do not sound promising. A meeting will be held shortly.

Just don't let it be Säpo, she thinks. *Don't let the Security Services take the case from us. Not now.*

She turns back to Frisell. Motley patches of color continue to dance across his face. He looks even more absent now, almost fearful. She leans over and slams the laptop shut in front of him, noticing just how ashen he is when the colors disappear from his face.

"What do you have to say about this?"

He blinks hard a couple of times and eventually replies hoarsely, "What could I possibly have to say about it?"

She studies him intently and then makes a decision.

"You look a bit peaked, Lukas. Here's what we're going to do. Head out on town for an hour. Walk around like you like to do, collect your thoughts, buy a cup of coffee, cash. And I'll see you back here in exactly one hour."

She stays in the conference room for a few minutes while the armed guard leads Lukas Frisell toward the exit. Only after he's gone can she bring herself to stand up.

59

Elias Shariq and his lawyer watch Anton Lindberg burst into the claustrophobic interview room and take a seat across from the mismatched pair. They watch him, not without concern, while he spreads out his documents across the interview table. He starts off with a kind of twisted enthusiasm: "Nice to have a day off, right? Nice to be able to have some extra time to think about how Hassan's going to react when he finds out you hoodwinked his posse, the Hjulsta Gang? I hope you've made the most of this extra day of life."

The lawyer clears his throat and announces, "My client highly doubts you've talked to Hassan, Inspector. That would be remarkably unethical."

Lindberg freezes mid-movement, as though suddenly turned to ice. He stays like that until both Shariq and the lawyer start to shift uncomfortably in their seats. Then he drops the petrification and says, "Unethical?" Just that. Then: "I've never heard the word used so perversely. By people who don't have the slightest idea what it means."

The lawyer whispers something in Shariq's ear. It goes on for a while. Lindberg says, "This is exactly how the Mafia got a foot in the door in the United States. Despicable, unscrupulous lawyers helped those bastards establish themselves—and then they turned consiglieri for their family businesses. It's a wonderful world we live in. Good to know we've learned the lessons of history."

Then Anton Lindberg turns to Elias Shariq and continues. "You're lucky, I've been very busy with the ongoing bombings. The ones you're involved in, Elias. But I have time now. Give me something right this second, or I'm going straight to Hassan. It's not an empty threat. He's sitting five doors down this hallway. I'll go right over there and discuss the picric acid with him instead."

He abruptly stands up. And then, even though Elias tries to hide it under the table, Anton sees him tugging violently on his lawyer's jacket.

The lawyer blurts out, "My client objects in the strongest terms—"

Anton Lindberg cuts him off: "All right, Elias, you just gave me something. Thank you for that." He pushes his face into Elias Shariq's.

"And because you did, I'm going to give you an hour to decide, Elias *Eriksson*."

Then he walks out.

60

Even though he knows Elias and his lawyer will be coming out soon too, he pauses five doors down the hallway.

He hesitates because he doesn't want to go in. He doesn't want to touch or be touched by their thoroughly corrupt world. Nor is he allowed to. And he can never tell anyone, least of all Nova. But he needs the leverage to get to Elias Eriksson, aka Elias Shariq. He needs this ace up his sleeve; he's not going to let that prick slip out of his grasp.

"So, what's it going to be?" the guard asks, jangling his keys.

When Anton Lindberg nods, he can feel in his bones how fateful that nod might prove. But he's been on this path for so long. Ever since organized crime took over his every thought.

The man in the cell looks unremarkable, the way most people do in prison clothes.

There are moth holes in both the joggers and the green T-shirt, his dark stubble's on the cusp of turning into a full beard.

The guard makes the prisoner sit on the bed and cuffs him to the table, which is bolted to the floor. On Lindberg's signal, he leaves the cell, but he also leaves the hatch in the door open. Lindberg hears him take up position within earshot.

"Hassan," Lindberg says, taking a seat on the chair across from him.

"Another copper," the leader of the Hjulsta Gang sighs, fixing him with an ice-cold stare.

"Picric acid," Lindberg counters. "You smuggle that?"

"Why are we talking about stuff that will never even come close to making it to court?" Hassan replies with a smile that's supposed to come off as sleepy.

But Anton Lindberg can see the veiled wariness.

"Because this isn't about your case," he replies, sharpening his senses.

And yes, Hassan's demonstrative ennui fails to impress. He's unable to hide his curiosity.

Or maybe it's all in Lindberg's overwrought brain.

"Come get this guy," Hassan calls out in the direction of the door. "He's boring me." Lindberg feels as though he's learned quite a bit about interview techniques from Sonja Ryd. Staying silent now would be the perfect move. Because it's obvious Hassan's curious.

Not a sound is heard from the hallway outside. No guard peeks in. And Anton Lindberg just sits there, silent and passive.

"So, whose case is it then?" Hassan asks eventually, a hint of temporary defeat in his tone.

"Picric acid," is all Lindberg says.

The only sound is a ventilation system, monotonous, persistent. Lindberg is struck by how difficult it must be to sleep with that sound.

In the end, Hassan spreads his hands, as far as the handcuffs allow, and says, "I don't even fucking know what picric acid is."

"It's an essential component of powerful homemade bombs. The kind that keep exploding all around the country right now, killing lots of people. And the Hjulsta Gang imports picric from the Balkans. We have proof. Soon, we'll be able to tie it to one specific load."

Lindberg studies Hassan.

"Let me know when you do," Hassan says at length.

"So you know which load I'm talking about?"

Hassan lets ice his icy gaze rest on Lindberg, who tries not to think about how many dead and tortured people those eyes have seen. Hassan doesn't take his eyes off him, not for a second. His eyes follow Lindberg even after he gets up and is waiting for the guard to unlock the door.

Only when the key is inserted in the lock does Hassan say, soberly and clearly, "I feel sorry for anyone who tries to stir our pot, Mr. Copper. Do you even know how easy it is to find out where you live?"

When the door swings open, Hassan quickly shoots Lindberg with his index finger. Then he blows away the imaginary smoke from his finger, and the thick door slams shut.

61

Shabir Sarwani is hunched over his computer screen. All around him, his colleagues are too: Lindberg, Ankan, and Ryd, in their own corners of the room, each surrounded by their team, similarly engaged.

It's like a competition.

Sarwani has been gathering information about the mysterious Börje Sandblom, creating a few alternative scenarios to explain his absence; listing all archives and databases where he might conceivably turn up; and finally, gathering and editing the known photographs of him, preparing them for professional facial recognition.

That's when he notices the small number above an icon in the menu bar at the top of his screen. He quickly opens his inbox and discovers a new email among the eighty-four unread ones.

He's had a reply. A match for the man who made an angry face when he was bumped by an army-green backpack on Odenplan. Not unexpectedly, the figure with the unmistakable violent tendencies has a criminal record. Also not unexpectedly he's a sex offender, but above all, he's a methamphetamine dealer. His name's Slobodan Jovanović, and his criminal record keeps growing before Sarwani's eyes.

He opens the picture from Odenplan again. The aggressive man who has just been lightly bumped by a man with a backpack who subsequently melted into the crowd to plant his deadly load among the onlookers.

And Slobodan Jovanović saw that person.

Sarwani studies his criminal record. Jovanović is no longer in detention, released six months ago after a three-year sentence for drug-related crimes. There's no work address, no permanent residence, no listed relatives or partners—only an address with a question mark after it, a flat in Farsta that belongs to a woman called Vesna Damnjanović.

Sarwani slowly pulls his jacket off the back of his chair and slips out of the office as inconspicuously as he's able. The others will have to continue their competition without Shabir Sarwani. He's playing in a completely different league.

62

Sonja Ryd isn't competing. True, she's hunched over her computer, but she's refusing to accept that there may be a connection between Börje Sandblom's red face and the Terrorist Bomber's ruthless and sophisticated series of bombings. Her objection is based on neither police instinct nor philosophical analysis; it's simply prejudiced.

She has her hands full with a different middle-aged man whom she finds far more difficult to read. And the hour's almost up. It's time to head downstairs and meet him at reception. She grabs her iPad and leaves.

In the hallway outside, she runs into Eva Nyman. They both halt their energetic steps. "Tell me it's not the Security Services" is the first thing out of Ryd's mouth.

"Best to say nothing," Nyman replies, holding her hands up. "But the threat has been averted for now. We've been given a forty-eight-hour respite."

Sonja Ryd heaves a heavy sigh and puts a hand on her boss's shoulder.

"Thank you, Eva. And let me be clear right now: I decline any future offers of a managerial role. Bloody hell, the wrestling you have to do with these bureaucrats."

"I hear you, loud and clear. Where are you going?"

"Reception," Ryd says, checking her watch. "I'm meeting Frisell in a couple of minutes."

"Part of our contract with Frisell is that he can never be late," Nyman reminds her. "If you don't have a call from either him or reception before those 'couple of minutes' are up, he's in breach of that contract."

Ryd checks her phone.

"I have to let Nova know we have forty-eight hours," Nyman says, pushing open the swing doors to the office before adding, "Let me know how you get on with Lukas."

Just then, Sonja Ryd's phone rings. They're still three minutes away from a breach of contract. Ryd expects the laconic voice from reception. But then she sees it's Frisell's number on her screen.

"We're meeting in three minutes," Ryd says coolly.

"I know," Lukas Frisell says in her ear. "I apologize. There's something I need to check out. I didn't quite have time to finish."

"What thing?" Ryd says, unlocking her iPad with her free hand. She opens the app. Sees the flashing red dot. Swipes over to the green one. The ankle bracelet and the mobile phone, respectively. They're in the same place. As they should be.

"Hard to explain," Frisell says. "You're just going to have to trust me. Can we push our meeting an hour?"

"I see you're in Östermalm, walking up Sturegatan. What are you doing there?"

"I'll tell you when I see you. I have to hang up now."

And then, Frisell does just that. Ryd finds herself staring at the phone for a moment. Then she swipes back and forth between the two maps again. The red dot, the ankle bracelet, is still in the same place as the green one, the Nokia phone, model 3310. Everything seems to be under control.

She contemplates the outer limit of Frisell's approved zone out on Gärdet. He's close to it, but not alarmingly so. Now."

"Something to check out . . . You're just going to have to trust me . . . I have to hang up."

Nothing about it is really all that strange. He called on time, if only just. Standard phrases. Establishing trust. Creating a familiar linguistic sphere. And a positive professional curiosity.

Everything's fine. They'll meet up in an hour. She'll find out everything then.

Sonja Ryd can't bring herself to move. There's a small but annoying speck of dust in her eye.

A mote.

Fuck. Something feels off. Why did he wait so long to call? Östermalm. Why Östermalm?

This is the very essence of Lukas Frisell: something feels a bit off—but she can't put her finger on what.

She stands motionless for a few definitive, rock-hard seconds, before she makes a decision. Right here, right now. She decides that there's no time to lose.

Sonja Ryd runs toward the garage, gets in her unmarked car, shoots out of the garage toward Fridhemsplan. Sets her course for Östermalm. At a red light, she checks the iPad again. The flashing red dot is passing Sture Park, continuing toward the major intersection with Valhallavägen, by the Olympic Stadium.

The light turns green. It's rush-hour traffic, and she's taking the inner-city route. She manages to get her portable blue light up on the roof. It's still crowded. She holds the wheel with her knees while she calls Lukas Frisell's Nokia 3310. No answer.

God fucking damn it. No answer.

She swipes from the red to the green dot. It's gone. There's no green dot on the second map.

Somehow, Lukas Frisell has managed to turn off his phone.

It could be innocent. Maybe he's meeting someone from the criminal underworld, someone who demands all phones be turned off. The shadow of trust is still there.

Until she realizes he can't turn off his phone. That's the whole point of the tracker they put in it. It can't be turned off.

She loops around Tegnérlunden Park, is sucked into traffic mayhem down by Sveavägen; there's no way of sirening herself past the congestion. She tries to make the vehicles on Tegnérgatan part for her. It's slow, and she gets half stuck, the siren wailing mercilessly. She has to turn it off to use her phone. Which means she's trapped in the middle of Sveavägen. The flashing blue light isn't enough to shift the hardened suburban motorists.

Ryd calls Eva Nyman. No answer, probably more meetings. As she pushes past Sveavägen in a cacophony of honking and accelerates up Tegnérgatan, she can't be more than five minutes away from Frisell and his bloody ankle bracelet. It has stopped now; she has an address for the location of the flashing red dot.

She reaches Birger Jarlsgatan and dials Ankan's number. Ankan picks up just as Ryd has to briefly start her siren up again. She hears Ankan shouting into the phone somewhere beyond the deranged howling. Then she shouts herself: "Lidingövägen twenty-eight. What is that?"

"Hold on, calm down, Sonja. I'm finding out . . ."

"Come on, come on."

"The Cavalry Barracks," Ankan says.

"I don't even understand what you're telling me," Ryd bellows, switching the siren off as she turns onto Sturegatan from Karlavägen, tires squealing. "What the fuck are the cavalry barracks?"

A major challenge comes into view. It's the massive intersection of Valhallavägen and Sturegatan, the latter of which changes into Lidingövägen on the other side of the intersection. But she can't turn the siren back on—she needs to be able to talk.

"I think it's the stables," Ankan says. "Our stables."

"Ours? Our what?"

"The police stable," Ankan clarifies. "The mounted police."

Just then, the flashing red dot begins to move again. As Ryd squeezes across the many lanes of Valhallavägen, she realizes the flashing red dot is now coming toward her. It has done a one-eighty and is quickly approaching, moving closer and closer to her, maybe three hundred yards ahead. A minor traffic jam makes her start up the siren again.

She's about to see Frisell and his ankle bracelet. According to the app, he's walking straight toward her.

Just then, she spots a small group of mounted police officers coming down the other side of Lidingövägen at a walk. Ignoring sirens is a skill all police horses have to master. Mild chaos erupts among the horses as she zigzags through the congestion.

Her sirens are still howling when she passes the horses. And, simultaneously, the flashing red dot on the map.

The place where Lukas Frisell is supposed to be.

One of the horses rears up dramatically. And around one of the animal's front legs, Sonja Ryd fleetingly spots a black ankle bracelet.

The howl of frustration inside the car drowns out the wailing of the sirens.

63

The unique fragrance of horse chestnut envelops Lukas Frisell as he waits outside a grand entrance in Vasastan. He turns his clear-blue eyes to the sky and sniffs the evening air.

It's strange: there are no chestnut trees nearby. Hasn't this happened to him before?

He can physically feel the transition from afternoon to evening. Even here, in the city, he can feel it. There's still nature here, after all. Observatorielunden Park isn't too far; Vasaparken's even closer.

While he waits, his mind works its way back over the past few hours. The temporary workshop on Inedalsgatan. The technical genius Alonzo waiting for him with a package and a car. The drive to Stureplan. The instructions he was given at the bottom of Sturegatan.

The memory of his own question: "Why the Cavalry Barracks?"

"I have a mate there. It'll be fun. Shits and giggles, amigo."

"Shits and giggles?"

"Walk up Sturegatan. Call them exactly three minutes before your deadline. Remember how to fix your phone?"

"It's been thirty seconds since you gave me the instructions, Alonzo."

"Make the call, fix your phone. Exactly three minutes, amigo. Even if they suspect you, they'll never catch you. But no copper would ever be that smart anyway."

"There's one," Frisell says, slamming the car door shut.

Then his mind reaches even further back in time. He's standing in front of a prison transport van, and he can see his own reflection in the window. He's wearing a police uniform, and his hair isn't wispy yet—more like an army buzzcut. A young man with black hair and light brown skin, wearing a tracksuit and leg irons, hugs him and says, "I'm trusting you to look after my family now, amigo."

"I'm probably the kind of person you can trust," Frisell replies simply.

A much younger Alonzo pats his cheek and flashes him an awkward smile. "See you in four years, amigo."

Then Alonzo shuffles over to the security guards who are waiting by the van.

The present-day, considerably more furrowed Frisell takes his disarmed Nokia out of his pocket and contemplates it for a long moment. Then he slips it back into the inner pocket of his old khaki jacket, briefly shaking his head.

Life is strange.

He did look after his informant Alonzo's family. He wished he could have done more, but Alonzo's massive online fraud scheme couldn't be overlooked. Frisell made sure his wife and daughter were safe from his enemies.

Completely unexpectedly, the technically inspired online fraudster and the young police officer had become friends. And Alonzo's early adoption of online embezzling opportunities had contributed significantly to Frisell's aversion to the internet.

Lukas Frisell looks around. Still not a soul in sight. This may be inner-city Stockholm, but his loitering underneath the opulent ornaments above the entrance to this building might soon draw the attention of some hypersensitive resident.

He hopes he doesn't have to wait too long.

His thoughts darken as he's transported back to a conversation he just had with a woman from his past. Who suddenly reappeared from the morass of suppressed memories.

He let Alonzo drive him to his present location from the Cavalry Barracks. His police instincts told him it would take infinite resources to identify them based on that short drive.

Almost a decade ago, Lukas and Sofia, one of his former students, had run into each other at Skansen after the end of the academic year. Some relative had secured her a rental contract in Djurgårdsstaden, two minutes' walk form Skansen, where she'd found a job as a vet. He suddenly remembered her naked body and above all, the tattoos wreathing around it.

The tattoos had faded considerably. But thankfully, Sofia herself still lived in Djurgårdsstaden. More than anything, he was curious about her split tongue. But it was just a regular tongue these days. Asking about plastic surgery had seemed superfluous. He'd only wanted one thing from her.

After digging deep, Sofia had been able dredge up an old address in Vasastan where some relative of her friend's had lived.

That's where Lukas Frisell is standing right now. Waiting.

The smell of horse chestnut has evaporated. Only the waiting remains.

It's a wait that involves a few strange moments of unfamiliar but unmistakable grief. Then a young man steps out through the front door. Frisell dashes over, managing to catch it.

In the same state of inexplicable but powerful grief, he walks up three flights of stairs. Rarely have his feet felt this heavy, not even when he was at his most malnourished in the woods. He'd had other sources of strength then.

It says "Eriksson" on the door. It should be the right place.

Frisell rings the doorbell; not a sound comes from inside. He waits a minute.

Somehow, he's still on the right side of the law. The way he sees it, his next step will be the most egregious. He rings the bell again and waits until the last reverberation of civilization has faded into silence.

Then he steps out into barbarism.

He pulls out his old lockpick and manages to pry the door open. He breathes in the darkness and slips inside.

It's not a big flat, and there's no whiff of diabolic stuffiness from the further reaches of it. But it's still clear that what Lukas Frisell quickly deems to be a turn-of-the-century two-bed is suffused with the smell of old lady. It's without a doubt the home of a widow.

What's more, it appears to be abandoned.

It's threadbare, dusty, dim. Frisell creeps though it with the wariness of a forest dweller. He finds nothing hidden, secret, concealed. And yet, he senses a recent presence.

People have been here. Not long ago. People have gathered here. In this flat.

In the far corner of one of the bedrooms, an old wardrobe turns out to contain what at first appears be a newer metal cabinet bolted to the floor. Frisell tries his lockpicks on the metal door—none of them are a match for the lock.

He pauses, composing himself, feeling one of the lockpicks really ought to fit. He's getting used to drilling down through his past. He tries again, slower this time. It takes a while, but then he hears the familiar click. He opens the metal door inside the old wooden one.

It's a disappointment. The cabinet's empty.

He illuminates the empty interior with the powerful, newly purchased torch he pulls out of one of the side pockets on his trousers. That's when he sees it.

In the top corner of the metal cabinet is a smaller compartment, a kind of strongbox. It's locked, and he can immediately tell it's a lock he won't be able to pick.

He grunts in frustration and is about to slam the metal door shut and leave when he spots a small balled-up piece of paper in the far back.

He picks it up. Smooths it.

It's a bill. He doesn't care what for. The only thing that interests him is the address: Midjegränd 13, Tomtjärla.

He slips the bill into his pocket and disappears. For real this time.

64

Shabir Sarwani studies his wounds in the mirror as he rides the lift in Farsta. It's the first time in a while he's been confronted with them so directly. The lift is the smallest he's ever been in; he's pressed up against the mirror and has no means of avoiding it.

On the whole, he looks insanely tired, pale, battered. There are cuts all over his body that keep reopening. He has a constant headache—and to what extent is his hearing damaged? There's an ominous ringing in his ears. Tinnitus?

He could really use a holiday.

Despite how cramped the lift is, he manages to pull on his red-and-yellow uniform jacket and adjust the gun he's stuck down the back of his trousers. He rings a door marked "Damnjanović" and studies the peephole for changes in light. When someone's clearly peering out, he calls out softly, "This is DHL. I need someone to sign for this package."

When the door opens a crack, Sarwani grabs it firmly and throws it wide open. Behind a sturdy woman, he catches a glimpse of a bedroom and a man snatching up his clothes and dashing away, out of his field of vision.

Sarwani pushes the woman aside, pulling his gun out as he chases after the man. Rubbish seems to have been strategically placed along the wall, and when he finally reaches the bedroom door, he glances in quickly to the left, spotting a balcony off the next room. But no people. He enters, wrestling his way through the clutter to the balcony, and sees a half-dressed man limping across the courtyard below and into an adjacent building.

For a moment, Sarwani considers hurling himself down after him. But perched on the railing, he has to acknowledge the miserable state he's in. Soberly and sensibly, he swings his legs back in, jumps down onto the balcony, and returns inside to talk to the woman.

She's still standing by the open front door, with her arms crossed over a flimsy summer dress that's not only rumpled but also on backward.

"Did I interrupt you and Slobodan in the middle of something, Vesna?" he asks without putting his gun away.

She just stares at him. There's open hate in her sharp gaze.

"Where did he go?" he continues. "What other hideouts does he have?"

The sturdy woman doesn't say a word. But her eyes continue to throw daggers.

"Why aren't you talking, Vesna? How do you figure silence will help you?"

"Like I would ever talk to an Arab," Vesna Damnjanović hisses.

Sarwani sighs deeply, sticks the gun back into the waistband of his trousers and says, "I'm actually from Afghanistan."

65

The tiny interview room is ridiculously crowded. Anton Lindberg is feeling slightly nauseous, has been ever since he stepped out of the cell down the hall. He's brought Ankan with him this time, and there's barely room for all of them to sit down around the interview table.

Ankan has only one job: to study Elias Shariq closely.

Lindberg keeps his secret trump card close to the vest as he leans in toward the pair on the other side of the table.

"I had a chat with Hassan. He knows nothing about this picric acid business. But he did find it, quote, 'interesting' that you've been using the gang's smuggling van for your private side hustle."

Lindberg isn't even looking at Elias Shariq; he's looking at Ankan. She nods briefly.

Lindberg continues: "Hassan's going to want to talk to you when you get to prison." There's silence. Nothing's said. Until Lindberg forges on: "There's also something very interesting about the fact that you've gone to such lengths to hide that your real name's Elias Eriksson. I suppose being half-Swedish is a bit of a problem if you want to be a gang member."

Lindberg shoots Ankan another glance, and she again nods briefly. He continues. "Thanks to various traffic cameras, we've been able to trace the route of the Hjulsta Gang's van through Stockholm on the night you were arrested, Elias Eriksson. On a couple of occasions, it got pretty close to an address in Vasastan. The one where your secret but real mother—Birgitta Eriksson, age seventy-four—resides."

The crisp gang lawyer comes off as slightly outmaneuvered when he half asks, half exclaims, "Are you seriously claiming my client stores explosives in his elderly mother's home?"

"Maybe he wouldn't if mummy dearest were there," Lindberg replies with a wry smile. "But he might if mummy dearest were in a nursing home." He turns to Ankan. She nods again.

Without another word, they leave.

* * *

In the car, Ankan says, "There was a very clear reaction when you mentioned his mother."

"I suppose we'll have to wait and see exactly what kind of reaction it was," Lindberg says, turning away from Odenplan to zigzag his way through the backstreets of Vasastan.

Ankan turns around and studies him thoughtfully. "How are you really doing, Anton?"

He just shakes his head. But Ankan's not that easily deterred. "You're not yourself. What's on your mind?"

When there's no response, she sighs briefly and changes the subject. "How much of what you said in there was true?" she asks.

"That he was christened Elias Eriksson once upon a time and that he has a mother by the name of Birgitta Eriksson, who had him late in life and now suffers from dementia."

"That's all?"

"The rest was intended as calibration," Lindberg says with a smile. "To help you adjust your aim before I asked the important question. Since you've become such a stellar judge of character lately."

"Because I'm dating, or what?"

"That's not the least of the reasons," Lindberg admits. "You seem to have some kind of precision radar switched on at all times."

"I suppose you have to as a woman on the dating scene," Ankan mutters.

They arrive at the right address. Lindberg parks right outside an entrance crowned with over-the-top ornamentation. Ankan's lockpick quickly gives access to the stairwell. They climb up three floors until they're standing before an unremarkable front door marked "Eriksson." Anton Lindberg has the search warrant in his hand, but when Ankan prepares to pick the lock and they realize the door's unlocked, he puts it back in his pocket. They simultaneously take out their guns, quietly pull the door open, and enter the flat, covering each other, calling out "Police!" as loudly as they can without announcing their presence to the entire building.

They systematically move from room to room. There's not a lot of them. Before long, the flat's been cleared.

Ankan pulls on latex gloves and sinks into a squat in the inner bedroom. She runs her index finger across the floor.

"Someone's been here very recently," she says.

Lindberg heads back out into the hallway, pulls the front door shut, and moves into the living room. Gun still raised.

On an old-fashioned mantel, a row of framed photographs is covered with a thin layer of dust. Lindberg glances at them in passing, noting an older wedding photo and a newer one, in which the groom is different but the bride the same. The bride also features in another picture, so old it's begun to peel, smiling broadly, alone in front of a temple in Palmyra, as text on it makes clear. It's almost certainly Birgitta Eriksson herself. Another picture, slightly yellow with age, shows a girl of about twelve with thick red hair and sharp green eyes sitting on Birgitta's lap—and then Anton Lindberg spots the last photograph in the row. After pulling on latex gloves, he picks it up. It's a picture of a ten-year-old boy with very faintly Arabic features.

It has to be a young Elias Eriksson, aka Elias Shariq.

"Here," Ankan calls out from the inner bedroom.

Lindberg puts the picture down and heads over. Ankan's standing in front of an old wardrobe. She opens the door, revealing a considerably newer metal cabinet inside, bolted to the floor and open a crack. They carefully open the steel door and spot some kind of secure compartment in the top right corner, securely welded to the inside of the cabinet.

"I know the type," Ankan says, pointing pensively at the strongbox.

"What do you mean you know it?" Lindberg asks. "That lock looks impenetrable."

"It's state of the art. None of the old lockpicks work. But I took a course a couple of months ago. And signed out a state-of-the-art lockpick. I have it here."

"Well, fuck me," Anton Lindberg says.

Ankan pulls out her impressive collection of lockpicks and selects the right one. She inserts it into the lock and gingerly finds her way through the lock's internal pins. At length, there's a click.

The sturdy little door opens.

Inside is a clear glass jar. In it, they can both make out two tiny grains of yellow swimming in a liquid.

"Picric acid," Anton Lindberg mumbles softly.

66

Eva Nyman is standing in front of a glass window, staring at a man in white protective clothing, moving about a dimly lit space. Only the eyes of the head forensic technician are visible.

"What's with the glass cage?" Nyman asks.

"It's necessary for our third order of business," the technician says, his voice muffled. "But let's start with the first one. You're certainly keeping us busy, Eva Nyman."

"I'd say it's the Terrorist Bomber who's keeping you busy, actually."

"First order of business: the flat in Vasastan. Yes, the yellow grains in the glass jar are picric acid. It's a highly volatile, explosive substance that can't be transported dry. Other than that, there were some signs of people having been in the flat recently. At least two different individuals, whose DNA we're now looking for. And there were faint indications that a third person may have been there just before your minions stumbled in. But that person left at most one footprint in the dust, and that has not been analyzed yet."

"Birgitta Eriksson has been in a dementia care home for over a year," Nyman says, mostly to herself. "The son clearly hasn't sold the flat, but rather, opted to use it as a kind of storage facility. And meeting place, I suppose."

"We're still processing the flat. I'll be in touch if we find anything else of note. We may have something to say about the bathroom. There are traces of an unknown acid in the bath. But don't hold your breath."

"I rarely do," Nyman mutters. "Next?"

The technician picks up something and lets it dangle beneath his white glove. It's black, circular, and severed.

"The ankle bracelet," the technician announces superfluously. "It took some doing, but we got it off the horse's leg. Our top electronics experts have worked all night to try to figure out how the bracelet was removed without the alarm going off, and subsequently attached to a police horse."

"Did they come up with anything?"

"It was taken offline with the aid of external electronics and then expanded through physical force. The swap from human to horse must have taken place inside the Cavalry Barracks just before the horse was taken out. Each step must have been executed with clinical precision while successfully avoiding detection. Our technicians were deeply impressed."

"But why a police horse?"

The technician pauses. His squinty eyes peer out of his white overalls with evident surprise.

"Surely you'd have be completely humorless not to see why?"

"Humorless?" Nyman exclaims.

"Well, disregarding the many serious legal aspects, you have to agree it's riotously funny that the bracelet was on a rearing police horse."

Nyman makes no reply. Pausing, she manages to slow down her frantic internal tempo. And then she sees it. It actually is hilarious. She smiles briefly, then turns the tempo back up again.

"I've put a couple of guys on interviewing the employees at the Cavalry Barracks. So far, how it could have been pulled off remains a mystery."

For some unclear reason, the technician seems to be searching for the right words. At length, he says, "This kind of ankle bracelet has become very popular, both here and internationally. But if you comb through their well-concealed history, you can find a couple of previous examples, one in Norway, one in Finland, of the bracelet coming off. No one has any interest in announcing that fact to the world. Maybe you can call it the cost of doing business."

Nyman sighs and is suddenly struck by a flash of memory.

"But what about the Nokia?" she says. "The tracker you put inside it was supposed to be impossible to turn off?"

"There's a built-in loophole," the technician replies. "You can turn off just the right microswitch in a hard-to-access circuit. If you hit the wrong one, the alarm goes off immediately. It requires a lot of skill."

"And Lukas Frisell is supposed to have done all of this by himself while strolling down Sturegatan?"

"I have to assume he has a steady hand. Or he had an expert with him during his stroll. Either way, he must have had the assistance of at least two people inside the Cavalry Barracks."

Eva Nyman nods and shakes her head at the same time.

"So, let's move on to the third reason we're here," the technician continues, pulling out a drawer and carefully placing a letter on his workbench. Nyman can clearly see the typewritten, old-timey-sounding address: Chief Inspector Eva Nyman, NOD, Police HQ, Stockholm.

"It arrived by post," she says. "Letter number four. You nabbed it before I even had a chance to read it."

"And so far, we've found nothing that sets this one apart from the previous three. Other than that we got hold of it sooner this time. Before it could be contaminated."

Even though only his eyes are visible, the accusatory expression on the technician's face is clear.

"It's definitely the same typewriter," he continues. "The same paper, the same tone. It was sent from the Rosersberg terminal yesterday."

"So, nothing new whatsoever?"

"Well, the message, of course. But nothing else. Not until I've had a chance to study it under a microscope and run DNA tests and so on. Which is why we need this glass to keep us separated."

"And I really need the text before you do all of that."

"I'll snap a couple of pictures and send them over."

A large stationary camera is pulled in over the workbench. A couple of flashes go off. The technician fiddles with a plastic-covered computer for a while, and then Nyman's phone dings.

She reads the text. When she walks away, her face has gone white as a sheet.

* * *

Sonja Ryd is standing in the late-morning sun on Inedalsgatan, five hundred yards from the station. She unlocks her iPad and changes the view from the map with the red lines to the log. She turns on a filter that shows a list of locations where Lukas Frisell stopped for more than five minutes during the time he wore the ankle bracelet. It's a long list.

But this was where he'd been when she called him in to talk about the symbol. The circle inside the circle. A conversation that had eventually made him both pale and upset. After that, Ryd had made the fatal mistake of giving him an hour's respite to collect himself and have a think. The memory of how he used that hour is still enough to block her breathing. She did two straight hours in the gym at five o'clock in the morning to punish herself.

He hadn't just been here when she'd called him in. He'd gone back here afterward too. To this exact address. And fifteen minutes later, he'd driven away from here in a car. It ought to be possible to track that car. It may have been a taxi, because it stopped exactly where taxis pull over at Stureplan.

A short flight of stairs at the address on Inedalsgatan leads down to a nondescript basement entrance with a mail slot in the door. She knocks. Nothing happens. She gets out her lockpick and makes quick work of the lock. She opens the door and steps into a simple workshop. There are a few broken bicycles, an old transformer, a couple of paint-stained chairs, and a table on which hammering and sawing has clearly taken place. A handful of vises of various sizes are attached along the short ends of the table. But there's no dust, no sign that the workshop has been abandoned or recently used. On the contrary, it simply seems very clean.

Maybe too clean.

Through the window facing the street, Ryd sees a pair of women's feet walking by out on the pavement, but nothing else. And yet, she can feel it.

She's trained in policing and philosophy. She doesn't believe in anything that has even a whiff of the supernatural to it. But suddenly, she's remarkably certain it was in this humble workshop that Lukas Frisell's escape had been planned, however it was carried out.

Just then, her phone dings. She reads the text: *Group meeting asap in Waiting Hall. Letter 4. Eva.*

67

When Sonja Ryd bursts into the Waiting Hall, the rest of the Nova Group are already there. She slides in next to Ankan. Without a word, Eva Nyman turns on the projector, which hurls an endless loop of typewritten words onto the wall. True to habit, she reads the fourth letter aloud:

> *This is no longer a warning, you soulless progeny of lost meaning. By now, you know what I can do, how easily duped you are. You're all so alike, all of you sitting there with your mobile phones, willingly selling your souls and even more willingly letting yourselves be brainwashed. You know what awaits you, and yet you do nothing; and yet life is allowed to go on as before; and yet the big betrayal is allowed to go unpunished. And now you also know that the home of the death birds will be flambéed in its own kerosene, transformed into the ruins of destruction, on Mother's Day, as a reminder of what awaits us all, not least he who betrays most deeply. Holy wrath is already washing over the land that forgot the meaning of life. I've duped you before, twice over, and I will dupe you again. You won't begin to fathom how it could happen, but you will be made fools of before the entire world. This is no longer a warning.*

Eva Nyman lets the ending that is also the beginning fade away and just there for a minute. There's not a sound in the Waiting Hall.

"Comments?" she breathes out at last.

Sonja Ryd sits motionless, letting insight wash over her. But it's Shabir Sarwani who says what they're probably all thinking: "'*The home of the death birds will be flambéed in its own kerosene, transformed into the ruins of destruction, on Mother's Day.*' It's a fucking airport. The death birds that run on jet fuel—which is a type of kerosene—and make their home at the airport."

"And Mother's Day is tomorrow," Nyman adds.

"It doesn't have to be Arlanda; it could be Bromma too," Anton Lindberg says. "If they're keeping to Stockholm. Otherwise, it could be Västerås, Landvettter, any Swedish airport. Malmö—or why not Copenhagen? Or military airports for that matter?"

"Is the Terrorist Bomber really capable of blowing up a Nordic airport?" Ankan asks. "Not to mention a military one? That sounds . . . difficult."

"He's done difficult things before," Nyman says. "So we're going to take this extremely seriously. Raised threat levels at all Swedish airports, with extra focus on the biggest one by far and the most symbolically important one, Arlanda—that's already been taken care of. Like I said, Mother's Day's tomorrow."

"He's going to blow up Arlanda," Sarwani says darkly.

"They're a terrorist cell," Lindberg says. "It's not a man, not a 'he'—it's an entire cell. And we have one of them in detention."

"And how much have you managed to get out of him so far?" Nyman asks coolly.

"It's not about that. I can put the screws to him."

"How many words has he said to date?" Nyman insists.

"Fine, zero," Lindberg admits. "But I found his lair anyway. I caught him red-handed. Let me put the screws to Elias fucking Shariq until he vomits the damn truth."

"You're going to smack him over the head with a statute book, are you?" Nyman asks. Linberg makes no reply. He shakes his head. Just sits there.

"What else does the letter say?" Nyman asks finally.

"That he's shown us up twice," Ryd says. "The first time must be Odenplan; the second, when he made his spectacular escape."

"If that's the case, Lukas Frisell really is the author of the letters," Nyman says. "Is he making a comeback as our main suspect? Is that why he escaped?"

"Or so he can go lie on a nudist beach on Tenerife," Anton Lindberg puts in. "Forget idealism, he just got sick of the woods. He wanted to sunbathe and get laid."

"What else would the second time he duped us be referring to?" Ryd asks.

"We're perpetually duped," Lindberg mutters. "I highly doubt Elias Shariq-Eriksson would take orders from someone like Frisell."

"If he's Frisell's hitman, he gets paid," Ryd counters. "He doesn't have convictions, or morals, but he understands money. He takes his marching orders from the money."

"All right, settle down, everybody," Eva Nyman says, standing up. "We were given forty-eight hours, but that was before an escape-proof Frisell gave us the slip. We have about thirty of those hours left. Any number of units are chomping at the bit to take this case away from us. We haven't been fired yet, despite the debacle with Frisell, but it's only a matter of time."

"Mother's Day," Sarwani says out of the blue. "Have his sights been set on Mother's Day this whole time? Does Mother's Day hold any specific significance? What about Elias's own mother?"

"Unless he's blowing something up right now, we should at least have until tomorrow to get closer to a solution," Nyman continues. "And the one solid lead we have right now is Börje Sandblom."

"It's not much of a lead, though," Ryd says. "Not unless there's a closer connection between Frisell and Sandblom than that they're both survivalists who lived relatively near each other for many years. That being said, it's only sixty miles from Frisell's dwelling to Kallfors. If Börje lives south of Kallfors, and thereby closer to Frisell, somewhere on the border between Uppland and Gästrikland, they might even have run into each other in the woods. Sandblom might have told him about Merplast's environmental crimes, and it fit right in with what Frisell was already working on. He incorporated it into his larger plan. We should have taken his talk of plans more seriously."

"And if we add Elias Eriksson as his hitman and picric acid smuggler, that's a complete cell," Lindberg notes. "Frisell's the brains, an enthusiastic Sandblom does the heavy lifting, and Eriksson takes care of the killing and smuggling. Together, they're the Terrorist Bomber Trio."

"But that means Frisell must have planned it all from his forest lair," Ankan says. "Or, more specifically, from his 'writing den.' And I've been talking to IT experts who say that if that's the case, he must really know how to wipe a computer. His own document, his 'book'—which is so close to nature it sucks you right in, take my word for it, and in which I haven't detected the slightest hint of any underlying hate—goes back eight years. Plus, are we saying Sandblom did Merplast all by himself? He installed the bomb in Rikard Albrektsson's office, watched him through a pair of binoculars, and pushed the remote detonator at exactly the right moment? Because the other two were both behind bars at the time."

"Perfectly possible," Lindberg replies. "He's the one with the local knowledge. That's the one attack he could execute, working according to Frisell's detailed instructions."

"I'm not sure all the pieces are in the right place yet," Eva Nyman says, "but it's good to look at things from a slightly different perspective. Can we uncover some demonstrable connection between Frisell and Sandblom? It would be in your videos if it's anywhere, I imagine, Sonja. Have you gone through them all?"

"Not personally," Ryd admits. "It's eighteen hours in all. But my assistants have. They're working on putting together a list of observations as we speak."

"Great," Nyman says. "I mean, how many lectures on survivalism were given in Sweden around that time? Shouldn't it have attracted at least some of the potential preppers in the area?"

"That's a good thought," Ryd says. "And there was the matter of attendance lists too. When I talked to the university earlier, they didn't think they'd still have attendance lists from that long ago. But apparently, there's a chance."

"Okay, so we all have things to get on with. Because we just had word from the Gästrikland police: they may have a lead on our mysterious Börje Sandblom."

The Waiting Hall stares at Eva Nyman. She says, "A helicopter's waiting for Anton and Ankan. You have ten minutes. It's likely going to be another over-nighter. You're going to get this guy—are we clear?"

68

A group of uniformed officers are waiting for them in a field outside Kallfors. The helicopter briefly circles the Merplast factory. Repairs are seemingly already underway, and a lorry is rolling in through the gates, bringing a delivery.

Life goes on. As does microplastics.

On the other side of the rotor blade tornado, Anton Lindberg and Ankan are greeted by a large, familiar woman in uniform.

"Hi, Ulla," Lindberg says with a nod, extending his hand. Inspector Ulla Hultqvist shakes it and cuts to the chase: "We've had reports that a man matching Börje Sandblom's description has been sighted in Baton Rouge."

"I'm sorry, where?" Lindberg exclaims.

"It's a commune located in the swamps northwest of Kallfors."

"A swamp commune by the name of Baton Rouge?"

"I suggest we head on out there; I can fill you in on the way."

* * *

No less than four vehicles—three patrol cars and a police van—drive in close formation toward Baton Rouge. Lindberg and Ankan are in the back of one of the patrol cars, with the unflappable Ulla Hultqvist in the passenger seat in front of them. Her alto voice is so stentorian she doesn't need to turn around to make herself heard. But Lindberg's wondering whether their intrepid driver might not be risking hearing loss. At least in his right ear.

"Baton Rouge is home to a mix of green wavers, marijuana enthusiasts, moonshiners, antivaxxers, and an American trailer park. The Libertarian founder, Tosh Larson, felt the area reminded him of the marshes of Louisiana, so he named it after the capital of the poorest state in the United States. Earlier today, a defector from Baton Rouge identified Börje Sandblom as someone who visits the commune regularly."

"Do you have a lot of communes like this in Gästrikland?" Ankan asks. Ulla Hultqvist chuckles.

"Don't underestimate the number of people who want to escape civilization," she says. "For many different reasons."

"Last time we were here, we asked you," Lindberg says, "and I'll ask you again now: Do you keep any sort of tabs on the preppers in the area?"

"I told you no then and unfortunately, I have to do so again now. We've considered it, but the woods here are enormous, and we can't keep track of everything that goes on in them."

The police caravan turns down a smaller forest road. The sky has darkened; there's rain in the air, and yesterday's downpour still covers the fields to the extent that they're no longer really fields. They're reminiscent of Vietnamese rice paddies. The caravan has reached the swamps. The road narrows further.

Just as they pass a hand-painted sign that says "Baton Rouge," the skies open.

* * *

By the time the caravan approaches a settlement that looks like something halfway between the American South and a hippie commune, rain is pouring down. Most of the idiosyncratic homes were once caravans, portable homes that have been rendered stationary with the aid of amateur architecture and by the merciless passage of time.

A scrawny man in a motorcycle vest steps out through the curtain of rain, approaching the arriving police. The precipitation is blurring the people behind him, but it's clear they're his bodyguards. At least a couple of shotguns hang across a chest here and there.

More than one safety has likely been disengaged inside the four police vehicles too. Lindberg and Ankan have definitely done so. When they climb out with their guns behind their backs, they find it hard to take in what they're seeing.

Ulla Hultqvist walks straight up to the scrawny man, nodding and saying, "Tosh. This is a proper shit day you've brought us."

The man's wrinkled face smooths out. It's probably his idea of a smile. "Ulla. To what do I owe the honor?"

She holds up a large, laminated photograph and takes a few firm steps forward. The scrawny Tosh wipes the rain from his eyes, studies the photo, and shakes his head in bewilderment.

"He goes by the name of Börje Sandblom," Hultqvist says, "but that might be an alias. He's been sighted up here a couple of times."

"No one keeps count of the number of dwellings here," Larson says, spreading his hands. "We all believe strongly in personal freedom and integrity. If someone has been 'sighted' here, you might have a hard time finding him."

"On the other hand, we all know that you—especially you—are very wary of strangers. Just look at this welcoming committee."

Tosh Larson's face folds into a smile once more. He calls his men over. Up close, it turns out there's only three of them. Earlier, behind the curtain of rain, there could have been considerably more.

Lindberg notices Ankan taking a step forward to read their facial expressions as they have a look at Börje Sandblom's face. They all shake their heads, but possibly not in the same way. Lindberg realizes he has no idea.

"We're going to go door to door and talk to every resident here," Ulla Hultqvist says. "Are you going to try to stop us?"

Tosh Larson crosses his arms, but he also signals his acquiescence, and he and his men back away into the deluge and are swallowed up by it.

Ulla Hultqvist gathers her officers. They form a circle, facing in, like a football team before kick-off. Hultqvist begins to speak. "As far as I know, only a few of these people are properly registered here, which means we have no idea what we're going to find. In other words, no one walks about alone out here. We have each other's backs. There are sixteen of us. We're going to split into two teams of eight. One team starts from the bottom, the other from the top. I suggest we split the Stockholmers up, so there's an expert on this case in each team.

A gap between Ankan and Lindberg breaks the circle. Then the officers divide into pairs. Lindberg pairs up with Hultqvist in the bottom team; Ankan, with a muscular local constable in the top one.

Ankan and Lindberg exchange a long look as the eight officers that make up the top team move out. Then Lindberg's eyes turn toward the dark sky. The rain looks like it's shooting out of the blanket of clouds. He runs a hand over his wet brow.

It's going to be an interesting afternoon.

69

The sound of a car squealing to a stop cuts through Sonja Ryd's thoughts. Blue lights are still flashing around her. Then they're switched off. The uniformed officer who looks back at her from the front seat has been unofficially ordered to drive fast. Which he has done, to Ultuna, on the outskirts of Uppsala. She gives him a nod and climbs out.

She has an overnight bag with her. She fears this will take time. But it may also be pivotal.

She walks toward the central administration building of the Swedish University of Agricultural Sciences. The older lady behind the reception desk isn't really supposed to be there since it's the weekend, but Sonja Ryd has talked her into coming in.

The woman is quietly reading a book. The activity level is low at SUAS today. It's Saturday afternoon, not much going on.

The old lady puts her book down, pulls her reading glasses toward the tip of her nose, and studies the new arrival.

"I presume you are . . ."

"Sonja Ryd," Ryd says. "And you're Vanja Pärn?"

The old lady nods and stands up.

"I'm sorry to make you come in on a Saturday," Ryd says.

"I needed to finish my John LeCarré anyway," Pärn says with a warm smile. "And I live nearby, so don't worry about it. I understand you need access to old attendance lists?"

"From public lectures on crisis preparedness given during the 2013–2014 academic year."

"I have a vague memory of those, yes," Vanja Pärn says. "But it's highly unlikely those attendance lists would have been saved. This could be an exception, however, because the public lectures were funded from a more central budget. Follow me, Sonja."

They slowly wander across the sparsely populated campus. Pärn turns to Ryd and says, "And I was given to understand you need overnight accommodation too?"

"That depends on how quickly I can go through the archives, but yes, please. If possible."

"I think you're going to need it," Pärn says, holding a key out to Ryd, who's not sure she likes those words.

That feeling only grows stronger when Pärn pulls open the door to the old basement archive and coaxes a reluctant fluorescent overhead light to flickering life. It lights up shelf after shelf filled with thick old folders.

"I know," Pärn says glumly. "The archive has not been treated kindly since I retired. But if your attendance lists still exist, this is where they'd be."

While Ryd is still staring at the shelves, the old lady puts a map into her hands. "To help you find your way home tonight. And here's my extra ID, so you can get in wherever you need to on campus tomorrow, Sunday. You'll need it to access the library, for example."

Sonja Ryd thanks her warmly. The first thing she does once she's alone to try to get an overview. The older documents are on the right, the newer on the left. She finds enough folders from the 2010s there to settle for that side. A few of the folders are neatly dated, but some lack any kind of timestamp, and the spines of some others are labeled with indecipherable combinations of letters.

The word *Sisyphean* doesn't even begin to describe it.

At first, she sits with her legs crossed; then she leans back against a shelf; and eventually she's lying down on her side, with her head on a stack of folders. She sneezes nonstop, sensing that her insides are now entirely coated with old paper dust.

What stops her from giving up is that she's always so close. She keeps finding old exams and attendance lists jumbled together, with dates that are almost in the right range, fairly legible names on reasonably well-preserved sheets of paper. And yet, she continues to strike out. And the thought that she'd be more useful elsewhere is increasingly crowding out the search.

In the end, she can't take it anymore. She steps out into air that has never felt fresher, unfolds Vanja Pärn's map, and sets off through the May evening, toward the residential part of the campus.

She finds it and is soon sprawled on a sofa, chewing a ready-made salad she brought with her and guzzling boxed wine. Her mind wanders. She pictures Lukas Frisell and is increasingly convinced she's overlooked something.

The sun hasn't even set yet outside the window. This would have been a wonderful time to go over everything again. Really collect her thoughts before Mother's Day tomorrow. But she just can't. She's too exhausted. She can feel her eyelids closing; she really can't stay awake. She'll have to get up early tomorrow instead. She thought she was more stubborn than this.

She should at least brush her teeth. If only to get all the dust she hasn't already swallowed out. Instead, she washes it down with more red wine. Then, her phone rings. She pushes up into a sitting position. Tries to focus her eyes on the screen. Reads the name. Pulls herself together. Answers.

On the other end, Eva Nyman says without preamble, "I'm in a meeting with several government ministers right now, Sonja. We're taking a five-minute break. From a heated discussion about whether to close all of Arlanda tomorrow. They seem to be leaning toward not doing it."

"Well, maybe the threat's too vague . . ."

"Closing the country's biggest airport is an enormous undertaking," Eva Nyman says. "I get where they're coming from. But my inner police officer is screaming in protest. The part of me that has sworn to serve and protect, as the Americans have it."

"Are we still on the case?" Ryd asks breathlessly. "Did they take it from us?"

"They want to get rid of Nova, but they need us. We're sitting on all the knowledge, and they know it. So, a compromise. A mixed management team on site at Arlanda, starting at midnight. Should I be on it?"

"Are you asking me if you should be part of the management team?"

"The meeting's starting. You're the only one I trust, Sonja. I personally feel I'd be more useful somewhere closer to the investigation. Yes or no?"

Ryd answers immediately, without hesitation. "Yes, Eva. One hundred percent yes. We need you there."

"Thank you," Nyman replies, unexpectedly warmly.

Ryd thinks she can hear the voice of the minister for justice in the background. And is that other voice the prime minister's? Eva Nyman ends the call.

Sonja Ryd stares at her phone for a minute, realizing she just spent what little was left of her strength. She falls back onto the sofa without taking her clothes off. Then, against her will, she falls asleep immediately.

70

It's been a long day. Lights have been turned on and back off in the strange houses in Baton Rouge. The swamp smell, the stink of bog, of wetland, has faded into the background by now, naturalized. And no one, absolutely no one, has seen Börje Sandblom in Baton Rouge.

Unlike in the night, now the rain has stopped falling. But the road between the houses remains as muddy as it is waterlogged.

Anton Lindberg and Ulla Hultqvist knock on the door of one of the houses near the middle of the commune. There's no answer, but the door's ajar.

They enter.

The shotgun that greets them is of an unbelievable caliber. If it were fired, it would hurl both Lindberg and Hultqvist through the flimsy walls, scattering them across the area like pink PVC pipe.

"Ragnar," Hultqvist says calmly, slowly putting her gun back in its holster. "I didn't know you'd moved out here."

"They said there would never be any coppers out here," the thin-haired man says, his rifle trembling. His mouth seems stuck halfway through a yawn. It's obvious he's onto something. Something hard and heavy.

Lindberg had almost begun to relax after working his way through a number of shacks with a feeling that anything could happen. Very rarely over the past few years has he thought so much and so often about his daughters.

And then this happens. A shaky, unpredictable junkie with a shotgun that could knock over a train carriage.

Lindberg knows he could take him out. He might be able to get his gun up and aim it at that almost yawning mouth before Ragnar could react. But that would require a kind of precision he's hardly capable of in this moment.

"Ragnar," booms an alto voice that's not primarily aimed at Ragnar, but rather at Anton. Ulla Hultqvist follows it up with a clear, two-handed lowering motion.

Lindberg finally gets it. He carefully puts the safety back on his gun and lets it disappear into the back of his trousers. Then he holds his hands up in front of him.

When he looks up again, Ragnar's no longer holding a shotgun. Instead, Ulla Hultqvist has taken possession of it and is ejecting shells as thick as a man's wrist. She looks larger and more imposing than ever. Almost superhuman.

Without looking at Lindberg, she hands the enormous rifle to him. He takes it, realizing he's barely strong enough to hold it.

Hultqvist tosses the shells out through the front door. They splash into the mud outside. Then she holds the photograph of Börje Sandblom out to Ragnar.

"You know him, don't you?"

The fact that Ragnar can speak with his continually yawning mouth is nothing short of a miracle. But despite the impediment, he says, "I have no idea who that is."

"But you've seen him around Baton Rouge, right?"

"Bloody hell. Yes," Ragnar says. "I thought you were here to nick my dealer. I feel calmer now. He's coming on Thursday."

Ragnar stares at them and at the picture of Sandblom. He seems to realize he's said something fundamentally wrong.

"Not this bloke, no. I've only seen him around. You know. But it was a pretty long time ago now. I think.

"Where did you see him?" Hultqvist asks.

"Up at Ugutz's. Fuck, did I say that aloud too?"

"We know Ugutz is his friend," Hultqvist lies smoothly, staring sternly at Lindberg, not Ragnar. Lindberg realizes the best thing he can do is shut up.

"Oh good," Ragnar says, shaking so hard the wind whistles past his open jaw. "Then I haven't put my foot in it."

"If you tell me where Ugutz lives, I'll give you back your rifle," Ulla Hultqvist says with a smile.

"Two houses over," Ragnar snorts. "But he's not there now. Not Friday–Saturday." "Thanks, Ragnar. Do you know what Ugutz and this man get up to when they get together?"

"Fuck? Get high? Sunday school? I don't bloody know. But they seemed pretty damn tight about six months ago. He hasn't been here since. Now give me my rifle."

"Soon," Hultqvist says, taking the shotgun from Lindberg. "So, Ugutz is coming back tomorrow, Sunday?"

"He's usually here when I wake up, yeah. I think he works in some bar in Gävle on drunk nights."

Ulla Hultqvist nods slowly and exits with Ragnar's shotgun under her arm. Lindberg follows.

"But you said you were giving me my rifle back," Ragnar shouts.

"You can have it when you show me a license," Hultqvist says, shoving the door shut. She blows out a breath. "I guess we have to come back tomorrow morning. I was really hoping not to."

"And don't forget Thursday," Lindberg says, allowing himself to relax.

"Thursday?"

"When Ragnar's dealer's paying a visit."

71

It's not just Mother's Day. It's also Sunday. The entire university is unstaffed. Sonja Ryd runs on autopilot all the way down to a vending machine she noticed the night before. She gets in with the help of Vanja Pärn's ID and eats a quick, exceedingly artificial breakfast before returning to her basement.

It seems to envelop her. She can feel herself literally desiccating. Time goes by monstrously slowly and at the same time far too quickly. After all, this is the day when the home of the death birds will be flambéed in their own kerosene.

In the end, she finds a folder with old attendance lists from the year in question. They're jumbled together, but eventually she locates the right date, and pulls out the attendance list from Frisell's public lecture about "Health and Medicine in Isolation."

Suddenly she can't breathe. This must be the list she glimpsed in the recording. She lets it sit on top of a three-foot stack of old folders for a minute. Then she takes a deep breath and lunges at it.

Unfortunately, it's a list of signatures, not neatly printed names. Half of the names are illegible; the other half mean nothing to her.

Until she reaches the bottom of the page. There, she spots a powerful signature that she can decipher with nearly one hundred percent certainty.

It almost definitely says Börje Sandblom.

The supposed survivalist who protested most vociferously against the pollution caused by Merplast in Kallfors—the man with only two fingers on his left hand—did in fact attend Lukas Frisell's lecture, during which he introduced the symbol of a circle within a circle.

Until now, Ryd has deliberately ignored Sandblom for the simple reason that she hasn't for a second believed he was the Terrorist Bomber. But something about those two fingers suddenly rings a vague bell.

She opens the pictures of Sandblom from the protests in Kallfors and studies the large, red-faced, perpetually worked-up man, but she's still not satisfied.

Regardless, the connection between him and Frisell is established. And now, she remembers something else. From the Facebook page "Fun With

Farming." She finds her saved pictures from there and takes a closer look at the corna sign in one of the party pictures where Frisell is flanked by two women.

Then, she curses herself.

Börje Sandblom, hidden behind the others with only his hand visible, isn't doing the corna sign; that's just what his hand looks like. She should have connected the dots sooner. Her prejudice against Sandblom has led her astray.

And he was definitely in the audience when a circle was drawn inside a circle on the whiteboard. At this point, she has to admit that quite a few things point to him being the Terrorist Bomber.

Or a member of the Terrorist Bomber Trio. Ryd calls Nyman.

"Börje Sandblom attended Frisell's public lectures."

"Excellent," Nyman exclaims. "And we should have him in custody soon. He has a friend in some kind of commune in Gästrikland. Ankan and Anton are still trying to pin down the friend. He'll hopefully arrive sometime this morning. He most likely knows where Sandblom lives."

"All right," Ryd says, experiencing a feeling of emptiness. This was what she came to SUAS for. Her work here is done.

"I'm sending Shabir up to join them. There'll probably be a raid before the end of the day," Nyman continues. "He'll take the same helicopter as me."

"As you, when you go to . . . ?"

"Yes," Nyman cuts in. "I took your advice. I'm going to be part of the management team at Arlanda. And you're going to drive straight up to Gästrikland, Sonja, aren't you, so you're there when they nick Börje Sandblom? An unmarked car is waiting for you at the police station on Svartbäcksgatan in Uppsala."

There's nothing left to do here. Sonja Ryd really doesn't have any reason to stay at SUAS. But even so, she hesitates. Something inside her is telling her she's not done yet.

"I'll be in touch," she says, ending the call.

72

Ryd doesn't drive up to Gästrikland. But she does leave the basement, moving over to the university library instead, to a deserted corner, where she manages to collect her thoughts and take a wide-angle view of the situation.

She goes back to the moment Frisell decided to leave the Nova Group and make them all look like idiots. Evidently, he'd decided he needed to be able to escape before the ankle bracelet was even put on his leg. Not that he would escape, necessarily, but that he needed to be able to, to have the option.

Why?

Sonja Ryd returns to the strange feeling she had during her exasperating interviews with Frisell, the feeling that he was interviewing her, not the other way around. What was that feeling?

He'd allowed himself to be caught.

Lukas Frisell had bloody let them catch him in his dwelling. He'd let himself be caught after Eva Nyman told him about the letters and that he was a suspect. He had to know what that meant. And he'd found out more and more as the interviews progressed, from her, from Sonja Ryd. Maybe it had slowly dawned on him that the perpetrator—who was pointing a finger at him—was to be found in his past. She could have sworn he didn't know who it was—she did trust her interview skills and gut that much, despite everything—but he'd sensed that he'd eventually connect the dots, and when that happened, he'd intended to take care of it himself, on his own, without Nova, without NOD, without the police.

That's scenario one: Frisell had waited until he knew who the perpetrator was and he had the opportunity to go after him.

Scenario two is more difficult.

Scenario two is that Lukas Frisell is the Terrorist Bomber after all. He'd certainly duped them with that ankle bracelet—what was to say he hadn't been duping them all along? The fourth letter did go on and on about "duping" people.

But the Frisell Ryd has gotten to know is a laconic person, he'd never use the flowery, apocalyptic language in the letters—unless he was deliberately imitating himself, his old self. He'd written the letters like the Frisell Eva Nyman knew, remembered, and might have even had a bit of a crush on. They were supposed to speak directly to her. Then he'd kept an eye on the investigation from inside the detention facility, directing his accomplices remotely, ordering Elias Shariq to commit the necessary murders and Börje Sandblom to plant the bomb in Kallfors. That way, the suspicions against him had subsided.

Could that actually be possible?

But he couldn't have known in advance that he was going to be allowed to wear the new ankle bracelet, which was still being trialed.

Or could he?

Who was this remarkable technical genius Frisell had hired, and how had he found him so quickly, without the internet, without a phone? Wouldn't everything have to have been planned far in advance? Maybe the technical genius was someone who worked with the ankle bracelets? At the company that made them? Who knew how eager the Swedish Prosecution Authority was to test them?

She stays in the secluded corner of the deserted library for a while.

When did she let herself down? When did she stop believing Lukas Frisell was guilty? When did he pull the wool over her eyes in earnest? Was it in that bar? When he convinced her he didn't know about cash-free bars?

Duped, duped, duped.

His plan had been to seduce Sonja Ryd the way he'd once seduced Eva Nyman.

73

Shabir Sarwani has waited an hour. He has pins and needles in his legs, and the wounds on his face are oozing. But he knows Slobodan Jovanović is on his way to his mother's home in Rinkeby—witnesses he's managed to dig up from the depths of the criminal register have informed him he visits her every day.

But Slobodan has also made sure his mother can't be linked to him. The name on the front door of the flat is something completely different. Somali?

Sarwani's pressed against the door of the neighboring flat, his eye glued to the peephole. The neighbors have been sent away.

The wait is becoming literally painful. He has to stretch briefly to regain mobility. When he looks back up, the lift dings.

The person who steps out of it is a shaky version of the notorious sex offender and methamphetamine dealer. There can be no doubt he's sampled his own wares.

Sarwani bursts out, pushes the large man up against the lift door, shoves his gun against his teeth, and says, "I don't have time to mess around today, Slobodan. You were in the crowd at Odenplan, the man with the army-green backpack bumped you. What did he look like?"

Slobodan Jovanović has gone deathly pale. He's shaking so hard his teeth rattle against the barrel of the gun. And yet he manages to squeeze out, "But it wasn't a man."

"Explain yourself, right now."

For a brief moment, Jovanović's eyes roll back.

Don't you pass out now, Sarwani thinks. Don't you fucking pass out.

After a few critical seconds, both the irises and the noticeably enlarged pupils return to Slobodan Jovanović's visual organs.

"It was a fucking girl carrying that backpack."

"A girl?"

"A woman. With binoculars around her neck."

74

Duped, duped, duped, duped. Sonja Ryd is so upset she has to pace around the empty library.

If it's true, her life has entered a new era. If it's true, then Lukas Frisell has genuinely run circles around her. Never before has she been so thoroughly hoodwinked, so seduced by a hardened criminal. She refuses to believe it.

On a deeper level, she simply feels betrayed. Her thoughts brush against her former husband before she manages to turn them away. She doesn't drink in the morning, but right now she could certainly use a glass.

Still, she's stuck on the betrayal. Two things in the most recent letter were slightly different. One was the smug bragging about duping them. The other was the betrayal.

She returns to her seat in the library and opens the letter on her iPad. Does a close reading. At the end of the fourth letter, the betrayal seems to tear free of the climate question. A couple of phrases stick with her.

She separates them from their context: the big betrayal is allowed to go unpunished. And: he who betrays most deeply.

Betrayal, betrayal, betrayal.

A less attentive reader would logically link the betrayal to the climate. But a closer look suggests that there's a major personal betrayal too, underneath the larger, more abstract climate betrayal.

The voice of Frisell's ex-wife, Nina Strömblad, rings out in Ryd's mind, sounding slightly tinny, like a recording. A secret recording made by a uniformed officer with a wide ginger moustache: "You must have gone at it pretty hard up in Uppsala, Lukas."

Ryd just sits there for several minutes, staring vacantly straight ahead. She can feel her brain cells casting about wildly. Hunting for connections, links; hunting for a coherent narrative.

Then, she sees Frisell's face. Who knew she had so many versions of that face stored in her memory? It so rarely revealed any kind of strong feeling. But it had happened a few times, not least in connection with Nina. And a couple of other times. But he'd only paled noticeably once.

When was it?

She frantically searches her already overtaxed mind. Patches of color on his face . . . ? Shifting colors. Yes, that's it.

They'd been sitting next to each other in the conference room at the station. The coffee urn, the cinnamon buns, the panic button, the guard outside the door. The recording from the autumn of 2013 reflected on Frisell's face. How genuinely taken aback he'd seemed when he saw his younger self draw the circle inside the circle on the whiteboard.

Then what had happened?

They'd talked about it. Ryd had muted the video and returned to her side of the table. Frisell's pensive face had continued to reflect the recording, which had kept playing in front of him. Ryd had held up her phone, showing Ankan's photograph from the tree in Vasaparken. A circle carved inside a larger circle. Had something changed just then?

Yes, it bloody well had. It had been a three-stage rocket.

It had begun with Ryd getting an email from Eva Nyman while she was sitting at the table. Her first thought had been *"Don't let it be Säpo."* When she'd looked up, Frisell had looked even more shaken. She'd closed the laptop, noting how pale his face was once the colors disappeared.

That was when she'd made the mistake of giving him an hour's respite to come up for air. By then, he'd likely already made the decision to escape.

The phases of the shock must have been as follows: Stage one—Frisell watched himself draw a circle within a circle on the whiteboard. Stage two—he saw that the murderer had carved a circle within a circle into a tree in Vasaparken.

Stage three?

It had happened while Ryd was distracted, while she was reading the email from Nyman. In that moment, there was only one thing that could have caused the third stage of shock.

The video.

But she'd watched the rest of it. She'd seen the Lukas Frisell on the screen dismiss his audience with the words "See you next Friday, on the other side of the ruins of destruction."

Wasn't that the end of the recording? Was there more to it?

She opens a different app on her iPad and fast-forwards to the end of the video, when the younger Frisell says his concluding words. Then he starts to pack up his things. That lasts about a minute; from its position diagonally above, the camera captures the attendees filing out in front of Frisell's desk. You can't really see much of them.

After about a minute, the crowd thins out. A young woman with short red hair pauses briefly in front of Frisell but then moves on. Ryd pauses the video to study her. She can't quite make out her face from the camera's aerial view.

Ryd unpauses the video and notes that the woman places something on the desk, possibly a note. She tries to understand the context.

Just before the woman with the buzzcut leaves the lecture hall, she turns toward the camera. Ryd rewinds and plays the recording in slow motion until she can capture a relatively sharp still of the woman. Even from a distance, there's something about her eyes.

Sonja Ryd freezes. The fragment of a memory is rattling around inside her. She goes back to the Facebook page "Fun With Farming" yet again, opening one of her saved photos.

It shows six women at a café table in a SUAS hall of residence. Sitting on the left edge of the group, both inside and outside it, is a sad-looking woman. Her shaved hair is red, and she has sharply green eyes.

Isn't she the girl from the video? The one who, after his public lecture, placed what might be a note on the desk in front of Lukas Frisell?

Sonja Ryd sends both pictures to her phone, shoves the iPad into her backpack, and leaves.

75

For once, Sonja Ryd is lucky. One of her two phone calls is to Leif Stierna, Lukas Frisell's former colleague at SUAS, who tells her he's in the middle of an intense exam period and can therefore be found in his office, grading papers.

After some initial difficulty, Ryd manages to find her way there. The man who still looks like a scholar is ensconced in his ergonomic office chair with a red pen in his hand and a stack of exams in front of him.

Without a word, Ryd holds out her phone, on which she has isolated the woman with the short red hair and green eyes at the café table. Scholarly frown engaged, Leif Stierna studies the picture, nodding slowly.

"I think I remember her, yes," he says, scratching his goatee. "But I'm terrible with names."

"This was taken in October of 2013," Ryd says. "I would be eternally grateful if you could try to cast your mind back."

Stierna keeps scratching his beard. Then he leans back and says, slightly more tentatively, "There was something very, dare I say, fiery about her. I seem to recall her suddenly shaving off a thick mane of ginger hair. But she wasn't one of ours; she was a vet, I think, did wildlife management or some such. But I don't remember her name."

"Do you know if she had anything to do with Lukas Frisell?"

"Can't say that I do," Stierna says. "But he was a bit of a Casanova back then . . ." And that's all Sonja Ryd manages to get out of him. She pauses outside his door, wondering if her second call, the one to Vanja Pärn, might have already born fruit.

Only then does the penny drop. The first time she saw the picture of the sad woman with the shaved head, sitting with the six other women around the café table in the SUAS hall of residence, during her visit to see city planner Jonna Carlgren in Södertälje, she'd thought she recognized her. And the reason she recognized her was that she'd just seen her. In an earlier picture, she was one of two women flanking Frisell in a party picture, only her hair had been completely different then.

She opens the picture again on her phone. One of the women has brown stubble on her head, tattoos all over her body, and a strange, split tongue. The other has a flaming red mane of hair—and her green eyes are positively devouring Frisell.

The flaming red hair is still there on the head of the woman moping on the edge of the group of her fellow vet students. But by then it's been shaved very short—and despite her obvious melancholy, she's surrounded by a strange kind of aura, one which Sonja Ryd can't quite put her finger on. The autumn of 2013 and spring of 2014, respectively. She's going to have to look up the exact dates later.

She walks through the hallways of SUAS. She's onto something now—she can feel it.

One-time receptionist Vanja Pärn is waiting for her at reception, as agreed. She smiles at Ryd and asks, "Did you sleep well in your overnight flat?"

"Too well, thank you," Ryd says, returning the smile. Then she takes out her phone and shows her the photograph. Vanja Pärn adjusts her reading glasses, taking her time, turning the picture this way and that. But in the end, she says, "Yes, Elin Eriksson."

Sonja Ryd sucks in a breath and repeats, "Elin Eriksson?"

"Yes," Vanja Pärn replies. "Veterinary student. Quit in the spring of 2014, right before graduation. Highly unnecessary."

"What does 'quit' mean?" Ryd asks. Shrugging, Vanja Pärn replies, "She dropped out. I don't recall the exact circumstances, but Elin was a top student, so it was very unexpected. I mean, really intelligent. I seem to remember trying to talk her into finishing her degree."

"Are you sure you don't remember, Vanja? Dropping out so close to graduating sounds remarkably dumb. Unless there were exceptional circumstances. Which I imagine the university would have been aware of."

Ryd can sense Pärn's initial openness fading.

"It was something personal," she says reticently. "She didn't want to cause a scandal."

"A scandal?" Ryd repeats, already aware that's as much as Vanja Pärn's going to tell her.

"I'm sorry, I don't remember. Elin probably didn't expand on it."

"But you tried to stop her? Persuade her not to drop out? Despite this scandal?"

Vanja Pärn shakes her head very slowly and starts packing up her things.

"Please, Vanja," Ryd says, gingerly putting a hand on the old receptionist's arm.

Pärn pauses. Stands there for a moment. Staring out into the void.

Ryd continues: "If there was talk of a 'scandal,' that almost has to mean a professor was involved, doesn't it?"

Pärn is eyeing Ryd now. It's clear the gears in the former receptionist's head are grinding hard. "Maybe. Possibly."

Maybe, possibly Ryd's next move is rash. She makes the somewhat unprofessional decision to ask, "Was it Lukas Frisell?"

And with that, some kind of line is crossed for Vanja Pärn. The gaze that meets Sonja Ryd's is suddenly of the unswervingly loyal kind.

On the other hand, that gaze speaks louder than a thousand words. Her phone rings; it's Eva Nyman. Ryd declines the call.

76

There are only two police cars in Baton Rouge this Sunday. But every officer except Ankan and Anton Lindberg is considerably more heavily armed than the day before.

The cars are concealed enough not to prompt an approaching Ugutz to turn around and initiate a dangerous high-speed chase.

They've waited for hours. Ankan's trying to bring a sleeping leg back to life, when the eccentric Tosh Larson raises a hand up in the lookout spot where he seems to spend most of his waking time.

"Car approaching," Ulla Hultqvist's deep alto voice translates. She has taken up position on a tree stump right next to the entrance to Baton Rouge, holding an MP5 as though it were a toy. The rest of her people are stationed farther up the road, at the edge of the commune.

Lindberg and Ankan place themselves on either side of the road, about thirty feet out from Hultqvist. A tank might be able to get past the trio, but probably not many other types of vehicles.

They hear the car before they see it. Because the entrance to Baton Rouge is preceded by a sharp bend, they only spot the aggressively accelerating vehicle when it's no more than thirty feet away.

Lindberg and Ankan step out onto the muddy road, meeting in the middle, right hands raised. But the car's going too fast, wheels spinning wildly in the slippery mud. Ankan and Lindberg throw themselves off the road in opposite directions.

Hultqvist steps out into the road, leveling her MP5 at the car.

It skids to a stop just feet from her. She can see the driver's hands clearly raised as he climbs out.

It's a young man with a Middle Eastern appearance, who freezes with his hands in the air. Ulla Hultqvist bellows, "Keep your hands where I can see them. Who are you?" The driver is very pale.

He finally blurts out, "My name's Shabir Sarwani. I think I just ran over my colleagues."

77

Sonja Ryd's back in the library. Elin Eriksson's personal identity number was still in the SUAS database, and with the help of the resources available in the office at Stockholm's Police HQ, Ryd has managed to dig up some interesting information.

Elin's registered as living abroad, has a younger with a criminal record and a mother with an address in Vasastan.

That all sounds far too familiar to have any chance of slipping past Sonja Ryd.

Because wasn't it in Vasastan Ankan and Lindberg just broke into a flat and found traces of picric acid? And wasn't their suspect Elias Shariq's real name Elias Eriksson? And wasn't he the late-born son of the now senile Birgitta Eriksson?

Ryd opens the report on Lindberg and Ankan's Vasastan raid. Among the technicians' photographs, one of a framed picture on an old-fashioned mantel catches her attention.

Ryd zooms in on the picture, which is of a girl of about twelve with flowing red hair and razor-sharp green eyes. Then, she pulls up the still from Frisell's lecture, the picture of the ginger woman with the shaved head and remarkable eyes, who placed something that was likely a note on the desk in front of him. Finally, she adds the picture of the young woman with the flaming red hair, staring at the partying Lukas Frisell. Three pictures side by side.

And there can be no doubt.

It has got to be the same person in all of them.

Her digitally competent assistants in Stockholm have also managed to access Elin Eriksson's SUAS records. What they discovered was top marks and effusive references that all mention her work with wildlife, one calling it "epoch defining."

"I might be able to dig up more," says Enok, the assistant currently on the other end of the line.

There's something tentative in his tone that piques Ryd's interest. "I'm listening," she says.

"But it may not comply fully with all current statutes and regulations . . ."

"I'm still listening."

"Theoretically speaking, I could access her medical records," Enok says cautiously.

"And how long would that take, hypothetically?"

"No more than an hour."

"You have thirty minutes, not a second more," Ryd says, and hangs up. She shuts her eyes, thinking deep and hard.

Elin Eriksson attended Frisell's public lectures on crisis preparedness and survival. As did Börje Sandblom, according to the signature on the attendance list.

After the lecture, which introduced the symbol of a circle within a circle, Elin placed something, possibly a note, on Frisell's desk.

Was that the moment the Terrorist Bomber was created? Börje—Elin—Lukas.

Ryd turns to her laptop, typing and clicking increasingly frantically. She's looking for a name, a phone number. *Eva Nyman went to Sandviken herself, right? With Shabir and Anton?*

She finds the note, dials the number.

"This is the local paper, Eva-Lotta speaking," a woman answers blandly.

"Is this Eva-Lotta Thelin? My name's Sonja Ryd, I'm working for Chief Inspector Eva Nyman on a case you discussed with her the other day."

"And not just any case," Eva-Lotta Thelin replies much less blandly.

"Correct. Other than that of Börje Sandblom, who attended the protests against Merplast in Kallfors?"

There's a brief silence on the other end.

"Just two or three people," Thelin replies. "They weren't from Kallfors proper. More like the surrounding countryside."

"But you don't remember their names?"

"I'm afraid not. But I sent you the photographs. I think Börje Sandblom's girlfriend's in them, or at least the ones from the unsuccessful protest meeting in Kallfors."

Ryd thanks Eva-Lotta Thelin and clicks through the Kallfors folder, finding the pictures. One in particular catches her attention. It's male-dominated. Börje Sandblom is in the foreground, sulking at a table on a raised stage. Behind him, an angry young man in a yellow baseball cap.

But in the background, half turned away, there's a third person. A woman with short red hair.

78

Eva Nyman has touched down. She has already walked quite far from the helipad, and now she's forced into a meandering powerwalk through the hectic departure hall at Arlanda Airport's Terminal 5, the big international terminal. She wonders if the sweat is showing on her classically cut pale gray pantsuit. Here and there, she sees discreet groups of people moving slightly too deliberately through the hall.

By all indications, police officers. Search teams.

But the controversial decision from the top still stands: the airport will remain open; the management team will try to do its job with planes still taking off and landing. Evacuating and closing down Arlanda on account of a "barely more than viable threat" has been deemed too difficult and costly.

But the National Bomb Squad is present, working their way through the airport, aided primarily by the National Task Force but also a growing number of regular officers from nearby districts. The goal is simply to try to find any potential bomb. Volunteer security personnel are also arriving from all over the region.

It's Sunday afternoon, Mother's Day, and the police are stealthily out in full force.

But Eva Nyman can see that some travelers, likely the more experienced ones, are reacting to the presence of the search teams. It's obvious they're getting suspicious. She wonders how long the decision to keep the airport open will hold up. The question is whether they're not courting disaster even more this way.

The crowd grows denser as she approaches SkyCity, the restaurant and shopping area between the terminals, next to Terminal 5's smaller security area. It's possible Eva Nyman's being hypersensitive, but she feels like there's a kind of panic in the air, still pent-up, not yet fully realized.

She squeezes past a couple of older women who are pointing at a far-too-conspicuous search team underneath the large information board.

Then she reaches the inner part of SkyCity, where a man who is unmistakably a plainclothes police officer is waiting for her.

A nod is all it takes, and she is led on.

79

Sometime after the incident, a still-flushed Sarwani is sitting on a tree stump farther into the swamp. His sheepish gaze is aimed straight out into the wilderness; the others are respectfully keeping their distance. Ankan's still stubbornly trying to wipe the mud from her clothes, but Lindberg has given up, accepting that sheets of caked mud are forming on his jacket and trousers.

That's when the next sign comes from Tosh Larson. Soon, they hear a car engine.

They've moved farther up the road, closer to the commune, so there's a proper straightaway in front of them. And this time, the uniformed officers are taking the lead. Hultqvist herself is the front row.

An old Volkswagen van is puffing up toward Baton Rouge.

The man who climbs out of it is a graying hippie with olive skin. He keeps his hands above his head, seeming more amused then scared.

"Are you Ugutz?" Hultqvist asks, surrounded by her colleagues.

"Depends on who's asking," the man replies with a wry smile.

"Don't play games with me," Hultqvist says with a humorless snort. Then she pulls out her large, laminated picture of Börje Sandblom.

Ugutz nods slowly and shrugs.

"Txomin, sure," he says. "An odd bird. But he's my bird." At this point, Ankan and Lindberg step forward.

"You might as well start from the beginning," Ankan says.

"But keep it snappy," Lindberg adds. "We don't have time for a tall tale."

"You don't deserve one anyway," Ugutz says. "We're childhood friends. I know he calls himself Börje now, but we grew up together in a very small Basque enclave outside Uppsala.

"Börje Sandblom's Basque?" Ankan exclaims in surprise. "He was born in Sweden. Txomin Larrazabal. Why did he change his name? To something as archetypally Swedish as Börje?"

"Well, he looks bloody Swedish, doesn't he? Kind of red-faced. It bothered him when people kept saying he shouldn't have a weird name like Txomin."

"He told you this when you met up with him here, in Baton Rouge?"

"He told me many things," Ugutz says, laughing. "But that was a long time ago now. I haven't seen him in six months."

"When you last saw him, what did he say he was up to?" Ankan asks.

"He was excited. For the first time in his life, he felt he was doing something important. To be honest, he was always a bit of a loser, poor Txomin. Unlike me, you know, who washes pint glasses covered with vomit in Gävle on the weekends. But I've never been involved in anything criminal."

"Get to the point." Lindberg sighs.

Ugutz shoots him another wry smile before answering, "When Txomin wanted to impress the eighth-grade girls, he blew off half his left hand."

While they've been talking, Sarwani has slowly approached from the swamp. Now, he springs into action, "He blew off half his hand? Was he into explosives?"

"Whatever—he was fourteen," Ugutz says with a shrug. "But sure, it was a hobby of his. Later, he become something of a Mozart of explosives."

Sarwani nods thoughtfully and gestures for Ankan to carry on, which she does after studying him for a long moment.

"Do you know what the important thing was that he was doing?"

"Well, he's mainly passionate about the environment these days, so that would be my best guess."

Ugutz seems genuinely uninterested. Or he's an accomplished actor.

"But you know where in the woods we can find Txomin's house, don't you?" Ankan asks.

"Even if I wanted to, I couldn't possibly call it a house," Ugutz says. "And I live in fucking Baton Rouge."

"Let's go," Ankan says.

* * *

The caravan pushes an hour further into the wilderness. Lindberg drives Sarwani's rental car, with Ugutz providing reluctant directions from the passenger seat, the two police cars following. Eventually, what might have been a road indisputably ends, and there's nothing but forest all around them.

Hidden under a dome of drooping branches is a van that has definitely not been parked there for six months.

Txomin Larrazabal, aka Börje Sandblom, has been active. And what's more, it would seem he's home.

Ugutz points into the trees, marking out a clear direction. "Somewhere between five hundred and a thousand yards that way," he says. "I can't be more specific. Just don't hurt Txomin. He's as meek as a lamb."

The officers huddle up. One of them launches into a futile protest when he's ordered to stay behind with Ugutz. The rest follow behind the vanguard, a quartet consisting of Ankan, Lindberg, Sarwani, and Hultqvist.

"You heard what he said, right?" Sarwani says, checking his gun.

"You're referring to the blown-up hand?" Ankan asks. "The perpetual corna sign?"

"I was actually referring to the Mozart of explosives," Sarwani replies.

80

Sonja Ryd studies the photo from the unsuccessful protest meeting in Kallfors intently. The woman's hair is even shorter than her own, but it's definitely red, and even though she's half turned away, there can be no doubt it's Elin Eriksson. Elin Eriksson some years post SUAS. Looking considerably more haggard than in the lecture video. Than in the pictures on the Facebook page "Fun With Farming."

An Elin Eriksson who has spent several years in the woods?

Ryd checks the dates on "Fun With Farming." The first photo—the one in which the woman with almost preternaturally red hair is devouring Lukas Frisell with her green eyes—is from late August 2013. The second one, in which she's moping at a café table, head shaved, is from March 2014.

Six months later.

A lot must have happened during those six months.

Ryd hurriedly opens the video folder again. Two weeks before the familiar October lecture on "Health and Medicine in Isolation," in which Frisell drew the circle within the circle, he gave another lecture entitled "Personal Hygiene as a Necessity for Survival."

She's watched it before, so she knows roughly where to look. At the end of a long soliloquy, Frisell says, "Briefly put, shaving off your hair is necessary if you are serious about living in the woods. Nowhere else are vermin so easily able to—"

Ryd pauses the film. Thinks the situation through.

Exceedingly talented veterinary student Elin Eriksson attends Lukas Frisell's lectures on exiting civilization. They've been partying together since late August. Just over a month later, from one lecture to the next, this intelligent young woman has most likely had her hair cut off. It was hardly a coincidence that she did it after a lecture in which Frisell talked about how necessary it is to have a shaved head in the woods.

That tells Sonja Ryd two things. First, that Elin Eriksson admired Frisell and took his words and ideas very seriously. And second, that she was potentially considering that same drastic step: leaving civilized society behind. It's not unthinkable that she was already a prepper by the time she attended the protest meeting in Kallfors.

Both Elin Eriksson and Börje Sandblom were inspired by Lukas Frisell. But only one of them left a note on his desk.

Just then, Ryd's phone rings.

"It's Enok," the voice on the other end says. "Hypothetically speaking, I might have something."

"Everything we say will remain hypothetical," Ryd assures him. "So, what did you find in Elin Eriksson's medical records?"

Enok clears his throat thoughtfully before saying, "A stillbirth three months after she dropped out of SUAS."

Ryd makes no reply. Just stares out at the spines of the library books.

"Close the file," she says calmly, "and cover your tracks. This conversation never happened."

She feels she can hear Enok nodding.

Ryd is thinking so hard her brain cells do somersaults.

She goes back to the picture of the six female vet students in the SUAS hall of residence, scrutinizing the melancholy Elin Eriksson, who does in fact seem to have the tiniest of baby bumps. Or is she imagining it?

Did Lukas Frisell have a fling with Elin Eriksson and knock her up? According to Leif Stierna, he'd been a "bit of a Casanova" back then. Did he leave her high and dry when she got pregnant?

The big betrayal, could that be it?

Maybe he'd had so many relationships at SUAS he didn't even remember going out with Elin Eriksson? Maybe he never found out she was pregnant? Or that their baby died at birth?

Or maybe he just didn't give a shit.

She casts her mind back to the conference room at the station. Seeing Elin Eriksson in the recording, seeing her put the note on the desk next to his backpack, must have made Lukas Frisell realize exactly what was being done to him.

Something as simple and timeless as vengeance.

The Terrorist Bomber's activities had never been just a violent climate protest. The whole thing had sprung from something personal, intimate. In this case, a woman betrayed.

Hell hath no fury like a woman scorned.

Elin knew how Lukas Frisell wrote and spoke. She very likely had access to his DNA. Together with her two partners in crime, Börje Sandblom and Elias Eriksson-Shariq, Elin Eriksson became the Terrorist Bomber.

And she put the blame on Frisell. The blame he'd earned.

Lukas had seen Elin in the recording, put two and two together, and gone off to find her, alone, without the police.

He hadn't escaped because he was guilty but because he was determined to find the person who was.

That's where things stand.

But how on earth is Sonja Ryd supposed to find Elin Eriksson—or Lukas Frisell for that matter?

She sinks into a sofa in the SUAS library, paralyzed by indecision.

But her brain's apparently still hard at work, because suddenly she has an idea. She picks up her iPad and opens the old surveillance app.

The ankle bracelet view is empty. Frisell's movements through Stockholm before the bracelet ended up on the horse's leg have been archived, and of course there's no flashing red dot anymore; the ankle bracelet has been deactivated and discarded. The other view, the one Ryd swipes over to, should look the same. There should be nothing there.

But there is. On a map that now covers central Sweden, there's a dot. A green dot. Lukas Frisell's turned-off Nokia 3310 has been turned back on. The flashing green dot seems to be burning a hole in the screen of her tablet.

81

Eva Nyman steps into the command center at Arlanda Airport, which has been set up in a conference room above SkyCity.

A few civilians are sitting in front of computers, doing their best to coordinate the search effort. Via monitors, they're in direct contact with the top management in a slightly more elevated room two minutes' walk away. On their screens, Nyman can see various maps showing the cleared areas slowly expanding on several floors.

But it turns out she's in the wrong place. Apparently, her job now is more practical, hands on.

She has been hastily assigned a team of police officers from the surrounding countryside, who have been tasked with searching a designated area over by the domestic terminal. They've gathered in a remote corner of SkyCity to go over the search strategy for their assigned territory.

She's just about to put them to work when her phone dings. She does her best to ignore it—right now, what she needs to do is give her team clear safety instructions and get them started. "If you run into anything out of the ordinary, no matter how minor, you have to report it to me or the nearest commander immediately," she instructs them.

Then, she can't stop herself any longer. She checks her phone.

It's a text from an unknown number. She hesitates for a few seconds before opening it.

It reads simply *6:43 pm, terminal 5. Booom. Good luck to you, Eva Nyman.*

She hands her team over to the man she's appointed her deputy and races back up toward the command center.

82

They push deeper into the forest in rhombus formation: Sarwani out in front, Ankan and Lindberg on either side, Hultqvist keeping an eye on their six. They can just about make out the rest of the officers about fifty yards behind them.

The forest is deep, dark, waterlogged, almost like a less accessible extension of the swamp where Baton Rouge was inexplicably built.

The lush deciduous forest seems to muffle all sound. They walk in a silence so compact they can barely make out the sound of their own footsteps.

Their attention is on detecting anything that could conceivably explode, mines, trip wires, kamikaze drones, anything. After all, Börje Sandblom is the one who most likely built the Terrorist Bomber's so far extremely accurate bombs.

Including the big one that has possibly been planted at Arlanda. Today, on Mother's Day.

They're making slow progress, moving very cautiously. Then, finally, they catch their first glimpse of Börje Sandblom's dwelling. They squat down behind a large bush. Compared to Lukas Frisell's dwelling, the residence before them fails to impress. It looks like little more than a pile of randomly stacked sheets of roofing tin. But they know appearances can be deceiving. And given Sandblom's skills with explosives, they have no intention of underestimating him.

There's something akin to a designated approach to the dwelling, a path that passes between two boulders. Ankan's the one who spots the wire stretched across the gap. A few more careless steps and all four of them would have been blown to smithereens.

After a rigorous search of area around the wire, they slowly and carefully step over it, one by one, and discover a barrel full of explosives behind the boulders.

It looks very homemade. And very, very dangerous.

They mark the trip wire clearly for the officers following behind, and forge on through the strange silence.

Just outside a camouflaged door in the cottage-like construction, their binoculars reveal a patch of ground of a slightly different shade of brown than the rest. There may very well be an IED hiding underneath it. They need to get the door open from a distance and then jump in from the side.

For the first person doing it, it'll be a genuine challenge. One little misstep and the IED will go off.

There's no discussion—Sarwani's the one who's going to take on that challenge.

Held up by Hultqvist and Lindberg, Ankan picks the lock on the door, hanging suspended above the possible IED. Lindberg's ready to pull the door open with a long stick he's found next to a chopping block.

Sarwani pulls out his gun and focuses on envisioning the entire scenario, eliminating the risk of mistakes.

He prepares to perform a long jump that absolutely can't be too long or too short.

Too long and he'll hit the lintel and fall backward onto the potential IED; too short and he'll land on top of it. Then he's going to have to tuck and roll into the dwelling, the ceiling of which appears to be low. Imagining the large-framed Börje Sandblom living there is downright absurd.

What's more, anything could be waiting for him in there while he's tucking and rolling. Lindberg and Sarwani exchange a glance. Five fingers from Ankan. Then four, three, two.

An odd little pause, and then: one.

Lindberg pulls the door open with his stick. Sarwani jumps. The stench hits him midair. It makes him stop in a crouch on the threshold, slowly tilting backward. Before he can fall, Anton Lindberg shoves him inside with his stick.

Sarwani falls forward, curling up and springing to his feet with his gun raised. Just as he hears Ankan jump in after him and start gagging, he sees, at the end of a short hallway, three more metal doors inside the foul-smelling dwelling.

He waits for Ankan. Together, they approach one of the doors. Despite her retching, Ankan has Sarwani's back; he hurls himself into the room. It's a storage room, filled with everything a proper prepper needs.

If anything, Börje Sandblom has slightly too much fertilizer.

When they come back out, Lindberg's standing over by the next metal door. Hultqvist has just made the jump through the front one. They both look like they're on the verge of throwing up. Sarwani gives them a nod and heads toward the third door. Ankan positions herself so she can pull it open unhindered.

Then, she does. Sarwani throws himself through it. The stench is now completely overwhelming. There's a table and a chair inside. Someone's sitting at the table, thoughtfully bent over something.

It's a man in camouflage clothing, with his back to them and a Kalashnikov in front of him. Sarwani bellows something unarticulated at him. There's no response. The rifle stays on the table.

Sarwani and Ankan step around the table, weapons raised. They hear Lindberg and Hultqvist enter the room just as they reach the man, who is leaning over, with both elbows on the table. His face is resting in his hands, the left of which has only two fingers, index and pinkie.

Corna, heavy metal's sign of the devil. Except the hand is faintly green.

As is Börje Sandblom. Greenish and falling apart.

Sarwani backs away. A pill bottle has spilled its contents across the table in front of the khaki-clad corpse.

Ankan says hoarsely, "Being a prepper seems like hard fucking work."

Next to the pill bottle is a ballpoint pen and a piece of paper with a short, sad, barely legible message written on it. Börje Sandblom, aka Txomin Larrazabal, seems to have composed a short but succinct suicide note that positively radiates bitterness at how his life turned out. Sarwani angles himself so he can read the letter aloud:

Goddamn fucking Elin. That heinous and wonderful devil woman got me good. She doesn't give a shit about the climate. I built all those bombs for her, but she's on her own damn crusade. Against the man she really loves. I'm going to die now, and I hope she'll do the same soon.

Sarwani straightens up as well as he's able in the cramped, reeking room. Still gagging, he says. "Slobodan Jovanović was right. The Terrorist Bomber's a fucking woman."

83

With three miles of road left, Sonja Ryd zooms in on the green dot flashing from somewhere in the deepest forests of Gästrikland. It's still there on the tablet, and it hasn't budged.

It's as though Lukas Frisell is calling out to her.

That had been her first instinct on seeing the flashing green dot. Technically, she should have called her discovery in immediately, made sure the nearest patrol car went straight out there to apprehend the fugitive.

But what she'd seen hadn't been the mistake of an escaped criminal. What she'd seen had been one police officer reaching out to another.

Which meant she couldn't use the unmarked car waiting for her at the station in Uppsala. Instead, she'd taken a taxi to the nearest car rental place.

Now, three miles away from where she has to turn off the main road and find her way along meandering forest tracks, Sonja Ryd decides it's time.

She slows down, pulls out her phone, and dials Frisell's number, the number of the Nokia 3310 he was given by the authorities. She waits. It's actually ringing, and she can feel herself breaking into a sweat.

Other than her, the road's deserted. Everything's strangely quiet.

Then the call is answered, without a word. Even so, she can sense someone on the other end. She, for her part, has two words to say, surprisingly hoarsely: "Elin Eriksson."

There's another long moment of silence, and then the call ends. She watches the flashing green dot on the tablet. After a moment, it disappears.

She understands. It's a sign. She goes over to her screenshots. Checks the approximate area from which Lukas Frisell's phone just disappeared.

Tomtjärla.

Some kind of summer house area. But completely unknown territory. Then, her phone rings. It's Frisell's number.

He must have turned the Nokia back on, as though to mark that they're now in contact. Maybe he's changed his mind. She answers and hears a reasonably familiar, deep man's voice say, "Number 13. Midjegränd 13." Then this call, too, is ended.

He hadn't changed his mind. Just wanted to be more specific. It's time to leave the main road.

* * *

It's hard to even imagine that there are summer houses in this forest. She finds it hard to raise her eyes above the treetops.

But then, a sign appears out of nowhere. Tomtjärla. The narrow road has a passing point just before it enters the area, marked by a sign. Ryd stops there, takes a mental step back, thinks.

At least there's reception out here. She picks up her iPad and starts by checking whether the flashing green dot is still there. It is, but with the map this zoomed in, it keeps jumping around; there's no way of determining exactly where in Tomtjärla the phone's located.

So, she searches for Midjegränd 13 in Google Maps, instead. Oddly enough, there are no hits. Why would Frisell tell her to go to an address that doesn't exist? For what purpose?

She's learned that she always has to look for purpose when dealing with Lukas Frisell. Is this how he's going to get to her?

To kill her?

She changes the search to Midjegränd 1. If the street exists at all, there should be a number 1. And there is. A tiny square about a hundred yards farther down the road is marked by a rust-red digital droplet. She moves on to Midjegränd 2, 3, 4, 5. They all exist. On to 6, 7, 8, 9, 10, 11, 12. But not 13. And not 14, 15, 16.

That means there are only twelve properties on Midjegränd, not thirteen. Elin Eriksson is thirteenth at the table.

Sonja Ryd changes the map type to satellite view on her tablet and zooms in on Midjegränd until the small road is completely pixelated. She pulls back out slightly, searching along the larger main road that runs through Tomtjärla.

Along a small dead-end street, she finds what she's looking for: a cluster of objects that could be a row of letterboxes.

That's what she sets her course for.

* * *

It turns out they are, in fact, letterboxes.

She spots them right next to the small dead end as the rental car rolls toward them. The Midjegränd boxes are grouped together on the right. Numbers 1 through 12. But there's also one labeled Midjegränd 13. The property that doesn't exist.

Sonja Ryd slips the iPad into her bag and takes it with her when she exits the car. She looks around. Not a soul to be seen. It's a grim, gray spring day. The strangely forlorn song of a bird she can't place accompanies her as she opens the letterbox.

Inside is a no longer turned-off Nokia 3310. She picks up the old-fashioned maroon phone and slips it into her pocket.

Then she slowly turns around.

Lukas Frisell is standing no more than three feet behind her.

84

Booom, she thinks.

Eva Nyman has been granted an audience with the head of the management team, upstairs at Arlanda. She has no idea who he is and doesn't even dare to guess what agency he's from.

His head is shaved and he's sitting ramrod straight in his chair among the temporary desks, with her phone in front of him, reading in a deep baritone, "6:43 PM, terminal 5. Booom. Good luck to you, Eva Nyman."

"I want you to focus on the interjection."

He lets out an odd chuckle and says, "'Booom'?" with an audible question mark.

"Go to the next picture," she says calmly.

He does. And sees a handwritten note that simply says, *Booom, motherfucker.*

"Three *o*'s," he says with a nod.

"The date," Eva Nyman says.

"I understand. Odenplan?"

"Alongside two pink balloons in a backpack on the commuter train platform, yes." "What do you want?" he asks simply.

"I want to be put in charge," she says. "And I want a big fat digital clock on the wall of the command center, counting down, second by second, to exactly 6:43."

That makes the head of the management team laugh out loud. But not for long. "You're in charge," he says. "And the technicians will have the clock up and running by the time you get there."

"It's two minutes away on foot," Eva Nyman says, bewildered.

"I'm afraid it may take you longer than that," the head of the management team says with a vague wave toward a large screen on which she sees a Zoom meeting grid, such a familiar sight since the recently ended pandemic. Among the many faces, she thinks she catches a glimpse of the National Police Commissioner.

"I don't follow," she says.

"A decision has just been made to close Arlanda," he explains, stroking his shiny head. "We're trying to do it in sections, but I'm afraid it won't be as easy as some of the people in there seem to believe."

Eva Nyman follows his finger to the Zoom meeting. It's clear they're all waiting for him.

All the government ministers.

* * *

The news seems to reach SkyCity just as Nyman steps out onto the ground floor. The first thing that greets her are three men in suits, running past, not even hesitating before charging into a family with children—the father only just manages to pull the three-year-old out of their path.

She slowly picks her way through SkyCity. Thankfully, the panic appears to be more sporadic than widespread. Both travelers and staff seem confused. There's fear and screaming here and there, but in the distance, she can tell most travelers in Terminal 5 are still queueing calmly. The disparate reactions create a sense of the surreal.

A screaming overweight man in pajama bottoms crushes Eva Nyman into a sushi stand before she can finally push her way through the dueling realities to where she needs to be. When she reaches the entrance to the command center, she pauses briefly, gazing out at the evacuation. It seems exceedingly tentative.

85

Shock makes Sonja Ryd drop her bag, its contents scattering across the ground. Without a word, Lukas Frisell gathers up her things, puts them in his own army-green backpack, and shoves Ryd's empty bag into the letterbox.

"That's not suitable for a day in the field," he says. "You'll have to come back for it later."

Only then do their eyes meet. There's too much to say. The words cancel one another out. So instead, Sonja Ryd says, "You cut your hair."

"More like shaved," Frisell says, running a hand over his scalp. "On the advice of an expert."

Ryd smiles briefly.

"Nice backpack," she says. Lukas Frisell lets out a chuckle.

"It's thirteen years old, Nordic Army Assault. And yes, identical to the two backpacks at Odenplan. It took me far too long to see it."

"Elin Eriksson really is mimicking you."

Frisell nods slowly. Then he changes the subject. "I assume you've already noted that Midjegränd 13 exists only as a letterbox. There's no property, no cottage. The property owners' association tells me they rent the letterbox out for a few thousand kronor a year."

"And what does that mean?"

"That neither one of us knows where Elin's dwelling is," Frisell says. "But I'm ready to track it down. Are you?"

Ryd nods, as though she knows exactly what "track it down" entails. They start walking.

"Why this direction?" Ryd asks.

"For reasons only years of living in the woods can explain," Frisell mutters. "But above all because Elin likely doesn't want to be seen when she picks up her post. She wants to avoid the road. Which means she's coming from the forest."

"You really are the perfect blend of prepper and detective."

"Survivalist and copper," Frisell counters with a snort.

They wander through a gray and grim Mother's Day, increasingly enveloped by a dense forest, not talking much. Frisell reads the landscape, testing its smells, winds, ground.

Tracking?

Ryd follows in his wake, forced to admit that she has put all her faith in him.

At the bottom of a small ravine, Frisell suddenly stops abruptly and sits down on a rock. He pulls a Thermos out of his backpack.

"Coffee?" he asks.

Ryd nods, takes a seat, is given a mug, and says, "I understand most of it, up to a point. Veterinary student and wildlife specialist Elin Eriksson worshiped you and idolized your ideas about crisis preparedness and survival. She initiated a relationship with you, possibly via a note left on your desk during a public lecture in October 2013. But then what happened?"

Sipping his coffee, Frisell winces slightly and comments: "Sometimes you really can tell the coffee's a few years old."

"So, you went back home to pick up coffee? Why?"

"I went to retrieve this from an undiscovered cache," Frisell says, pulling out a Sig Sauer 226, the gun previously used by the Police Authority. She takes out her virtually brand- new Glock 17.

They place them next to each other on a boulder.

"One of the few places where the passage of time doesn't show," Frisell says, studying the two weapons.

"You're a civilian," Ryd says. "I hope you have a license for that."

Frisell just shakes his head. Ryd continues, "I note that you're avoiding answering my question." Frisell smiles and takes another sip of his vintage coffee.

"'You made me see my true self,'" he says.

Ryd waits, sipping her coffee. It really is a tad bitter.

"That's what the note Elin left on my desk said," Frisell clarifies. "But my mind was already elsewhere, here, out in the woods, and my slightly raucous bachelor period felt like a closed chapter."

"But you still let it happen? And then you forgot all about her?"

"It ended after just a few weeks." Frisell sighs. "My heart was never really in it. I'd already found a part of the forest I wanted to make mine. I'd started to build, to lay the foundation."

"But Elin was into that stuff too, wasn't she?"

"Very much so. But I wanted to do it for real, completely alone."

"So, you told her about your place in the woods of Uppland?"

"No, never. As far as I was concerned, she was a thing of the past. Even though our relationship was ongoing. Possibly ongoing."

"And you didn't connect Elin with the Terrorist Bomber until I showed you your lecture on 'Health and Medicine in Isolation'?"

Frisell heaves a deep sigh, shaking his head.

"I honestly didn't," he says. "It was like a hole in my head. I was on the cusp of fundamentally changing my life. She was, at most, a distraction. I know that makes me sound like a prick, but it's the truth."

At that, Ryd almost lets the cat out of the bag. But ultimately, she decides not to. This isn't the time to tell him about the pregnancy.

About the stillborn child.

She needs Lukas Frisell. His survivalist focus must remain sharp if she wants to survive a possible encounter with Elin Eriksson on her turf.

She opts for a more cautious approach. "But for some reason you told her about Eva Nyman? Because why else would Elin be addressing the letters to her of all people?"

"From what I remember, she badgered me until I told her about my past. I must have mentioned Eva as part of that, but only in passing."

Ryd pauses again. Changes the subject again.

"Were you aware she dropped out of the veterinary program?"

"No," Frisell replies. "I was working on my dwelling that winter, gradually easing myself into the world of the woods. When spring 2014 came around, I stepped it up quite a bit. I was mostly waiting for the year to end at SUAS, so I could cash my final paycheck and leave, never to return."

"Is it possible she followed you out to your forest?"

Frisell pauses, staring out into eternity. At length he replies, "I never saw that degree of fixation in her. Not back then. Our relationship simply ended. That was all. Petered out."

"Not back then? But later?"

"She didn't make herself known to me until I'd already made the decision to leave the forest. She carved that circle within a circle symbol into my doorpost."

"The technicians haven't found anything like that in your dwelling."

"I cut it out, wanted nothing to do with it. I realized someone has somehow found me—since it was my symbol—but it never occurred to me it could have been Elin. It was too farfetched. I only realized I'd been framed when you came out to arrest me. I had to wring as much information as possible out of you so I could find the perpetrator myself."

"She was obsessed with you, Lukas. She familiarized herself with the language you used back then, that apocalyptic tone; she saved your DNA; she's mimicking you. You must have betrayed her on so many different levels."

The sorrow in his face cuts her like a knife.

Before they set off again, Frisell picks up his Sig Sauer and shoves it into the waistband of his trousers. Then he hands Ryd a pair of binoculars and hangs another around his own neck.

They push ever farther into what feels like a primeval Swedish forest. The light is extraordinary. It wouldn't surprise Sonja to learn this forest has existed undisturbed since the last ice age.

Imagining the amount of life that's still reproducing in this forest is mind-boggling. She is and will forever remain a big-city girl, will never fully grasp the power of nature. She doesn't understand it, but she can feel it.

She feels it when they finally reach a clearing that opens up like a theater stage in the ancient forest, a stage from a long-distant past. It's like an Ancient Greek amphitheater. The struggle between nature's barbarism and newly invented civilization is in full swing.

And this forest might be older even than the oldest Greek civilization.

They slowly enter the clearing. Afternoon sunlight is trickling down through the foliage, sifting into shafts of light. Where the shafts meet, at the center of the clearing, they spot what appears to be a small monument.

Ryd and Frisell walk closer. Squat down next to a small grave, a low mound no more than two feet long. Only big enough for a child.

An infant.

The cross marking the mound is made of wood, and where its wide boards meet there's a carved symbol.

It's a ring inside a ring. A circle within a circle. An icy north wind sweeps through them.

Inside the inner circle is a small but unmistakable dot.

Lukas Frisell falls to his knees, staring into the center of the circle. Where he sees everything.

86

In the center of the circle, Lukas Frisell feels himself slipping back in time. It's October 2013, and he's just returned to his small flat on the Ultuna campus. He's still dressed in khaki from top to toe. He's come from what's going to become his forest. He hasn't even had time to set his army-green backpack down when the doorbell rings.

He shows no sign of surprise, just waves the young woman with short red hair and penetrating green eyes in. He tries to smile at her.

But that's his last smile in a while. She lunges at him before he can even close the front door, kissing him passionately. He can't help but respond.

She jumps up on him, wrapping her strong legs around his hips, and he feels her lust flare up, powerfully, instantaneously.

But it's not the multifaceted smell of strong, mutual desire that surrounds him, not even when their clothes somehow fall off, leaving a couple of entangled, unprotected bodies to reflect the last dying light of the autumn day.

No, it's a completely different smell. Probably a perfume of some kind. But it feels so incredibly natural.

It's still in his nostrils when they fall onto the bed, when her legs part and a completely different smell reaches his already overwhelmed olfactory organs.

It could possibly be the smell of horse chestnut, but there are no chestnut trees on campus. He can still smell it when he enters her, as slowly he's able, inch by inch. He rests in there, and she rests too.

It's the calm before the storm.

Then the storm breaks, sucking in the light from the hallway outside, which is trickling in through the gap in the still-open front door at first and is then transformed into a crackling shower of brilliant colors.

Her smell, that distinctive horse chestnut smell, never dissipates in the room where the tempest of passion refuses to stop howling.

87

Eva Nyman's graying brown hair is disheveled, and her pantsuit is covered with sushi stains. She looks up at the command center wall. The head of the management team had promised too much when he claimed they were going to have it up and running before she got there, but he hadn't been too far off.

The technician gives her a curt nod, and then the countdown begins. It says 48:00, then 47:59.

It's counting down to 6:43 PM, the time mentioned in the text sent to her phone.

They're less than forty-eight minutes away from a possible explosion.

The very first thing she did after receiving the text was to check the departures and arrivals scheduled for around 6:43 PM. There were at least eight flights that would have a large crowd of people either gathered on a plane or on their way into or out of one, depending on levels of delay.

Which was to say at least eight gates in Terminal 5.

The search effort was immediately redirected to those eight gates, out of a total of around fifty, but nothing of note was found.

By now, Eva Nyman has adapted to being in charge. She's standing by the screens in the command center, with a view of SkyCity and the chaos of evacuation down below, a stark contrast to the apparent order upstairs.

On the monitors, she has a clear view of the police and security personnel clearing section after section, each meticulously marked on the digital maps by the staff that is now hers.

The counter on the wall reaches forty-seven minutes.

88

Lukas Frisell returns to the present and studies the tiny dot at the center of the circle. A searing, burning mark. That's what both he and Sonja Ryd see as they kneel next to each other by the small cross.

Ryd can sense that for the first time in a long time, Frisell is overcome with emotion. Genuinely human emotion. At least that's what it looks like. But she's not entirely sure. She can't remember the last time she was overcome with genuinely human emotion herself.

Yes, she can. But she can't go there now.

Frisell's neglected child is buried right here, underneath his feet. Mummy Elin has repurposed his old circle-within-a-circle symbol to mean human within a human.

A child in her womb.

At the center of the circle is the child that didn't get to live. On Mother's Day.

Booom, motherfucker.

Lukas Frisell's arrogance is what set this spiral of violence in motion. He seems floored by the realization, but Sonja Ryd still manages to pull him to his feet.

They slowly leave the grave and the clearing behind. Ryd can tell Lukas Frisell is waking up more and more as they move deeper into the forest. She doesn't quite understand what it is she sees in his face, but she watches it closely.

Frisell is moving about, observing, seemingly comparing things, examining them. Then he throws up his hands.

"What's the matter?" Ryd says.

"Well, I mean," Frisell says, sounding puzzled, "it feels like home."

"And what does that mean?"

"That it really feels like home. These are my own, I don't know, surroundings . . ."

"Your surroundings are located a hundred miles south of here, Lukas."

"I know that. But this is a replica."

"A replica?"

"If what you're saying is true, Elin followed me to my surroundings, memorized everything, maybe photographed it, and tried to recreate it up here. Everything's far too similar for it to be happenstance."

They continue through the woods. Even the inexperienced Ryd notes the similarities.

Elin Eriksson has found and continued to build a world that is alarmingly reminiscent of Lukas Frisell's.

They reach a pond that lies dark and mirror-like under the leaden sky. As though it concealed the darkest of secrets. Sound and smell, noise and stench blend together.

Next to the pond is a trap set with explosives. It is an eerily exact copy of the trap Frisell set up next to his own pond. He sniffs the air, and Ryd can tell he can smell the explosives. Their reflections in the pond are blurred. As though the people reflected don't quite exist.

They keep pushing through a forest that's now growing denser again. Once they get close enough, Frisell seems to locate the well-concealed dwelling with relative ease.

It takes experienced forest eyes to recognize the vague outline next to the hill as anything other than constantly shifting nature. But he can tell it's something else. Where the hill turns into a ravine, the foliage has taken on an unnatural shape. The underlying layout of the well-camouflaged dwelling looks like Frisell's, but this one has been expanded in several directions.

"As though she's trying to tell me something," he whispers, squatting down in the moss, watching the dwelling.

"What do you mean?" Ryd asks in a low voice as she pulls out her Glock.

"That she's better than me," Frisell replies. "She watched every step I took for years—and the worst part is that I never saw her, never even sensed her presence."

"She must have taken a lot of pictures of you and your world," Ryd says, and Frisell nods.

"She stalked me, imitated me, duped me, outdid me. I betrayed every ideal she had. Not just our relationship, the dead child I never even bothered to know about. But I also betrayed her on a professional plane."

"How? You mean, survivalist-wise?" Frisell nods again.

"The greater ideal is to live in genuine harmony with nature, no climate footprint at all. I betrayed that ideal by installing electricity, purchasing a computer, hiding beer and wine and whiskey in the woods. But I also betrayed it on a smaller scale. According to her dogmatic worldview, I cheated. On every level."

"Maybe she even knew about your little outings to Uppsala . . . ?"

"She was there," Frisell says. "At my house. Not long after I went to Uppsala to meet a woman, she came creeping around."

"What makes you say that?"

"A day or two after coming back from Uppsala, I took a walk down to the pond to take down my trap. I'd decided to leave the forest, and I'd talked to my date at Flustret about it. When I got back to the house, that carving had appeared on my doorpost."

"The circle inside the circle," Sonja Ryd says, nodding as she lets out a breath. "After all those years, she wanted to mark her presence."

"Maybe even more than that," Frisell says thoughtfully. "Maybe she followed me to Flustret and listened in on our conversation. It made her even more disappointed than she already was, and she wanted to let me know she'd begun. That my time was almost up. That I was going to be sacrificed, cast in the role of the Terrorist Bomber. For my infinite betrayal."

Ryd takes another deep breath. Exhales.

"I'm sure you're right," she says. "But what do we do now? Right here and now?" Frisell raises his binoculars and takes another long look at the camouflaged dwelling.

Then, he scans the surroundings and says, "I can make out at least four locations inside that would serve as lookout posts." Then he pulls the Sig Sauer 226 out of the waistband of his trousers.

Squatting in the shrubbery, Sonja Ryd's only impression of the house is that it looks very peaceful in the pale light of the bleak day.

89

The clock on the wall has ticked down to twenty-nine minutes, and the evacuation is still in full swing. Several of the monitors on the desks in front of Eva Nyman are showing more or less chaotic scenes from an increasingly deserted international terminal. When she changes the feed on the screen in front of her, she gets an outdoor camera instead, overlooking the entrances to Terminal 5.

She watches the media arriving, vans full of reporters and photographers racing toward the barriers that were thankfully put up in time.

Eva Nyman thinks she might have caught a brief glimpse of Eva-Lotta Thelin from the local paper in Sandviken. Whom she may have given an insincere promise. Or maybe she just imagined it.

One of the screens shows a map of the terminal, on which the cleared area is slowly expanding. Soon, half of the building will have been searched.

No bomb has been found.

Eva Nyman refuses to sit down. Instead, she paces around the command center. While still managing to stay laser focused.

When the alarm goes off, she reacts instantly.

She taps a free keyboard in front one of the screens and finds her way to an image divided into four squares, each showing the feed from a police bodycam.

In one of them, a heavily armed National Task Force officer, who is evidently facing the officer with the bodycam, is waving his arms to get their attention. He says, "This is unit 129. Do you copy, command center?"

"We copy," one of the seated civilians says into his headset.

"We're underneath gate six," the officer says. "I'm told there's an unidentified object further in. Closer to the planes, in an area with no CCTV coverage. We're going in."

"Proceed with caution," the man with the headset replies.

Eva Nyman leans across the wide desk, snatches up another headset, and asks, "Where did this information come from?"

The armed officer returns, staring into the camera. “Three evacuees passing unit 129 informed us.”

“Evacuated from where?”

“They were wearing yellow vests, so I assume they do some kind of technical work down here.”

“Hmm,” Nyman says. “Fine, proceed.”

The heavily armed officer briefly shakes his head and then slowly moves off, at a crouch, toward a dark passageway between two columns. The bodycam feed shows another five or six Task Force officers joining him, with their weapons raised, disappearing between the columns.

The officer with the bodycam follows.

Darkness descends on the screen in the command center.

90

Crouched in the shade behind the big bush, Sonja Ryd studies Lukas Frisell. It's as though he's wearing a different face now. Watching him is like watching an animal. He's breathing in the atmosphere around the barely visible dwelling on the other side of the bush. She can see he's come to a decision.

"Remember how you got into my home?" he asks.

"We split up," Ryd replies. "Shabir and I went in through the back." Frisell nods.

"I'm afraid the same thing has to happen now," he says. "Elin's copied my dwelling. It would be too easy for her to slip away if we don't cover both exits. And we don't want her to get outside."

Frisell studies Ryd. She remembers how she felt entering his house. The near-death panic that had to be converted into undiluted determination.

"I understand if you don't want to," Frisell says gently.

"I don't want any of it," she mutters. "I just want people to get along. How are we doing this?"

He looks at her until she waves her hand impatiently.

"I'll take the front," he says. "You follow your internal map to the back entrance. It will look the same as at my place. Then we break in as simply and silently as we can. If everything's the same as at my house, there will be no locks on the doors."

She nods. He slides over toward the left side of the shrubbery. She has already moved over to the right side when she whispers, "She's your stalker, Lukas. She built her world to be a better, more orthodox facsimile of yours. She sees herself as a superior version of you. She thinks she knows you better than you know yourself. This has to be done in a way she doesn't expect. You have to think unlike yourself."

Frisell pulls back a little. "So, swap places?" he says. Ryd nods.

"It's a bigger change than you might think," she adds.

Frisell continues, frowning: "Worst-case scenario, she goes for you instead of me."

She smiles briefly. "But you'll rescue me, right?"

Their eyes meet. Frisell's curt nod seems to be in earnest. Then they set off, roles reversed.

At first, there are bushes and rocks to hide behind. Every time Sonja Ryd crouches down behind cover, she raises her binoculars and peers down at the dwelling. She's filled with a strange serenity. It's as though she has moved beyond the near-death panic. She feels focused, as though she's moving with the precision of a Norrland Ranger. But she can't be sure. Maybe she's just imagining it. Maybe that precision exists only in her head.

And then, she runs out of cover. She crouches behind the last bush. Binoculars raised. The door is close now. If she can just reach it, she'll get inside. That's the agreement.

There's no lock on the door.

When she lowers the binoculars, the door seems a lot farther away. As though she's not quite present in reality. Or reality's not quite present in her.

Just as she slowly stands up to initiate the last, fateful part of the approach, she wonders how a wasp could have gotten inside her jacket and crawled up her arm.

As she turns to looks at her suddenly tender left shoulder, Sonja Ryd sees nothing but spinning, swirling skies.

91

The bodycam seems to move through the darkness and come out on the other side. The passageway between the columns underneath gate 6 at Arlanda widens into an open space next to the runways. There are a few seconds of shaky chaos on Eva Nyman's screen before the image stabilizes.

There's enough light and activity now to make out a team of Task Force officers advancing. Nyman turns up the sound. She can hear heavy breathing, excited, worked up.

Thirty feet away, a lone officer is pointing at a large cardboard box. It certainly looks out of place in the otherwise empty space.

The bodycam stops, slips in behind a corner, sinks lower. Nyman recognizes a voice that should belong to the heavily armed Task Force officer who talked to them just a minute ago. He asks frantically, "Do we have time to wait for the bomb squad?"

"Last I heard, they were working at the other end of the terminal," says a voice so loud it must belong to the wearer of the bodycam.

"Okay, fuck, we have to check it ourselves. We're just having a look. Mustafa?"

A Task Force officer with his visor lowered enters the frame, nodding curtly. Then Mustafa turns around and walks up to the large box.

He slowly folds the cardboard flaps back. Even at this distance they can see his hands shaking.

But nothing happens. No bomb goes off. Mustafa returns to the camera.

"It was supposed to be delivered to one of the restaurants upstairs," he pants.

"I have no idea what you're telling me," the group leader hisses hoarsely.

"It's an espresso machine. It must have been delivered to the wrong place."

Eva Nyman groans and hears the door to the command center open. Three people in civilian clothing enter, two absolutely covered in muck. It's Anton Lindberg, Shabir Sarwani, and Ankan. It's the slightly less muddy Sarwani who asks, "Why aren't you answering your phone?"

"I kind of have my hands full here," Nyman says, checking her mobile. She has more than ten missed calls, from Sarwani, Lindberg, and Ankan. She points up at the clock, which just then passes 26:00. They're less than twenty-six minutes away from 6:43 PM, when the bomb is supposed to explode.

Sarwani nods and gives her a brief report. "Börje Sandblom has been dead for over a week. The Terrorist Bomber appears to be a person called Elin, whom Börje was unrequitedly in love with."

"Sonja's not with you?"

"We never heard from her. So, we're 25:41 away from an explosion here at Arlanda?"

"Unless we stop it," Nyman replies, staring intently at the screens. "You'll have to fill me in on all that other stuff later. I have to put you to work now."

"Where? Here, at the airport?"

"Checking the places no one has covered yet, yes. As you can see, we don't have much time. The evacuation is pretty much complete, and we need to clear as much of the building as possible before we pull out too, to avoid casualties. I'll email you a link. Split up as you see fit."

She points to the screens, to opposite ends of the search area. None of the three hesitates for a second.

92

Something about the smell makes Ryd feel trapped, even before she realizes she can't move.

It smells like soil, real soil, soil as origin, as end.

Ashes to ashes, dust to dust.

And it's absolutely pitch-black.

Even so, it takes Sonja Ryd several seconds to realize where she is, what she is: she's buried alive.

She breathes slowly and deeply, in the icily clear knowledge that she absolutely can't afford to panic.

Except breathing is unexpectedly difficult. It takes her a while to figure out that it's because of the rag shoved into her mouth.

Once she has regained some measure of control over her vision, she realizes there is in fact some light trickling in through gaps between the boards above her. She tries to think rationally, logically.

Could it be that she's in a coffin, in a grave, but that the dirt hasn't been piled on top of her yet?

Then, she's overwhelmed by sound. The coffin lid creaks and groans as it's opened.

It's attached with hinges and folds back along the long side.

The light knocks her out. It feels like her brain's going to explode. And yet the light doesn't seem to reach down into the pit. She focuses on everything she can see, on memorizing as many visual impressions as possible. She sees the wooden coffin with its hinges; she sees her hands and feet tied with thick rope made of natural materials; she sees dirt trickling down from the edges of the pit above her.

Possibly six feet above her.

Which means she'll soon be six feet underground.

The coffin lid must have been opened from ground level, and it's from up there that a harsh woman's voice with no visible source rings out: "I assume you're dear Lukas's latest conquest. I wonder what you would say your name is if you had the chance."

Ryd tries to shout through the rag in her mouth. Just to make noise, to give Frisell a bearing. It doesn't work. Almost no sound comes out. What does come might be the muffled, wordless noises of near-death panic.

Ryd hears a deep sigh and sees someone glide into her field of vision, leaning over the grave. It's a woman with short red hair, in khaki clothes, who steps into the backlight and fixes Ryd with her green eyes.

"I've seen the two of you," she says. "It figures the cheater would bring his mistress here. Who I'm guessing is also a police officer. And I'd wager there aren't any other officers around."

Ryd kicks at the edge of the coffin, pulling and tugging on the rope. But no sound she can produce rises above the quiet voice of the ginger woman: "This does disturb my circles. I have to give that to you. It was supposed to be Lukas in that coffin, not you. He was the one who was going to experience what it's like to lie in the womb, rejected, only to then die. At the center of the circle. But now, you can do it together instead."

She reaches down toward the coffin lid with a sturdy shovel but pauses before she shuts it, saying, "I'm heading out to kill your darling now, my friend. I promise I'll be back. I'll throw him down to join you, and you'll journey into eternity entwined. Doesn't that sound romantic?"

The last thing Sonja Ryd sees is the redhead arming herself with a rifle and a pistol, picking up a mobile phone, tapping briefly on it and saying, as though to herself, "'Gate F29. Booom.' With three *o*'s."

Then she sends the text, waves sweetly, and disappears from view.

The coffin lid slams shut in front of Ryd's face, and she can hear thudding, another thud after each time the shovel bites into the soil above her, and she sees a layer of dirt covering gap after gap between the boards of the primitive coffin.

Until Elin Eriksson achieves what is likely her goal. The last of the light disappears.

93

The countdown clock in front of Eva Nyman lets her know they're nineteen minutes away from 6:43 PM, the time the Terrorist Bomber has announced the bomb in the airport is going to go off.

The last few minutes have been interminable, completely pointless in their uneventfulness. The good news is that the cleared area on the monitors in front of her keeps growing. New police officers have arrived, and empty spaces are being filled with red. There aren't many parts of Terminal 5 that haven't been checked.

And yet, Nyman suspects it's not enough. There could be hidden explosives smuggled in by staff or in deliveries, which the bomb squad won't be able to reach with their cumbersome, high-tech equipment.

Maybe it's time to insist on a complete evacuation. Maybe everyone, including the management team, needs to leave Arlanda.

But not just yet. Nineteen minutes to go.

Over the course of the last few, short minutes, she's tried to launch an additional search, sending newly arrived police teams to places that have already been cleared. The green color denoting their progress only covers a tiny fraction of the map so far.

Nineteen minutes turn into eighteen. A hopelessness she struggles to push down at any cost is growing inside her.

Her phone dings. Another text from an unknown number. It's simple and unambiguous: *Gate F29. Booom.*

Nyman hurriedly reports it to her superiors and bellows to the civilians in the command center: "Redirect all search parties to F29. But no more than ten minutes. Then we're initiating a complete evacuation."

Considering how many patrols are searching Arlanda's Terminal 5, there are very few in the F part of it. And there's a reason for that.

Nyman walks over to another screen, peering over a civilian's shoulder. She can tell her drastic regrouping has slowly begun. But since the F section of the terminal is completely covered, completely red, it seems to be considered done. There are hardly any search teams left there. Most importantly, the bomb squad is as far away from it as it's possible to be. They'll never make it back in time.

Nyman makes sure the civilian fixes his pointer as close as possible to gate F29. A click of the mouse brings up a shaky bodycam from the farthest reaches of Terminal 5. The camera is approaching gate F29, one of the eight gates originally identified as serving flights taking off around 6:43 PM.

And the area really is red on Nyman's screen, because it's already been thoroughly searched.

Unless something was missed the first time around, something new must have arrived. And if so, it must have been delivered very recently.

Just as the countdown reaches seventeen minutes to detonation, Eva Nyman sees via the bodycam that a familiar figure is part of the group running toward gate F29.

It's Shabir Sarwani.

16:56 now.

94

As soon as Lukas Frisell steps through Elin Eriksson's back door, he realizes there's no one home. Even so, he searches the dwelling, room by room, with a mounting sense of unease. He doesn't like that he's still alone in here. Sonja Ryd should have come in through the main entrance by now. He should at least be able to hear her.

He enters a room with a chemical smell. It's a smell from the past that he tries to place while his eyes get used to the pitch-dark room. And yes, that's what it smells like: like a dark room, a darkroom. Developer, fixer. He pulls outs a torch and turns it on. A few scattered photographs are dangling from clothespins, but the walls are completely covered with pictures.

And every single one of them is of his dwelling, his forest. From every conceivable angle. Elin Eriksson must have entered his home countless times without him ever noticing.

And, he notes now, there's a battery-powered lamp in the photo enlarger. No electricity as far as the eye can see.

With a feeling of revulsion, he heads toward the main entrance, through which Sonja Ryd should have entered. He takes out his gun, looking around warily. There's really no trace of her.

He moves forward with his turn-of-the-millennium Sig Sauer raised. In a previous life, it was his backup weapon when he patrolled on foot the pockets of urban deprivation that have since been termed "vulnerable areas." Now, it feels woefully inadequate against Elin Eriksson's presumably highly sophisticated arsenal.

At least he's outside now. Granted, it would have been better to take Elin down inside the house, but ultimately he prefers to be outdoors.

He was a good shot, once upon a time.

He can picture the route Ryd must have taken. Where she must have taken cover. He moves toward her last possible shelter, a bush about thirty feet from the door.

A handful of patches of slightly flattened undergrowth indicate that someone doubled their weight in this exact spot. As though that someone picked up and carried someone else.

Then the tracks end.

He's back in the forest. The forest that's so similar to his home, and yet not. He turns his face up toward the pale blue sky, briefly sniffing the air. But all he can smell is the still-distant coming of the May evening.

Dusk is far off yet, but Mother's Day is undeniably coming to an end. To its culmination.

Lukas Frisell lets himself become animal again, sharpening his hearing, vision, smell. He can't overlook any conceivable sniper position, even for a second. He moves forward slowly, his eyes everywhere at once.

He has the experience and originality; she has the flaming fury and a strangely creative ability to mimic. He knows that what he's up against is a more advanced and motivated clone of himself.

After taking out a reasonable bearing, he moves slowly through the silent, deserted forest. All his senses straining. The forest is a living organism, and it envelops him. He knows it so incredibly well.

A couple of times, he registers a deviation, a sound, a flash of something, but both times his senses quickly grasp that the event is part of the natural aural landscape of the forest.

The third time is different.

Since he both sees and hears the sudden movements in a shrubbery and then watches them subside, it must be serious. Frisell glances down at his gun, noticing how badly it's shaking. It's certainly not out of the realm of possibility that the scope of an advanced hunting rifle is already trained on his chest or back.

His gun continues to shake.

When the movement finally resumes and a deer comes bounding out of the bushes, Frisell manages to stop himself from firing.

95

Eva Nyman tears her eyes away from the monitor and sees the countdown reach eleven minutes. The thoughts running through her are too myriad to be put into words.

10:59 now.

The complete evacuation is underway. But she's failing to get in touch with the search team at gate F29.

On the screen, she watches the shaky bodycam feed that shows the group approaching the gate. The designation F29 is clearly visible on the illuminated sign above it. The area around the gate is completely deserted and appears to have been abandoned in a hurry, much like the plane. Watching the heavily armed National Task Force officers moving in obscure patterns through the desolate airport borders on ghostly.

So far, panting breaths into the bodycam microphone are virtually the only sound. During their quick sweep, which includes an abandoned nearby café, Nyman occasionally catches a glimpse of Shabir Sarwani.

Nyman shouts at them through her headset for what must be the tenth time. No one reacts. It's becoming increasingly clear there's something wrong with the connection.

The group huddles up. Nyman's drawn into a discussion—but without being able to participate. Her orders fall like seeds on rocky ground.

"The gate's open to the plane," says a big man who seems to be the group leader.

"But the plane's been searched," another male voice counters.

"If there's a bomb, it's in there," a female officer with her weapon raised puts in.

Eva Nyman once again attempts to bellow at them to evacuate the area immediately. No sound reaches them. Either one of them has blocked communications with the command center, or it's simply not working.

The bodycam has turned toward the gate. The glass doors at the start of the jetway are indeed wide open. It's as though the staff ran away in a panic.

The group leader and the female officer exchange a long look. Even though the feed is shaking wildly, Nyman can see them say, "Fuck it" and launch themselves into the jetway.

The bodycam doesn't follow. It sinks down low as its wearer takes a seat on the floor, with his back against a wall, emitting a kind of whimpering sound. The camera is still aimed at the gate. All told, five officers charge in.

The camera wearer is now sobbing loudly. The image goes dark when he puts his head between his knees. Eva Nyman notes that Sarwani wasn't among the five who defied orders and ran into the plane.

96

Frisell's eyes follow the deer for a fraction too long. For a few seconds, he loses sight of the bigger picture, which could prove fatal.

But nothing happens. The silence that follows in the wake of the small roe deer is deafening. He identifies a spot with full cover in a stand of trees and sinks onto the ground, sits right down on the moss. He takes long, deep breaths through his nose while he studies his old Sig Sauer. His heart rate slowly returns to manageable.

He doesn't really give a shit that the gun in his hand is shaking. It was always like that for him in critical situations—if anything, it was a sign of heightened focus. He hopes that's still the case. He takes three more properly deep breaths through his nose. Then he gets up and moves out.

Elin has left no trace, even though she is by all indications hauling Sonja Ryd through the rough terrain. But where to? He was following his internal map, the map of his own dwelling and its surroundings, but now he has nothing to go on anymore. There's nothing to tell him where Elin's headed.

There's only one thing left inside him. A promise. A promise he intends to keep: his promise to rescue Sonja Ryd.

He keeps moving, operating on pure instinct now, on the conviction that Elin's doing what he would do, move like he would. He looks down at the Sig Sauer again. He was a crack shot once, and the few times he'd hunted wild game in the woods during his isolation, he hadn't felt rusty in the slightest. But now? Fuck knows.

These aren't exactly regular circumstances.

The smell of oncoming evening is growing stronger in his sensitive nostrils.

But then it mixes with something. His nose picks up the faint, faint traces of another smell. He recognizes it but can't place it. It probably takes him no more than a second to search his olfactory memories, stronger than any other memories.

And then he knows where he remembers it from.

It was after he took the trap down, when he returned to his dwelling and found the carving in his doorpost. The circle inside the circle. And only then does he realize that what he's smelling is horse chestnut.

After that, everything happens very quickly.

Frisell turns around with his Sig Sauer raised and sees Elin Eriksson standing behind a thicket about a hundred feet away with an advanced hunting rifle aimed at his chest. The shot rings out just as Frisell gets his gun up and fires while hurling himself aside.

He can feel the impact of the bullet, can feel his entire being crisscrossed by pain the likes of which he has never experienced before despite his long life.

And through it all, he can smell the chestnut.

97

Eva Nyman has two screens going in front of her. One shows a CCTV camera feed the civilian on her left has managed to dig up. It's the empty entrance to gate F29. Nothing's happening there. A large part of the search team has disappeared into the plane. Only the bodycam wearer is sitting on the floor, racked with sobs.

But the other CCTV camera, the one the civilian on her right is still adjusting, shows three men who have managed to work their way down to ground level, underneath gate F29.

One of the three is Shabir Sarwani. She notes that they've entered a workshop-like area that's mostly open to the newly refueled plane parked outside.

Then, all three police officers disappear once more. Nyman peeks up at the countdown clock. It says 03:27.

She's no longer breathing.

On the other screen, one floor up, the officers are now exiting the plane. Sprinting away from gate F29. The bodycam wearer gets back on his feet and follows them, still sobbing.

* * *

Sarwani checks his smartwatch, on which he's added the countdown.

It's ticking down from 01:24.

On the way down, the three of them introduced themselves, to make communication easier. Sarwani's running through the deserted ground-level workshop at Arlanda alongside Anders and Nicke. It feels infinitely large.

They split up and spread out. Forty seconds left.

Sarwani's just about to give the evacuation order when he hears Nicke, the officer farthest away from him, shout, "What the fuck is this?"

Sarwani moves over until he can see Nicke's finger pointing at something that triggers a color memory.

It's the same color as on Odenplan. The color that was very nearly the last thing he ever saw.

Only after focusing his eyes does he see that the color's army green. An abandoned backpack leaning against an equally abandoned truck of the type that delivers food to aircraft.

But this time, Sarwani's too far away. Nicke's closer. Sarwani thinks, *Primary and secondary explosive.*

Backpack and truck.

The smaller charge sets off the larger. Which in turn blows up the fully fueled plane parked less than fifty feet away.

The tertiary explosive.

"The home of the death birds will be flambéed in its own kerosene."

Sarwani bellows, "Throw the backpack away and take cover."

He sees Nicke snatch up the backpack and rush off in the opposite direction, away from the truck.

"Fucking throw it," Shabir Sarwani shouts as he hurls himself in behind a column.

* * *

Eva Nyman is staring at the workshop area underneath gate F29 on two different screens. And yet she can't see any of the three officers. She can't see Shabir Sarwani. What she can see is the countdown clock as it reaches 6:43 PM. And she still hasn't breathed.

00:01 becomes 00:00.

98

Lukas Frisell manages to hold on to both his consciousness and his gun when Elin Eriksson's bullet hits him. He stays down on the mossy ground, sweeping his Sig Sauer this way and that. He can't tell which way is up and which way is down. But he's keeping his eyes open. Strangely enough, he's keeping his eyes open.

Where is she going to come from? When is she going to come?

How is she going to kill him?

There's movement in the woods—but it doesn't happen. She doesn't come to finish him off.

Or does she?

As some kind of rationality slowly returns to his battered body, he asks himself why. But the moment he lowers his guard, the pain's going to take over completely.

He can't let that happen.

The why question will have to wait. As he has done so many times before over the years in the woods, he forces himself back to wariness—but no Elin comes.

What does come is a moment when he can focus on his injury. Rationally. His shoulder—he's been shot near his left shoulder. It looks like a major artery's been hit; blood is gushing out.

He makes a quick attempt at bandaging it, filling his jacket with plants to create a kind of pressure dressing. But what he really needs is a way to keep going despite the blood loss.

He needs to find Sonja Ryd. It should be possible now. To at least try.

But where the fuck is he going to look for her? How is he going to find her when the pain is killing him?

He stands up, noting that his backpack must have fallen off him, letting rationality linger.

He remembers Alonzo, Alonzo sitting in his workshop on Inedalsgatan, saying, "If they're using the standard app to keep tabs on you, they'll see the ankle bracelet as a flashing red dot on a map. Your Nokia should be flashing a different color on a parallel map in a second tab. And I'm sure they can access the app on something portable, like a tablet or whatever."

It was then, on Inedalsgatan, that Frisell first struck on the idea of leaving Sonja Ryd a message in the form of the Nokia's flashing dot once the time was right.

That's when he condemned her to death.

Now Frisell remembers Ryd dropping her bag instead, its contents scattering on the ground by the letterboxes. He remembers himself gathering up her things and shoving them into his own army-green backpack.

He manages to bend down and dig through the backpack, panting hard. He pulls out Ryd's iPad. It's still on, and the only thing on it is a surveillance app.

Lukas Frisell has had nothing to do with modern technology in years. Faced with the tablet and app, he feels genuinely helpless. All he can see is a map of Stockholm. There's nothing else on it.

When he gingerly runs his fingers over the map, he notices that it moves, that he can zoom in and out. But that doesn't help him. Nothing's flashing on this map.

He hears Alonzo's voice: *"Your Nokia should be flashing a different color on a parallel map in a second tab."*

Increasingly annoyed, Frisell tests every type of motion he can think of on the screen, and in the end, he does manage to swipe the map aside. Suddenly, he's looking at a different map, and in the middle of it, there's a green dot.

Not even in his exhausted state is the irony lost on him.

In the autumn of 2008, Liselott Lindman died because Lukas Frisell refused to use digital tools. All these years later, he can save Sonja Ryd with the aid of, yes, digital tools. If he can stay alive, that is.

He zooms in on the flashing green dot and works out how to move to get closer to it. Without putting his gun down for even a second, he drags his wounded body in the direction of the green dot, toward the kidnapped Sonja Ryd.

Moving through the forest is sheer torture. And yet, he can barely feel any physical pain. All the pain has migrated to his soul. It's one big open wound.

He reaches a steep hill. If he's read the map correctly, the green dot should be on the other side of the hill. It's like climbing Mount Everest. The pain is chewing its way through him. Every step is pure grit. But he does reach the top. He climbs the steep slope and crouches down behind the summit.

He shuts his eyes for a moment. Then he quickly sticks his head up over the top of the hill and sees Elin Eriksson filling in a hole in the ground. It's a grave. Now he can see that it's a grave. He feels himself shudder. His entire being. It's his soul shuddering. Sonja Ryd is in that grave.

Dead or alive?

The hunting rifle is slung over Elin Eriksson's shoulder. But it's not hanging right; it's at an odd angle. And her shovel is moving slightly feebly and awkwardly. That explains why she didn't come to finish him off when he was lying wounded on the mossy ground. She was wounded too. By the bullet he fired as he threw himself down. And because she was probably convinced she'd got him, she opted to save her strength for the murder she had yet to complete.

For the funeral.

Which might mean Sonja Ryd is still alive inside that coffin.

He drops the iPad and raises his Sig Sauer. He wants to get as close as possible before she sees him. He wants to minimize the distance between them. He creeps closer, closer, closer, until she hears him.

Despite the distance, it's a piercing green gaze that meets his. Eyes as bright green as the forest.

Like a flashing green dot on a digital map.

99

Eva Nyman watches the countdown clock go from 00:01 to 00:00. The only feeling she has in that moment is that she doesn't want to die. She still has a phone call to make.

One of the screens in front of her abruptly goes dark. On the other, she sees the world explode. Smoke and gravel and debris is pushed into the workshop space underneath gate F29. The bomb has gone off.

The bloody bomb has gone off.

She and the nearest civilian stare at each other. His face is deathly pale, but his eyes are increasingly puzzled. The questions echoing between them are these: Shouldn't they have heard that? Or at least felt the vibrations? Or is this just a short delay, an illusory respite before the home of the death birds really is flambéed in its own kerosene?

Soon, they'll all be blown up. Any second now.

She holds the man's gaze until the spell is broken somehow, and a more ordinary type of terror ripples through the command center.

"Get me every camera feed near there," Eva Nyman shouts. She doesn't recognize her own voice.

The civilians around her manage to pull up several different camera feeds. Officers at the far end of Terminal 5 seem to be reacting to the explosion. Some are running toward it, others away from it. A couple of cameras have gone dark. Others show smoke, ash, fire.

She gets more far-flung perspectives from the airport's runways and aprons. There's not much to see there.

The camera at gate F29 is lost, but the feed from the next gate over clearly shows that the plane parked at F29 is intact. Smoke is billowing out next to the plane's front wheels, from the workshop space on ground level.

An explosion did take place. But it was much, much smaller than it should have been. Or was it?

"What the fuck just happened?" Eva Nyman shouts to everyone and no one in the command center.

100

Lukas Frisell is propped up against a tree branch, but his gun is firmly leveled at Elin Eriksson's green eyes about sixty feet away. She's standing next to a pile of dirt in front of a tall pine tree, hunting rifle over her shoulder, a pistol in a holster, leaning hard on her shovel.

She shouts hoarsely, "You're not hitting me again, not from that distance. You got lucky before. This time, I'll get my rifle up in time."

"Are you ready to bet your life on it?" Frisell asks in a voice that seems to have curdled like a sauce gone bad.

Elin smiles wanly. "Even from this distance, I can tell your face is very pale, Lukas. I knew that hit was fatal. The plan was to bring you back here so you could be reunited in death with your beloved. It's a shame I wasn't in a state to drag your corpse through the woods."

Frisell can feel himself leaning more and more heavily on the tree branch. "I'm not going to miss, Elin."

"Did you ever call me Elin? Did you ever say my name? I'm trying to remember. But I promise I'll make your death look like a suicide. And that I'll make it look as though Lukas Frisell, the Terrorist Bomber, buried his little police lover alive first."

Frisell can feel the world spinning. It's all he can do not to lose consciousness. Elin continues: "It was a girl, Lukas, in case you're interested. You had a daughter. But this time, the world will see how guilty you are. A conviction for a dead man, Lukas. On Mother's Day.

Booom, motherfucker."

She lets go of the shovel and takes the rifle from her shoulder.

Frisell tries to stabilize his Sig Sauer, betting everything on a single card, emptying his magazine.

Elin slips in behind the pile of dirt. She still has her rifle.

Lukas falls forward, crawls across the ground, inch by inch, fully aware he might be shot at any moment. But he reaches the pile of dirt without any new gunshot wounds and stops in front of it.

It's colder than before. The air feels strangely thin.

A heavy black raincloud plunges the clearing into early evening.

He takes a deep breath, thinking it might be his last. Then he crawls around the pile of dirt and sees Elin Eriksson sitting with her back against the trunk of the pine tree. She's cradling the hunting rifle in her arms, staring at him with her bright-green eyes.

Her dead green eyes.

There's a lot of blood on the front of her jacket.

Apparently, the muscle memory from his firearms training still lives inside him. Stronger than all other memories.

Frisell drags himself back to the other side of the dirt pile to peer down into the grave, where he sees a corner of a coffin sticking out from under the soil.

"Sonja," he shouts as loudly as he's able.

But there's no answer. He shouts again, with everything he has.

Feeling the blood streaming out of him, he pulls the jacket tighter, making the most of the woefully inadequate pressure dressing.

This is where he's forced to give up. So close to the finish line. Then he hears something from down below.

It's the briefest of sounds, a knock, a foot kicking against wood.

101

When Eva Nyman clicks her way back to the CCTV camera in the workshop area underneath gate F29 that still works, the cloud of dust has finally begun to settle, and the contours of the space are slowly becoming visible again, covered by a thick layer of still-billowing dust.

Suddenly, something's chirping in the command center. It takes Eva Nyman far too long to realize that it's her phone ringing. Video call, FaceTime. She answers, still far too shaken to understand what she's looking at. Her best guess is a ghost.

Here and there, bloodstains have sucked up the white dust that otherwise covers the entire creature from top to toe.

When it finally speaks, the voice is Shabir Sarwani's. "The primary charge," he says.

"Huh?" Nyman manages.

"That's what exploded. Not the secondary one. Not the plane. Just the picric acid. But I don't know if he made it."

"Who are we talking about?" Eva Nyman says. It feels like she's not quite at home in her own body.

"Nicke," Sarwani replies. "Nicke's the true hero here today, Eva, not you, not me."

"To be frank with you, I don't understand a word you're saying," Nyman admits.

"Just get a medical team down here right now," Sarwani says, ending the call.

As though it were poisoned, Eva Nyman puts her phone down on the desk in front of her, staring at it.

Then it rings again.

Nyman composes herself, answering soberly, "I'm not sure I will ever be able to speak another word for as long as I live."

102

Drawn from some unknown source, a last burst of life surges through Lukas Frisell. When he hears the sounds from the coffin down below, he doesn't hesitate. He lets his battered body roll over the edge, falling what might be three feet down into the ground. Landing with a thud on the half-covered coffin. The pain is indescribable.

With his back against the side of the pit, he somehow manages to heave himself onto his feet. He throws his arms up over the edge and grabs the shovel lying there.

Every movement is hell. He wonders if he has any blood left in his body at all. He has to raise the shovel to head height again and again. It's a Sisyphean undertaking. By the end, he's running on sheer willpower. There's no strength left in his broken body.

But maybe he's uncovered enough of the coffin lid. He manages to wedge his feet in next to the coffin. With what feels like his last ounce of strength, he works his fingers in under the edge of the lid and pries it open.

Sonja Ryd is staring at him. Her eyes are unnaturally wide. He topples onto her, down into the coffin.

They lie there together.

With strength drawn from unknown depths, Lukas Frisell manages to untie the rope around Sonja Ryd's wrists. Then his body goes limp on top of hers.

She manages to slip out from under his fallen body, fighting her way free of him. She pulls the rag out of her mouth, coughing and spitting. She moves her stiff, numb limbs, getting the blood to flow freely through her veins again. Then she unties the rope around her ankles and pulls the fallen Frisell into some kind of standing position.

Together, they stick their heads out of the depths of the grave. She drags herself up. Then she pulls him out.

It's like a birth.

She hauls him around the pile of dirt and then quickly jumps back. But the abnormal has become normal, so she props him up against the trunk of the pine tree, right next to the dead Elin Eriksson.

She pulls off his jacket and shirt, removing the plants he used to bandage his wound. Blood is streaming down his shoulder. She tears off her own jacket, pressing it hard against the wound, using the sleeves to tie it on tight, a more effective pressure dressing.

Frisell's face is ashen.

She goes through his pockets, but there's nothing in them. His backpack's gone too.

Sonja Ryd sits there, watching the life seep out of Lukas Frisell, with no means of calling for help. She's stuck in the wilderness with what will soon be two dead parents, not far from their daughter's grave.

Maybe there's some kind of sick justice to it. Then she turns to look at Elin. One last chance.

She sticks her hands into Elin's blood-filled pockets and feels something.

She pulls an object out of one of the pockets and sinks onto the ground, leaning back against the pine tree so that each of them takes up a third of the trunk's circumference. A deranged symmetry.

Then, she starts frantically wiping the blood from the object. It's a maroon Nokia 3310. It's Lukas Frisell's phone, which Elin Eriksson must have taken from Sonja Ryd. Pushing the buttons is virtually impossible. The entire phone seems saturated with blood that's in the process of coagulating. It would be nothing short of a miracle if it worked.

But it has to. It has to. Lukas Frisell's life depends on it. She pushes a button. The display lights up. With trembling hands, she dials Eva Nyman's number.

"I'm not sure I will ever be able to speak another word for as long as I live," Eva Nyman answers in a strange voice.

"It's me," Ryd says weakly. "It's Sonja."

"Why aren't you here? If you only knew—"

"Ambulance helicopter," Ryd cuts in. "Right fucking now. We're losing Lukas Frisell."

"But what's . . . "

"You should be able to follow the flashing green dot."

She drops the phone and leans back, thinking she could really use a drink right now.

Epilogue

103

It's no longer Mother's Day when Sonja Ryd opens the door to the small observation room behind the interview room. It feels like visiting a former life.

She's greeted by four pairs of sharp eyes. Nova has gathered. Despite everything, this is where she belongs.

Behind the two-way mirror she can see the ancient interview table where she questioned Lukas Frisell so intensely. It's still empty.

Chief Inspector Eva Nyman is sitting on the room's only chair. Her hair finally seems to have made up its mind about what color it wants to be. It has turned gray.

"We were just wondering where you'd gotten to, Sonja," she says with a small smile. "Lukas is alive," Sonja Ryd says.

The four pairs of eyes remain intently fixed on her. They are all eyes she can bring herself to meet. That she's happy to meet.

"Surgery's done and he's awake," she clarifies. "The bullet from Elin Eriksson's hunting rifle caused a massive loss of blood, but he was able to save me and thereby himself. We'll see how long they manage to keep him in the hospital."

A collective sigh soughs through the small room.

"And speaking of heroes," Shabir Sarwani says, "the hero of our part of the story is called Nicke."

"Nicke?" Sonja Ryd asks.

"Have you seriously managed to miss every single breaking-news notification and headline over the past twenty-four hours?" Ankan exclaims, letting down her blonde hair.

"After being buried alive, I spent most of the night at the hospital," Ryd counters grimly.

"Nicke's real name is Nicolas Adeleke," Sarwani says. "And it's very possible I sent him to his death."

"Explain, please," Ryd demands. Sarwani shakes his head.

"He was the closest. We had at most ten seconds left. I yelled at him to hurl the backpack away and take cover. He grabbed it and ran. He'd just let go of it when the picric acid exploded in his face."

"In his face?" Ryd exclaims.

Sarwani spreads his hands, saying, "The reconstruction indicates he did attempt to throw it away at the last second. That's what saved his life. But I don't know. He's in the ICU at Löwenströmska and may pull through. Every Swedish and international news outlet is calling him the 'Stockholm Bomb Hero.'"

"Because he separated the primary explosive from the secondary?"

"Yes. He ran far enough that the picric acid in the backpack couldn't reach the main DDNP charge in the truck."

Eva Nyman nods and says, "Which in turn would have reached the fully fueled airplane, the explosion of which could have reached the plane at the next gate, which could have reached another and another and so on all around the terminal. Police Constable Nicolas Adeleke from Tensta has earned his hero status. And also it steals some of the attention away from Nova."

Sonja Ryd is nodding slowly. "So, what are we doing here?" she asks.

"We're desperately hoping to tie up all the loose ends."

Anton Lindberg takes a step forward. Ryd notes in passing that his unruly light-brown hair has grown far too long. And there's a worry line on his forehead she's never seen before.

"I'm going to do my best," he says with a nod.

"And I'm going to observe with great interest."

Lindberg lets out a chuckle and says, "I can't do it without you."

Sonja Ryd blinks several times. Struggling to put the pieces of a very large puzzle together.

"Me?" she says.

"Everyone knows you're the best," Anton Linberg says. Eva Nyman clears her throat to call for silence.

Ryd turns to her.

"But I haven't prepared," she says.

"You'll be given all the information you need," Nyman says. "But I know you have the whole case in your head anyway."

104

First in is a lawyer, then a member of a criminal gang. They sit down next to each other at the interview table, exchanging a smile that's not entirely amiable.

A door opens and a burly man with unruly hair enters the interview room.

"I'm sorry to have to tell you this," he says before falling silent and taking a seat. The lawyer and the accused exchange a quick glance.

"My client—" the lawyer begins to say.

"—is actually going to have to make a decision now," Anton Lindberg cuts in. "He has to decide if he wants to know how his sister's doing."

A brief jolt runs through Elias Eriksson, aka Elias Shariq. The man who has not said a single word so far.

"The situation just became crystal clear," the lawyer announces. "From now on, it's no comment. Right, Elias?"

"No comment," Elias says, looking a little bit brittle for the first time.

It's also the first time Anton Lindberg hears his voice. It's less cocky than Elias's general vibe. More high pitched.

"We're still going to go through everything, one question at a time," Lindberg says, smiling. "I just want to start by informing you that our old friend Hassan, leader of the Hjulsta Gang, has been given a life sentence, to be served at Kumla High-Security Prison. A prison that also houses terrorists, like people who try to blow up Sweden's largest airport. I tell you this as a reference point for your 'no comment' strategy. Understood?"

The lawyer and Elias Eriksson both remain silent and attentive.

"Then with no further ado, allow me to introduce my partner, Sonja Ryd," Anton Lindberg says.

Ryd enters the interview room, placing a thick folder on the interview table before stroking the stubble on her head.

"I'd like to start by showing you a photograph," she says. Then she places it in front of Elias.

It's a picture of Elin Eriksson, sitting with her back against the tree next to the open grave. She's staring straight ahead and is quite clearly dead.

It's a gamble that was hotly debated in the small observation room. For and against. Here and now, though, is where it's decided. Whether they're going to learn the whole truth. Or whether "no comment" is the only answer they're ever going to get.

Ryd and Lindberg study Elias Eriksson very closely. He shut his eyes when he saw the photograph. Now he's sitting motionless, eyes closed. Without a doubt, there's a lot going on inside him.

"I'm sorry for your loss," Ryd says quietly.

Elias opens his eyes. He's staring straight into hers.

It's still a draw. The emperor's thumb is pointing sideways. Within the next few seconds, they'll know if it's turning up or down.

Sonja Ryd was the person in the small room on the other side of the mirror who was certain Elin was genuinely important to her brother. But the answer is still unclear.

"It's over, Elias," Ryd continues in that same calm, mild tone. "I'm sensing you loved your sister very much."

He holds her gaze. She doesn't look away.

"What was your mother like?" she asks. "A bit difficult, right?"

"No comment," Elias replies, but Ryd can see that his eyes are saying something else entirely. That he wants nothing more than to somehow pay tribute to his sister.

"We don't have to talk about your mother," Ryd says, placing her hands palms up on the table. "We can talk about Elin instead."

"No comment," Elias says. The lawyer whispers a few words in his ear. Elias pulls away from him slightly.

"Let's take a step back," Ryd says in the mildest voice Anton Lindberg has ever heard come out of her mouth. "What was your mother Birgitta like, Elias? We know she met your Syrian father, Najeeb Shariq, in Palmyra in Syria."

Elias Eriksson, aka Elias Shariq, says nothing. He's staring at an invisible spot on the wall of the interview room.

Ryd continues, "It's important to remember one thing, Elias. You're going to be convicted of murder and acts of terrorism whether you talk or not. But you have an opportunity here to serve your sentence away from your partners in crime. They will also not be told of your betrayal and will therefore be unlikely to send an assassin your way. You'll probably even get off easier if you tell us everything. But above all, you'll feel better."

Sonja Ryd shoots Anton Lindberg a quick glance, allowing herself to be briefly surprised at how deep the worry line on his forehead has become.

The lawyer turns to his client again to whisper some more. But Elias pushes him away and says, "She was my mum. She wasn't a good mum. But I loved her."

Ryd and Lindberg exchange a quick look.

"Elin did too," Sonja Ryd says. "Which is why she took over her role when your mum started drinking too much. Elin was almost ten years older than you and didn't hesitate to step in as your mother when she was fourteen years old."

"We lived in the countryside," Elias says, staring into space. "Had a lot of animals. I don't know how she did it. She became a parent to both me and Mum."

"She liked living in the countryside," Ryd says with a nod. "But you didn't?"

"Not when I was sixteen. It was completely dead out there."

"So you moved in with your father's relatives in Hjulsta and took his surname. But you never officially changed it?"

"It wasn't important," Elias says, shrugging. "I was never interested in him. And he'd gone back to Syria long before that. I lived with my cousins."

"Or maybe you kept the surname Eriksson because you wanted that link to your sister? The two of you were very close, weren't you? You loved her?"

Elias shrugs again. But something else is happening in his face now. A single tear wells up and then slowly trickles down his cheek.

"Should we start from the beginning?" Ryd asks, putting her hand on his. To the surprise of many observers, he lets it stay there. They sit like that for a moment before she continues. "How did all this start? Just tell us the whole story from the beginning."

Elias wipes the tear away with his free hand.

105

Sonja Ryd catches Elias's eye and can clearly see her possibly overbold approach being processed in a brain that functions completely differently from her own.

"Just tell us the whole story from the beginning."

He opens his mouth. It's decision time.

"I was in the nick when Elin moved out into the woods," he says. "She just vanished—it wasn't like her. It was a few years until I heard from her again. She and some bloody prepper mate of hers, Börje fucking Sandblom, had cooked up a scheme."

"When was this?"

"Like, a year ago? It had to do with the climate or whatever. The two of them had—how did she put it?—'realized how urgent stopping the climate offenders was.' They needed me. I mean, fuck, it was Elin, my sister. Elin and Elias, the dynamic duo. Of course I was going to help her. Even though I didn't give a shit about the climate."

"What did they need you for?"

"The hands-on stuff. And the import of some yellow fucking acid that was unstable as fuck. I brought it in from the Balkans via the Hjulsta Gang. Nothing could lead back to Elin."

"But there was the small matter of your mum's flat . . ."

"Mum pulled herself together at some point when I was already involved with the Hjulsta Gang. She sold the place in the countryside Elin had made all kinds of improvement to and bought that flat in Vasastan. Elin didn't object. It gave her the chance to finally become a veterinarian, her childhood dream, saving wild animals or whatever. By then, Mum already had dementia and was in a home. Elin and I kept the flat. And it was a good thing we did, because later on it became our headquarters, kind of."

"The Terrorist Bomber's HQ," Sonja Ryd says with a nod. Elias Eriksson chuckles.

"Right, yeah, the newspapers and their fucking nicknames, seriously . . ."

"How did you plan it?"

"I wasn't particularly involved. It was more like Elin told us what to do. Börje was a clown, obviously, with his farmer's face and missing fingers, but he was a whiz at making bombs. To be completely honest, I think he might have been a bit retarded."

"So Börje never studied at SUAS?"

"Absolutely fucking not. Börje, study? Nah, but he attended some talks at the university. About becoming a prepper or whatever. Though I think he was already living in the woods when he and my sister met."

"And how did the three of you start working together?"

"It was a bit James Bond–like at first. I was supposed to follow this BMW from some house in Uppsala, staying close but not too close. When we got to a place with a large yellow field, I called Elin. She was waiting on a nearby hill, spotted the BMW through her binoculars, and blew it up. It went shooting straight out into the yellow. And I just kept going, drove into town."

"Do you know how the bomb ended up inside the BMW?"

"Not really. I know Elin and Börje went out to that house the day before. That's it." "And then it was Vasaparken . . ."

"Yeah, that was a bit trickier. We needed to get a bomb into the offices of some company with a weird name. Elin was after this one bloke, Jesper Something-or-the-other. I followed him to Tennstopet, where he had lunch with some mate of his. He whinged up a bloody storm about a delivery that was running late and wouldn't arrive until Saturday afternoon. I hung out in Vasaparken the next day until the delivery arrived. Then I picked up the DHL courier and the package and drove them both around the corner to Elin and Börje in Vasastan. Börje made a bomb to fit in the package. Then I drove back to the PR company, wearing the courier's clothes, and handed the package to some good-looking girl. I told her it was fragile."

"And what happened to the courier?"

The lawyer has looked positively taxidermied for a while, but now, he has a knee-jerk reaction. "All right, this is definitely a 'no comment' situation."

"What this is," Sonja Ryd replies, "is the whole story, if you want us to be able to offer Elias the kind of deal on which his life may very well depend. An edited version of the story won't be enough."

Elias just shakes his head and carries on. "First, I parked the delivery van in the DHL car park in Västberga and put the keys in the glove box. Then I kicked Elin and Börje out for a few hours while I gave the courier an acid soak in the bath. I know a good, effective blend."

Ryd hopes he can't tell that it's with a shudder—of both horror and smugness—that she asks, "But Elin wanted to watch the Vasaparken explosion, right? How did she know when she had to be there, behind that tree? Wasn't there a risk Jesper would already be on his way to the office when you dropped off the package? When Frida Söder from the PR firm told him it had arrived?"

"I'd put some Hjulsta kids in a car outside Jesper's house in Täby. The kids are well trained; they kept an eye on things, sleeping in shifts, so they were awake when he set off early on Sunday morning. They called us at the flat, and Elin went over to Vasaparken."

"And then it was the data center in Västerås. Did all three of you go out there?"

"No, Börje wasn't there for that. He'd built the bombs for Västerås, the plastic factory, Arlanda, but at that point he suddenly went missing. For a while, we were worried the police had nicked him, but no one came after us."

"So he'd already built the bomb you used in Västerås?"

"Yeah. I know a guy who works in that hell hall—that's why we picked it. And I'm not going to tell you who he is. He told me how the delivery of spare parts works, that packages from the United States are left in a certain place so the data center manager can pick them up. Thanks to my mate, Elin got a link so she could access one of the CCTV cameras and watch the whole thing live from Mum's flat. We knew what the packages usually looked like, and we knew what their delivery vans look like. We lay in wait on a back road off the airport and used Elin as bait to get the van to pull over. Girl with car trouble, you know. I knocked the delivery guy out, and we transferred the address sticker from the US package to ours. Then I drove over to the server hall and delivered it. And after that we went to Hjulsta and told the kids to take the van and burn it in the woods. And another courier got an acid bath."

"How old are these kids?"

"That's more than the whole story, Sonja Ryd."

"Fair enough. And then it was time for Odenplan . . ."

"That was a piece of cake, actually. I placed one of the backpacks on the commuter train platform. Elin took the other and planted it in the crowd in the square."

"What do you know about the letters, Elias?"

"Nothing. I know she wrote letters that she sent to some copper, but that's it. That wasn't my thing."

"But then you got caught, didn't you?"

"Yeah, by the Järva police of all people. Pretty embarrassing."

"Which meant you weren't there in Gästrikland when Elin blew up Merplast."

"She didn't need me there. She had Börje's bomb. She knew her way around. Her place was in the woods nearby. She broke in at night and hid it in the CEO's office, in his sofa. Assuming it worked as planned, she aimed it just so and then sat outside the next day to trigger it remotely."

"Arlanda, on the other hand, must have been very complicated," Ryd says.

"First, we had to smuggle in enough secondary explosives to fill one of those catering trucks. Those deliveries have been going on for a while now. I have my contacts. We stashed the stuff all around the workshop. We got the timing mechanism in well in advance too."

"But then, you were arrested."

"My mates had Elin's detailed plan. And she was bloody particular about the date. They weren't allowed to bring the backpack with the primary explosives in until that exact day. Then they were supposed to wait until the evacuation got underway, fill the truck with the secondary explosives, and finally lean the backpack with the primary charge up against the truck. Then they just had to start the timer and get the fuck out of there."

"You must have promised your mates a lot of money," Ryd says.

"Or maybe they're just proper mates," Elias Eriksson says, studying the deathly pale lawyer sitting next to him.

Then his thoughts seem to return to his dead sister. He closes his eyes. Maybe he's done talking.

But she can't let him stop. Not just yet. Sonja Ryd has one important question left to ask, and she has to ask it the right way.

"And was it only about the climate issue for Elin?" she asks. "There was no other motive?"

Elias opens his eyes again, shakes his head, and asks indifferently, "Like what?"

She prays her question hasn't sowed a seed in Elias's mind. She absolutely doesn't want to set him on Lukas Frisell's trail. Elias Shariq is not a man whose contacts, kids, or mates anyone wants to have sicced on them.

She stays seated, feeling drained, while Elias exits the interview room ahead of his stunned lawyer. Her index finger traces a carving in the table.

It says FREE.

They're all free now. Everyone except Sonja Ryd. She's still stuck in her own, personal betrayal. Tyskertøsen. But at least she's not buried alive.

At length, she turns to Anton Lindberg. But he's not there.

She turns around. He's standing in the doorway to the small room behind the mirror, waving for her to join him.

106

The small space behind the one-way window feels very crowded again. Eva Nyman gets up from the only chair and nods to Sonja Ryd.

"I'm glad he doesn't know about Lukas," she says. "As for the rest, that was all pretty unexpected."

"Not really," Ryd replies. "His actions hinted at a deep love for his sister. He would have done anything for her."

"Including letting two delivery boys get sucked down the drain," Shabir Sarwani mutters. "Dedik Jaya and Wilhelm Bock."

"I imagine a reduction of his sentence is pretty much out of the question," Ankan summarizes.

Eva Nyman nods and says after a long pause, "The group in the office is going through CCTV footage from Arlanda. They just found a clip that likely shows Elias Shariq's 'mate' right after he planted the backpack with the primary explosive. He seems to have known exactly where the cameras were, but in one spot he slips up briefly. This is what he looks like, at least from behind. We've already put out a nation-wide alert."

All eyes turn to the screen in front of Nyman. It's a short clip. The man's only visible for a fraction of a second as he rounds a corner. His only identifying characteristic is a turquoise tracksuit jacket with three distinctive Adidas stripes.

"If that's all we have, we're going to have a hard time finding him," Ankan says.

"I know." Eva Nyman sighs, looking as though she has more to get off her chest. She clears her throat and continues. "There are two more things I'd like to say, other than that we've found the typewriter, carefully hidden in Elin's dwelling. The first is that you've done such an insanely outstanding job that the Nova Group is being made permanent within NOD as an 'extraordinary crimes unit,' whatever that's supposed to mean."

Total silence descends on the small room. Nyman goes on: "I assume this is agreeable to all of you. If not, I need you to voice your objection now."

There are none. Only a speechless, stunned, and ecstatic silence.

"The second thing I wanted to tell you is that I have today, with the full backing of the NOD, submitted an application to the National Police Board to have Lukas Frisell reinstated."

Everyone nods. Nyman continues, "Since the group currently has no vacancies, Frisell will serve as an extra resource within Nova until further notice."

Then, Ankan pushes the door handle down and everyone is sort of sucked out of the room. Except Sonja Ryd. She's held back by Eva Nyman. Ryd finds it difficult to read the expression in her eyes.

Nyman sinks back onto the chair. Ryd leans against the edge of the desk. "You did an extraordinary thing in there," Nyman says with a nod to the one-way mirror.

"You didn't keep me back to tell me that," Ryd replies. Nyman smiles. Then, she says, "I don't know if we're a good team, Sonja. You and me, I mean, not Nova. Nova is definitely a good team."

"But the two of us?" Ryd says. "I don't know either."

"You ran your own race at the end there, together with Frisell. You didn't trust me. You went behind my back. But you should know I trusted you and looked the other way when you hung up on me and stopped taking my calls. We also had diametrically opposed views on how to approach the interview with Elias Eriksson. And you were right, I admit that."

There's a brief silence in the small room.

"I'm going to make a call now," Nyman says finally, "a private call that I've deliberately been putting off this whole time."

"And you want me here as a witness?"

"For moral support," Nyman corrects her. "Because you're my best friend, put simply. I have no one else to turn to."

Ryd nods curtly. Nyman looks around, heaves a deep sigh, stares at her phone. "Actually, never mind," she says, slipping the phone back into her pocket.

Ryd grabs her arm and says, "It's obvious this is important to you, Eva. Stop putting it off. I'm here. Right now, I'm doing exactly what you want me to. Make the call."

Nyman takes her phone back out and once again tries to stare it down. "I promised myself I wouldn't call. I'm fine on my own."

"But it might not be as fun. Although, who am I to say? I have an extremely hard time picturing myself in a relationship ever again."

Nyman takes a deep breath and dials a number. Ryd hears a woman's voice answering on the other end.

"Hi," Nyman says breathlessly. "It's Eva."

Ryd hears a long initial silence, then that words are spoken, just a handful, and she can't make any of them out.

"I'm so incredibly sorry about everything that happened," Nyman continues. "I have to apologize to you. On my bare knees."

Ryd hears a few more syllables on the other end. She even thinks she might be starting to recognize the voice.

Then, Eva Nyman smiles, wipes something from the corner of her eye and says, "I would love to come over for dinner, Nina."

107

The doctors objected vociferously when Lukas Frisell insisted on leaving the hospital. Now, sitting in his small police flat on Agnegatan, at least he's not alone.

"It feels as though the blood pumping around inside this body belongs to someone else," he says.

The man with the Latin American appearance sitting across from him on the sofa leans back, shakes his head, and says, "Don't be an idiot, amigo. You know exactly who you are."

"Do I, though, Alonzo? There are a lot of things that need putting back together inside this brain. Inside the ruins of goddamn destruction."

Alonzo keeps shaking his head.

"We should be celebrating," he says. "I should have brought a bottle of tequila or something. You're a bloody copper again, Lukas."

Frisell flashes him a quick smile. "Tequila would have been invigorating, sure. But probably not particularly good for a person in my situation."

"Come on, amigo. We'll have to hit a bar instead. The hospital's nearby—don't worry, we can roll you there. But don't think I don't know what's bubbling around in that mysterious head of yours."

Even in the old days, Alonzo had always been able to read him like an open book. Even after everything they've both been through, that ability seems intact. "Liselott Lindman," Alonzo continues. "And don't try to deny it."

"I keep picturing that fucking Dick Lindman, free as a bird, smoking weed on a beach in Goa."

"You'll get him this time, amigo. But what was that call you were in the middle of when I got here? It sounded like your wife on the other end."

"Her name's Nina Strömblad these days. Divorced for a second time. *Re*-divorced."

"Well, what do you know? But what were you talking about? You sounded a bit shocked."

"I'm not sure I fully understood. She told me she'd 'reconciled with Eva Nyman.'" "That Eva Nyman? The one you used to work with?"

"Who was also the person hunting me this whole time—and who is now my boss. She and Nina became friends after our divorce, remained friends through her next marriage, and then 'one thing led to another.'"

Alonzo lets out a raucous laugh. "What the fuck, amigo? You turned Nina into a dyke?"

"Her and Eva both, I guess," Frisell says with a wry smile. "Bloody hell, we could really use a drink right now."

They sit there for a moment, chuckling softly, the way middle-aged men often do. Resting in the past. In a completely different tone of voice, Alonzo then says, "But who was she really? The killer girl who tried to frame you?" A darkness falls over Frisell.

He pictures Elin Eriksson, her immense strength and grit, the extraordinary personality that he'd just cast aside and allowed to morph into pure, unadulterated hatred.

Their child, whom he hadn't even known he was ignoring.

Only now does grief catch up with him. Grief for his stillborn daughter crashes over him.

Grief at being the kind of man he is.

"You'll have to tell me later, amigo," Alonzo says, patting him on the shoulder. "Let's go out and knock back a couple." Just then, the doorbell rings.

The doorbell shouldn't be ringing.

Lukas Frisell heaves himself up, drags himself to the door, and tries to look out through the peephole.

He sees nothing. There's no one there. In the end, he still decides he has nothing to lose. He opens the door. Sonja Ryd's hiding just to the right of it.

She sniffs the air, holds up a box of red wine, and says, "How about some ethanol?"

108

It feels strange to come home when the terraced house in Huvudsta is empty. Normally, his home is filled by the constant movements and talking of his two—according to the unanimous assessment of their teachers—dynamic daughters. But since Anton Lindberg's mother-in-law insisted, his family has extended their Mother's Day visit to Tärnaby by another day or two.

It's been a long day at work, but at least things have finally calmed down. He would almost go so far as to call it harmonious.

They did it. They put an end to the Terrorist Bomber's campaign of terror. Sweden and Stockholm may just be able to return to some kind of normalcy now.

If there's any normalcy to return to.

Anton Lindberg pauses for a moment on the gravel path leading up to the terraced house.

Home, he thinks with a contented sigh. *I'm finally home. There's no place like home.*

He unlocks the front door and turns on the hallway light, continues into the kitchen, finds a beer in the fridge and gives himself permission to open it. Then he sets his course for the living room, where the Champion's League play-offs are hopefully waiting for him.

The first sip of beer is still in his mouth when he reaches the living room and turns on the light.

Two teenagers are sitting on the sofa, each leaning on a semiautomatic rifle. They both flash him crooked smiles before reaching for another fistful of crisps from a bowl on the coffee table.

"You'll have to excuse the kids," says a voice from an armchair in the shadows. "Their table manners leave something to be desired."

The last thing Anton Lindberg sees before the blood freezes in his veins is a turquoise tracksuit jacket with three distinctive Adidas stripes.